PRAISE FOR DR. SOMMER'S
PREVIOUS NOVELS:

"I love psychological mystery/thrillers, and have to say that this is one of the best. I've found most doctors turned writers try not to show too much of their psychology backgrounds in a story they've written. But, I found this book was the opposite and I loved every minute of it…It was fascinating to watch the story unfold and I was completely shocked at what the whole truth entailed."

—*One Book At A Time*
(http://pagese.wordpress.com)

"As soon as I picked up this book and read the first chapter, I couldn't put it down. It kept me wondering until the very end. The character development pulls you in and won't let you go."

—*Through Him*
(http://goingthroughhimtofindme.blogspot.com)

"Unlike most psychological thrillers, Heath Sommer's debut novel is chock full of actual psychology. Marriage counseling, abnormal behaviors and other real psychological themes are represented…People are represented in this book, not just as characters that drive the plot, but as real, flawed human beings. People that you can relate to in some way…It's a fast-paced read that keeps you wondering what the heck is going on…"

—*Reading with Tequila*
(http://readingwithtequila.blogspot.com)

"One word can pretty much summarize this novel and it has to be amazing ... one of the best psychological thrillers I have read. Dr. Sommer honestly put it together in such an amazing way that left me completely breathless."

—*The Chick That Reads*
(http://thatchickthatreads.blogspot.com)

" ... every character that the reader interacts with, both good and bad, is as layered as a character can be. They are real people with real psychological issues ... One of the best you will ever read in the genre."

—*Salt Lake Examiner*
(http://www.examiner.com)

THE GRAND
DELUSION

A MANUFACTURED IDENTITY
THRILLER

THE GRAND
DELUSION

HEATH SOMMER

TATE PUBLISHING & Enterprises

Published by Tate Publishing & Enterprises, LLC
127 E. Trade Center Terrace | Mustang, Oklahoma 73064 USA
1.888.361.9473 | www.tatepublishing.com

Tate Publishing is committed to excellence in the publishing industry. The company reflects the philosophy established by the founders, based on Psalm 68:11,
"The Lord gave the word and great was the company of those who published it."

Book design copyright © 2010 by Tate Publishing, LLC. All rights reserved.
Cover design by Kellie Southerland
Interior design by Stefanie Rooney

Published in the United States of America

ISBN: 978-1-61663-559-6
1. Fiction, Thrillers
2. Fiction, Psychological
10.08.30

OTHER NOVELS WRITTEN BY HEATH SOMMER

The Human Obsession, Tate Publishing, 2010.
The Manufactured Identity, Tate Publishing, 2009.

DEDICATION

Thanks to my wife, children, family, and friends who saw in this manuscript only the finished product from draft one. A special thanks to Meghan Barnes for her dedication, friendship, and insight throughout the editing process of this and my other novels. Finally, to all who suffer under the term "mentally ill" and wonder if anyone notices or cares, you are noticed and cared for by more than you know. These are your stories...

So from dust cometh man; whence cometh the dust?

PROLOGUE

With fleeting energy the weary man lay motionless underneath his desk and stared into the quiet of the darkened room, straining himself to breathe without sound. *This is not the way it was supposed to happen.* He slowly shifted his body and turned his head toward the oscillating siren blaring through the cracked window. Silently he prayed that the speeding police car would zoom past his home, but underneath his consciousness he feared that he had been found.

After long seconds the siren passed, and the man heaved a carefully measured sigh. Taking pause, he recalled the faculties of his mind into focus and reminded himself that simply because one black-and-white passed him by didn't mean he was no longer being monitored.

Stealthily, he moved from the office and into the parlor, deliberate to avoid stepping on the loose boards in the middle of the room leading up to the door's threshold. For an intense moment he thought he heard a crackling off to his right. Quickly, but with control, he surveyed every corner of his periphery before taking another step. Satisfied the parlor was void of life, he closed the door behind him and retrieved the vintage copy of *Animal Farm* from off the fifth shelf of the middle bookcase. With mildly trembling hands, he opened the novel to page sixty-two and carefully handled the loose photograph resting in the crevice of the page, gazing upon the solemn face in the picture before turning it over to read the long-since memorized phone number. Fighting the urge to blink the sweat from his eyes, he lowered himself to the telephone and held his face over the keypad. It was time.

Reaching up, he grabbed the phone and listened to the dial tone; let it sink into the depths of his mind; let its drone nearly induce in him a deep trance. Not acknowledging the subtle nausea mixed with adrenaline, he brought up his curved right-hand index finger and softly depressed the seven digits. The phone rang once, then twice, then a third time. He exhaled silently but sustained.

"Hello?"

At first he couldn't respond; he could only catch his breath. He didn't like this part of his work.

"Hello?" the woman on the other side tried again.

More quiet breathing.

"Hello, who is this? I can hear you breathing."

He finally spoke but only in a soft, strained whisper. "Is this Sally, Sally Strathers?"

"Yeah, it's me, but who are you? Why do you keep calling me? What's your name?"

"I am … a friend," he breathed, his mind racing, his fingers wet.

"What do you want? How did you get my new number? Why do you keep calling me?"

He looked at his laptop. "You'll know soon," he said, his voice beginning to quiver.

"What will I know soon? Listen to me. Don't hang up! Why do you keep calling me? What do you want?"

He closed his eyes and fought a horrific urge to scream. With tears, he slowly cut off the woman on the other side of the call.

PART ONE
FEAR

CHAPTER ONE

When she heard the sound, Sally Strathers dashed behind the pillar support to the minimarket and quickly threw her trench coat around her shivering body. *That feels so good,* she thought as the coat's fabric trapped a pocket of warm air around her skin. Her body responded to the comforting heat by slipping at the knees a bit and by sending a chill up her spine that stretched across her back and neck and rolled up to the hair follicles atop her head.

The police siren grew in pitch and became increasingly symmetric in highs and lows. The red and green lights lit up the street, highlighting the bustling travelers and coloring Sally's frozen breath. She watched the puffs of air as they left her mouth and dissipated like psychedelic cigar smoke.

Through the vapor she could see the regulars hiding on the other side of Monroe street; Betsy, Rachel, Cindy, the Heather sisters, all laughing and carrying on as if dorm sisters out for a girl's night.

When the officers zoomed past her, the police siren changed in pitch, and its acoustic trail now sounded like a drunken donkey as the taillights became soft, blending with the illumination of the larger city.

It's too cold. Maybe I'll take the night off. She rapidly

rubbed hands against arms and then plunged them deep into her pockets again. *But rent has to be paid, and I like nice things, so let's do it, Sal,* she motivated herself as she stepped back onto her corner spot.

Lifting her right hand from her pocket, she felt the crisp air strike against her bony black fingers. She grasped her top button with her thumb and forefinger and flipped it and each succeeding button until her coat fell bidirectionally away from her body. Shifting her weight to her left foot, she bent her right knee. Forcing a smile, she flipped her long dark hair over the collar of her coat and smoothed her miniskirt over her charcoal legs.

Twenty minutes, she thought as she watched Betsy disappear into an oversized limousine. Sally recognized the car. It was Ben. He had been a patron of hers many times. She hated the way he spoke to her. "How you doin' tonight?" he'd always ask in that mafia-like baritone voice, as if he cared. Sally hated talking to clients. Everyone knew that wasn't the point, and she'd rather just get it done and back to her corner for the next round of business.

"Excuse me, miss. Twenty dollars?"

Sally whirled around and saw a young boy, couldn't have been a day over seventeen, staring back at her. He was dark haired, tall, slightly chubby, and neatly dressed.

"*Excuse me?* Did you say twenty dollars? Maybe in Vegas, baby, but not here! Now run along before you get hurt and someone thinks I'm with you."

"I'm sorry, I've … I've never done this before," the boy said.

Sally looked at the quaking young man. His face was red and his knees knocked. He was obviously telling the truth. *First lay.* It wasn't uncommon for her to entertain recent high school graduates who could never muster the courage to ask a girl out.

"Look, kid, twenty's real cheap. You got any more cash?"

"All I have is sixty-five dollars. What'll that get me?"

Sally looked at the boy as he pulled out three twenties and a five. Her body wouldn't stop moving in the cold night air. She looked down the street and at her watch: three twenty-five a.m. *This might be my best offer for this time of night,* she reasoned as she grabbed the boy's hand and kissed him on the cheek; it was cold.

"An hour," she said, moving up his face and blowing into his ear canal. The boy winced, took a step backward, and looked into her eyes as if terrified.

"Let's go quickly, please. I don't want to be found out here," he said, leading her away from the curb.

"Don't none of them want to," Sally said. "Don't none of them want to."

CHAPTER TWO

Chief of Police Frank Murphy gasped for breath as he lurched up from his bed, clutching his chest and inadvertently hurling his body pillow across the room.

"What is it? Are you okay?" Lucy, his wife, asked.

"I'm okay. I'm okay," he said, shaking his head as if to further convince her there was no cause for alarm and that she should go back to sleep. The chief looked up at the clock: three thirty in the morning. Why was it that these dreams always came at three thirty in the morning? It was enough to make a man crazy.

"Just another one of those, you know, kind of dreams," he said. Lucy rolled back over and pulled the blanket higher on her shoulder.

"Ah, another one of your prophecy dreams, eh? I really do hate those."

"Yeah, you and me both, but they're kind of a blessing and a curse in my line of business, no?"

"If you say so," Lucy said. "What was this one about anyway? Some kid being tortured or raped, or just a drug dealer spreading disease and addiction to the homeless?"

"Ah nothin' like that, hon," Murphy said, leaning over his wife's body and gently kissing her on the cheek. "Just a minor traffic accident or something," he lied. Murphy'd learned that the true content of his dreams was too much for his wife, and this one was getting really bad.

Walking to the bathroom to briefly relieve himself, he observed that his wife was already snoring by the time he was ready to lie down again. But although Murphy's body was willing to snooze, his mind was full of worry and conjecture, and so he knew sleep just wasn't going to be an option. He headed for the kitchen and grabbed a glass of milk and some stale donuts from the cupboard.

With a sigh he plopped down on his recliner and thought of the recurring dream that had originally started by entering his mind once every few weeks, then weekly, and now was occurring nightly.

Truth was, he was not exactly sure what the dream was about or who was in it or where it took place, but he knew enough to know that there was a woman—a dark-skinned woman lying dead in the middle of everything else going on in the dream, but he didn't know why.

With a sigh he clicked on the cable news and bit into his stale maple bar. It was going to be a long day.

CHAPTER THREE

"What're you laughing at?" the young solicitor demanded of Sally Strathers as he careered toward a beige Geo Metro parked on Elm.

"Nothin' kid," the prostitute said as the two reached the young man's car. "What's your name?"

"You can call me, uh … uh … Cambo," he offered, opening the passenger side for Sally.

She smirked. "Well, that's definitely an original."

Sally slumped into her seat and watched the boy sprint around the car and slip into the driver side, clumsily inserting the key into the ignition. After a few rumblings, the engine sputtered into action, inciting a cacophony as the vent, radio, and seat belt alarm competed for the title of most annoying sound. The boy snapped off the radio just as the chorus of Handel's *Messiah* began.

"Church boy?" Sally marveled.

The twitchy boy shot a series of incalculably brief glances at his guest. The first few were without verbal response; the final was followed by a question. "Why do you ask?"

"Well, uh, I guess because, you know, not too many of my patrons have a CD of Handel's *Messiah* playing while solicitin'."

"I like that song. Have you ever heard it before?"

"I'm a prostitute, not an idiot," Sally said while glaring at the boy with a masterfully crafted face of anger and disgust. *Why is it that no one ever thinks of hookers as having culture? Just because someone has a questionable profession doesn't make one a moron. Besides,* she considered, *I like the job. It pays well, and I can do it on my own timetable.* Sally's head nearly hit the ceiling of the little car as Cambo drove straight over a speed bump.

"In a hurry?" she said, rubbing her neck.

"You know, you're not the most friendly of prostitutes. Maybe you oughta consider some more tact," Cambo said.

Sally laughed quietly, musing over the idea that a guy picking up a hooker was lecturing *her* about tact.

"Look, kid, how far away is this place we're goin'? You know the clock's a-tickin' already?"

"Almost there," Cambo said as he rounded the corner onto Fifth.

CHAPTER FOUR

All through the morning, Chief Murphy thought of the intensity of the dream that was about nothing, but also something; something so important he could almost feel it, almost taste it. Murphy had been a police chief a long time and a human being even longer. He had learned to trust his instincts; he had learned to trust the paranormal. He believed that God was capable of telling a man how to do his job and whom to trust and not to trust, and he believed God was doing so now.

Although busy, he spent the day thinking about the dream and its impact on some black woman he didn't know. He knew, without a doubt, what the dream meant. He had been down this road so many times before. A murder was going to happen. Problem was that although he got the dreams from time to time, they didn't always save the girl. And with this one, he just didn't know the when or who or how of it. But he had to keep the faith, had to believe that in this case he was going to find out. God was giving him the dream for a reason, and the reason was so that he could stop it.

After a rigorous eleven-hour shift, Chief Murphy breezed into the nearly vacant police precinct and fumbled with his keys in his office door. Once in, he crossed the stained gray carpet toward his chair and tossed his badge onto his desk, peering with mild irritation at the flashing light on his "urgent" message machine. *I'm not answering you, so forget it! My shift's over, and Lucy'll be mad for the fifth night in a row.*

Taking a step toward the door, he extended his arm outward, catching the light switch with his finger. He sat for a moment in the darkened doorway as his eyes adjusted slowly to the absence of light. Something was off. In his heart he felt the familiar onset of intuition, the feeling that something important awaited him on the machine. He wondered if it was connected to the dream.

I really can't this time, he told himself while watching the tiny plastic circle on the answering machine repeatedly illuminate. He scrunched his dark eyes, raised his cheekbones, and brought his right hand upward to massage his temples. Taking a step out into the hall, he again fought the overwhelming phenomenal urge to check what was on the machine.

Stopping himself and growling, he turned and clicked the light back on as he moved toward his desk. Grabbing a mint from his candy bowl, he lowered himself onto his swivel chair and brought himself up snug against the oak workplace. He paused for a moment and rubbed a finger across the scratch he had made on the desktop two days prior. After grabbing a pen and paper, he sat and stared at the machine, thinking of the fight he and Lucy had a couple of months prior when the emergency with the fishing boat kept him out until two a.m.

"Well, crap, Lucy, whaddaya want me to do? I'm the frickin' chief of police," he said, moving a finger toward the play button.

CHAPTER FIVE

After a twenty-minute or so drive through town, Cambo steered the Geo Metro carrying himself and his prostitute companion onto a side street with only one house. The edifice was a beautiful two-story Victorian spread. Well lit with meticulous landscaping and a sprawling fence, Sally couldn't help but be excited. In all her years tricking, seldom had she been taken to a ritzy dwelling. She was more used to the Johns taking her to little dumps or Travel Inns.

The boy depressed the garage door opener fastened to the middle of the driver-side sun flap and pulled the car into one of two empty slots in the three-car garage. The occupied slot housed a top-end, black Mercedes-Benz in pristine condition.

"Hey, kid, what's with the sixty-five bucks? Looks to me like you got more to give," Sally said as she emerged from the car and followed him into a kitchen area.

"Take off your shoes," Cambo said as he led her to the living room.

"Seriously, what's with the measly sixty-five?"

"First of all, a deal's a deal. You agreed fair and square to sixty-five dollars, and the time to negotiate was on the street, not in my home, which, second of all, isn't mine—it's my folks. They're on a religious trip to Europe and won't be back for a long time," he said, finding a seat on a large leather sofa.

"Whatever," Sal said. "Let's just get goin'."

"No."

"Listen, I told you your time's tickin' away. Now or never, baby! I ain't waiting around for you to resolve your conscience."

Sally took off her trench coat and began unbuttoning her blouse. Cambo fixed a direct stare on her then stood up and walked briskly across the carpet to her.

"I said no! Stop it! Don't undress anymore! I don't want to have, you know, *relations* with you. That's not why I brought you here. That's not why I bought you."

"Bought me? First of all, no one buys me; they buy my services. Second of all, if you don't want sex, what in the world are you doin' driving me all this way? What do you want from me?"

Cambo stood silently, wearing a subtle smile across his face.

CHAPTER SIX

Chief Murphy hit the play button on his answering machine and readied himself for whatever might be coming.

"You have two messages," the machine whirred. "First message: Wednesday, four oh seven p.m. *Beep!*" The chief listened uncomfortably as the caller breathed heavily into the phone. It didn't sound like an obscene caller, more like someone who was winded.

"Shut up!" a male voice whispered intensely, followed by continued breathing, some whispers, and then more breathing. "Shut up! Please! Go away!" the voice pleaded again. "I'm sorry to scare you, Chief Murphy. I hope you don't mind my calling. I was given this number by someone in your office." The chief lowered his ear toward the machine's speaker and strained to make out the strange noise in the background. The man on the message began crying. "Stop it! Please stop it!" he sobbed, gasping for breath.

Suddenly the speaker output became distorted as the man screamed into the phone. Murphy jerked his head back.

"I know what's happening to me, but I don't know how long I can fight it! I'm going crazy! I'm losing my mind! Please help me! Please, God almighty, save me from this plague! I don't want to hurt anyone! I'll do whatever you want me to, just come pick me up right now before—"

"*Beep!* End of message."

"Stupid machine!" the chief yelled, punishing the desk with a thundering right hook. The chief hit the repeat button and processed the message once again. Beyond the message itself, there was something discomforting about the tone of the man's voice. He leaned forward and puzzled over the message. After a few moments, the chief sat back in his chair and let his body slump into the cushion.

"What in the world was all of that about, anyway?" he questioned, listening to it a third time. After a few seconds, he sat up and checked the source of the call: unknown name and number.

"Well, there's nothing I can do about it now!" he said, looking contemptuously at the message machine. Suddenly he remembered there was another message.

"Next message: Wednesday, four twelve p.m. *Beep!*"

"Hey, Chief, we got another stolen car. Don't worry about nothin', though. I already put out the APB while you were checking out that 1040–02 earlier. Just leaving the message, FYI, like you always ask us to. Anyway, identifying info is a missing Geo Metro: beige, nineteen ninety-five, two-door. It was reported stolen this morning and last seen two nights ago parked on the street at its home residence at fourteen twenty-one Cherokee Court. All right, that's it. I'll catch ya later, Chief."

A frustrated Murphy blasted the desk again.

You have no new messages.

Murphy sat for some time worried about the caller. *Who are you, and who might you hurt?* he wondered, nursing an oncoming headache. He looked up at the large city map fastened to the wall. Seconds transformed into minutes. Finally, he rubbed his eyes and with a sigh grabbed his logbook and inscribed the missing vehicle information into the auto theft section. He then reclined in his seat for a few moments, still uneasy about the first message, which he listened to again in its entirety. Pushing his body forward, his feet caught hold of the floor. He grabbed the phone receiver, dialed his home number, and sat patiently, listening to the onset and offset of ringing.

"Hello?" said the familiar voice.

"Hi, Lucy," he said, bracing himself. "I'm sorry, hon, but I'm running a few minutes late again."

CHAPTER SEVEN

Sally Strathers was frightened and on her feet. "Listen, kid, I don't know what you got in mind, but this night is over. Take me back to my corner now, or you don't even know how messed up my friends'll have you!" Sal lied. She had learned not to trust pimps a long time ago. It was hard to make it to middle age as an independent hooker but would be even harder with the company of a guy named Pierre who smacks you across the face for only making four hundred dollars a night.

"No, wait a minute. You'll get your money," Cambo said. "I just don't want to have ... sex. That's not why I brought you here. I just wanna talk."

Sally's stomach churned. She had a friend who was picked up by a guy like this once. Next thing you know, she was found in a dumpster on Applegate, two bullets in her cranium and a knife wound just below her left scapula.

"Look, just take me back to my corner. You can keep the money, really," she said in a soothing voice, fastening her clothes and retightening her trench coat.

"No, really, I just wanna talk. I promise. You don't need to worry. I'm not a freak or anything. I'm not going to hurt you."

Sally wasn't sure how much she liked the whole scene but sensed that it would be in her best interest not to press the issue and get the boy all riled up. A better plan would be to go along with him for a while then slip out when he was in the john or something.

"Well, a'ight. What you wanna talk about?"

"You," he said, looking pleased she had given up her resistance. Abruptly he turned and walked into the kitchen.

"What about me?"

"I want to know why you became a prostitute," he said, grabbing mugs out of a cupboard.

"Why?"

"I don't know. I'm fascinated. I've always wanted to talk with a real, live prostitute. Get their story. See what's behind it all."

Sally watched him pour milk and cocoa into the cups. It was a bit odd. She hadn't had cocoa since she was a teenager. She wondered where the coffee was. Impulsively she opened her mouth to ask for some and then thought better of it. There were worse things in life than hot cocoa. She turned her attention to her discomfort with his questions and wondered how to get out of talking to him without aggravating him. "Why am I a prostitute? I don't know. I learned it from my mom, I guess. We have a long line of call girls in our family."

"She still alive?" Cambo asked, pulling the cups from the microwave and walking back to the seating area.

"Who, my mom? No," she said, grabbing a cup from his hand. "What's this for?"

"You look cold," Cambo said.

"You didn't, like, poison this or anything, did you?"

"No. Look, I'm a minister type of guy. Honest. I have no desire to hurt you."

"Minister? Yo' church know you picking up street girls?"

"I'm a street minister; the world is my congregation. And I'm not ashamed of talking to you, as my intentions are pure; therefore, why would I be ashamed of anyone finding out?"

"Oh, yeah? Well, if you ain't ashamed of being seen with me, why were you so panicked of being seen on the street?"

He looked blankly at her.

"What kind of minister are you?" she asked.

"Like I said, I'm a street minister type of person. I was a youth minister, and I have been on a religious mission or two, and now I just have local missions. You religious?"

Sally pulled out her necklace and displayed the cross her mother gave her.

"So you're Catholic?"

"Was," she said, tucking her necklace behind her shirt.

"Why'd you quit going?"

"Why do you care?"

Cambo shrugged his shoulders. "Like I said, I'm just interested in people's stories. Tell me, if you don't mind."

Sal thought it over for a minute. She decided she didn't mind. "I don't know why I stopped. There's just things I don't like about religion."

"What? Like hypocrites and stuff?"

"No, no, not that. I mean, yes, I hated the hypocrites, but I figure, you know, that's just human nature and no church's fault."

"So what is it? Why'd you quit going?" he asked, leaning back in his chair and kicking his feet up on the coffee table.

"I don't know. I just didn't think some of it made too much sense, that's all," she said as she set her cocoa on the table next to the boy's feet.

"Like what?"

Sally looked at his young face and noted his soft eyes. They were blue, entrenched in dark lashes, and hidden under bushy eyebrows. He looked friendly, trustworthy, but still…

"Look, I don't know how comfortable I am telling you this stuff, and I don't think it's right you're being so pushy."

"Well, that's a fair comment," he said, pausing to sip his cocoa. "How 'bout if I yak awhile?"

"It's your dollar, kid."

"Do you call all eighteen-year-olds kid?"

You do when you're thirty-nine, kid. Thinking better of the sarcasm, she simply leaned back into the couch and made a circling motion with her hands as if to gesture him on.

"Well, I believe there is a God. I really do. I have no idea what he looks like or who he is *really*, but I believe there's one out there. And if that's true, we all must be connected somehow. And if that's true, then why shouldn't I be concerned that my sister is out prostituting herself to gain money? There has to be a better way."

Sally rolled her eyes. Now she was getting the point of being here. "So you're soliciting me to save me. Okay, I get it. Well, you could've saved yourself some money, kid. I already believe in God, and I've already been saved."

The boy looked over at her and laughed. "I have no desire to convert you by paying you. I just wanted to do something nice. You looked cold, and I doubt you get many people coming around wanting to *talk* with you. Is it so bad what I'm offering?"

Sally had to admit that the boy had been nice to her, and she did like feeling like someone respected her enough to talk with her, yet she was still hesitant. "Well, what do you want from me then?"

"Nothing," the boy said. "What I want is from me. I'm just using you as a means to an end."

"What do you mean?"

"Simple. I was having a bad day and wanted to feel good about myself. Helping other people makes me feel good. Therefore, I have what I want."

It was corny logic, but there was something believable and honest about the boy. Against her better judgment, Sal conversed more freely with him. They talked about their childhoods, parents, and dreams. They discussed politics, pet peeves, and compared favorite media stars. Suddenly Sally noticed the clock: five fifteen a.m.

"It's gettin' late."

"All right," Cambo said, pausing for a few seconds and smiling wryly at her. "Thank you for talking with me."

The two persons walked out to the garage, boarded the Geo Metro, and sped out into the night air. Neither of them spoke as they passed the bridge, crossed the tracks, turned onto Monroe street, and slowed to a stop at Sally's usual corner. Sal looked over at the boy and thanked him for the night.

"It was fun, really. I actually enjoyed myself. Thank you," Sally said.

The boy pulled out a piece of paper from his wallet and wrote his number on it. "Call me if you would like to do it again sometime," he said as she took the paper and got out of the car. Cambo rolled up his window and pulled away from the curb. Sally watched the car merge into the right lane and then stop in front of the traffic light. Suddenly, the reverse lights came on, and the car awkwardly found its way back to the spot where Sally was standing.

"Hey, I almost forgot. You never did tell me why you stopped going to church."

Sally thought for a moment as she looked at the grinning face seated in the car, left arm propped out of the window, right arm hanging lazily atop the steering wheel. She hesitated and then told him that she stopped attending after her first solicitation.

"Ah, you felt too ashamed to return?"

"No, it wasn't that. I just couldn't reconcile how I fit into God's plan."

"What do you mean?" he asked, furrowing his brow and resting his head on the side of his door.

"Well, why would a loving, perfect God not stop me from choosing to be a prostitute?" she asked, the comment hanging in the night air as she turned and walked toward the mini-market.

CHAPTER EIGHT

The man looked up from behind his sweat-filled eyes at the woman on the street corner and tightly clenched the knife in his hand.

Igniting the engine, he sped away from the intersection and traveled a few miles. Quickly, he pulled next to a vacant underpass where he fished for his cell phone and brought it rapidly up to his mouth, darting glances over his left then right shoulder.

"Yeah, it's me. They've made contact. What do you want me to do?"

PART TWO
SUSPICION

CHAPTER NINE

John Joe struggled to relieve the tension in his thighs caused by the tightness of the desk space. Scowling, he first tried rubbing the pain away, but this seemed to only make it worse. Desperate, he sat straight up, pulled his toes backward, and slid his heels out.

"They must not have expected fat people to attend college classes," he muttered with contempt as the blood once again flowed down his leg.

"Here," the girl next to him said curtly, throwing a stack of syllabi onto John's desktop. She was a young girl, fashionably dressed, with well-crimped dark hair and a self-evaluation that was probably too cool for the likes of John. Dropping his gaze to the syllabi, he reluctantly separated the top syllabus from the remaining stack and handed the pile to the sluggish student next to him.

"Whatever happened to a one-page course outline?" John said as he scanned through the lengthy packet. The girl next to him shot him a disgusted glance; he ignored her and kept reviewing the syllabus. Centered atop the document in bolded, sixteen-point Times New Roman font read the Course title: "Philosophy 114: Comparative Religion."

John always felt inadequate when discussing religion with others. His family was not the church-going type. In fact, the only Sunday ritual in his familial history included a newspaper, a porcelain seat, and thirty to forty minutes of slight to moderate discomfort.

Skipping the introductory paragraphs and class mission statement, he flipped to the first thing any reasonable college student would want to know with regard to a new course: the study requirements and grading.

> Ten extra credit points will be awarded for each community religious session attended up to a maximum of fifty points. The religious leader must sign a form stating that you were present for the whole sermon.

Extra credit's always a good thing.

> Assigned texts will include English translations of the *Koran*, *King James Bible*, *Bhagavad Gita*, *The Book of Mormon*, and Darwin's *The Descent of Man*.

Good thing I happen to be both a millionaire and lifeless, he thought, taking time to calculate the page amount of required reading and money necessary to buy all of the books. *Why is it the two-credit classes are always more demanding than the three-credit upper-level courses?*

"Good morning, and welcome to Comparative Religion. Please take your seats and be sure to obtain a copy of the course syllabus that should be floating around."

John looked up to find the source of the voice. It came from a short, slender Caucasian male standing at a lectern housed in the front of the classroom. He wore a double-breasted suit, had diminutive white hair, with an anterior whorl that disappeared over the left side of his head. The man caught John's gaze, and quickly John dropped his eyes, refocusing on the syllabus.

"Class, my name is Doctor Harold Haddelby, and I am a god in embryo."

Ah yes, typical wacko college professor, John concluded as he mused over the notion that a requirement for any Ph.D. in American society must include the severing of the neural areas that correspond with reality, social skills, and sanity. A scarlet-haired female in the front row raised her hand and asked the professor if he were a hippie.

"No, my dear," the old man replied with an unyielding facial expression, "but thank you for your adept insensitivity. Anyone with a brain care to wager a guess?"

A man in the front row raised his hand. "You're a Buddhist?"

"No, but why do you guess such a thing?" the old professor asked.

The man shrugged his shoulders. "'Cause I heard they all, like, believe that when you're good you turn into a cow or something, which is like a god to them."

The professor's apparent interest in the man faded as quickly as it came. "No, but again, thank you for your display of ignorance. It is true that some Eastern religions do believe in reincarnation and that certain animals that are the sustenance providers in terms of life support are a sanctimonious emblem of worship and reverence in some of these religions. Of course, in this country, we don't bother to live a good life with the hopes of someday being a sanctimonious cow. We simply do the job ourselves by stuffing our faces with greasy fast food on a multiple-times-per-day basis."

Several people in the class including John laughed at the sarcasm.

"Now, does anyone with a functioning frontal lobe have a real guess as to why I am claiming to be a god in embryo?"

No one in the class moved.

"Ah, it appears the metaphorical cat has got your tongues. Well, let's see, to answer the question, we must start with basic terminology. First, what is the definition of God?"

"God is whatever you make him to be," said a man in the second row.

"Or her," said a girl on the west side of the class.

"Or it," another said.

"So, if I hear the class right, we are unsure of the identity of God. Is God a person or a thing? Is God a sovereign male, female, bi-gendered individual, or a free-floating energy mass that expands across the far reaches of outer and inner space?"

"Or is there no God?" said a man in the back row.

"*Indeed.* Is there no God?" repeated the professor with emphasis. The question hung in John's ears, running through his mind over and again. It was the question he had asked incalculable times, the very impetus for John's enrolling in Doctor Haddelby's class in the first place.

"Well, I don't know if he's real or not, but I did a whole lotta praying to him during finals last semester," someone at the front of the class joked. A moderate rumble of laughter swept across the room, leaving John to sit back in his chair and become disinterested once again. *Why do all the lamest jokes get laughed at in big group settings?*

"What is your name, sir?" Haddelby asked the impromptu comedian.

"Merci," the student said with a lingering smile.

"Merci what?"

"Bowku," the student said, a wild smirk painted across his face. "My name is Merci Bowku. I think my parents were drunk when they came up with the idea, but that's the name." The class became uneasy as a roar of silent laughter overpowered all of the conscious students.

"Well, Mr. Bowku, I'm curious about something. Did you break the silence after I asked 'is there a God' because you inherited a comedic appreciation from your parents, or because humor is a way for you to cope with the most important question asked in both prerecorded and recorded history? Now, don't answer, but my suspicion is the latter. In fact, my suspicion is that many of you signed up for this elective because, like me, you struggle for the satisfaction of that most evasive question. Specifically, does God exist? Does God actually reside somewhere in the expanse of eternity? And if so, what does he, she, or it want me to do?"

CHAPTER TEN

Bored, Merci Bowku lounged back in his classroom chair and watched his classmates leave the stuffy lecture hall like every classroom of students in the world finishes out a lecture period. First of all, 70 percent of the students leave in mass, thankful to get the heck out of there. Ten percent stay and talk about work, friendship, the news, or tonight's party kinds of things. The rest gather around the professor, offering patronizing platitudes and remarking on how much they learned from his or her infinite wisdom. It was the latter group that always disgusted Merci.

"Suck ups," he mouthed at the backs of the group around Doctor Haddelby. *Guess I better get going.*

Merci huffed to himself and gathered his things. He slid to the side of his desk and stood up, facing the door. *I am so sick of the college thing.* He groaned as he rolled his eyes at a couple of chicks to the right gabbing about some stupid girly thing.

As he walked onto the quad, Merci wondered briefly what to do. He had another class in ten minutes, but...

He turned himself toward the parking lot and decided his car was the best destination for himself at present.

Slowly meandering across the walkway, Merci looked about the quad and took in the smells and sights of campus living. He'd always wanted to go to college, and he loved learning, but the classes were so long and so boring sometimes that he just wished he could go at his own pace.

Turning the corner at the Johnson building, he walked through a crowd of guys talking about last night's game when someone called him out by name.

He turned and looked but didn't see anyone he recognized.

"Merci, Merci Bowku!" the voice came again. Finally, the third time he heard the voice he was able to hone in on the location of the speaker and stared at a fat, unkempt, hygienically challenged male who looked like he'd never met a Twinkie he didn't like.

"Merci? Merci Bowku, right?" the man said again, sticking out his hand but oddly not getting out of his chair, as if Merci should go to him for the privilege of a handshake. Merci complied.

"Hi," Merci said with all the enthusiasm of a five-year-old in front of a plate of broccoli. "Do we know each other?"

"Not yet, but I know your mama, if you know what I mean," the guy joked. Merci wasn't laughing. The man, aware his humor was not being appreciated, cut his cackle off and introduced himself.

"Name's John, John Joe. We got Comparative Religion together with Dr. Haddelby."

Oh, joy.

"Oh," Merci said, looking everywhere but at the guy he was talking to. "Yeah, seems like an interesting class."

"Yeah, I heard Haddelby's pretty good, so I'm kinda looking forward to it," John continued.

"Yeah, me too," Merci said, checking out a chick in a bright pink top and jean pants walking diagonally across the aisle.

"Yeah," John said again, letting his voice trail off. Merci grew bored with the conversation.

"Well, hey, maybe I'll see you around some more some time," Merci said, patting John once on the shoulder.

John smirked. "I guarantee it."

CHAPTER ELEVEN

Adnyl "Addy" Siwel sat behind the group of students and listened to their patronizing comments.

"Wonderful lecture, Doctor Haddelby."

"I loved your use of Kant and how you tied his works into the neo-reformationist theological movement."

"What was it like to win the Cleric's award in Belgium last year?"

"Would you sign this Bible, please?"

What an odd thing to watch someone ask for an autograph on a Bible, Addy pondered, thinking such a thing might just infuriate the being the Bible was about. Haddelby smiled and wrote his name across the inner flap. *Then again, what do I know?* Addy self-deprecated as she sat observing the students shake hands with the widely renowned theologian, only to talk briefly and then slip across the classroom floor, out the door, and into the exterior hallway. After what seemed a decade, the last student finally left the doctor to pack his materials into his briefcase. *Okay, here goes.*

"Doctor Haddelby," she ventured. The old man lowered the top half of his black case and took great care to fasten the latches before elevating his gaze to match that of the nervous young woman.

"Yes, my dear?" The old professor smiled.

"I have a couple of questions for you, if you have a minute?"

"Certainly, my dear, only I ask that you accompany me on a walk toward my next class. I don't like to be late, whenever possible."

Addy felt stupid for approaching the man. She always felt uncomfortable asking serious questions, and she felt especially stupid when it seemed like she was being a burden to someone.

"I'm just curious, sir, or doctor, or…I mean, as to what religion you are?" Her face became flush, and she nursed her anxiety against an urge to run away. Life had been hard lately, however, for Addy, and now more than ever she wanted to know if there was a point to life at all. Any reason to keep herself around another day.

"Now, why do you bother yourself with such a question as that, my dear?" the old man queried, pausing for a moment in the hall.

"Well, if you're the most respected doctor of religion in America, I thought it would be useful to know what religion you settled on, that's all."

"Oh, I see. You want advice on your journey to religious acquisition, is that right?"

Addy nodded.

"If I told you what religion I was, would it really matter?"

"Yes," she said faster than she intended.

"Well then, let me leave you with this thought. Today we live in eternity, whether you believe in evolutionary biology, the Buddhist's nirvana, or Judeo-Christianity's heaven and hell. We are given only guesses in this life as to religion. Is there really any proof that any of the religions, including the religion of science, is ultimately correct? I would be so bold as to offer a no to that question. Therefore, I consider myself a-religious; that is, I belong to none of them and yet all of them at the same time. They are all a part of me, and yet none encapsulate me. The same is true for you."

The old man's stare lingered a moment longer than his voice, and then he offered a grin and a wink of the eye and disappeared through the classroom door.

CHAPTER TWELVE

"Doctor Haddelby's an idiot," John said to Merci, who ate more of his eggs in response. Merci stared incredulously at his new acquaintance, amazed that for some reason he was actually hanging out with him. John and Merci had started hanging out after the first week of class when almost improbably they happened to sit by each other in the large lecture section, and both took to making sarcastic references back and forth about the class and the people in it. John was a little bit of a goofball, but he was better company than the television, and so Merci had been meeting with him every morning for breakfast at the university café.

"I mean come on, dude, you gotta admit the guy's half-baked. I mean, all last week all he could talk about was 'faith this' and 'faith that.' Every week it's the same thing. 'You've got to believe,', 'evidence is nothing,' 'only belief can save the race.' What does that mean, anyway? Are we dying of some plague?" John said in between bites of sausage.

"Well, maybe we are," Merci said. "Abortion, fatherlessness, depression, anxiety, and mental illness are all on the rise."

"Wah!" John said. "I need my Prozac! Help me! I have serotonin deficits!"

"*You're* the idiot," Merci said. "I'm trying to be serious here."

"So am I. But I just hate how all of you religious freaks are always pushing faith on everyone else. It just seems awfully suspicious that there is no *shred* of evidence for *any* of religion's beliefs—and the defense of this problem is always, 'Hey, it's not about proof, it's about believin'. Well, I don't buy it."

Merci furrowed his brow. "Look, I gotta go," he finally said, throwing fifteen dollars on the table and signaling the waitress.

"Well, hey, I'm not trying to tick ya off. It's just

how I feel, man. I mean, I'm not sayin' it can't be true, just that I want evidence, that's all."

"It's not that; I just need to go and process all of these ideas for a while. I'll catch you in class tomorrow."

"All right, man. See you later," John said, obviously concerned he'd made Merci mad.

Merci didn't worry about John's fears for the moment and burst out of the café and dashed across the one-lane road. A light wind tickled his nose and ears and quickly distracted his mood. He grabbed his coat collar and flipped it upward. Burying his chin under the lip of his shirt, he started across the quad to the library. Classes had just ended, and the quad was quickly filling with fast-moving students and slow-moving clichés.

Merci grinned at all of the characters. When he was a child, he used to ponder on the billions of people in the world, each playing a unique part. How each had his or her own social life, family, and dreams. He liked to wonder about where they went home to, who their secret loves were, and what their silent fears consisted of. *If there is a God, how can he keep up with all of the people in the world?* he would question. It just didn't seem plausible. When he was a kid, the thought of God was too much for him. It would even kind of freak him out. And the truth was it still did, so when John started talking about faith and religion, Merci recognized the same old familiar symptoms coming out. He knew he had only moments to get away and turn it around or else …

Merci felt a bead of sweat and was now walking full force, moving as fast as he could across the quad and toward the parking lot. Merci breathed and rehearsed something relaxing in his mind. The trick seemed to work. His heart started pounding less. He tried to think of girls, movies, anything but religion. He just wanted to get into his car, drive home, and go to bed.

He approached his mostly brown station wagon from behind the stadium lot where he had parked it earlier for class. It was a classic of an automobile. Three-toned from the salvage yard and room enough to house the meatier part of the college wrestling team. Nearing the wagon, he fished for his keys in his right pocket while pinching his books and school supplies in between his left arm and ribs. "Urgh!" Merci groaned as he removed his hand from his pocket with only some lint. *It's some kind of supernatural rule that my keys will always be in the opposite pocket of my free hand.*

Determined not to suffer from the intolerable inconvenience of having to shift his books and supplies from his left to his right arm, he thrust his right hand into his left pocket, contorting his body like a yoga master in order to pull the keys out. With no small measure of satisfaction, he sequestered his keys and angled them into the keyhole. As he unlocked the door and pulled it open wide, a horrendous scent filled his nostrils. Merci's eyes fell with his gut upon the partially consumed fish sandwich in the community landfill otherwise known as the passenger-side foot area. He took a mental note to throw the sandwich away when he got home.

Lowering himself into the vehicle and latching his seat belt, he ignited the car, threw it in reverse, and backed out westward a safe distance to allow himself room to push forward toward the freeway. As the wagon slowed to a stop, John knocked on his window.

Merci jerked in his seat and let out a ghastly sound while clutching his chest. "What're you doing?"

"Dude, chill! You left your wallet," John yelled through the rolled-up window. Merci's heart thumped.

"Look, I'm really sorry if I got you riled up this morning. I guess sometimes I don't know when to keep my mouth shut," John said. "Let's try this thing over again sometime, all right?"

"All right," Merci said, giving a little head nod. Awkwardly he sat still until John waved and then paced off into the distance.

As the aloof breakfast companion flirted with the distant buildings at the mouth of the quad, Merci became uncontrollably conscious of his aroused physical state. He was breathing heavily and searing. He tried intensely to distract his mind, but it was too late. Rapidly observation turned to panic, and panic to acceleration. His heart pounded harder. His sweat flowed through his linens.

"Not here!" he pleaded softly, quickly reclining his seat and unbuckling his belt. A surge of tension and energy attacked his knees and spread like wildfire up to his throat. He gasped for air. Great beads of sodium water trickled from his brow and fell silently downward, stinging his eyes and streaking his face.

I'm going to die! I'm going to die!

His gastrointestinal areas erupted with discomfort and pain. The constriction in his throat was unbearable, and he felt himself becoming faint. His visual plane grew distorted and wavy then narrowed. His head was on fire, and his heart felt as if it would burst on any given beat. A crowd of students walking by looked toward him and began pointing and talking. One approached his window and asked if he was okay. Merci tried to nod yes but was actually not sure. *Please, God, get me out of this! Please! Please! Please! I'll do anything! Anything!*

Merci's eyes rolled back as he let his awareness slip away.

CHAPTER THIRTEEN

Addy Siwel lay in her bed, lost somewhere in time and space. *Even though my eyes are closed, I can still see light streaks,* she thought, concentrating on the soft but complex light patterns barely detectable with her eyes shut. *I wonder if this is what blind people see?*

Addy had been lying in her bed for nearly four days. Today she had only left the mattress twice to eat and several times to use the restroom. She currently lay in a supine position with a blanket lying atop her waist and lower body and her feet poking out. Her room was muggy and smelled of stale clothes and exposed food. Addy didn't care for the smell, but it didn't bother her much either. Nothing really bothered her lately, except life.

With great effort she opened her eyelids and, turning her head as minimally as possible, glanced at the time. "Four thirty-one a.m," she read, pulling her eyes away from the clock and fixating on the ceiling fan directly above her.

Whir, whir, whir.

She watched the blades circle endlessly. It was hypnotic, soothing.

Whir, whir, whir.

Addy felt the heaviness of the blankets on her tired extremities. She tried lifting them, but the cost was too great. Her legs and back were sunken in the cupping formation the bed had melded with her body. Time moved horrifically slowly.

Poca-a-poca, she heard in her mind, remembering childhood piano lessons at the orphanage. *You must play slower. Back straight. Now that's it! Slow, like a cat stretching after a nap. Stretch it out, Addy!* Addy hated that piano teacher, Ms. Fadalgo. She remembered being even a bit happy when she died.

Whir, whir, whir.

What is the point of life? she thought, forcing her arm up and then bringing it down to rest against her forehead. Addy saw an image of her father in her mind, or at least she thought it was her father. She was so young the last time she saw him, she couldn't be sure. In the memory, they were playing catch. Her father had thrown her a football, and Addy caught it.

"Good job, Addy!" he said. She smiled a bit and then started laughing out loud as she remembered throwing the ball back to her father. Only she had actually overthrown the ball and hit a nearby dog. The dog let out a terrific yelp and jumped what must have been thirty feet straight into the air, finally landing on its back where it let out the second painful howl. "No, Addy!" her Father scolded her as he chased after the animal. That night she went to sleep, and the next morning he was gone forever. Her mom would follow not long after.

I wonder what they were really like, Addy pondered, now resting her hand on the bridge of her nose. *I wonder why they left me? Why would God let them?* she thought as she rolled to her left side.

"What does it matter anyway?" she said audibly, her voice trailing off before finishing the sentence. She noticed a dirt mark on the wallpaper and wondered about its origin. It was approximately the size of a half dollar and was almost in perfect eye line. Moving her eyes slowly, she followed the ambiguous line patterns of the wallpaper as they weaved in and out of the dirt spot.

I can see why they didn't want me, she thought as the lines and dirt spot formed an image of a donkey riding a horse with a small cloud trailing. *I wouldn't want me either. In fact, I don't want me. I just don't know how to get rid of me.*

The donkey morphed into a mouse, then a lion,

then back to a donkey. Addy rolled onto her back once again. *What's the point of life? What's the point of God if this is what life can be like for someone?* Pressure built in the top of her throat. Her lips pursed, and her breathing became more labored. Small pools of liquid formed in the lower halves of her eyes, causing her sight to become unclear.

I don't want to die, she whined silently, ejecting a tear out of her left eye and curling her trembling lips. *But I don't want to live like this anymore either.* She tried to swallow the pressure in her throat unsuccessfully. Tears were now streaming down her cheeks, making the bed under the back of her head moist and unpleasant to lie upon. She rolled over again and picked up the bottle of aspirin resting on her oak nightstand.

"If I take all of you, will it just end?" she wondered out loud, bringing the bottle of pills to her chest. "Or will it only be different?"

Whir, whir, whir.

CHAPTER FOURTEEN

The man ignored the beads of sweat speckled across his forehead as he sat by the disposable phone and listened to the ringing over and over again. Without variation the phone would ring seven times, then go to voicemail.

Hey, you've reached Sal. I'm not able to talk right now. Leave a message.

"Sal, pick up the phone. You know you want to. You know you need to. Don't be afraid. I'm the good guy. I'm not going to hurt you; that is not my calling. But beware of strangers; they know things about you. They have plans for you," he whispered then hung up and dialed the number again and again, leaving the same message until finally the disposable phone ran out of minutes.

Carefully, he took out a wet wipe and cleaned the phone from front to back, then emerged from his car and found the nearest trashcan, where he dumped it, careful to rearrange the top layer of trash to hide the phone.

Slowly he took in a deep breath and then traversed the short distance back to his vehicle from the trashcan, where he took out a pair of binoculars and peered through the magnified air at Sal. He took his time to take in her gorgeous frame, beautiful hair, and curvaceous posture.

How come sometimes doing one's job can feel so devilishly good?

PART THREE
OBSESSION

CHAPTER FIFTEEN

Doctor Haddelby cleared his throat loudly as if to signal that the class should quiet down and attend to him. "Class," he said, holding up the course syllabus. You'll all notice that due in some number of weeks is your final project. Now, we haven't spoken about it much as to this point in this semester, but in the words of Paul, 'Fear not.' The project is fairly easy and will involve the following: you are to attend a religious service of any faith. In fact, you must attend three services, and I would encourage, although not require, you to sample different theological paradigms, such as one Hindu service, one Jewish service, and one Catholic service. However, if you prefer to attend, say, three Episcopalian services, that would suffice.

"Once you've attended your three services, you will then write a summary report of the main content themes of the service. So if the lecture is on faith, write of faith. If the lecture is on obedience, write the main tenets of obedience as defined by the observed religious leader. Once you've attended your three services, you will then meet with your group members, whom you will choose shortly, and prepare a class presentation to be delivered at the end of the semester. Now I'll entertain any questions regarding this matter after you've broken into small groups."

Addy looked at the three men seated in front of her and wondered why she was always the one who had to break the ice.

"Hi, I'm Addy. Looks like you guys need one more. Mind if it's me?" she asked, wishing Haddelby would have just assigned groups himself.

"Of course not," the man on the left said. Addy smiled and sat down. "I'm John Joe," he said.

"Cameron Bo," the man in the middle said.

"Merci," said the man on the right.

"I remember your name." Addy giggled. *He's cute,* she thought, analyzing his soft eyes and unsettled hair. The group sat silently for a moment, no one sure what to say next.

"So what should we do? Should we all go to the same sermons as a group, or should we divide and conquer?" John asked. Addy looked briefly at him. He was sporting sweat pants and a faded football T-shirt that exposed his lower abdomen.

"I don't care. What do you all think?" Merci asked.

"I'd really prefer to go to services alone," said Cameron, squinting his eyes while he spoke.

"Fine by me," John said, slipping his hand under his shirt and scratching his now very exposed stomach.

"I'd actually prefer to go with someone," Addy said, looking invitingly at Merci, who quickly changed the subject.

"Well, maybe we should take an inventory of where we are religiously and see how we fare as a group.

I'll start. I was born Jehovah's Witness, but my folks aren't practicing. I kind of consider myself Methodist, although I'm not officially a member of the church," Merci said, fixing his gaze on John as if to signal the passing of the unseen torch.

"I'm nothing; heathen type, pretty much," John said, finally taking his hand off his stomach.

"I'm still exploring. I don't know what I am," Addy said, stealing glimpses at Merci.

The group looked toward Cameron, who was staring into his cell phone. Suddenly he looked up and smiled. "Oh, I guess it's my turn." He seemed to reflect for a moment.

"I don't know," he said, looking eerily into Addy's eyes. "People are my religion, not books."

CHAPTER SIXTEEN

Sally peered through the windowpane, observing the passage of the desert soil that rolled on for miles, only to disappear over the arc of the earth.

"How much longer 'till we're there?" she asked.

"Couple more minutes. We really *are* almost there this time," Cambo said while sporting a playful grin.

Sal reached down for her water bottle. "Yeah right," she said. "We're *real* close until we take another one of your shortcuts," she said, unscrewing the cap and taking a swig.

"Hey, it was one of those shortcuts that brought you and me together in the first place, you know?" Cambo said, turning his face toward her and protruding his chin while raising his eyebrows. Sal reflected the gesture with more than a hint of derision.

"So what's this date all about anyway?" Sal asked.

"It's not a date. It's an outing."

"Well, we sure go on a lot of outings lately."

"Hey, you don't *have* to go," Cambo said as he thrust his left hand upward into the turn signal stick.

"I know, I know. I'm just kidding! Look, you gotta lighten up a bit, kid, 'cause it ain't funny when you gotta label it all the time, you know what I mean?" she said, worried she may have offended him. The truth was, she did like their outings. He was a real sweet guy and kinda cute too. Mostly, though, she liked having a man who was willing to hang out with her without any intimate favors in return—although it did make her feel a bit unattractive at the same time. No one had ever turned her down before, and she couldn't help wondering if maybe she was too old or too fat nowadays, or just not attractive in general. Maybe guys only liked her because they were desperate, and they would have picked up anyone on the street corner at those times. Maybe there was nothing special or beautiful or desirable about her at all.

The car veered off the main highway onto a long gravel road. Every few seconds the vehicle would shake violently as the rocks under the tires grew larger and more implanted in the parched soil. Approaching fast was a tiny square house about as big and wide as a half-sized singlewide trailer.

"Where in the world are we?" she asked, sitting up and whirling her head around. A trail of dust was visible for at least a half-mile behind the speeding little car.

"This is Auntie Deb's place."

"This is where your aunt lives? How sad," Sally said, assessing the entirety of the approaching house could fit into her living room.

"It is kind of sad," he said, braking and throwing the stick into neutral. "And just so you know, she's not my real aunt. That's just what she likes to be called."

Sally rubbed her neck a little, irritated at the unnecessary abruptness of the stop. She grabbed the door latch and pulled it toward her. Dropping her shoulder, she thrust her weight into the door wall which, hesitating momentarily, flung open awkwardly. Stepping out of the car and grabbing her purse, she surveyed the expanse around the house. Sally didn't like the desert plains much, but she was awed by the beauty of the roaming clouds that stretched like shedding cotton fields across the picturesque sky.

"Well, is she a friend of the family or something? I mean, how did you meet her?" Sally asked as she followed the boy to the front door.

"One of my minimissions," he explained as he grabbed the knob. He turned and obviously noted her confused facial expression. "I met her when we were doing the rural outreach marathon, which is this project my old church had to proselytize to families that live far out of the cities and towns. The idea is to bring the good news to everyone without discriminating against them just because they live far away."

"So you, like, converted her or something?"

"No, just the opposite. She wouldn't have anything to do with me."

"Then why in the world are we out here?"

"Because she's still human. She's still one of God's children. And on top of that, well, her husband died, and she has three little children, and I just want to make sure she's okay," he said. He finally turned the knob and opened the door. "C'mon, she's a real nice lady. You'll like her. Just don't bring up politics or religion unless you got three hours to kill."

Sally watched Cambo fondly as he disappeared into the tiny house. She mused upon the unusual attraction she felt toward him. How it had been building over their increasing time together; walking in the park, or debating philosophies and politics, or eating in cafés. How she felt almost a compulsive urge in her bosom every time they were together, compelling her to touch him, hold him, feel his warmth. Not in a sexual way, but more of an intimate holding, a connectivity. The feeling was very foreign to her; typically, she felt nothing toward men except boredom and disgust.

"He's twenty years younger than you, Sal," she muttered under her breath as she cracked a smile and pressed forward into the tiny residence.

CHAPTER SEVENTEEN

John picked up the remote control and fell sideways onto the couch. He lay for a moment, feeling the plastic device in his hand and observing his thumb resting on the power button. *I shouldn't do this,* he thought, grabbing a pillow and shoving it under his head. Depressing the button, he waited as the screen hissed its high frequency electric sound and produced an initially blurry picture that progressed into an amalgam of crisp hues and contrasting lines and figures.

Turn it off, he weakly commanded himself while concurrently searching the satellite menu for his viewing options. "*The Cosby Show, Dick van Dyke, Friends, Roseanne, Whose Line Is It Anyway?*" he read, flying through the channels. Finally the screen displayed the adult movie varieties. He glanced at the clock on the in-screen menu: 12:13 a.m. *Why do I do this to myself?* he pondered, reading through the descriptions of each movie. He felt a surge of energy in his thighs and loins and shifted his weight on the couch to accommodate the discomfort. *Turn it off!* he repeatedly instructed himself. He began to feel a rush of excitement as he committed himself to viewing one of the programs. He selected the text and read the price per view: $12.50. Quickly he turned off the set and threw the remote across the room. His body ached and grew sweaty.

Why do I think there's something wrong with watching that stuff? Is it because of my dad? My religion? Above him he could hear the sounds of movement. There was obviously some kind of party on the upstairs floor. John lay quietly for some time, listening to the excessively loud music and numerous bumps and footsteps above.

Those people don't care about morality, he thought, *and they all seem to be doing fine. They get decent grades, get married, have kids. Am I just being stupid?* John brought the palms of his hands to his face and fought an urge to retrieve the remote control. He lay quietly for a few more moments, analyzing the distorted rhythms from the party's music track. For a moment he considered going upstairs and finding a girl to spend the night with. He quickly dismissed the thought. *She wouldn't want you anyway.*

Rolling sideways over his arm, he clumsily flung himself off the couch and headed across the floor to the bathroom. He adjusted his clothing and leaned over the porcelain seat, resting on his left arm while dangling his face over the bowl. *What's the big deal anyway? I'm not even religious. I really don't buy it all anyway, so why do I feel this way every time I start doing this kind of stuff?* John flushed the toilet, reset his clothing, and washed his hands. He caught his face in the mirror and looked himself in the eyes. *What's wrong with you?*

CHAPTER EIGHTEEN

Addy Siwel looked up at Doctor Haddelby and wondered what his private life was like. Was he a father, a husband, a louse? What made him so famous, respected, or knowledgeable about God? Does eight years of college really make someone spiritual or actually just the opposite?

"That's my point exactly," the doctor said, moving on for a third iteration of his main points to the mostly attentive students. Addy surveyed her classmates. Most of them were well groomed, white, and looked like they came from upper middle class homes. She glanced at Merci, who was writing some notes about the lecture. His pen moved as if in organized pandemonium, filling line after line with indecipherable scribbles. Randomly seeded amid the scratchings were key words from the lecture: *evolution, faith, infinity, beliefs.* She smiled at him. He saw her do so and smiled back.

"Ms. Siwel, what do you think about the woman's comment?"

Addy jerked her head forward, encoding every detail of Haddelby's posture. A few seconds of awkward silence engendered tension in the silent classroom. To her left, a chair squeaked as a large man attempted to rearrange his body.

"Well, I think of it this way, professor," Merci said, briefly placing a hand on Addy's knee as if to calm her anxiety; she fought showing another smile.

"There must be a beginning and an end to creation, whether or not one believes in creationism or whether one believes in evolution."

"Any other thoughts?" the professor asked.

Another student raised her hand. "I think there must be a beginning and an end as well. How could it be possible otherwise?"

"Fine, fine," the old professor said, grinning. "It seems the majority of you feel that regardless of whether a deity was involved, life began somewhere and life will end somewhere. There are alternative explanations, however. For example, the idea that there was a beginning, but there will be no end. And there is also the thought that there was no beginning, but there will be an end."

"Except evolutionary theory has proven that there was a beginning, that we all evolved from basic cells and stuff," said a freshman student in the front and center section of the classroom.

"Oh, excuse me, class. Here I am prattling on about endless theory when apparently Darwin has already incontrovertibly resolved the riddle of life! Well, I have nothing more to say then," Haddelby said then approached the freshman and glared down at him disapprovingly. The freshman looked uncomfortable. "Now before I get into the real problem with your statement, let me first just refute your premise of evolution explaining a beginning by pointing out that evolution runs up against a significant problem, in that any evolving process must have something to evolve from.

"A basic scientific law is that matter cannot be created. Therefore, Mr. Lewell, where might you suppose matter came from in the first place? Where did matter begin? How did matter begin where there was nothing there in the first place? And if you can tell me where matter was created where there was actually nothing in the first place, then you have just violated your basic law that matter cannot be created!" Doctor Haddelby said. "Now beyond that, who can tell me the grave mistake this young man just committed?"

The class sat uneasily for about a half minute. Finally John raised his hand. "He assumed evolution had occurred."

"Precisely!" the doctor exclaimed, repeating what John had said slowly and clearly. "And do we actually know that evolution has occurred?"

"Well, yes!" the freshman persisted, regaining his composure and looking indignant.

"Oh, really, Mr. Lewell? You know it occurred *for sure?* My, I didn't realize you were around to see it! You know, for as old as you must be, you hide your age well. Freshman well," the professor said.

"Well, no, of course that's not what I'm saying; look, maybe I wasn't around to see it, but I don't have to see it! I see the residual, the living evidence today!"

"Balderdash! I can say the same thing about religion. We are the living evidence of creationism, right? The earth is God's handiwork, right? Wrong! No reputable academic accepts that kind of primitive logic. Now give me hard *facts,* man, not tautologies! Tell me something irrefutable to validate your naïve assertion that evolution occurred. Case closed!"

"Well, I can't do that, obviously, which is why you're so bold about it. But, well, I feel I *can* say that if it didn't occur *for sure*, then it is at least very, *very* likely that it occurred, because numerous studies say it did. And these studies hold up in different countries, and with different cultures. And they explain issues like genetic mutation, and sexual selection, and phobias, just to name a few," the freshman said.

The professor looked at the young man with an intrigued smile. "Has anyone ever received junk mail in which a young, attractive stock broker on the cover of the letter claims that he has been sending you numerous letters full of free advice on what stocks to invest in, and if you had only listened to him and invested in the stocks, you would now be two or three hundred thousand dollars richer?"

A few students nodded their heads.

"How can this be explained, if he actually lists the dates of the previous letters with the past recommended stocks?" Haddelby looked around the room tauntingly. "And the answer is simple. He just makes enough predictions that some small number of them will be right. Then after he has guessed a couple rounds correctly, he advertises only those things he got correct and looks prophetic. Of course, the man actually has no idea what the market will do in the future and never has! He was just manipulating the data! But too late. The money is in and the dice are rolled, and the only people hurt were the idiots who couldn't sort good from bad conclusions! Now, do you finally get it, Mr. Lewell?" the professor asked in an over-controlled verbal staccato.

"You see, the stock broker can convince people by taking current data and showing how it got here from the past. That is not real research! Real, meaningful research can take current phenomena and tell us how it predicts the future! Since evolution, if it is real, happened millions and millions of years ago, then the best we can do with it is to retrofit ideas of how it *might* have worked, but we can never test it with a future predicting method. Therefore, all of your studies are fundamentally flawed and yield little to no meaningful data! They are no more meaningful than lining up a thousand studies that show how religious phenomena such as faith, repentance, and belief in deity prove the existence of God! That's just not how it works here, son! Maybe in biology, but not in philosophy! Here we see evolution and religion for what they are worth: theories! They are nothing but ideas about what might have happened! Ideas that may ultimately discontinue being theories by becoming fact or by being disproven. But right now, all any of them are, are ideas. Nothing more, nothing less!"

Secretly the man fantasized over Sal as he listened to Dr. Haddelby's naïve insights about evolution versus religion. "Tell them to shut up!" a shrill voice from nowhere commanded. He ignored it. An ethereal female image emerged from the chalkboard at the front of the class, took a step toward him, and opened her mouth.

"Tell them to shut up! Tell them you are the prophet of this people!" she said before dissolving. The man continued to ignore the images and voices, pretending rather to be interested in the class lecture.

"Kill the freshman!" another voice commanded. His body shuddered as he recognized the familiar sound.

"Kill the freshman!" the voice repeated. The man was frightened but dared not budge. He didn't want the others to notice anything different about him. He wanted them to trust him and not throw him in some loony bin. He knew what those were like.

"Kill the freshman now with the gun in your backpack!" two voices commanded in stereo. The man was now sweating, his heart expanding, ready to burst. He had to get away. He spun his head around; the debate around him was getting more intense. Time seemed to stand still. The voices repeated commands unceasingly. The ringing in his ears grew deafening. He thought of the gun in his backpack and began raising his right hand toward the zipper.

"No!" he whispered sternly to the lead voice, clutching his head as discreetly as possible. He had to leave, immediately, but no one could know or suspect anything, so he had to leave nonchalantly, as if nothing were wrong. He extended his sweaty arm across the desk and grabbed his book bag, trying not to think about the metal object inside.

"No! They'll know about you if you leave!" the

male voice whispered. "I'll tell them, and they'll lock you up forever!"

Stop it! he screamed in his mind. *Leave me alone!*

Instantly the voices left. The ringing lowered in decibel level. The images and sensations were absent.

The man stood up and started walking toward the door, breathing heavily. No one seemed to notice his plight as the debate raged on and on, sucking up the group's attention. Reaching the hallway, he walked quickly into the nearest restroom. He hurriedly checked under the stalls to verify that they were empty. After a last look over his shoulder, he entered the farthest stall, closed it, and latched the door. Tears streamed down his cheeks as he lowered the seat cover and sat down. He opened his mouth and strained his face, choking back the pain in his throat. With fervor he unzipped his backpack and grabbed the small revolver pistol. Deliberately, he brought the gun to his face and examined the silver plating and burrows of the revolving pin.

Help me, God!

PART FOUR
COMPULSION

CHAPTER NINETEEN

Addy leaned over and dimmed the light. Finding her resting spot on the couch again, she leaned back and looked silently at the man slumbering on the recliner. She smiled as she watched his eyes move violently under their slender fleshy veils. *He's not sleeping well.* She wondered what might be keeping him awake at night. Addy closed her eyes and enjoyed the feeling of having a man sleeping in her presence. It'd been a long time since she spent the night with someone, and she longed for the companionship of another human being. She imagined his body next to hers, not in a romantic way, but rather she longed to just cuddle with him; feel the warmth of his being beside her.

Addy opened her eyes again and chuckled silently as Merci's breathing became increasingly heavy and audible. At first the noise was a semi-high pitched wheezing, but after several minutes, a unique snore stumbled in and out of his vocal register, ultimately becoming so loud that Addy didn't quite know what to do with herself. Finally Merci emitted an acute, ghastly blend of grunts and wheezes, causing him to tremor violently and wake up. He jumped up so quickly that Addy couldn't help but scream.

"What's happening?" Merci asked.

"It's okay! You're all right," Addy said. "You just fell asleep, that's all. Just relax."

Merci breathed heavily while rubbing his hands in his eyes. "I'm sorry … I'm so embarrassed. I totally didn't mean to do that. Oh, geez, I, uh, I'm really sorry. I didn't mean to do that."

"It's no big deal, really. Truth is, I like that you felt comfortable falling asleep here."

"You like that? Okay. Well then, glad I can float your unusual boat."

"What? I'm the freak because I like people feeling comfortable enough to fall asleep in my house? That makes me crazy?"

"No, it's that voice that keeps telling you to get a sex change that makes you crazy," Merci said. Addy launched a throw pillow toward his head but tagged him in the chest.

"What time is it?" Merci asked.

"It's ten. You were only asleep for about fifteen minutes. You could go back to sleep if you want. It's really okay with me."

Merci smiled at Addy for a few moments and then looked down at his legs. "Thanks," he said, making eye contact with her again, "but I'll pass. I'm too afraid I'd say something awkward or snore real loud or something."

Well, you're already one for two. Addy grinned.

"What?" Merci asked. "What're you smilin' at?"

"Oh, is it a crime to smile these days?" Addy rose off of the couch and walked toward the kitchen. "Hey, you want something to drink?"

"Sure, just for a minute, then I really ought to go," Merci said, standing and following her into the kitchen. "So where were we anyway?"

"I don't know, and I don't care either," Addy said while grabbing pops from the fridge.

"What do you mean you don't care? The project deadline isn't getting any further away. We really need to get serious about doing it, instead of just messin' around every time we get together," Merci said, taking a pop from Addy.

"I know, I know. It just gives me a headache, you know? The whole school thing," Addy said, popping open her beverage and taking a large swig. The carbonation from the soda caused her throat to tingle initially before escalating into an uncomfortable burning sensation. She opened her lips and let out a pocket of the carbonized air.

"We'll, why d'ya go to school if you hate it so much?"

"I don't know."

"Seriously, I just want to know. Why?"

Addy looked over at him and pondered over how serious she wanted the conversation to be. *Is he ready for this?* she thought, noting the scar on her left wrist. She reached over with her right hand and pulled her sleeve over the scar. "I just go, okay, is that all right with you?"

"Yeah, I don't care. I mean, I do care, but not like, you know, if you go get educated and all, but like, you know, I'm glad to, well, you know…" Merci finally retreated into his Sprite.

"What're you talking about?"

"Nothing, I don't know. Let's change the subject, all right?"

"You trying to say you enjoy me?" Addy said in a bad imitation of a proper English voice. "You trying to say you like me?"

"Well, not when you do that Princess Diana after a lobotomy impression."

"Really, so you're not denying that you like me? Interesting, well, time to make my head big. What do you love and worship about me so much? What inspirational qualities do I possess that render you powerless to follow me around like a lovesick lemming?" Addy asked, feeling a tingling in her stomach and a quiet sense of desperation that Merci would tell her he was kidding and leave.

"Lovesick lemming? Wow, I can honestly say I've never been called that before in all my days."

"*All* your days? You're so old."

"To answer your question, I don't know. I just like you, I guess. I don't know, I just think you're attractive, that's all."

"I'm 'attractive, that's all.' So effectively you are admitting to me that you're a shallow, stinking pig who lets attraction rule your relationship interests, is that it? Well, you sure know how to make a lady feel good about herself," Addy said, making a dopey looking face and saying to herself in her best redneck voice, "Hey, yur like, real pre-tee, lay-dee."

"Seriously, you have got to cut out the impressions. Honestly. And no, I am not saying I only think you're attractive. There are lots of attractive women in our class that I—"

"What are you, like, the world champ o' stupid? You're actually sitting there, trying to come on to me, and now you're telling me that you've noticed that I'm in a class full of outstandingly attractive women? How dense can you be? That's like 'Asking Girls on a Date One-oh-One' kind of stuff. Rule one: don't tell her she is one of a sea of attractive women you check out."

"Hey," Merci said, placing his pop off to the side of the table and grabbing Addy's hands. "You don't make it easy for a guy to ask you out do you?" he said, looking her in the eyes. "Now look, I'm going to start over, and you're going to astonish the world by shutting up and letting me finish before you take this honesty and use it against me. Now, as I was saying, there are lots of attractive girls in the class, but you are the only attractive *woman*."

Addy felt tingles climb up her spine and basked in the warmth of his firm hands on hers. She gazed into his eyes and surrendered to the telling smile that formed on her lower face. After several silent moments, she lowered her head and moved it closer to his. He brought his face dangerously close to hers; so close they could each feel each other's warm breath on each other's skin. A large smile crept upon Merci's face as he lifted his hand to her head and gently rubbed the left side of her jaw line and across her neck. Addy brushed his face with hers, letting his stubbly bristles scratch against her cheek, until she found his ear.

"Merci," she said softly, pulling herself back away

from his ear until she could see his eyes again, "that was the cheesiest line I think I ever heard."

Merci laughed, hung his head low, and dropped his hands on the table in a synchronized slap. "Look, if I promise to dispense with the pickup lines, and you promise to dispense with the corny impressions and the sarcastic, not to mention highly insensitive banter, do you think we could start a relationship tonight?"

Addy smiled and picked his hands up off the table, leaned over, and kissed him for several seconds. "Does that answer your question?"

Merci looked back at her from across the table with an involuntary grin. "Not quite," he said, leaning over for another kiss.

CHAPTER TWENTY

That's friggin' cold! John groaned silently as he jerked the car door closed. *Maybe I'll wait just a few more minutes,* he considered as he looked down the empty street. *Or maybe I should just go home.* Sitting back in his seat, he felt the chill of the vinyl against his neck. Leaning forward, he grabbed the hood attachment to his coat and spent a few frustrating minutes snapping it on before pulling it clear over the top of his head. He sat back again and picked several potato chips out of the grab bag in the passenger seat. *What time is it?* he wondered as he shoved his keys into the ignition.

The small radio clock struggled to illuminate. "Eleven twelve p.m.," he read, again wondering if he should just go home.

Grimacing, John looked out the fogging window while reclining his chair several inches. *What am I doing here?* he pondered as his eyes meandered up to the heavens. It was an overcast winter night, the kind that puts one in a subdued mood. John looked in his rearview mirror and saw the light of an oncoming car. Quickly he slouched down to a level he thought would hide the fact anyone was in his parked vehicle. With his right hand he adjusted the mirror so as to follow the progress of the approaching car.

The focused light grew steadily brighter on the white two-story house several dozen feet behind John's car. Soon, a slow-moving vehicle with one headlight drifted lazily around the curve, highlighting each house as it went by. John squinted his eyes as the light contacted the rearview mirror. John yawned as the car passed on his left and flowed in an unceasing manner down the remainder of the street, pausing only for a stop sign every so often. He blinked his eyes several times, seeing the residual image of the singular headlight dance around his visual plane with every shutter.

Okay, seriously, this is stupid. I'm going to go home now, John decided, sitting up and igniting the vehicle's engine. The engine first hesitated, then sputtered into action, racing initially, and then retarding to a slow, steady firing pattern. Depressing the brake and shifting the car into drive, John reached his left arm around the steering wheel and turned on his lights. Blankly he stared across the streams of light and fixated on a one-story house approximately fifty feet ahead of him. His body began to ache and yearn for satisfaction. John tried desperately to shift his thoughts to something else, but to no avail. *C'mon, John, you're better than this. What're you doing?* he thought while killing the engine and clicking off his headlights.

CHAPTER TWENTY-ONE

Sally leaned forward and grabbed the back of Cambo's neck with her left hand. He looked over at her and then let his gaze drift back toward the road ahead. She smiled at him and leaned sideways to give him a kiss before nestling into her chair.

"What're you thinking about?" Sally asked.

"I dunno. Nothing, really. What're you thinking about?"

"Why are you dodging the question? Is it something bad?"

"No," Cambo said flatly, switching lanes.

Sally looked at the young man, encoding his every detail. He was obviously concentrating on something. She could always tell when he was processing something because he consistently made the same face: brow scrunched together, eyes somewhat dissociated on a fixed point, his tongue moving repeatedly across the upper ridge of his teeth. Sally watched as Cambo briefly took his hands off the steering wheel and rubbed his temples.

"Feeling all right?" she asked.

"Uh, yeah, just my head's hurting."

"Got a headache?"

"No. Well, yeah, a little bit. More like I'm just having a hard time concentrating. My head's kind of stuffy, ears are ringing a bit. I dunno, I feel like I'm not seeing all that well."

"I'm sorry, babe," Sally said while gently rubbing his leg. "Anything I can do?"

"No, I'll be fine. Thanks anyway," he said, turning the corner to Cottonwood Lane. "So, you hungry?"

"Starved. Where do you wanna eat?"

"Joe's Place."

Sally rolled her eyes. "Why do you like Joe's Place so much?"

"I don't know. They have the best fries in the world, for one."

"Not really. I mean, the food's fine, but I wouldn't say it was anything *special.*"

"I like it. Besides, it's never crowded, which makes it, you know, a good place to just sit and think. Or talk. Or whatever. You know, it's always kind of vacant that way."

That should clue you into something, Sally thought, deciding she would get the French dip again. Looking outside her window, she watched as the people on the sidewalk zoomed by, some in groups, some in dyads, and a few in solitude. *More than six billion people in the world. That's hard to imagine,* Sally thought as the car turned down a practically vacant street. She knew this part of town well; it was dangerous. The only people stupid enough to be out on this street at this time of night were suicidal maniacs or unfortunate souls whose cars broke down.

Sally laid her head back on the headrest, closed her eyes, and tried to imagine six billion people all at once. *Do they all eat, love, think about life, miss people, hate people?* Sally opened her eyes again and looked at the incoming stream of streetlights. *How would a God keep track of all of them? How could you answer six billion people's prayers? How could you keep track of so many different people at the same time? There's just no way.* Sally adjusted herself in the chair, pulling her skirt back down over her legs to buffer against the chill in the car. Off to her side she could see the reflection of the vehicle in the passing store windows. She sat mesmerized for several moments as the compact Geo Metro danced back and forth from large and small reflections across the numerous store fronts.

"It's starting to snow," Cambo observed, flicking on the windshield wipers. Sally looked out the front window, smiling at the white flecks descending with such simple beauty. She secretly loved the snow season. It reminded her of Christmas when she was younger and her mom wasn't working the street. She used to pretend to be fast asleep long enough for her mom to stop checking in on her late Christmas Eve, then she would leave the bed and pass the night sitting on the window ledge, breathing the chilling midnight air through the window screen and spying for Santa's sleigh. She closed her eyes and recalled the sensation of the freezing air filling her lungs.

"Now you're the one who's thinking," Cambo said, smirking in her direction for a few seconds before returning his gaze to the road ahead.

"Yeah," Sally replied, still closing her eyes. "Just a little nostalgic."

"What're you remembering?"

"Oh, I dunno. Being a kid. You know, that kind of stuff. It's been a long time now."

"Don't you mean an *extremely* long time?"

"Don't push it, kid. Just 'cause I ain't no spring chicken doesn't mean I can't kick your butt."

"Seriously, what are you thinking about? Those fond childhood nights hookin' with mom?"

"Shut up! Really, I don't even know why I put up with you!" Sally said, socking him in the arm. "Actually, I was just thinking about Christmas when I was a kid, if you must know."

"Well, I must. Do tell."

"Nah. It's really not all that exciting."

"I'll be the judge of that. Seriously, what about it?"

"Oh, I don't know, I'm just remembering, you know, what it was like to be a kid. To feel safe and loved and that the world is so big, all of that. Don't you ever think about that stuff?"

"Not really. Sometimes, I guess."

"You don't *ever* think about being a kid again?"

"No."

"What is wrong with you?" Sally said as she rolled her eyes. "Don't you have *any* positive memories?"

"Yeah, I guess. I just don't care much, that's all."

"'Cause you're a man."

"Yeah, that's it. It's just that simple."

Sally looked back defensively at her recently formalized boyfriend. "Well, hey, don't get your panties in a bunch."

Cambo looked back at Sal and spoke with an unusually cross voice, "Well, don't go asking about stuff you don't really want to know."

CHAPTER TWENTY-TWO

"Forget this," John muttered, popping the latch and thrusting his shoulder into the door while swinging his left leg out onto the frozen street. Pausing for a moment to grab his black leather gloves, he then awkwardly swung his right leg street-ward as well, rubbing his upper thigh on the lower steering wheel.

"I really need to get a man-sized car," John said as he tossed the door shut. He stood for a moment looking up the street ahead. All was silent. Slowly he slipped his hand into his pocket and felt the hard metal object. He ran his fingers silently across its smooth surface contours, debating his next move. After grasping it a few seconds, he could feel the cold transferring across the material of his gloves and into his aching fingers. *Let's go,* he thought, initiating forward motion.

The street was icy, and a light flurry of snow began to descend from the skies. The tip of John's nose burned. His breath visibly fled from his mouth, spread wide, and vanished with every few footsteps. Toward the end of the first block, he slipped somewhat, recovered, and adjusted his speed to a slower, more careful pace. *It's not too late to stop,* John thought as he turned down Wakeland Lane and headed for the adjacent court. Although he thought of his alternative options, he knew that he could not talk himself out of it at this point. He was too excited, and the urge was unrelenting. *Maybe better to just get it over with and go home. Start fresh tomorrow; handle it before it builds up so bad,* John reasoned. He began to breathe more rapidly and could hear his heart pounding as he approached her corner. Standing by the icy street sign, he looked at the brown duplex and its neighboring homes. Only two had lights on from the front view.

With a sigh, he strode briskly toward his usual path alongside the bushes. Despite the cold, he felt a rush of energy and heat overcoming his body as he approached her gate. With haste he peered over the gate to make sure there was no activity in the backyard. After being satisfied he could enter without incident, he reached up to unlatch the lock.

Suddenly the duplex three houses down let out a loud mechanistic noise. It was a moving garage door. Panicked, John dropped to his hands and knees. He looked over toward the noisy house and saw an old

Buick fire up, its reverse lights illuminating. John tried to remain motionless as the oversized vehicle ventured out into the open air.

Please nobody see me, John thought, ashamed and fearful of being caught. *How would I explain this to everyone?* Through the frozen night air, John saw the brake lights of the car shining, casting added illumination to his hiding spot.

From the duplex John could hear laughter. *She's got company tonight,* John noted, wondering if maybe he should just go home. *Nah, even less reason to worry about being caught,* John reasoned as the Buick drove away. *Besides, that might make it more interesting.*

CHAPTER TWENTY-THREE

Sally let a few moments pass in silence before she responded to the irritated comeback Cambo had just made. Finally, she broke the silence.

"Why is it whenever I ask you how you feel, you seem to just clam up? It's like you don't trust me. What have I ever done for you to have problems trusting me?"

Cambo looked her direction with a hardened face for only a few seconds longer, and then he physically relaxed his expression, as if to say he was sorry.

"It's not that I don't trust you. Truth is I don't really feel much about things. I just sort of do what

I think's right, but I don't ever really get emotional about it. That's why I don't talk about it. It's not like I am keeping stuff from you; it's like there is nothing to share."

"So, like, if your parents molested you, you wouldn't be upset about that?"

"No, I'd be mad. Just not—I don't know. It's just not the same as what I hear most people talking about."

"What do you mean?"

"I don't know. It's hard to explain."

Sally studied his face for a few moments, confused. Sometimes he was so vague. It always seemed like he was thinking about something deep and hidden. She wanted to know what was troubling him, but whenever she asked, he'd just get quiet and say nothing was wrong.

"Did I ever tell you about when my grandfather died?" Cambo asked.

"No, what of it?"

"Well, I dunno. My grandfather and I were, like, close. I used to go over to his house all the time when I was a kid. He'd buy me clothes, toys, take me out to eat, that kind of stuff. We had a lot of fun together. For a few years I was probably as much raised by him as my parents."

"Must have been hard to lose him," Sally said, stroking the back of Cambo's neck.

"That's the thing about it. Even though I was *so* close to him, I never cried. I never felt sad. I remember staying up late one night in my room, pinching myself as hard as I could to make myself cry because I

95

thought I was some kind of freak for not being more messed up about it. Truth of it is, I was fine."

"That's awful!"

"I know. It's always bothered me. But, I'm like that. Things happen, and I just keep going on, unaffected really."

"So, nothing ever bothers you? If I died right now, you'd just say, 'Oh well, on to the next part of my life.'?"

"No, it's not like that. A lot of things bother me. Too much, even. And I do *care* about things and people. I mean, I do have my passions. It's just I sometimes don't think I feel the same as other people do about things. That's all. I just feel sort of removed from my emotions, you know?"

"No, I don't," Sally said, a little unhappy with the disclosure.

"It's really not that I wouldn't care if you or someone else died. It would bother me. It's more that I don't know what to do with those emotions, maybe? I dunno."

The two of them sat silently, looking at the road ahead. Lights from the passing store signs danced across their bodies and the interior of the car. Their heads remained motionless, except for the episodic synchronized bobbling that occurred when the car passed over a pothole or malformation in the road. Sally no longer felt hungry. She wished she could just go away, leave the car, and think for a while. She couldn't help to wonder why her boyfriend would even want to be with someone when he could care less about whether they died or not.

Suddenly the car slowed to a full stop then began inching backward.

Sally looked at Cambo. "What are you doing?"

"Quiet," he said, rolling down his window. Sally could hear a man's voice screaming, but she couldn't make out the muffled words.

Sally's spine sent a rolling chill northward. "What's going on?"

CHAPTER TWENTY-FOUR

Okay, let's do this, John commanded himself, rising up and finding the gate latch again. Slowly he pushed the gate open, pausing with horror whenever the gate made any kind of sound. Frequently he looked over his shoulder and strained his ears to hear warnings of potential discovery. His mind was racing with an amalgam of perverse, self-deprecating, philosophical, and moralizing thoughts, yet his body convincingly urged him into the backyard. Taking care to close the gate but not latch it, he snuck along the distal fence wall and positioned himself behind the shrubs opposite the bedroom, bathroom, and living room windows.

The bedroom and living room lights were on dimly, and inside John could make out her profile. It looked like she was wearing flannel pajamas and had her hair in a ponytail. The flannel pajamas were John's favorite, and they always made him uncomfortably excited. He reached into his pocket and felt the metal object that was digging into his side. Grasping the binoculars, he lifted them to his eyes. *There she is.* Unexpectedly the backyard lights flickered. John's heart leapt violently, and he choked back a lump in his throat while retreating deeper into the bush.

CHAPTER TWENTY-FIVE

"What're we looking for?" Sal asked, trying to look around Cambo's head.

"I dunno. But I could swear I saw some guy trying to hit some lady down that street over there."

"Where?"

Cambo thrust his finger at the far alley. "Right there."

"Well, what do you think you're doing backin' up?"

"I just want to make sure everything's all right," Cambo said. In a flash, a red-haired woman emerged from the proximate side of the alley and slammed into the opposite alley wall.

"Stop it!" the woman screamed, bringing her hands to her eyes and hunching over herself. She was bleeding on the left arm and right knee and was perhaps fifteen feet from the now motionless Geo Metro.

"Hey, lady, you okay?" Cambo yelled, unbuckling his seat belt and leaning out his window.

The woman waved Cambo off without lifting her

head. A burly man, must have been five feet eleven inches and about 245 pounds, stepped onto the scene. He wore a tight leather jacket with a long, drooping chain attached to his belt that disappeared into his left front pocket. Walking slowly out into the middle of the alley, his oversized black leather boots made a pattern of snow tracks quickly covered by the ever-increasing falling powder. His right hand was clenched around a lead pipe, and his left hand swayed with each step.

"This ain't none of your business," the man shouted at Cambo while raising his pipe, "unless you want it to be."

Sally's body shook uncontrollably. She reached for Cambo's leg and whispered that they should go and call the cops.

Cambo said, "I don't want trouble, pal, but it looks like you're handling the lady a little rough tonight, that's all."

"Shut up, *pal*. I said this ain't none of your business. You don't know what she done. Now get outta here before I bust up your pretty little face in front of your old lady!" The man took another step toward the Geo Metro.

"Cambo, let's get out of here right now!" Sally said, now clenching onto his leg.

"No! It's not right. He might kill her!"

"You're right, and that's not okay, but if you don't leave, he might kill us! We didn't get her into this—it's not our fault whatever happened here. Let's just go. We can call the cops as soon as we're away. Let them handle it."

"No!" he said, turning toward the perpetrator and elevating his voice even louder. "I'm not going anywhere, and you're a little too drunk and stupid to hurt me. Either you drop that pipe and walk away right now, or you're spending the night in jail. Now those are your options. What's it gonna be?"

The perpetrator lowered the pipe and took a wobbly step backward. He stood seemingly dumbfounded for several long moments; glancing for a few seconds at the battered woman, then at Cambo, and then back at the woman again.

"I said, what's it gonna be?"

The woman against the wall took a step closer to the fuming man, raising her arms toward him and catching him by the right elbow. "Leave 'em alone, Joe, this ain't got nothin' to do with them." Joe looked at her with a prolonged stare and then looked back at Sally and Cambo.

"Screw it," Joe said and raced toward the Geo Metro.

"Watch out!" Sally screamed as Cambo threw the car into gear, which clumsily slid forward just as the man swung the pipe into the air, bringing it down on the rear of the vehicle, where it bounced off the back left bumper and fell inelegantly out of the perpetrator's hands and into the cold street. Sally looked behind her as the burly man retrieved his pipe, faced the fleeing vehicle, and then, leaning back deep, hurled the pipe after the car.

"Ah!" she screamed, covering her head with both hands.

Clang!

The pipe touched down on the roof of the car and bounced off into the dark night. Carefully the car swung right. Sally watched as the man disappeared around the corner.

"He's gone!" she screamed under her breath while still looking behind them. She shifted her gaze to fall upon Cambo, observing his laser-thin lips and furrowed brow. "You could have killed us, you idiot!" she shrieked inches from his ear.

Cambo turned his head and looked into her fuming eyes. The car bumped over a pothole. "Watch out!" Cambo said as he popped open the glove box. Sally looked in horror at the small, shiny, silver object inside.

CHAPTER TWENTY-SIX

It's okay. It's okay. Nobody saw you, John assured himself over and again as the backyard lights failed to remain on for the next several minutes. *She must've just hit the wrong switch.* Fighting a heart attack, John breathed himself slowly back into a normative respiratory pattern and reengaged in his voyeurism. His subject slipped from the living room and into the bedroom. Peering through the magnifying device, he could see her broken profile through the poorly shut blinds. He watched as she took off her shirt and began fussing with her brassiere. *Here it is,* he thought, his body excited and on fire. But as a feeling of grief and anger enveloped him, he lowered his eyes at the last possible moment, not allowing himself to see her completely undress. He sat on the ground and battled some of the twigs poking at his eyes.

Why do you do this? he scolded himself through abundant tears. *You never even go all the way! You go through all of this trouble to see her, and then every time you get to this point, you look away and cry like a little child. I hate you!* He wept for several minutes while rubbing his temples under his frosty hair. *Maybe you should be caught,* he thought, tearing up more intensely again. *Nobody loves you, and nobody should! You're a loser! Look at yourself; you're a millionaire who won't spend any money. You don't talk to your own mother, who is probably the only reason you're even alive! And you're turning into the man who raped you night after night for nearly seven years. What is wrong with you! Why would you do this to yourself?*

John bled his last reserves of dignity through his eyes for another ten minutes or so before deciding to go back to his car. He took one last look at her and admired her beautiful face and shiny brown hair. *I love you,* he thought, sad that she would never go for a guy like him.

Out of the darker corner of the room, her visitor stood up and walked toward another farther room, which John figured was the kitchen. He looked about six feet tall, average build. John tried to peek at him through his binoculars but couldn't make out his face. *C'mon, c'mon, I want to see who the competition is. See the guy I have absolutely no chance against.* The man emerged back into the living room area. He had on his coat. She piled into him, throwing her arms around his body and kissing him passionately.

"I can't watch this," John said, upset with himself and now longing for his bed. He struggled to get out from behind the bushes and backtracked out of the yard the way he had come in. With few strides he crossed the court and turned himself back onto Wakeland Lane. Rounding the corner again, he focused on his car from a good distance away, trying to keep his attention singularly on the car and avoid thinking about any of the rest of it. *I need therapy! I know it's wrong, so why do I do it?* he asked himself, pulling his leather glove off his right hand and fishing for his keys as he approached the driver side door, but not finding them.

He reached for the handle and tried jostling the door, but to no avail. The car was locked.

CHAPTER TWENTY-SEVEN

"What's that for?" Sally asked in horror as Cambo reached in and retrieved a silver-plated nine-millimeter pistol.

"What's that for?" Sally asked again, springing backward and tearing up. "Why do you have a pistol in your car?"

"Relax, it's not even mine. It's my father's. He carried it around for cases."

"What cases?" Sally asked, a lump forming in her throat. "I thought your dad is some kind of preacher. Why does a preacher need a gun?"

"Even preachers need to protect themselves," Cambo said, his eyes hardening as they looked at the road ahead. The car navigated around two corners and aimed for the alley where the scuffle had taken place.

"Cambo, you're scaring me, please let me out if you're really gonna do this!" Sally asked, grasping for the door.

"That is absolutely out of the question!" Cambo screamed, his words sounding off like a rapid-fire weapon. "I can't let you out, not now, not with him out there, not in this neighborhood. He'll kill you. Don't worry. I'll protect you. I'm not gonna shoot him. Just wound his soul a little. Wanna wound his soul. It'll be okay, okay! There he is!" Cambo screamed as he burst out the door, shouting at the man named Joe who had just given his girlfriend a devastating right hook. Her body fell clumsily to the pavement with a thump.

"Stop it!" Cambo shouted, raising the gun into the night and firing off two loud shots. The burly man turned and squatted, frozen, covering his ears, and then held out his right hand to Cambo.

"Easy. Easy, buddy. You don't want to do that. I'm a cop. Let me show you my badge," the man said, slowly reaching into his breast pocket.

"No!" Cambo said, pointing the pistol directly at the man's face and stepping closer. The man ceased reaching for his breast pocket and turned his head to look at the girl on the floor beneath him. The woman was groaning but was otherwise not moving.

"It ain't what it looks like," he said. "Just let me explain. You don't want to do this, man. You're gonna be in a lot of trouble if you do."

Sally looked around for anyone else on the streets behind her. She could see no one. "Cambo, I'm begging you, let's just go," she said out the driver-side window. "I'm really freaked out now. Please, this isn't like you."

"It's gonna be okay now. Don't worry, it's gonna be all right. Quiet! Let me do my business with this bad guy," Cambo said. He inched closer to the man in the alley. "You think you're tough, beating up on some woman, don't ya? How about I beat up on you a little bit? Would you like that?" Cambo asked. The man in the alley looked frightened. He kept glancing over his shoulders as if to ascertain his options. But the alley wasn't conducive to escape plans, and the man had to know it.

"Look, I'm sorry. Really, it won't happen again, all right, pal? I learned my lesson. Just let me be, and you and your lady can be on your way to whatever you was all gonna do, all right?"

Cambo looked at the girl on the floor and then back at the man in the alley once again. Time retarded to a dreadful pace. All seemed still, surreal, uncoordinated. Sally struggled to regain her composure, but she was stricken with the most pervasive sense of terror that something horrible would serve as the conclusion to this exchange. In a weak and crackly voice, she pleaded with Cambo one last time to leave with her. But Cambo just stood there, almost dissociated, as if he wasn't even aware of the terrified woman he had left helpless in the car.

The woman on the floor started to stir. "Oh!" she moaned, struggling to land her feet on the ground.

"You all right?" Cambo asked without changing his aim. "We're here to help you. This guy is not going to bother you anymore. We can take you anywhere you need to go. The hospital, police, anywhere!"

The woman rested her elbows on her knees and played with her bloody lip for a few seconds before pulling herself up to a standing position. As she stood erect, the light revealed several badly bruised areas on her body, extending from her partially bare stomach to her neck and head. She looked up at Cambo.

"Thanks, man. I owe you one," she said, turning herself around and walking into the darkness.

Sally nervously checked behind her again. She couldn't help but feel uneasy. *Something is wrong here! Something is wrong!* She thought of calling Cambo back to the car again, but she felt afraid to talk to him. He was acting so strangely, and she never would've thought he was capable of shooting a gun at someone. It just didn't make any sense to her.

"All right, pal, we're all good then," the perpetrator said, easing his way back down the alley. "Why don't we just go our separate ways now, huh?"

"No," Cambo said, taking a few steps closer to the man. "Just because she's gone doesn't mean you received your justice. I have to make sure I punish you so that you don't think scum like you can do whatever you want and it's okay."

"Easy, man, you ain't like that. I know. I can tell. You ain't the kinda guy who can mess someone up and not say anything about it. Think about what you're saying. Now look, I'm just gonna walk away now. You won, all right? Game over. I lose, you proved your point. I've learned my lesson," the man said as he slowly stepped back another few feet.

"I don't believe you!" Cambo said. "I don't think you've learned jack squat! I think if you find her, you'll beat her all over again. So I think you have to be punished, and if I don't do it, who will? There're no witnesses here, and I'll never find the girl to get her to testify against you. You'll just spend a couple of nights in jail, get out, then beat some other naïve chick to a pulp, only no one'll be around to keep you from finishing *that* job. So here's what I'm thinkin'. Maybe I just save the world the trouble of having to deal with arrogant thugs like you and just become the judge and jury right now, huh? What do you think of that?" Cambo punctuated the offer by raising the gun a little higher and tightening his grip around the trigger.

Sally's mind raced with unprecedented speed. "No, Cambo! He's right, think about what you're saying! You're not like that and he is. You've made your point, so let's go, please!" Sally's request rolled out of her mouth and off into the distance, resonating slightly before dissipating into a low hum that grew into soft but steady bipolar contrasts of high and low pitch.

"The cops!" Sally yelled, looking frantically out the back window.

CHAPTER TWENTY-EIGHT

"Don't tell me that I locked my keys in the car!" John said, now frantically searching all of his pockets for the missing keys. *See! It is wrong, and you're being punished for what you're doing,* he thought in a fleeting, almost indiscernible mentation. *That's ridiculous. This is just random chance, that's all this is,* he countered, noting that he was actually having a conversation with himself and wondering if everyone did that, or if he was just a little crazy. *Course not everyone is a peeping tom, so maybe you shouldn't be worrying about whether talking to yourself means you're crazy or not,* he countered again, still frantically searching for his keys. He looked up at the path he'd just taken, wondering if maybe he'd lost his keys on the walk to the car. *Oh no,* he thought as he began jogging back toward Wakeland Lane. With every step he scrutinized the ground below him, searching for anything resembling small metal objects.

Nothing, he thought as he reached Wakeland Lane. He looked across the lane toward the direction of the court where she lived and started retracing his steps. After a few strides, he stooped down to poke at something that shimmered as it passed his line of sight. Upon inspection it revealed itself to be a gum wrapper. *Where are my keys?* he pined, still slouching in the middle of the street and putting his cold hands into his jacket pockets. He buried his head into the neck flap of his coat and breathed out some warm air in an attempt to counter the frost.

As he captured the air against his neck flap fibers, his nose relaxed, and he felt a warm, soothing feeling rush across his face. *I better get out of the road,* he concluded as he heard a car from the court start up and throttle forward. Standing up, he set his sights toward the sidewalk leading into the court and began a fast-paced trot toward that end. After a few steps, however, he slipped and fell backward onto the street, just as the approaching car appeared from the court and turned toward him.

"Hey!" he screamed, waving one hand in the air while scrambling to get up with the other. "Watch out!"

CHAPTER TWENTY-NINE

Cambo turned his head to look toward the sound of the still distant but fast-approaching police sirens. While he was distracted, the burly man burst into flight and disappeared down the backside of the alley. Cambo jerked his head toward the man in flight and let off another shot into the night air.

"Hey! Come back here!" Cambo ordered, starting after him.

"No! Cambo, let's go now or we'll be in trouble!" Sally screeched.

Cambo looked toward the car, then toward the

back alley, then the car again. "Okay," he said, bustling toward the car. Nearly diving into the driver's seat, he forced the shift into drive and dropped his foot on the gas pedal. The car made a terrible screeching sound as it half-slid and half-jumped off the curb where it had been parked and soared down Fifth Avenue toward the freeway. The police siren grew louder, and green and red lights began to mingle with the night air. Sally's head whipped to the right as the car cornered left into the delivery area behind Ragstar's Deli.

"Watch out!" Sally said as the car hopped over a large speed bump and jostled a bit before regaining its course.

"I got it!" Cambo said, whipping the car toward the freeway on-ramp. Sally watched through tearstained eyes as Cambo merged across two lanes of the sparsely populated roadway and eased into the car-pool lane.

"Why are you slowin' down? Those cops aren't very far away."

"No reason to look guilty. Our best shot is to go the speed limit. Besides, we haven't done anything wrong. It was defense of another human being."

"No, you shot at a guy! There *is* something wrong with that! That's called attempted murder!"

"Oh, I'm sorry, I'm the cretin, I should've just let the guy kill his girlfriend, is that it? Look, I know you're scared, but you've gotten to know me a little bit now. Do I seem like some callous murderer? I was just trying to help that lady and save some future victim from being raped or worse! If that makes me a mur-derer, then fine. I'll wear the badge, but you just consider for a moment that in some countries the offensive thing to do would be to just drive on by, like you wanted to. Besides, I didn't shoot at him. I just shot into the air to scare him a little."

Sally looked at Cambo's beet-red face, studying the pattern of his furrowed brow and droopy bangs. His breaths were shallow and rapid. Angrily he jerked the car into the fast lane and accelerated. *Why would he do this to me?* she lamented, unwilling to move her gaze. Her right cheek felt a sliding tickle as a tear slowly dissolved across her skin. *What should I do now?* she wondered, finally shifting her body forward and gazing at the streams of light beckoning beyond the freeway retaining wall.

"Look, I'm sorry," Cambo said, grasping at her hand. She jerked it away and tucked it into her right armpit. Cambo tried again. "Look, you don't have to … urgh!" They sat in silence for a few moments as Cambo adjusted the rearview mirror and looked over his right shoulder.

"What are you doin'?" Sally demanded as he crossed the lanes toward the Twenty-seventh Street off-ramp. Cambo ignored the question.

"What are you doing?" Sally asked, starting to again escalate in nervousness. The car cruised down the off ramp and rolled to a stop at the base.

"What are you doing? You're really scaring me, Cambo," Sally said. "Talk to me. What are we doing here?"

Cambo sat silently for what seemed like an eternity. Sally looked at his narrow eyes and focused gaze.

He was hunched over the wheel, staring at the speed-ometer, his chest rising and falling in a rapid but even pattern. After some time he brought a hand up to his hair and ran his fingers entirely across his scalp, finally letting his hand descend for a surprisingly loud slap on his knee. He leaned back powerfully and dramatically held up two tight fists to his temples, hitting them lightly and repetitively.

"I don't think I can do this anymore, Sal," he said, starting to rock while now applying constant pressure against his temples. "I mean, who are you to judge me? I mean, you're a freakin' hooker! You prostitute yourself for a living, and yet you get off telling me I'm some kind of crazed lunatic going around try-ing to murder people! I mean, what's your problem? Have I *ever* judged you? Have I called you a hypo-crite because you wear that cross around your neck? Have I ever told you your mother is a whore too and that she's rotting in flames for what she did to you? I thought of all people you would understand what I was about! That I didn't believe in living all of the lies of this world like everybody else! That somehow there is a right and there is a wrong, and we've all lost our ability to know it! But now you're acting like the rest of them! You call good evil and evil good because you don't realize that what I did tonight, not you—because all you could think about was yourself—but what *I* did tonight was not bad but good. That's right, good. I helped some lady live, and that makes me a murderer? Well forget it! I don't need this in my life! I got enough of my own problems, and I don't need your condescending, ignorant, and annoying nagging anymore, okay? We're finished! Got it? Now, get outta my car! Get outta my life! And don't ever come crawling back. You hear me?"

Sally looked dumbfounded at Cambo, who was now screaming at an ear-shattering decibel level and nearly frothing at the mouth. She felt numb, in shock, not knowing what to do. Tears were uncontrollably streaming down her face, and she sobbed out loud.

"Out!" Cambo repeated, leaning over and forcing her door open. The sharp chill of the night immersed her, sending tremors up her back and goose bumps down her barren legs. The door alarm pinged systematically, as if sending a distress signal down the empty street.

"What do you want me to do?" Sally asked, looking at his rage-laden face. "It's freezing outside, and we're in the middle of nowhere. I mean, if you hate me, okay, I can deal with that. But can't you at least drop me off at home?"

Cambo stared callously at her. His breathing was now labored, and his body trembled violently. Sally couldn't believe the way he was reacting. She stared into those fixed eyes and searched for something deep beyond the surface but couldn't find anything. Her body began to ache from the cold, and her tear-stained face felt as if tiny icicles were forming under her eyes and on her cheeks.

"Please go now!" Cambo said, but something was funny in his voice. When he screamed "now," his inflection faltered momentarily. Frightened as she was,

Sally couldn't help but to stare blankly into his face and wonder what'd happened in his mind. They were having such a good time laughing and joking before this had all started. They were starting a romance.

She turned and looked at the open passenger door. *I should get out of the car now.* She leaned away from Cambo a few inches and glanced over her shoulder at the silent street behind her. She knew the area. It was a rough neighborhood; she'd been there several times with customers. There was a bus station about ten blocks away. She could probably get there in a half hour if she was quick.

"Go now," Cambo instructed one last time, turning away from Sally and leaning the back of his head against the driver's side headrest while shutting his eyes. Sally stifled her tears, grabbed her purse, and unlatched her seat belt. As she clumsily flung her right foot out onto the increasingly snow-covered street, she felt Cambo's hand on her arm.

"I'm sorry," he whispered as she defiantly wrestled her arm loose and stepped out into the biting cold.

CHAPTER THIRTY

John lay in the middle of the street frozen with fear as the car barreled toward him. Finally the driver jerked the car to the left and slammed on the brakes. John scrambled upwards and stepped away from the car like a drunken man avoiding an oncoming crowd. The car fishtailed for some feet before spinning almost completely in the opposite direction. The person in the car threw on the emergency brake, making a fast-paced clicking noise.

"Hey, man, are you all right? I totally didn't see you! You okay?"

"Merci?" John ventured, squinting into the driver's face as he stopped in front of him.

"John?" Merci said. "John, is that you? What in the world are you doing out here?"

John's mind scrambled for a believable reason. "Just, uh, checking on an old friend. What're you doing here?"

"Me? Oh, I was just meeting for a study session, for our religion class, with Addy," Merci said, picking up John's gloves and handing them to him. "Hey, I'm so sorry. Are you okay? Geez, I mean, what are the odds of this, huh?"

"Totally. Small world, huh?" John said. "Yeah, I'm okay." He let his friend pull him up to a standing position. Merci's face hung with a doubtful grin.

"This is crazy, John!"

"I know."

"So, whose your friend out here?" Merci asked as he wiped some ice and snow off of John's coat.

"Uh, just an old college buddy—from Texas."

"Well, where's your car?"

"Down that road over there," John said, pointing in the car's direction.

"Well, why are you all the way down here then?"

"Well I was, um, actually looking for my car keys. I guess I lost them somewhere in between my friend's house and my car, and so I was retracing my steps."

"Well, hey, I'd be glad to help you look for 'em. Least I could do seeing as how I just about ran you over."

"No, that's all right. I got it. You can just mosey on home or wherever you're going."

"Nonsense, it's freezing out here. I'm not about to take off and leave you here in the cold when you can't even get in your car. Hey, where does your buddy live, anyway?"

"Just down that court over there," John said, growing increasingly anxious.

"Really? That's actually where Addy from our group lives. Huh, that's crazy. Say, why don't we go see if you left them over at his place on accident?"

"Um, actually, he wasn't home."

"Oh," Merci said, looking back to where John had showed him that he had parked his car, then back toward the court again. "So, you always make a habit of parking a quarter mile away from friend's houses?"

"Well, no … I think I got bad directions. I went and knocked on the door and no one was home, so I figured either my address was wrong, or maybe it's just too old and he's already moved away," John said, trying to think if anything he just said made any sense.

"Oh." Merci said then grinned widely at John. "I just can't believe I'm sitting out here talking to you, of all people. Man! Small world. Well, hey, Addy literally just lives right down there in one of those duplexes. Why don't you go use her phone? I know she's still up."

John looked up the street and back toward his car then shrugged his shoulders and agreed. The entire way to the duplex John and Merci feverishly examined every bit of road.

"It's this one right here," Merci explained, leading John up to the front door. John pretended to be surprised. Merci gave the door three brisk raps, and after a few seconds a light flipped on.

"Hey, it's Merci. Let me in," he yelled into the wood door.

As Addy unlocked the bolt, the two men waited in anticipation for her appearance. Suddenly the door flew open, and Addy looked at the two men initially with a smile and then a look of surprise.

"John? What're you doing here?"

John briefly looked down at the floor and then slowly up at her flannel pajama bottoms and oversized nightie. "It's a long story," he said. "Can we come in?"

CHAPTER THIRTY-ONE

Sally Strathers walked as if on a mission straight away from the car without turning her head to the right or left. She heard the pinging of the door alarm begin to fade as she put distance between herself and the Geo Metro. *Don't look back. He's a creep. He's probably some kind of murderer. He shot at that guy like a lunatic! You've got enough problems. You don't need that guy!*

The pinging was barely detectable now. *Why is he not driving off?* she wondered, fighting an urge to see what Cambo was doing. *Maybe he's coming after me.* She walked more briskly for a few feet but then stopped rapidly. She wiped her freezing tears from her face and held her breath in as best she could. *What's that noise?* she queried, straining her ears to analyze the sound. At first she could only detect the distorted sounds of the door alarm, but quickly she discerned another very similar noise being emitted from the car.

Sally whirled around and gazed at the car. Squinting her eyes through the now lightly falling snow she detected the outline of the car. *Where is he?* she wondered as she forced her eyes to focus on the outline of the driver side door, which was now also wide open. A car rushed by on the lonely freeway above the off-ramp. Sally began to be worried about the noises coming from the vehicle as she rehearsed the events of the night in her mind and Cambo's angry tone and demands of her to leave.

Maybe he hates me? Maybe he wants to hurt me? she thought, stepping backward. *That's ridiculous! I know this guy. He's not a creep. He's never taken advantage of me in any way, even when I offered. He feeds old ladies. He tends to orphans. He only called me his girlfriend for this first time last Saturday. What am I so scared of?* she reasoned as her head began to pound. *I just need to go.* She stepped back again and turned around into a full pace away from the scene. Suddenly she stopped dead in her tracks and thought a moment. *How could I be so stupid!* she screamed in her mind as she turned around again and began rushing as fast as one can in such slippery conditions toward the car.

"Cambo!" she screamed out loud, frantically searching the wintry scene. The car alarms grew louder, and soon she could visibly peer into the illuminated car passenger area. *No! No! Cambo, don't do it! Don't do it, baby!* she silently pleaded, pouncing on the passenger door and thrusting her hand first under the car seats and then the glove compartment.

"It's not there!" she said. Violently she burst back out of the car and spun full around, hurriedly surveying the lay of the land. *Where is he?* She strained her eyes, fixating on the underpass that led off to a small park. She began an all-out rush for the other side of the underpass, slipping a little from time to time in the snow.

"Cambo!" she screamed, racing out of the underpass area and into the park entrance.

"Go away," Cambo said.

"Cambo?" Sally repeated, whirling around to see the solitary figure slouched against the wall of the underpass.

"Leave me alone!" Cambo said louder, holding up the gun at Sally.

"What are you doing here?" Sally demanded while inching closer.

"Leave me alone. I'm warning you. I'll do it!" Cambo said, raising the gun directly at Sally's face.

Sally took another step closer, her tears starting to fall once again. "I just want to help."

"Seriously, stop right now!" Cambo screamed, rising to his feet, his extended arm unflinching.

Sally froze.

"Look, I'm sorry, okay? I know I messed up. Now just leave me alone. Get outta here! You don't need some guy like me ruining your life! Okay?" Cambo wiped some snot off of his face with the sleeve of his arm.

Sally watched him momentarily, unsure of what to do. "I'm sorry too," she said, waiting for his reaction.

"For what? For freaking out as I shot at some guy? You didn't do anything wrong! You think I don't know that?"

"It's okay. We'll work it out, all right?"

"There is nothing to work out. I'm a freak. I know that. I tried to hide it from you, but it always comes out. Why do you think I'm such a loner anyway, huh? There's a reason I go around picking up call girls for friends. This side of me always surfaces, and I hate myself for it!" Cambo beat himself in the chest several times with the gun.

"Why? Why does this side of you have to be hidden? Who are you hiding it from?" Sally asked, taking another step closer as he briefly wiped his eyes.

"From myself! Myself! Okay? I hate myself! I hate everything about myself! Okay? Is that what you want to hear?" Cambo said, his voice becoming hostile again as he raised the gun toward his temple.

"Sometimes I just want to end it all. *Bang!* And it's over. No more worries. But I can't. I'm too scared. Ugh! I tried to warn you not to talk to me about this stuff. Now you see why! I'm not who you think I am, see? I'm not some great guy who just goes around helping people, see? I'm really this lunatic! I can't even keep a relationship with a hooker! I'm such a loser!"

"You're not a loser!" Sally took several large steps toward him. "And you're not a lunatic. So you got some problems. Who doesn't? Like you said, I'm a hooker. I got problems too, but that doesn't mean I ain't worth being around and that I'm not worth getting to know. I want to help. Let me in. Tell me what's wrong. I like that you're finally opening up to me. I like what I see. I'm here for you. Look, I came back. I didn't run away. Let me in. I want to be let into your world. Please share it with me. Tell me what it's like for you. Tell me where all of this pain is coming from. I want to be a part of it with you, baby!" she pleaded, finally reaching out and grabbing him by his cold neck.

"No you don't," Cambo said, slouching against the overpass wall. "You don't want to know anything about me," he whispered, descending into a sitting position and dropping the gun into a patch of white.

PART FIVE
DOUBT

CHAPTER THIRTY-TWO

Merci Bowku looked across the small room at Stephen, his student therapist, in the recliner chair. Stephen was tall—about six feet—big boned and plain. He had a hair full of cowlicks and a mole on his right cheek. His nose wore itself prominently across his face.

Why do I feel like this is gonna be a big mistake?

"Merci, um, I said hello. But you seem to not have heard me. Are you okay?" the therapist asked.

"I'm all right, just thinking," Merci said, coming out of his daydreaming.

"About what?"

"Nothing."

The therapist eyed Merci in a way that seemed to say "I don't believe you," but let it go. "Well, I was just saying hello and asking if you had ever been to a therapist before?"

"No."

"Okay, so what brings you here now?"

Merci thought about the question but decided to ask his own question instead of answering.

"What makes you think you're so smart and can help me with my problems?"

"That's a good question," the therapist said, leaning back in his chair while crossing his left leg over his right. "I think it's interesting that you assume it takes someone smart to help others with their problems. Let me ask you, what're you hoping I'll say in response to your question?"

"I don't know. You're the doctor, or doc-in-training anyway," Merci said. The therapist looked back at him silently for an eternity.

"Do you think that *I* think I am so smart? Or are you just trying to get a rise out of me?"

Merci felt stupid. He eyed the door and considered leaving. Visions of his anxiety attacks made him stay, however—they seemed to be getting worse again. He tried to relax his stiff body. "Look, I don't mean to be rude, just once I went to a psychiatrist and he put me on medications, which seemed to really help. But now they really aren't doing the trick, and you're, well, you're—"

"Not a medical doctor?"

Merci dropped his eyes to the floor and shrugged his shoulders.

"Why does that bother you?"

"Just because you don't know anything about medicine, and that's what worked before."

The therapist nodded several times. "If your previous visits to the psychiatrist were successful in reducing your panic attacks, why did you come here?"

"Because I can't afford the medicine anymore, and you're free with my student benefits."

"That's honest, and I'm glad you can be so forward, but the fact that you're here generates a few hypotheses for me. First, you're likely being very affected by these panic attacks, or you probably wouldn't seek services in the first place. Second, I suspect you're not sure I can't help or you wouldn't be talking to me. Third, you haven't got up and left, and based on your forwardness that's not due to your worrying about offending me, so it must be that you're here in desperation regarding something you can't seem to break yourself, which begs the question, what is it I can do for you today?"

Merci read the young clinician's face and contemplated telling him the full truth. He decided to stick with only part of it for now.

"Well, I don't know. It's like I told the gal who assessed me here the last couple of weeks; I just have a long history of like, freaking out."

"Why do you think you 'freak out'? Or stated differently, what kinds of things occur that make it more likely you'll have a panic attack?"

Before Merci could respond, there was a knock on the door, and an older man in a suit asked the therapist to step out for a moment. "I'm sorry. I have to respond to this. I'll be right back," the therapist said, quickly moving out of the room. Merci observed the empty room for a few moments, analyzing the tired old couch and recliner. *I wonder how many quacks've been through this place?* he thought, running his hands across the seat cushion next to him. His eye gaze caught sight of his case file on the recliner. He reached forward and grabbed it with his thumb and forefinger. "File number 9162," he read as he opened the folder and set it on his lap. He thumbed through the cover sheets, evaluation case notes and personality protocols, finally locating his intake report.

"Merci Bowku is a twenty-two-year-old Caucasian male presenting with concern over anxiety and ruminative thoughts," he read, skipping down a few paragraphs. "Psychiatric history is notable for a diagnosis of panic disorder without agoraphobia."

Merci had forgotten the formal name of his disorder, which his previous doctor had explained as anxiety attacks without fear of public interactions.

"Familial history is remarkable for maternal bipolar disorder: type one with psychotic features, and a paternal grandfather with schizoaffective disorder: bipolar type."

Merci heard the doorknob being jostled, and he jumped. With haste he snapped the file shut and tossed it onto the empty chair. The student therapist entered the room, grabbed the folder, and sat down, but did not speak for some while. Finally, with apparent soberness, he looked up at Merci and apologized again.

"Look, I'm really sorry about that. It's actually quite rare that our sessions will be interrupted." More silence as Merci waved off any need to feel guilt. "Remind me where we were?"

Merci looked at the therapist. He seemed distracted and upset. "What's wrong?"

"Nothing, really. Thanks for asking. Now I believe we left off talking about triggers for the panic episodes?"

"Oh, I get it. I'm the only one required to be honest and open in here?" Merci said. The therapist matched Merci's stare for a moment then softened his expression and opened his mouth.

"You're right. Look, I was not trying to blow off your question so much as trying to remain confidential. I just received a very worrisome call about another client, and to be honest, I'm concerned for the client's welfare."

"What happened?"

"That I really am not allowed to tell you, by law."

Merci looked into the clinician's eyes, which seemed troubled and disturbed by whatever news he had just heard. "How long have you been seeing this client?"

"Since my first year of Doc school," the therapist said. "I must apologize again, but I really should respect the client's right to privacy and not answer any more questions."

Merci watched the therapist speak to him and responded to the therapist's unending questions, all the while picturing the concerned look on the student's face after returning from the phone call.

"Well, we're out of time today. Thanks again for your patience with the interruption. Will you be back next week same time?" the therapist asked, the question lingering in the air.

Merci thought for several seconds, still contemplating the long face and concerned tones of the professional opposite him.

"I will," he finally answered.

"Well then, I'll see you next Wednesday. I sincerely hope you have a good week," the therapist said, extending his arm for a parting shake.

"I believe that," Merci replied, catching his hand.

CHAPTER THIRTY-THREE

Addy Siwel glanced up at the three young men seated upon her couch. The one in the middle had been talking for some time about his religious beliefs and why the three of them had traveled from various regions of the country to proselytize in the area. "It's our belief that God is a lover of all persons and not a discriminator of anyone. We know that God has a plan for us all, and that you are part of that plan. What we would like to do is present to you six lessons about that plan and how it relates to you and your divine destiny."

Addy relaxed in her chair and listened for twenty minutes or more, responding every few minutes to a question or two and wondering how much longer they'd talk before giving her a chance to ask her questions. Finally, the man on the right put his hand on the middle missionary's shoulder and cut him off.

"Obviously we're excited that you were kind enough to let us into your home," he said, the other two sporting a validating smile. "The point is we really believe the things we're saying to you. Enough that we come on these missions and spend our own money to share the message with people like you. But, that doesn't mean you will or have to believe it. We're simply asking you to give it a try. We only ask that you allow us to come several times and present the messages to you, and you can read our materials and pray for yourself to see if you feel this message is correct—if it's right for you."

The missionary stopped speaking, and all three of the young ministers fixated upon Addy, anxiously awaiting her response. She never really liked being in the spotlight and felt extremely uncomfortable. Truth was she really wasn't interested in their message as much as she was to get some insight into other people's answers to her questions about God, the world, and the afterlife.

"Well, I don't know," she said. "Actually, I just wanted to ask a few questions, if that's all right."

"Great," said the missionary on the left. "That's what we're here for. Fire away."

Addy sat for a few seconds eyeballing the group. "Well, why do you all believe in God anyway? I mean, like, were you all born into your faith, or did some of you find it later in your life, or what?"

"Well, that's a great question. I was a convert to the church, and Elder Jones and Kershaw here were born into it," he explained, tapping each missionary on the shoulder as he addressed them.

"Okay," Addy said, addressing the one in the middle, "then what made you decide to join your church?"

"I had some friends introduce me to it. After a while I just knew it was right!"

"You just knew, *poof!* Mysteries of life unfolded?" she asked, hiding her sarcasm poorly.

"Well, I don't know. I guess it wasn't just overnight. I spent a lot of time pondering over the materials. Praying to God. Fasting about it. And then one day I got my answer, and I knew."

Addy rocked in her chair slightly. "What did you,

like, pray to God? I mean, how'd you ... like ... 'Hey, God, you there? And is this right for me?'"

"Actually, that's about right." He laughed.

"And then what? Like, I mean what happened? God talk to you or something?" she asked, raising her eyebrows.

"Well, yes and no—I mean, he sort of answered me, but in his own special way."

"And what 'special way' did he use?"

"Well, I guess it was sort of, I don't know—for lack of a better word—a feeling, in my heart. Like I said before, I just knew it was true."

Addy bit her lip as she thought about the young minister's response. "You guys like can't drink or have sex before you're married. You have to pay money to your church and all this other stuff, right?"

"Uh-huh," echoed the missionary on the right.

"How do you know it's all worth it? I mean, seriously, that's an awful lot to stake on a *feeling* that you suppose came from God. I mean, how do you know you're not wrong—that it wasn't just indigestion or made up? That you're really just deceiving yourselves? I mean, how do you know that you didn't want there to be a God so bad that you just made him up as some kind of grand delusion?"

The missionaries looked back at her blankly for a moment, then at each other. Finally the one on the left spoke up. "We don't. All we can do is have faith. That's the point of the whole thing. We believe in what we can't see; but what we can feel. It's like the

Bible says, 'Faith is the evidence of things not seen.' That's the process. That's the plan."

The missionaries all sat alike with their elbows resting on their knees and fingers interdigitated under their chins. Addy sat back again and rocked somewhat in her chair, taking it all in. No one moved for several minutes, but rather they all sat quietly, listening to the creaks from Addy's chair, the heater whirring up from the ground vent, and the rain splattering on the roof. Addy's mind drifted back to the classroom with Dr. Haddelby and what he said about evolution and religion and how we can't really know anything in this life. It was frustrating. What's the point in being if we do not know the purpose of our being? With an elongated sigh, Addy ceased her hypnotic rock and broke the silence by thanking the missionaries for coming by, adding that she'd like to politely decline the offer that they come back.

The missionaries rose and thanked her for her time. One by one they grabbed their trench coats, throwing them effortlessly onto their shoulders as if the maneuver had been performed a thousand times. After handing her a card, the one who'd been sitting on the left of the couch opened the door and stepped into the night air. The freezing rain fell terribly onto the landing area, soaking the young men as they reached for their bicycles. A flash of electricity sparked in the distance, framing the urban landscape.

Addy thanked them again for their time, feeling bad for not offering them a ride home. Stepping backward she pushed the door toward the young men.

Suddenly the door ceased in its path. Addy looked up in surprise as the missionary who had been sitting on the right of the couch stepped back into the entry way, water dripping from his coat onto the stained linoleum.

"Can I just say one more thing?" the missionary requested but didn't wait for an answer. "How do *you* know there is *no* God? Isn't your evidence the same as ours that there is a God?" Addy gazed blankly at the missionary, her stance uncomfortably quiet.

"I mean, you say our belief in God is based on just that—a belief, a hunch, a feeling, an educated guess. But so is your belief that there is no God! It is likewise based on a belief, a hunch, a feeling, or an educated guess. The plain truth is we can't prove for sure, none of us can, which side is true. The world has scientific theories that support notions like evolution, but society has millions of anecdotal stories that support creation and theology. Any time of the day you can approach people the world over, and you'll always find that in every culture, religion is practiced and believed in, to one extent or the other, by the majority of the people! The names may change, the deity may change, but the underlying belief is that religion is real, serious, practiced, and believed in. How do you know that all those people are wrong? Doesn't it make sense that if we don't know the answer for sure, either way, that we pick the one with the least amount of consequences?"

"What do you mean, 'the least amount of consequences?'" Addy queried cautiously, clinging to the doorknob and sporting a confused look on her face.

"I mean this—if we're wrong and there's no God, we just die and cease to exist. Then at the end of this life, we're no better off than you are. It doesn't matter if I were Catholic, Muslim, Baptist, Jewish, Hindu, Mormon, agnostic, atheistic, a murderer, a Nobel laureate, a rapist, president of the United States, or anything else. If there's no God, we all wind up in the same place—dead. Eternally nonexistent. But if the believers are right, and there is a God, then God must have an order. And God must have a plan. And God must abide by eternal principles. And if so, then words like *faith, obedience, prayer, suffering,* and *religion* become more than words; they become real and meaningful. If we're right, then it makes an eternal difference what one did in this life, what their religious title is, or more personally, what their beliefs and character are. Are *you* willing to risk *all of that* on a belief, or a feeling, or an educated guess that says we're all wrong?"

The rain fell in droves, descending from the darkened skies above and splattering violently across the concrete pathway, the missionaries, their bicycles, and their sober facial features. "Just think it over is all I ask," the missionary requested, his face morphing from a hardened stare to a soft and sad expression. Removing his hand from the door and mounting his bike, he turned and pedaled away from the dim porch light and into the expansive black.

CHAPTER THIRTY-FOUR

Sal looked across the couch at Cambo and studied his facial features. *He really is an attractive young man,* she thought, feeling something pleasant deep within her chest. She wiggled her toes along his leg and grabbed his feet in her hands and began rubbing them.

"What're you doing?" Cambo asked, seemingly startled.

"Relax, paranoid; just giving you a foot rub."

"Why?"

"Cause I want to, geez! What is it with you and the million questions all the time?"

"I don't know, I just—"

"Just what?"

"I don't know," Cambo said, looking off in the distance.

They sat in silence for several minutes. Down the hall a large grandfather clock rang a portion of some classical tune, followed by three loud bongs.

"Why does anyone ever have a grandfather clock?" Sal asked.

"What do you have against grandfather clocks?"

"Nothing," Sal said, switching to the other foot, "except they're loud and obnoxious, and they ring all night long, like when you're trying to sleep. But other than that, they're just great."

"Well, you're loud and obnoxious and never shut up all night, but I like you."

"Cute," Sal said, smacking him hard in the kneecap. The two existed in each other's presence for a quiet few moments. Outside, a loud motor engine growled down some distant road.

"Well," Sal said, propping herself up on an elbow. "Maybe we should talk about it?"

"It?"

"Don't be stupid. You know exactly what I'm talking about."

"I don't have anything I need to talk about."

Sal rolled her eyes and fell on her back. "'Course not."

"Well what's *that* supposed to mean?"

"I'm sure you can figure it out."

"Well, I can figure out that you're angry."

"What is wrong with you?" Sal said. "We just went through something fairly traumatic together, and it's like we're pretending it never happened."

"I'm not pretending. I just... can't... talk about that."

"Well then, talk about anything. I don't know anything about you!"

"Because there's really nothing great to talk about."

"I'll be the judge of that. Tell me more. Tell me more about your family and childhood and all that stuff. Please, I want to know. I think it's important."

"I don't know," Cambo said, sitting up and tossing Sal's feet off of him. "I really don't like talking about it much. It wasn't that great."

"Well, don't say anything you don't want then. Okay?"

Cambo closed his eyes and shrugged his shoulders

while giving a slight head nod. "All right, fine. What do you want to know?"

"Anything."

"No, no, no," Cambo said, smiling. "It doesn't work that way. You ask me, and I'll consider responding. That's the deal."

"Fair," Sal said, bringing her right fingertips up to her forehead and looking at her lap while considering what she wanted to know. "Okay, I got it. Tell me about your favorite childhood memory."

"Eating lunch on nacho day. Next."

"Eating nachos? That's your favorite childhood memory? That's so lame," Sal said.

"Wow, I sure am glad we are playing this game. You sure are making me want to talk some more. I am glad we are opening up to each other," Cambo mocked in a robot-like voice.

"Yeah, yeah, yeah, just shut up and answer the questions. Tell me about your worst childhood memory."

Cambo looked over at Sal, seeming to study her face for several moments. Sal smiled back at him.

"My worst childhood memory? Well…" Cambo looked Sal in the eye. "I guess that would have to be the time I watched my dad rape my mom."

"What?" Sal asked, letting out a gasp of breath. She examined his face closely for some seconds. Suddenly she felt a rush of laughter envelop her. "Okay, that was a good one. You got me, I admit it. But you're not taking the game seriously. C'mon, I really want to know this stuff. Play along," Sal said. Cambo's face remained motionless. Sal began to feel uncomfortable.

Is he serious? she wondered. *I can't tell.* Cambo continued to hold a stone face and unflinchingly stared into her pupils.

"I'm not kidding, and you're failing the test," Cambo said.

"What? What test? What're you talking about?"

"I told you, no one likes to talk about this stuff. It makes them uncomfortable. It made you uncomfortable. You don't really want to talk about *my* memories; you want me to talk about *edited* memories. The ones that are funny, or unusual, or inspiring, or have some laudable emotional quality. I told you the unedited truth assuming you were right in knowing what you want, and now I'm regretting it because of how you're reacting."

"What do you mean the way I'm reacting? I do want you to tell the truth, whatever it is," Sal protested while rubbing his leg.

"Then why is your face blushing? Why are you rubbing my leg as if you did something wrong that you want to make up for? Why did you assume I must've been kidding?"

"Baby, I'm sorry. I don't mean to act shocked, but I am. I had no idea. You're right. I shouldn't have reacted this way. I ... I thought your dad was a preacher; it was just the last thing in the world I thought might happen. Him doing something like that. Please tell me about it. What happened? I really *do* want to know," Sal said, reaching for him. "Go on, tell me about it. *Please.* What happened?"

"Why would you want to know that?" Cambo

asked, pulling away from her and standing on his feet. "I don't want to know about it," he said, wiping tears away from his face. Sal looked at him for half a minute puzzling over what to say.

"Why would he do that?" she finally asked.

"I don't know," Cambo replied back meagerly. He walked over to the recliner opposite the couch and sat down with his elbows on his knees, his head hung clumsily between his legs.

"When you say 'rape,' like do you mean *rape* rape, or like—"

Cambo cut her off. "Like do I mean I walked in on her saying she had a headache and would prefer not to? No, a lot more serious than that. Like violent, unspeakable, forceful kind of serious, okay? More serious than you want to hear about, I promise you." Cambo grabbed his head with his arms and shook violently. He let out a scream that made Sal jump. "I shouldn't have done this," he said more quietly.

What do I say? Sal wondered although she remained frozen in her chair. She worried that saying the wrong things might make him snap, like he did in the alley. On the other hand, saying nothing might make him snap as well.

"Cambo," she ventured, unsure of herself, "I wish I knew what to say to make you feel safe with me right now. I didn't mean to make you so upset. You're right, I reacted badly, but I'm not put off by you saying this to me. I want to know about it, if you feel comfortable telling me. No matter how bad, I'll listen. I want to know."

"No you don't," Cambo said, his voice high and nasally. "I promise you that you don't want to know. No one does. I don't want to know."

Sal rose and took several steps toward him. She knelt down, facing his left side, and raised her hand to rub the back of his neck. "Cambo, I'm here for you. I sense you want to tell me. And I really want to know. I love you, and I would never purposely hurt your feelings. I'm not going to take advantage of you, just like you have never taken advantage of me. If you feel you can trust me, I'm listening."

Cambo sat hunched over pitifully, hyperventilating. Sadly, he raised his head and looked at Sal. She took his head and laid it on her shoulder, rubbing his neck. She could feel the moisture from his tears seeping through her shirt.

"I've ... it's just, I've never told anyone," Cambo said in a broken, strained voice.

Sal ached inside. Her stomach churned, and her head throbbed with tremendous pressure. She wanted desperately to help him out of this. Tears began to roll away from her eyes onto Cambo's matted hair. "I want to help. I really do. Please let me in. You can trust me."

"Promise?" Cambo's broken voice asked, his head still heavy on her shoulder.

"Yes."

"Swear?"

"Oh, Cambo, I swear, I swear, I swear. Tell me everything."

Cambo lifted his head off of her shoulder and leaned back against the recliner, letting his head collide with the upper cushion.

"It happened about a year ago."

Sal reached up and grabbed his hands. "Go on."

Cambo looked down at Sal then leaned his head upward and stared off at the ceiling. "I, uh, had just come home from a school thing, and it was pretty late. My parents were out celebrating their anniversary, and well, I guess they got a little drunk."

Sal reached up and wiped tears from Cambo's face.

"I tried sneaking in because it was way past curfew. But they didn't even notice. They were fighting in the den upstairs. They were screaming so loud. I ran to see what was wrong."

Cambo cried more profusely, his voice choked for breath. "As I got to the door, I heard them screaming at the top of their lungs. My mom was screaming at him about something like, 'How can you tell me you love me when you do this kind of stuff to me and your own son?' He screamed back at her that he wouldn't have to find other women if she'd just give him what he needed. I sat frozen outside the door in the shadows. They didn't see me. They were too mad at each other. I started crying and got real scared. I don't know why. I just got worried and felt something dark and evil, like, come over me, you know?"

Sal matched Cambo's level of tears and squeezed his hand. "Then what happened?"

Cambo's voice became barely decipherable through the choking and crying. "Then he raped her." Cambo bit on his lip and strained his face for a moment. "Right in front of me. He just kept going and going, and I sat frozen like a baby not knowing what to do. Listening to her cry. Begging him to stop. Crying out desperately for help. And there I was, practically within reach, not doing anything."

"I'm so sorry."

Cambo looked through his tearstained eyes into her face. His eyes grew thin, and his jaw line bulged. "I'll never forgive myself for not intervening," he said, his voice deep and intense but giving way to more tears. His jaw began quivering, and he squinted while squeezing his fingers into tight fists. "I told myself I'd never again sit idly by while someone was being hurt. See? That's why I had to stop and help that girl in the alley. See? I just couldn't let it go!"

"Of course, of course."

"I couldn't just sit there and let him—"

"I get it now, Cambo. I love you. I get it now, I'm so sorry. I'm so sorry."

"Just couldn't sit … "

The two of them sat for an hour or more, crying on and off and kissing sporadically. As the grandfather clock let out five loud bongs, Sal lowered her mouth toward Cambo's ear. "Thank you for telling me. Thank you for trusting me."

Cambo looked back at her through his teary eyes but said nothing. She sat rocking his head and stroking his hair until she heard him begin to snore. The snoring was quiet at first and then grew loud and encompassing. She smiled, glad he was able to pass away from the conscious reality of the memory. Thrilled he was able to leave the cruel and heartless world. Thankful he could pass the rest of the morning safely in slumber. She stroked his head one final time. "Sleep," she whispered, tearing up once again and looking out the window at the shadowy images beyond the glass.

CHAPTER THIRTY-FIVE

Chief Murphy reclined heavily into his chair and let his hands hang off the sides of the armrests. The phone rang loudly, irritating his ears.

"Murphy."

"Yeah, Chief, it's Jones."

"What's up, Jonesy?"

"Not much. Hey, we got a lead on a stolen vehicle."

"Which one?"

"Geo Metro: beige, nineteen ninety-five, two-door."

"Yeah, yeah, I know which one you're talking about. So what's the lead?"

"Prostitute we picked up this morning claims to have seen a beige Geo Metro she figures must have been a ninety-five 'bout three weeks ago, with two passengers, one male, the driver, and one female, also a prostitute."

"Why would she remember this car from three weeks ago?"

"That's what I asked. She said the guy driving it busted outta the car like Rambo and took it to some clown who was pushing her around for a meth payment."

"Whaddaya talking about? What d'ya mean he 'took it to' this meth dealer?"

"Uh, I guess he busted outta the car and started brandishing some metal, yelling at the dealer to move on or eat some lead. Apparently the guy popped off about a buck fifty in shells."

"Wait a minute. How long ago did ya say this happened?" the chief asked.

"Three weeks-ish."

"Hooker couldn't remember the exact date?"

"No, said she was kinda spun that night. Apparently she dropped the meth earlier that evening before her dealer approached her."

"We had that random shooting report 'bout three weeks ago, remember? Bob and Edwards went out to take statements. Do you remember what they found by chance?" the chief asked, opening a file to search for Edward's report.

"Not really. Why d'ya ask, Chief?"

"Shut up a minute. Let me think," the chief ordered, finding the report. He opened it up and groaned aloud when several of the papers fell across his desktop from the file.

"You all right, Chief?" Jones asked. Ignoring Jones, the chief searched madly through the stack of papers, separating out the Edward's report from the other unimportant documents it fell among. Finding the report he snatched it up and began reading through the incident description.

"Friday night, eleven thirteen p.m., two shots heard fired in the red light district off Elm and Broadway. Suspects were seen driving off in a beige compact car. Specific make and model unknown to witness."

"Chief, you still there?" Jones asked.

"Jones, you still a moron? I said shut up for a minute."

"Lucy and you fighting again, ain't ya?" Jones asked. The chief ignored him and continued to read.

"Secondary witness was not found to corroborate report; however, possible tie-in to gun found by the Twenty-seventh Street off-ramp. Approximately twenty minutes after the reported shooting, a passerby called in for a vehicular distress signal when she noticed that a small car was parked at the base of the aforementioned off-ramp, approximately four miles from the red light district. Car was not found when officers arrived at the scene. Officers did find a set of footprints under the bridge, and noticed a silver object sticking out of the snow several feet from the underpass opening. Gun was a silver-plated custom made nine-millimeter with five empty shells in the cartridge. The gun was not registered and looked foreign made. Dusted for prints: negative, too obfuscated to ID."

The chief looked up from the report and scratched his head.

"Jonesy, did the hooker say where this Rambo thing went down?"

"Yeah, 'bout Carvener and Elm, by the Oyster Bar. Why, you got something?"

"How'd she know the passenger was a hooker?"

"She said she guessed by her outfit. Besides, she said she looked vaguely familiar."

"You run her through the photo albums?" the chief asked, glancing down at the report again.

"Yeah, turned up nothin'," Jones said, letting out a nasty cough.

"Quit coughing in my ear, what's the matter with you anyway? Didn't your mother never teach you to sneeze into your hand or nuthin'?" Murphy said. "Hey, what about the Geo being a ninety-five? How'd she know that?"

"Said she's been in enough to know."

"What's that supposed to mean?"

"What? I gotta spell it out for you? She's a h-o-o-k-e-r, get it? Look, I gotta run. You need anything else from me?"

"Yeah, I need you to watch your mouth and show some respect to your superiors, that's what I need."

"Yeah, yeah, I bet that's what Lucy said to you this morning, eh?" Jones said, cracking himself up.

The chief scowled at the handset and then slammed the phone down. He stood up and paced the floor for a moment, pondering over the correlation of the Geo Metro and the shots fired. *What kind of criminal steals a car and then runs around saving addicts from their suppliers?* he wondered, sitting down again. Suddenly he sat up and snapped on his computer.

"C'mon, c'mon!" he grumbled impatiently while the drives booted. Finally he had access to the stolen vehicle database. Carefully, and with two hands and two fingers, he typed in the theft incident number of the Geo and pulled up the registered owner's address: Cameron Bo, 1421 Cherokee Court.

CHAPTER THIRTY-SIX

Cameron Bo looked up at Sally and noted the way she was smiling back at him.

Kill her! A voice commanded from a distant corner of his mind. *Kill her now!* the voice repeated as a vision of a severed chicken passed through his mental field.

"Hey, Cambo … what're you thinking about?" Sal asked.

"Nothin'," Cameron said, straining his eyes closed and trying to block out the sounds. Another vision of a chicken's severed head entered his mind. He felt his stomach churn and a momentary surge of excitement charge through his body.

"You okay? You seem so tense today," Sal noted. "You really haven't talked all afternoon. Is something wrong?" Cameron looked her in the eye and grimaced. He began laughing out loud while fighting an impulse to place his hands around Sal's black neck. Suddenly he had an impression of a blue jay and smelt a faint scent of burning incense. He took a deep breath and closed his eyes.

"You seem so disconnected lately," Sal continued. "Not that I expect you to talk all the time or anything, but once and a while would be nice. Seriously, I don't think I've heard you really say anything all day. Or last night, or the night before that, come to think of it. Or all week since you told me about…" Sal looked at Cameron, waiting for a response. He looked back at her, now smelling rotten eggs and popcorn. A woman slipped behind Sal and disappeared through the refrigerator.

"Stop this! You know better!" a loud voice said.

Cameron looked toward the voice and saw an image of his father speaking to him. The image was fuzzy. Cameron couldn't tell if the image was real or fake, or even if it was his father, until he heard him speak again.

"I raised you better than this, boy! Don't you become a fruitcake on me just like your mother was! Don't you give me that crazy talk and impaired look of retardation in the morning. You're a Bo, and Bos are winners. I don't want to have some loser for a son. Don't you ever go crazy on me!"

"*Cambo! Hello!* Anyone there? Why aren't you responding to me?" Sal asked. She let out a loud and voluminous load of breath. "Honestly, I don't even know why I try. What's the point in talking to mannequin boy over there? I swear, sometimes I wish you'd just left me on that 'ole corner street. At least the customers would acknowledge my presence once in a while. Not you! All I ever do with you is sit and wonder what in the devil is going on in that mind of yours. And I'll tell you another thing too, I don't think I ever am gonna know. And truthfully, I don't ever know why I bother. I mean, what's the point? I've been killing myself to be here for you when everything seems to be so rough for you right now, and it's like all you can do is sit and make things awkward for me. I mean, what's the deal with you anyway? Are you healthy? Are you angry? Do you want to talk? Do you know what it's like to go seven days with someone without them speaking back to you? What? What is it?" Sal asked, pausing for several moments and looking into Cameron's eyes.

Cameron listened to every word she said, wanting but being unable to respond. He kept eyeing the man with the gun behind her.

"*Save her!*" screamed a female voice that sounded like it was being stabbed. "*Save her!*" the voice said again, this time full of resonation and distance, like a fading echo stretching a deep chasm.

Cameron caught Sal's eyes. She looked mad. She began shaking her head. Packing up her things she leaned over and gave him a kiss on the cheek. "I just don't know, Cambo. I love you, it's true, and I'll be there for you, whenever you need me. But *sometimes*, forgive me, sometimes you're a little crazy, you know?"

With a few hastened steps, Sal made her way toward the door to the garage, opened it wide, hesitated a moment while looking back at Cameron, then disappeared into the garage. Cameron had difficulty keeping his eyes open. His head felt ablaze with heat. His heart palpitated like a drum in a hailstorm.

Whir! The garage door made a clumsy sound as it reeled the metallic door links upward and around the overarching garage axis. Cameron heard the Geo turning its engine over and over, finally igniting. The severed chicken popped into his mind again.

"Stop it!" he screamed in a whisper.

"*Stop it! Stop it!*" his father mocked. Cameron

looked up to see his father's disappointed expression, then he looked down again at the floor. *I hate you,* he thought with regard to his father. He began pacing the floor back and forth. Every so often he stopped to observe his father's blurry presence in the room.

"I'm not going away," his father resisted. Cameron raised his hands suddenly and emitted a muffled scream. His ears deafened him with stereophonic ringing and pressure.

"Stop it! Please, whoever is doing this to me, please stop it!" Cameron ordered in a slouched over position while grabbing his ears.

Keep it hidden! he told himself over and over again while rocking himself back and forth. The strategy seemed to work after some time: the ringing dissipated, the loudness faded, the voices fled, and the smell turned into the waft of a winter afternoon. Still, Cameron rocked for another twenty minutes, not daring to look up, sensing his father's presence still bearing down upon him. *What do you want?* he thought. His father breathed down on his neck and began stroking his hair. The severed chicken popped into his mind again.

"What do you want me to do, Dad?" Cameron asked, still afraid to look at his father. Cameron listened quietly to the birds chirping somewhere in the house behind him. He wondered why the birds hadn't migrated for winter and what they were doing in his house. He listened to the birds some more, straining with all his might to hear them while ignoring his father's constant gestures for attention. Cameron honed in on one bird in particular. There was something different about it. Its voice was lower, arrhythmic, and piercing. He became infatuated with the noise and let his mind wander from the confines of his own private thoughts to join with the bird's. The bird chirped louder and louder until reaching a painful level. The low and long tones became short and high pitched, and finally Cameron could make out a message from the bird to him.

What is it you want to tell me, little bird? he asked telepathically, careful to not give any clues to his father that he was communicating with the bird.

"I want you to save the world," the bird said, playing it cool. Casually, without moving his body, Cameron rocked his head in an affirmative manner. *I know this is my destiny. I hear the calling to save the world. I've started my journey already, but I need more time. What would you like me to do?*

"*You must kill the girl!*" the bird growled, putting the decapitated chicken into his mind again. *Kill the girl! Kill the girl! Kill the girl!*

Cameron shrieked inside himself. *No! Go away, I love the girl!* he said emphatically in his mind, trying to distract himself. *Get away, devil bird! I know your work, and you can't control me. I've got heaven on my side!* Cameron hissed quietly at the bird, grinning triumphantly as the bird disappeared before him.

"Cameron," his father said.

"What?" Cameron asked, turning around and catching his father's eyes.

"You let her know your secret. Now she's going to

tell the police, and then they're going to know what you did to me. The bird is right."

Cameron looked behind him and saw the bird hadn't disappeared at all. *How did he hear us?* Cameron wondered, looking back at his father then at the bird again.

"I told him," the bird said defiantly. "I told him because you wouldn't listen. Now listen to your father and do what you're told!"

"Yes, Cameron, do as you are told. You wouldn't want to disappoint me. I am your father, and I have forgiven you for your sins. Don't make me hate you again. Listen to the bird. It's right. She knows too much. Do you know where your girlfriend is? She's going to tell the police about your secret. Do you know that? She knows. She has always known. Ever since the first day you picked her up on that whore street, she has known there was something evil and bad about you, and now she's going to tell. She's going to tell before you have a chance to show your power to the world and make it right. She wants to take away your power to be a messenger for God and truth by going to the police. She's sending them over right now, and they *are* going to find you. Do you want that? No, I didn't think so. You must kill the girl before she figures it out. She'll be fine. God loves girls with hearts like Sal; she'll have a special place in heaven. It's not her fault she's a whore. She said it herself; her momma got her into it. Nothing she can do. So send her home, Cameron. In fact, you'll be helping her, because if you let her expose you, she'll only stop the special mission you were appointed to fulfill, and then she'd be in trouble, right? Then she couldn't go to heaven because then she'd be punished, right?

"And so would you. You'd be punished too for letting her ruin your legacy! Your mission! Your divine errand! So what're you going to do? Sit and cry and doubt your gifts? You're not crazy. No, *she* is wrong! You are special, and she wouldn't understand that. You are special, and the world needs someone special. The world needs you. Their prophet. Thousands, even millions will die without you. Maybe not in this world, but in the world to come if you don't fulfill your mission. So go now. It is better that she should die than that all of those you could help perish in the next life because they're ignorant. Get up, son, and save me. You owe me that! And your mother too. We'll be watching you from above, from heaven. Please avenge our deaths. Make right the wrong. Kill the girl!"

Cameron's brain was on fire. He could smell burning. He grabbed his head and vigorously rubbed his temples until one side began to bleed. He let out a yelping scream and shook violently. Everywhere he looked all he could see was Sal's head being decapitated like the chicken. He scrambled around with himself, grabbing at his shirt collar as if it were choking him. He gagged on his breath and began blacking out. His visual plane grew dark, and he felt himself hit the linoleum floor. Thousands of visual pictures of every variety raced through his mind.

"Kill her!" A myriad of voices shrieked so loudly the physical integrity of the house seemed to falter and shake.

No, I can't do it! I can't do it! You're not real! My father died a year ago in a car accident! Please go away! Please go away, demon voices of sin! Through his tears he pulled himself up from the floor and rested his forehead on the counter, looking down into the utility drawer. His gaze fell upon the large butcher knife, and he stared at it for what seemed hours.

After receiving numerous impressions to grasp the knife, he finally lowered his hands into the drawer and picked up the plastic handle. As he pulled the knife out, he briefly caught his reflection and that of his smiling father behind him.

"Good boy, son," his father said as he dropped a hand onto Cameron's shoulder.

CHAPTER THIRTY-SEVEN

"Doctor Haddelby, can I ask an off-topic question?" Addy asked. The old professor discontinued his discourse on Catholicism for a moment and found Addy's upraised hand. John smiled as he looked at the curves of her body, even though they were nestled too close to his now good friend Merci. Who knew John would have a classic case of "Jesse's Girl" syndrome? He leaned back and closed his eyes and thought of all he'd seen of Addy from the many nights he had watched her outside her bedroom window. As he put his arms on the rests, he accidently knocked Cameron's arm.

"Sorry, man," he whispered. Bo nodded back briefly. John wondered what was up with that guy. He seemed a bit weird to him. He never spoke during the group project nights and refused to answer questions about himself.

"Yes, my dear," Haddelby said with a wink to Addy, mentioning that he had noticed that Addy had missed a few classes. She'd been crying a lot, John knew. She seemed to get very depressed at times. Sometimes, when watching her from the backyard, John would feel such a surge of energy to break through the sliding door and wrap his arms around her and tell her it would be okay. It didn't seem to John that Merci knew just how serious Addy's depression was. But then again, Merci was always a little bit wrapped up in himself. John could tell Merci had his own demons to work on.

"We'll, maybe you covered this while I was gone, but I'm just curious," Addy said, "the first day of class you started off by saying you were, like, a potential god, or a 'god in the womb' or something like that. I guess I never really got why you did that." The old man slowly shuffled his way toward her side of the classroom.

"That's more than a bit off topic, but I've been waiting all semester for someone to point that out, so I'll be happy to address your question for a while. But first, tell me, why do you care to know why I said such a thing?"

Addy shrugged her shoulders and looked at him blankly. "I guess it was just an odd thing to say. I'm curious as to what you were gettin' at."

"Fair enough. Well, you all heard the young lady, now answer her question, class. What was I getting at?" the doctor queried as he raised his eyes to the mass of bodies. "Anyone have a guess as to where I was going with that statement?" The class was unusually silent. "Cat got your tongues, eh? Well, allow me to restructure my inquiry—what do you know about me automatically by my saying that I'm a god in the womb, or more accurately, a god in embryo?" A large man in the back raised his hand.

"Well, we know you're religious."

"Okay, explain?"

"Well, just that—you're religious. You believe in God."

"And how is it that you know I in fact do believe in God, based on the statement of interest?"

"Because you said *you* are a God in embryo. Therefore, you obviously believe there is such a thing as God if you can become one, right?" a girl on the left side of the lecture hall interrupted.

"That's a tautology, and circularity does not satisfy conclusion in this course. Now, someone give me some substance! What do you know, or what are you not able to know about me from my statement that I am a 'god in embryo'?"

"We know you believe in religion and not in science. Is that what you're looking for?" someone tried.

"Not quite, but I'll accept your logic as a tenable conclusion from my statement. However, let me ask you something. Why do you assume that I could not be both an evolutionist and still be 'religious' as you defined it?"

"I'm not sure I understand what you mean?" the student said.

"What I'm trying to say is that from your comment, it seems to be that you believe that a person can be either religious or a scientist, and nothing in between. But is that right? Consider: is it possible that I can actually believe I am a god in embryo yet *not* be religious—that is, believe I am a potential, blooming god, but I believe exclusively in evolutionary principles that were not put into action by a deity?"

"No. That part we *can* rule out from your statement that you are a possible God," John said.

"Class, anyone disagree with Mr. Joe?"

Addy raised her hand. "Yes." Haddelby whirled around, led by an intrigued smirk.

"Why?" he asked.

"I don't know. I guess because even if you believe in God and all that stuff, it all had to start somewhere right?"

The old man looked down at her and smiled a minute then turned his attention toward the larger class. "Any of you get what this young woman is trying to point out?"

The class stared back at the old man blankly.

"Who here is exclusively a scientist—meaning you buy the evolution thing hook, line, and sinker—and are completely atheistic; there is no God before, during, or after this life?" A few hands crept upward.

"Aha! Thank you for your honesty. You, sir, Mr. Zway, why do you believe in science?"

"Because it's gotten results. It works."

"Balderdash!" Haddelby attacked teasingly. "What kind of results? I mean, what can we *really* do with science?"

"Tons: fly to the moon, build computers, save lives, and tons more stuff."

"Okay, but there's a limit, right? Computers can't think, and humans can't create life."

"Actually, some researchers have developed computers that can think. I mean, it's not a bunch of big deal stuff, but they have machines that can learn simple patterns and stuff on their own."

"And what about cloning?" another man suggested from the back of the class.

"What about it?" Doctor Haddelby said. "Cloning is not creating life. It's replicating a produced mass of cells that was already created by two human beings. It's not manufacturing life, but rather just duplicating it once it's already made."

"True," Zway agreed, "but it's just a matter of time until we discover how to manufacture life, not just Xerox it. That's why I buy the science argument. All of the religious explanations seem unnecessary when you can just do it yourself. Who needs God anymore to help explain the mysteries of life? As they become less mysterious, religion becomes useless, a waste of time."

The professor looked at Zway for a few moments, as if processing his arguments. "Do you really believe all that you just said, Mr. Zway?"

"I do."

"How long until you think we discover all of those life-creating mechanisms and fancy science stuff?"

"I dunno. Fifty years at most would be my guess."

"But what's off limits to science? Astronomy, atomic creation and manipulation, ecological control?" Haddelby asked.

"Nothing, I suppose. The sky's the limit. Science has a hand in all of those fields, and we're progressing in them all. Some may take a lot more time than others, but I really believe we'll figure them out."

"Given enough time, that is," the doctor pressed.

"Right. I mean we're a long ways off now, but unless we kill our planet too quickly, we'll only get more and more able to do all that stuff."

"Okay, now, I am just a simple, humble old man, so let me make sure I got this straight. You're saying that *if* we do not kill ourselves *or* kill our planet off, *then* given enough time we can learn to create life, control the ecology; in essence, manufacture and manipulate all biological, social, and environmental processes through established laws and principles of science. Well, Mr. Zway, thank you for educating the class on my point," Doctor Haddelby announced triumphantly, seating himself on his desk and facing the class center.

"I'm sorry, Doctor Haddelby, but I'm not sure I follow?" Zway said.

"Well, the point about how I'm a god in embryo. You see, it's all very simple. If I am a scientist and believe the sky is the limit, and that we can learn all of the essential parameters of life functioning, then I believe that the end stage of evolution is to evolve a species that acquires godlike powers. You see? Literally, then, my point is to say that whether or not one is religious or claims dogmatic science, we all arrive at the same conclusion: the nature and destiny of mankind is the potential to be a creator and controller of life!" The doctor held out a hand and stepped to the side, beginning a dramatic pacing across the center of the room.

"Isn't it ironic? Two opposite sides of the coin ending with the same summary chapter, but by so very different means." He stopped abruptly and turned toward the attentive students once again, his presence presiding over the silent class for several long seconds after delivering his opus, searching all present. Finally, he loosened his rigid stance, checked his watch, and turned to face Addy.

"Well, I guess if there're no disagreements, then the class agrees with me. I'm a god in embryo. But if that's true, I'm not the only one. You, Ms. Siwel, are as well."

CHAPTER THIRTY-EIGHT

Chief Murphy sped down Fifth Street, irritated at the traffic. "No, hon, I promise I am *not* trying to make you upset, it's just—you know how much I hate your parents coming to visit." The chief hit the brakes as the light faded from green to yellow. He eyed the funeral procession and rolled his eyes.

"No—"

"No—no, but—"

"Honey, I—"

"Yes, dear, but if you'll just listen to m—"

The chief shifted in his chair as a hydraulically powered Volkswagen convertible meandered across the intersection with two passengers leaning into the tilted vehicle.

"Look—"

"Look, hon—"

"Look, I—"

"Okay, quiet for a minute! Look, I'm sorry I don't like your parents coming to visit. It's not them. I just have things to do, and all they want to do is show me pictures of their grandkids. Can't you just tell 'em I'm on a job? Or that you divorced me? Or that I died in a terrible accident or something?"

"Yeah."

"Yes."

"Yeah, you're right."

"I am only kidding."

"No, seriously."

"They are good people."

"Yep, like you."

"Okay gotta go, love you, hon. Bye."

As the last car passed through the intersection, Chief Murphy flashed his lights and motored through. *It must be that Victorian-looking house over there,* the chief thought as he turned onto Cherokee. *Nice digs,* he considered as he rolled into an appropriate stopping position in front of the large two-story house. Quickly he surveyed the landscape, noticing the poorly trimmed bushes in their varying artistic shapes. No one seemed to be around. Dropping his hand into the driver's side door latch, the chief gave a pull on the handle, and the door swung wide. With some effort he angled his left leg onto the pavement. His leg tingled as it moved out from the car to the street. Moaning, he ran a massaging hand up and down his thigh before grabbing the top of his door and pulling himself out of the car. Slowly he walked up to the front porch, noticing every detail about the landscaping, yard, and house. He noted that the three-car garage was open, but no cars were inside. The foundation block of the first garage, however, seemed to have some fresh oil droppings.

As he made his way closer to the front door, he saw someone peek out the window at him then vanish back into the house. The chief lowered his hand to his gun—he had a bad feeling about this, but he was unsure why. Quickly he looked around, seeing if anyone would hear him if he hollered for assistance. Unfortunately, the house was set aside just enough from the other dwellings that it would be highly unlikely anyone could hear him if he yelled. With an invisible shoulder shrug he approached the front door. Just as he depressed the doorbell, the wind picked up, blocking his ability to hear if the doorbell rang or if it was broken. He sat for a moment, straining his ears in order to hear any response. The wind blasted him so hard that he had to hold his hat to keep it in place. He looked out across the city horizon and noted the rolling cumulus clouds that seemed to stretch forever.

Okay, it's definitely been long enough for me to try again, the chief thought as he hammered on the door. There was no response. He leaned into the door and angrily announced his presence, including that he knew someone was home and they'd better answer the door.

"Can I help you, Officer?" came a voice from behind him. The chief spun around while still grasping his gun handle.

"You live here, son?" the chief queried, recognizing the youthful face as the peeper from the window.

"Yes, sir, I surely do. What can I do you for?"

"Well, I'm looking for a, um, just a second there," the chief stalled as he scrambled for the name on the auto theft complaint. "Oh yes, here it is, looking for a Cameron Bo. You know where I can find him?"

"Sure do, that's me."

The chief looked at the young boy then back at the complaint. "How old are you, son?"

"Eighteen and two-tenths," Cameron said with a grin.

The chief looked down at his sheet again. "I hope you'll not mind my saying that you don't look a day over sixteen," Murphy marveled, taking a few steps toward the boy and extending his hand for a shake. "Look, I don't want to take up much of your time, but I have a few questions to ask you about your auto theft. Mind if we step inside for a moment."

"Not at all," Cameron replied, "but you might. The house is a mess, and I just set off some debugging fumigators. Air is all full of poisonous gasses and stuff."

The chief looked over his shoulder into the front room as much as the broken shades would allow but couldn't tell if the boy was lying. The wind picked up again, and the chief quickly surveyed the landscape for a more conducive setting to converse.

"I have a couple of chairs on the other side of the garage," Cameron offered. Responding to the boy's motioning gestures, the chief followed the youth across the driveway and around the side of the house to a small grassy area that had a barbecue and several lawn chairs. The chairs were frozen from the high winds.

"Sure has been a cold spell lately, hasn't it?" the chief commented, throwing a hand in his pocket to retrieve his pad and pencil.

"Yes, sir," Cameron said while surveying the skies. "Weatherman says it's only going to get worse too." He shifted in his chair for a moment, lowered his head, and seemed to whisper something to himself. The chief watched closely as Cameron shook his head back and forth slightly, whispered something again, then looked directly up at the chief like he'd forgotten he was there.

"You all right, son?"

"Yes—sorry. I, uh, I just forgot I was supposed to be somewhere in a half hour, that's all."

"Oh, I see. Whereabouts?"

"Well, cross town actually. But uh, it's okay, I can

be a little late. What can I do for you, Officer? Do you have any leads on the car?"

"Well, it's funny you mention it, son. We actually got a lead today, and you won't believe it, but it appears your car has been doing some pretty heavy traveling right here in town."

Cameron sat up. "Really, so you've found it?"

"Not quite," Murphy said, eyeing the boy for a moment.

"Oh, well, I'm sure you get a lot of thefts. Probably hard to retrieve these kinds of things."

"Actually, we usually get to the bottom of these cases fairly quickly. In fact, I pride myself on our auto-theft division. Head it myself. But this one seems a little tough to solve, and I'm not sure where we stand on its progress," the chief explained, sitting back in his chair and letting his notepad lay across his left thigh.

"Why? What makes this one so hard?"

The chief shrugged his shoulders for a moment and looked off to the side of the house before answering. "Well," the chief started as he turned toward Cameron again, "to be perfectly honest, I'm starting to feel something's off about this case."

Cameron looked at the chief for several moments as if trying to process the chief's intent. "What do you mean by that?"

"Well, I'll tell you, but first, can you show me your driver's license?" the chief requested, sitting back comfortably in his chair.

Cameron smiled at the chief. "No can do, boss.

Unfortunately, my wallet's been missing for several weeks now."

"Well, that's too bad. You know you're required to carry ID around all the time. I could cite you for not having it now, you know? You'll have to call that in and order a new one."

"Yes, sir, first thing in the morning," Cameron said, laughing sheepishly. An awkward silence passed between them.

"Well, fine. Now I know you have to get going, but let me tell you why I came here in the first place. It appears your car was seen about three weeks ago as part of a robbery."

"You're kidding me," Cameron said wide eyed. "Did anyone get shot?"

"I didn't say anyone used a gun. Why would you ask that?"

Cameron popped his head back and hung his mouth open for a brief moment. "Well, I don't know. I just figured if you're going to rob something, you likely wouldn't hold up your dukes, you know what I mean?"

"So if you were going to rob someone, you'd use a gun?"

Cameron looked aloofly at the aging police officer. "I didn't say that."

Murphy stared unflinchingly at Cameron. "Then what are you saying?"

"Just that I can't imagine someone would try to pull off something that illegal without use of a weapon or something."

"You'd be surprised. As a matter of fact, shots were fired, although no one was hurt."

"Oh my heavens!" Cameron said, running his fingers through his hair. "What happened?"

"Well, can't get much into the details, you know police business and all. But we have a description of the perpetrators," the chief said matter-of-factly while looking off into the distance.

"What'd they look like?"

"Well, funny you should ask. That's actually why I wanted to see your driver's license."

"Oh?"

"Yeah, see the passenger was a woman: dark hair, thin figure, provocatively dressed. But see, the driver, the one we think fired the shots, well, he was described in terms very similar as I might describe you."

"Really, what do you mean by that?"

"Well, the witness saw this at nighttime, but the witness said the driver was, you know, dark hair, taller, and most of all, youthful in appearance. What do you make of that?"

"I think I might know what to make of that, officer." Cambo laughed. "Oh boy, my parents would sure like to kick my butt for this one. Well, there's no way to say this but straightly. Some months ago, I, well … oh, geez. Well, here it is straight. I brought home a girl. You know—a call girl. It was my, well, my first experience with this sort of thing. I guess I'm the world's biggest idiot, but when we—when the night was over, I guess I fell asleep. And when I woke up, my car was missing. I suppose I'm naïve for thinking maybe she didn't take it, but she just seemed so nice. Wow, I feel really stupid right now. You know, I bet you she's the one who took my wallet too."

"Wait a minute, wait a minute. I thought you said you lost your wallet only a couple of weeks ago. This car theft has been on the books for *well* over two weeks. How could that be? You still tricking with the girl?"

Cambo looked pale. "No, of course not, Officer. It was a one-time deal. I swear."

"Then how'd she get your wallet?"

"Well, isn't it obvious? She had my keys, not just my car keys, but my house keys too. She must be watching the house for when I leave. Geez, I'll have to change the locks or somethin'."

"Sounds like a good idea."

"It does."

"Wouldn't want a bad guy to be livin' in your home."

"No, I wouldn't. I don't like bad guys. Or a bad girl in this case, right?"

Murphy leaned back in his chair again and nodded his head. "Yeah, I guess that's right. A bad girl. In fact, a bad call girl. Which, I might add, that trickin' with a call girl is also illegal."

"Well, it was sort of, uh, you know, an eighteenth birthday present to myself. Guess it wasn't such a smart gift after all, huh?"

"No, I'd say not. A very poor choice indeed."

"Well, she seemed really nice, and I have a hard time believing she'd get all caught up in a shooting.

But, then again, guess if that's your profession you're probably not the most moral of persons, right?"

The chief forced a laugh. "Guess not. Did she give you a name by any chance?"

"Yeah, she said her name was Sal."

"Sal, eh?"

"Yep. Sal. In fact, I guess her specialty is young boys doing that sort of thing for the first time."

"Really?"

"Yup."

"Then I guess she was perfect for you, wasn't she?"

"I guess you could say that."

"Well, I guess that also conveniently explains the whole perpetrator that looks just like you thing, huh?"

"Well, yeah, I guess it does. I hadn't thought of that. That's an interesting point, Officer."

The two men sat in a slow motion staring contest for several moments before Cameron broke his gaze and looked at the ground.

"Well, I appreciate your time, son. I'll let you go," Murphy said as he found his feet and stood upright. Cameron matched his movement.

"Sure. Let me know how the investigation goes. Will I see you again?"

"I've a feeling you will," he said, grabbing Cameron's outstretched hand for a parting shake. "In the meantime, I'll be out watching for you. Your car I mean."

CHAPTER THIRTY-NINE

Addy squeezed her stomach while trying to not draw attention to herself. "You okay?" Merci asked.

"Yeah. Just, ah, girl cramps," Addy replied, her face slightly strained.

"Say no more," Merci said, knocking back the remainder of his drink.

Addy smiled and looked down at the table.

Merci smiled back. "This is nice," he said.

"What is?"

"Being here. With you. I like it a whole lot, actually."

"Yeah?"

"Yeah. These last weeks have honestly been the happiest of my life. I just feel so open with you. I feel like I can tell you anything. Like you don't care. You don't judge me. I've never had that feeling with anyone before, and I like it."

Addy looked down at the table. *He doesn't really mean that. He wouldn't say that if he really knew you; how high maintenance you are. How stupid.*

Despite her insecurities and doubts, Addy played along with the lover's dance, looking back up at Merci's face and rubbing his hands. Merci leaned in and kissed her lips. He was such a bad kisser, but Addy didn't have the heart to tell him. Besides, she liked the attention. She liked how much he liked her. It made her feel special, wanted, desired. Of course, she didn't know why he was into her, but she decided she didn't care for the moment. She was having fun in this relationship, and for some reason, she really didn't want it to end. Not yet, anyway.

"Hey, can I ask you a totally random question?" Merci asked.

"Okay."

"What do you think about crazy people?"

"Like what do you mean?" Addy asked, picking up a French fry.

"You know, like loony people. Schizophrenics, bipolars, wack jobs, that kind of stuff?"

"Are bipolar people crazy? I thought they just got depressed and happy and stuff?"

"Well, I don't know, but that's beside the point. I mean people who, like, hear things and stuff. Would you ever go out with someone like that?"

"I dunno, like how crazy? Are they gonna kill me or something?" Addy asked, dipping her fry in the mayonnaise then the ketchup.

"No."

"So, like, would I date a guy who's crazy? Hears voices, sees things, speaks gibberish, but wouldn't kill me?"

"Not all crazy people speak gibberish and see things, you know."

"No, I didn't know that. How do you know all this stuff? Your therapist been telling you all this stuff?"

"No, I'm just wondering about it. Guess I was thinking about it at the clinic. Actually, I saw some guy there who was, like, hearing voices, and I started thinking: what chance does this guy have of getting married or having kids? That kind of stuff."

"Well, to be honest, I'd be more concerned about having kids with someone like that than getting married to him, although I can't say that I see a point in getting married if my husband doesn't even know who I am."

Merci pulled a long face at her. "Well, it wouldn't be like that. I mean, I'm not talking about the completely insane. I'm talking about someone who is a nice guy but who, like, hears voices once in a while."

"Are you trying to tell me something?" Addy smiled, then turned to a serious face. "So, let me get this straight, would I want to marry a guy who wasn't insane, meaning he wasn't going to kill me or talk in riddles or anything, but wherever he went he heard voices?"

"Yep," replied Merci.

"And who wasn't all 'blah, blah, blubbity, bloo blah,'" Addy asked.

"Well, I'm not sure what that means, but yep," Merci responded again. Several silent seconds passed as they looked at each other.

"It depends then."

"Depends on what?"

"On what the voices say."

"Okay, they say lots of things: some good, some disturbing. The point is the guy never acts on it, though; he just hears them all the time."

Addy remained silent for several minutes thinking it over.

"Well?" Merci finally prompted.

"No."

"No? Why not?"

"Cause, I don't believe him that he would never act on them."

"Well, in our pretend world, we decided he wouldn't ever act on 'em."

"Still no."

"Why still no?"

"Because."

"Because … what?"

"Because, well, first of all, it would make me uncomfortable living with someone crazy. Second, I wouldn't want to pass on that trait to my kids, and third, and to be honest this is the biggest deal, I don't like living with fake people. How would a guy who couldn't even explain his own thoughts know how he feels about me? If he couldn't be real with me, then I could never trust he actually loved me. Maybe that part is as pretend as his voices. If he couldn't decide if he ever really loved me, then I could never really trust him. If I could never really trust him, then no, I wouldn't want to marry him."

Merci sat back in his chair and stared silently at Addy, apparently processing her comments. After some time, Addy's thoughts meandered with her eyes around the room. She watched a trio of men playing pool, drinking alcohol, and laughing boisterously. She examined for a while another group of men huddled around the large-screen television, all watching a sports game. She noticed the couples at their varying tables, some talking feverishly, and some eating dinner in silence, hardly noticing one another. She observed the man at the bar, formally dressed in a tuxedo with several empty bottles around his personal space. He was knocking down another glass at the moment, and Addy mused upon his professional-looking appearance. *What's a guy like that doing alone in a place like this?* The man stooped forward, grasped at his back pocket, and wrestled a picture out of his wallet. He held the picture close to his eyes then set it down and took a large swig of alcohol, pausing every so often to lift up the picture and rub his eyes. *How sad,* Addy thought, now completely absorbed in watching the old man. *I wonder who's in the picture?*

"Who are you looking at?" Merci asked, breaking into Addy's trance.

Addy turned her eyes to her grinning date. "There's some guy over there. Looks like he's getting drunk over some memory or somethin'. He keeps pulling out this picture, kisses it, then drops down a glass of wine. Looks like he's been at it for a while."

Merci swung around, watched for several seconds, then glanced back over at Addy before looking at the old man again. Addy looked curiously at Merci as he got up from his chair, tiptoed several feet away from the table, and then returned to his seat with an enigmatic look of intrigue on his face.

"Do you know who that is?"

Addy strained to see, but she couldn't make any distinguishing features out from her angle. "No, do you?"

Merci looked over his shoulder again then snapped

his head back and whispered in an over-controlled voice, "That's Doctor Haddelby!"

"No way," Addy dismissed, leaning over to try and make out more of his face.

"No, seriously. I'm not kidding you. That's him. Check it out!" Merci said, stealing another glance over his shoulder at the old professor.

"I don't believe it. You're right. What's he doing way out here on a Saturday night?"

"I don't know. Kind of a crusty place for the most distinguished church dude this side of the Mississippi, don't you think?"

Addy watched the old man for a few moments.

"He looks so sad," Addy said. "Maybe we should go over there and talk with him?"

"I don't know. He also looks kinda drunk. I'm not sure he really wants us around if he's tipsy."

"Well, I'm going over there," Addy announced as she grabbed her purse and began rising out of her chair.

CHAPTER FORTY

"Doctor Haddelby?" Addy asked, the words floating out like a frail soap bubble. The old man slowly set down his drink and turned to look at the woman on his right. He stared motionless for several seconds before allowing his face to form a smile.

"Ms. Siwel and Mr. Bowku. I should've guessed. Out for a furlough, are you?" the old man inferred clumsily. Addy could smell the strong scent of alcohol on his breath. "Come, sit down," Haddelby said, patting stools on his left and right. Addy found the stool on his right and lowered her body onto the hard wood. "So, what brings the two of you out to a place like this? Love is in the air, I suspect?"

Addy and Merci exchanged an awkward smile. "You know, kids on the town is all. We were surprised to see *you* here, though," Addy said.

"Well, I come here every year at this time, don't you know? Every blasted year, to the same raunchy, dirty, old bar!"

Addy eyed the bartender, who made a disapproving look toward the professor. "Sounds like you've been drinking a bit tonight."

"Of course! What other reason would I have for coming to a bar?"

Addy had to admit that seemed like a good response even for a drunk old professor.

"Why d'ya come here every year?" Merci asked. "What's the big occasion?"

The professor poured another glass of wine and lifted it to his forehead. "Oh, that feels *so* refreshing," he moaned, rubbing the glass back and forth. Addy was beginning to regret coming over.

"Ms. Siwel, let me ask you something," the professor requested while laughing. "Let me ask you something," he repeated, now laughing hysterically.

"What?"

"Final exam! Ready?" Haddelby howled, barely able to contain his voice.

"Ready!" Addy said while smirking and winking at Merci, who was also grinning wide.

"What do you call a Hindu, a Christian, a Buddhist, a Reformist, and a Restorationist?" the professor choked out in between chortles.

Addy shrugged her shoulders. "I don't know. What?"

"Morons!" the professor squealed with delight followed by a long burst of drunken laughter.

Addy worked hard to bite down on her laughter, but she was helpless to the uncomfortable scene. "Okay, well, it was nice to see you. We're gonna get going now, okay?" Addy motioned to Merci to start leaving when suddenly the professor's hand caught her arm.

"Wait a minute. Don't go yet. I have something to tell you," Haddelby pleaded, his voice and posture turning serious. Addy and Merci both sat down again, eyes on the drunken man.

"Let me show you something. Here, take a look." The professor grabbed the picture he'd been looking at and handed it to Addy. "That's my wife, my sweet Lynda, gone now for exactly forty-two years."

Addy stared at the woman's prominent chin, high cheek bone, and fair skin. "She's beautiful," she said, handing the picture across to Merci.

"Stunning is the word I always use to describe her. She was nothing less," the professor said.

"What happened to her?" Addy asked.

The professor grew awkwardly silent. His jaw began to twitch, and his body rocked unsteadily. At first the shaking was mild, but then it grew into a raging tremor, culminating in a full-fisted blow to the bar counter, which caught the barkeep's disapproving look once again. Addy waved him off and dropped a couple dollars into his tip jar.

"What is it?" Addy asked. "What happened?"

The old man stopped shaking and looked into Addy's hazel eyes, a tear forming under his left eyelid, cresting over the bumpy skin layer and streaming slowly down his wrinkled face. "She was murdered. Forty-two years ago tonight. She was raped, tortured, and dismembered by a pack of men all drunken with their religious dogma!"

Addy felt a pit in her stomach. Her eyes grew moist at the pathetic sight of the old professor recapping the story. "I'm sorry. I never knew. How could something like this happen?"

"I don't know," the old professor said while raising his glass to his lips once again, taking a swig, and then setting it down. "I don't know. In fact, I have spent my whole life searching for an answer to your question, my dear. And truth is, I still don't know."

Addy sat uncomfortably, wishing she could leave and cry somewhere in private. "I'm sorry," she said once again, the words stumbling out lamely.

"Don't be sorry. It's not your fault; it's his!" the old man said in a threatening voice while looking upward and waving a fist toward the ceiling. Soon, the look of anger faded back into despair and the old man low-

ered himself back down to the chair he had been resting upon for the majority of the evening. "Oh, what's
the use? I'm screaming at a non-being. That's the
point, don't you see? Nothing, there's nothing there to
protect us. Nothing there to keep us safe."

Addy reached out and grabbed the professor by
his arm. He looked up into her eyes and smiled. "Ms.
Siwel, did I ever tell you that you look strikingly like
my wife did at your age?"

"No. Tell me about her," she said, trying to hide
her shock at what her religion professor had just
admitted.

"You mean, tell you about the folly I just committed in front of a religious student?" he said, unwaver-
ing in his gaze. Addy quickly thought for a response,
looking to Merci for help.

"My dear, I'm drunk, but I'm not senile—yet. I've
been handling my liquor for a long time now, and
there are some things I can still do pretty well, even
when I have passed beyond practical limits of alcohol consumption. I'm sorry I did that in front of you
and your male friend here." He flung an identifying
thumb in Merci's general direction. "I have a harder
time repressing the emotions when I'm drunk. It's the
emotions that get you, see? It's this stuff right here,"
he said, tapping on the wine bottle. "This stuff'll go
right to your frontal lobes and impair the executive
inhibitor that keeps us from getting our foot in our
mouth in day-to-day living, no? Well, here I am need-
ing either a podiatrist or a shrink, but since you're neither, I'll tell you exactly what it was you saw there."

"What?" Addy asked cautiously.

"That was the answer to your question. That's what."

"What question?" Addy asked, very uncomfortable to have this conversation in front of Merci.

"The question you asked me the first time you came to my class. The question everybody around the world likes to ask me, and I am too chicken to tell them my real feelings about. The question that begs for an answer as unsatisfying and useless as the very theoretical underpinnings that engendered the question in the first place. Now don't play stupid with me, young lady. I'm an old drunk man, and for once I'm feeling a bit candid, and all I ask is that you attend well and be honest as I give it to you straight. Now, you with me? Or should I go gargle with some of the other insignificant creatures inhabiting the tavern?"

Addy didn't know what to do. She felt confused, offended, and curious all at the same time. She motioned to Merci to sit back down and shooed the bartender away once again. "Okay, I'm listening. Not wasting your time. You're talking about my question about God, right? And religion, right?"

"That's right, girlee, the Big Kahuna himself, God almighty, or the myth of God almighty, because here is your answer: there ain't a-one of them worth attending because they're all pretense, you see? They're all as phony as the sincerity in your voice when you ask someone how their day is. Their tenets, powers, and doctrinal diamonds are but, how does the *Bible* put it, 'tinkling brass.' Cowards, thieves, liars, destitute of logic and reason, and hypocrites. The every one of 'em. All succored by the allure of the inexplicable, the enigmatic, the unpredictable. They cheapen their lives with the false doctrines of a God who loves them and will help them. Well, I've been around the world, studied with the leaders of virtually every religion, prayed, read, pondered, and written about every religious exercise, book, ritual, or practice there is to engage in, and you want to know from all of that which church you should join? Here is my answer: save your money for wine because it is cheaper, more fun, and just as temporary a fix as that reified institution of faith you call any religion."

Addy looked incredulously at the man, who was near foaming at the mouth in his rage and disgust over the topic. *How could he be so hateful inside if he is a doctor of religion? How could he lead thousands of people to a religious lifetime when he can't believe it himself?*

Doctor Haddelby swigged another bit of his wine, set his cup on the bar top, wiped his face, and started in again. "I know what you're thinking," he said. "You too." He pointed a finger at Merci. "You're both wondering how I could be so apt to defend religious philosophies in class when I don't believe in any of them. Well, the answer is simple; I value the teachings as much as a teacher of the *Star Trek* series values his literature. Neither's real, but it's a living, and a lie you can believe in whenever you don't feel like facing the truth. That's it. How do you think religion got started in the first place? This is it. This is, in the words of Marx, our opiate. In the manner of Nietzsche and

Camus, our self-deception. And in the words of logic, our desperate nature. The ugly face of life is too much for the evolutionarily based coping systems we have. The answer was to evolve religion. Religion is the tool whereby nature strings us along from one insignificant life event to another. But in the end, it doesn't matter. None of it."

The professor grabbed his wife's picture and held it up to Addy's face. "It didn't matter for her." He held it up to Merci's face. "It didn't matter to her husband when he screamed out for help, having been hand-cuffed to an alley pipe, where he was forced by cruel and insane barbarians to watch his wife be known over and over again by a pack of viscous wolves, all who wore the cloak of the 'priesthood.' All who swore God was in them, and they in God. And all who will never burn in hell for their horrible deceptions of the con-gregations, of their rhetoric, and of their true natures."

Professor Haddelby began shaking fiercely. "That's the part I hate the most, knowing that for all the evil they've caused me, they will receive no different treat-ment in the next life, or shall I say next nothingness, than will you and I, even though we have tried to live honorably. Whatever that is."

The old professor was now teary, as were Addy and Merci. Even the barkeep must've had sympathy for the old man, because he stopped coming around to motion to Addy to control her guest. Addy took the professor in her arms and stroked the back of his head while tell-ing him she was sorry for what he'd experienced. After several long minutes, he raised his hoary head from her shoulder and put his hand on her cheek.

"You know, it's people like you. That is why I still preach it. It keeps people like you from giving up. The world needs people like you. Without anything to believe in, what authority is there to appeal to? Without anything to believe in, how do we prevent anarchy? How do we appeal to evildoers to change? How do we inculcate a common thread of decency in the world? That's why I still go on. But inside my private hell, I know what I did was wrong. And, Ms. Siwel, worst of all, I was the one who suggested we join the cult. Of course, I didn't know that's what it was, and I never knew my company had such skeletons in their closet. They told me it would be fun. They told me it was normal. They told me it was what had been done for centuries. A few odd rituals and a whole lot of philosophy. See, that's how they sold it to me.

"First an animal sacrifice, then another. Join us for the secret ceremony, and then … how could I have not seen? How could I have not detected? You see, I thought I had a revelation from God that this new 'church' was correct. I thought I knew it! Don't you see? I joined a cult! Me! The man who would become the world's most brilliant theologian, duped into a con my first year of adulthood! And my wife, Lynda, she knew. She always knew there was something wrong with it. But I was the head. I was the thinker. I was sure of my choice, and I made her go. You know, I never once thought it would ever get worse than animal sacrifice. I never—" He looked first with all the pain in the world at Addy, but quickly his face devolved into contempt.

"And *you* think there is a God? No! I refuse to believe he would allow me to be victimized in such a manner when I had dedicated my entire existence to him! I refuse to believe that he would allow my precious wife to be mutilated, tortured, and raped before my own eyes! You know they let them go? Yes, they did. Some nervous DA paid off the jury without my knowing it just to ensure the conviction. When the defending attorneys got wind of it, the judge closed the case and sealed the proceedings to protect faith in the legal system. Sounds impossible, doesn't it? Sounds too complex to be true, doesn't it? Well, Ms. Siwel, it happened, just as I say, and don't think I'm embellishing just because I'm drunk. No amount of depressant chemicals could impair my ability to recall the facts of *this* case! None! Now, go with your date and leave me alone. I'm a bitter old man, but I do not need a babysitter or a therapist, and you have taken quite enough of my time, young lady!"

Addy sat helpless and paralyzed while the old man turned away from her. She didn't know what to do now that he was crying again. *Do I go?* she thought while wiping tears from her eyes. She jumped as she felt a tug at her arm. It was Merci.

"Come on, let's go," he whispered as he pulled her away from the barstool. As Merci paid both their bill and Haddelby's, she looked back at the sobbing man with one hand holding up his forehead and the other framing a small black and white picture.

CHAPTER FORTY-ONE

"Is he ever gonna shut up?" John asked, leaning over to Cameron and laughing quietly. Cameron moved his eyes briefly in John's direction before focusing back on Doctor Haddelby's lecture.

John thrust his hand into his pocket and grabbed the lump of tissue under his keys. He always seemed to put his tissue in with his keys, which, given the tightness of his pants, created the right set of variables to yield useless shredded wads by the time he actually got the tissues out of his pocket. Achieving success, he wiped his forehead with the shredded wad, peeling off the residual strings of paper that stuck to his sweaty brow.

"Doctor Haddelby, what do you think about premonitions?" a student asked. John looked over at the student. He'd seen him all semester but never talked to him. He was tall, about six feet, gangly, with an acne explosion across his face. John always thought the guy's skin looked like a hot dog left in a microwave for about four minutes too long.

"You know, Mr. Smith, I had a feeling you were going to ask about that," Doctor Haddelby said. The class fell into immediate laughter as John rolled his eyes. *I don't know if I can stand another lame Doctor Haddelby joke in this class,* he thought while scanning the room for attractive women.

He had his favorites. There was Trisha, who always sat in the back left making out with her boyfriend whenever the old professor got into long chalk-board-writing spells. Barbara sat in the front and had dark, flowing hair and a great body to match. John had thought about asking her out a time or two and then remembered his gruesome nature and the fact that most women would rather take a flaming arrow to the retina before passing a night with him, and he reconsidered. Still, it amazed him that all the ugly people he knew seemed to find women.

He couldn't figure out what it was about him that was so hideous above and beyond his friend Jake, for example, who had an evil and unnatural odious scent about him but still landed that attractive girl he met at the post office. Then there was Frank, who was a jerk, both interpersonally and on the eyes, and he had a whole slew of women proposing to him. Ned was the biggest dork he'd ever seen, and yet he landed a hot babe from Germany that he met in a chat room last September.

And finally there was Merci. He'd landed John's favorite girl, the one he felt overwhelmingly attracted to; and what was more, she seemed to like Merci even though he wasn't all that good looking either. Besides, John was convinced that he was a bit of a nut job, although he really liked him a lot. But Merci was forever getting down, depressed, and self-deprecating, and on and on. John was convinced that Merci's student shrink had been making him actually worse, but Merci got real defensive about it when he brought it up one night, saying he felt he was all better and making progress. Professor Haddelby's voice raised and took John away from his musings.

"Hey, what's he talking about, Cameron?" John asked. Cameron looked over at John and opened John's book to page 319. With great care Cameron pointed to the heading upon which Haddelby was lecturing without actually saying a word.

"Thanks," John said, straightening out and tuning into the lecture again for only seconds, then slyly dropping his eyes back to his textbook, where he fished out a couple of pictures of Addy changing that he'd taken the week before.

She is so beautiful, John thought, becoming uncomfortably aroused. He quickly looked around to see if anyone was attending him and adjusted his seating arrangement. His heart began to beat faster, and he could feel sweat breaking through his clothing layers, causing his cotton shirt to stick against his body. *I've gotta get outta here,* John thought, eyeing the door. He rose out of his chair and stepped over Cameron's legs while ignoring the curious look on Haddelby's face. Quickly he trudged down the stairs and out the door into the hallway. Students were everywhere, conversing and laughing with one another. John headed for the nearest bathroom and dove in.

Out of breath, he swallowed a big gulp of air and rested his hands on his knees. *Nasty men's bathrooms!* he thought, irritated. *Why do they always have to smell so rank?* He made his way into the stall and spent some time just sitting and collecting his thoughts. *What is wrong with you?* he asked himself. *You're out of shape, and slave to your obsession with this girl, who happens to be dating your only real friend around here. You're so pathetic,* he chastened, flushing the toilet and refastening his trousers.

Pulling the door latch to the right, he squeezed in his stomach to allow the door to pass across him toward the inner stall wall. Washing his hands first, he strode back into the hallway and found the classroom door. Briefly he entertained feelings of embarrassment and worried that he might have toilet paper or an unzipped fly or anything else that would be noticed and mocked as he made his way back to his seat. Discretely he checked himself to make sure he was zipped up. *Yep, all good,* he thought, checking a second time anyway. Cautiously he opened the door and proceeded inward toward his seat. When he reached his row, his eyes fell upon Cameron, who was staring intensely into John's face, almost threateningly.

"What?" John asked, lowering his body into his chair. He kind of bounced when he hit the plastic seat, as he dropped in too quickly. Cameron continued to stare at him.

"I know," Cameron said.

"Know what?" John asked, noticing he'd stupidly left his book open with the pictures of Addy in sight. Without voluntary thought his eyes widened and he moved toward the book and quickly picked the pictures out and shoved them into his backpack. He could feel the judgmental stare of Cameron throughout the whole production and longed to find a rock the size of New Hampshire that he could lie under. Forcing himself against the urge to run away, he clenched his jaw and faced Cameron's piercing gaze.

"Hey, you wanna back off? I don't care what you think you know," John said. Cameron didn't adjust himself in any way; he just kept looking at the back of John's soul. Abruptly, the judgmental stare seemed to break into a controlled smile.

"Don't worry," Cameron said as his face grew into a subtle smile. "No one will ever find out what you are doing."

CHAPTER FORTY-TWO

"Jonesy, come here a minute," Chief Murphy said out his doorway and into the hall. After several seconds Jones's head appeared in his office.

"Whaddaya want?"

"The company of a half-wit. C'mere," the chief ordered, finding his way back to his chair. Jones followed, offering some lame comeback to the chief's jab.

"Yeah, yeah, bring a chair over here," the chief ordered.

"Whaddaya want with me, Chief?" Jones asked again while grabbing a chair.

"Set it down right there," Murphy instructed, motioning to the empty space in front of the computer. Jones fumbled with the chair a moment before letting it drop clumsily into place. "Feel free to break government property while you're at it," Murphy said.

"Does that include your face?" Jones said with a smirk. The chief forced his lips and eyes into a goofy expression and nodded his head mockingly in response.

"Just log on to the search engine, will ya?" the chief asked.

"Sure thing, Chief. Whadda we lookin' up?"

"Fella named Cameron Bo."

"Okay," Jones said, typing the name in. "Who's that?"

"Beige Geo Metro."

"Oh yeah. I thought you went over there and he had a story that checked out?"

"Yeah, well I'm not convinced just yet," the chief explained, scooting his chair closer to Jones's spot.

"Been having some of your crazy dreams about it?" Jones queried as he sat back to let the computer search. Murphy looked over at his long-time friend and gave a silent nod. They both watched as the computer indicated it was searching records. *Cheap government computers*, Murphy thought. Finally the name popped up.

"Okay, Cameron Bo, fourteen twenty-one Cherokee Court. That's it," the chief said triumphantly. "Now, what does it say about his parents, anything?"

"Just a minute, Chief. I'll cross-reference this with the federal file." Jones worked harmonically with the computer; clicking the mouse, typing words in, pulling up web pages. The chief was growing impatient. *I hate computers,* he thought. *It was so much better when we used to do all this stuff by phone. Maybe it was slower, but at least any idiot could do it.*

"Okay, here it is. Looks like Mr. Cameron here is born of one Dominique and Tasha Bo. What else do you want to know?"

"Everything," the chief said.

"Okay, just a minute. Let me just access the pedigree reference, and ... we're in business," Jones said, framing the monitor like a model caressing a sale item on a game show.

"All right, let me look here," the chief said, pushing Jones out of the way.

"Uh, I guess I'll just move," Jones said as he stumbled to his feet.

"How 'bout out of the state?" the chief suggested, cracking himself up but not diverting his attention from the screen. He grabbed the mouse and navigated the specs on the Bos. "All right, says here that Mr. and Mrs. Bo are shrinks who run a non-profit psychiatric clinic in the downtown area."

"*Were,*" Jones said, pointing to the line that read *deceased* on the monitor.

"Interesting," the chief commented as he read on. "How'd they die? Can we look that up?"

"Sure, if you would kindly remove your computer-illiterate self out of the way and let the wizardry of Officer Jones back in the captain's chair." The chief moved over mechanically. Jones worked for several more minutes pulling up web pages and government databases.

"All right, here we go. Looks like the cause of death: car accident."

"When?"

"Uh, looks like it was a year ago. Here's the write-up from *The Times*. Wanna hear it?"

"No, I want to print it out and fly to Hong Kong with it. Read it already, will ya?"

"All right, all right. Let's see ... 'Wednesday, November twenty-first, accident report. Local heroes Dominique and Tasha Bo were killed today when their car was found at the bottom of the Garberville Gap. Emergency services arrived on the scene at approximately ten thirty p.m. and deemed the crash an enigma. According to Sheriff Ramsey, head of the county law enforcement agency, the accident was highly atypical.'"

"Ramsey's such an idiot," the chief said.

"Hey, I'm readin' here. You mind? I could read to myself, you know."

"That's amazing. Say, why don't you go read to yourself a little bit about the line of authority in the department and look for reasons why you might be fired when you disrespect your superior, eh?" the chief said. Jones continued.

"'This kind of thing doesn't normally happen, and the case is a little baffling to put it frankly,'" Ramsey said. 'Typically you'd expect to see some skid marks or something, but these folks just went clean off the road for no reason. No one seems to have witnessed the accident, which makes sense. This is a very lonely road after dark. It appears the deceased were returning from a church service held in Garberville, and best we can tell, lost control of the vehicle coming around the bend and just broke through the safety rail, plummeting to their untimely demise. A vacationing resident heard the explosion and contacted 911, who dispatched an emergency response team. The team, upon arrival, found the car in flames with the bodies charred badly.' The sheriff denied any concern over foul play or suicide, remarking that, 'It looked like a clean accident. This is exactly why we caution drivers to slow down on these old roads during the winter season in particular.'"

"And that's the article, Chief. Anything else you want to know?"

"Yeah, how many surviving relatives?" the chief asked.

"Well, just a second." Jones spent several minutes searching various pages from the newspaper and federal and county databases while the chief pondered the peculiarities of the case. "Okay," Jones said, "according to the obituary, there was one surviving relative."

"Our Cameron Bo," Murphy filled in.

"Looks like, according to the state endowment records, that Mr. Bo was the full beneficiary of the estate, with certain stipulations barring him from full access until he turns eighteen."

"Which he already has."

"Court granted him the status of major at the time of death, excepting the noted provisions, and he was named the sole executor of the estate," Jones said.

"So, let me get this straight. Cameron Bo, the only

son of two psychiatrists, wakes up one day, finds his parents have both been in a car accident and died. He inherits the estate and then, nine months later, reports having a car stolen. The car, a beige Geo Metro, nineteen ninety-five, is seen some weeks later, manned by a call girl and boyishly looking male, who hauls out of the vehicle and fires off a couple of shots at some dealer who's harassing a junkie? Something about that seem goofy to you, Jones?"

"Well, I don't know, Chief. You're the one with the sixth sense on these things, still—," Jones replied in a rare, serious tone, "sounds like a bad year, maybe a little strange. But doesn't sound like an evil criminal plot to me. Why? What're you thinking?"

"I don't know," the chief answered, scratching the stubble on the underside of his chin. "I don't know. But something *is* off. Not just because of the dreams. I can feel it. You know? You ever have one of those cases where you know something's wrong, even though you can't place your finger on why?"

"No. When I do police work, it all comes from here, not here," Jones replied, pointing to his mind before his heart.

"Well, not me," the chief said, thinking of the many cases he'd solved based on initial hunches. "And remember, I was promoted to be the chief for a reason, intellect, boy."

"Yeah, your sexy figure. If I had that body, I'd be rising to the top too."

"The only rising you're gonna do is in an obscure lake if you don't learn to can it once in a while."

"Yeah, I know, I have a problem with that. My mouth's like your marital skills, always getting me into trouble."

The chief gave him a dirty look, and the two sat quietly, thinking over the case. "Tell me this. What motive do you think someone would have to report their own car stolen?"

"You *really* think this Bo kid would do something like that? Why?"

"I don't know. Forget this kid for a minute. Why would anyone do something like that? Other than to collect on the insurance. I checked up on that, and the kid's clean. He hasn't claimed anything with the insurance company."

"He hasn't? Now that's odd. Hasn't it been like three months or something?"

"Yeah, it has. So if it wasn't insurance fraud, why would someone do something like that?"

"Well, my guess is he wouldn't. Unless he's planning on doing something real bad with the car he doesn't want to be linked to."

"Yeah, but what? What crime would you commit in a car that you didn't want to be linked to?"

"Well, I can think of a lot if you put it that way. But why would he have this master plan that includes reporting the car stolen? He'd have to know that makes him look funny. Besides, why wouldn't he have already committed the crime? What, is he taking his sweet time to plan or something? Seems like you'd have the master planning completed before the car was stolen. And why's he out gallivanting with hookers and trying to save the world if he's some kind of criminal mind? That doesn't make sense at all. Why would he go through all of this trouble and expose himself in such a visible way with that shooting if he's just manufacturing the whole thing?"

"I don't know," the chief said, bringing his hands over his eyes and rubbing his forehead.

CHAPTER FORTY-THREE

Cameron Bo listened to the phone ring four, then five times before he heard the familiar sound of which he had become so fond. That he had come to know so much more than he ever thought possible since his mission began. But now he was afraid he was going to lose the fight against his father. He realized that he may not be strong enough to save this woman after all, and it was time to come clean.

"Hello," Sally answered.

"Is this Sally, Sally Strathers?" Cameron whispered into the disposable phone.

"Do you really have to ask by now? Look, if you haven't gotten the clue, I'm not afraid of you. Never gonna be. If you were gonna do something, you would've done it by now. So give up. Quit calling me. I'm not gonna change my number anymore because I am not going to give you the satisfaction of thinking I'm scared. I'm done running. And oh yeah, I got a boyfriend now, and he's real tough. He'll kill you if you ever try to get near me. So what do you think of that, deep throat?"

Cameron choked down the tears and silently opened his mouth, unsure if he would be able to spit out what he knew he must.

"I'm sorry you are going to die. I tried to warn you. It may not be too late, if you leave now. I wouldn't suggest relying on your boyfriend to save you. You are both in grave danger."

"Oh yeah, why don't you come meet us, and we'll see who winds up in the grave."

Unable to keep the tears from streaming, Cameron breathed one last time into the phone. "This will be the last time I call. Good-bye, Sally Strathers."

PART SIX
THE GRAND
DELUSIONS

CHAPTER FORTY-FOUR

Cameron lay at the foot of his bed, staring at the darkened sky outside of his window. Flashes of his childhood days raced through his mind. He remembered glimpses from his fourth birthday. He could see his father scolding him for spitting in the candles. He heard his mother's laughter ringing through his ears. He smelled the eucalyptus trees fresh in bloom. He saw the scattered clouds lying across the atmosphere.

He remembered his father teaching him how to ride a bicycle in the third grade. Remembered his first academic competition in the sixth grade. He observed his friends beating him up in middle school. He still could feel their adolescent-sized hands grabbing him by the trousers and neck, forcing him downward into the trashcan. He remembered the rotten food streaking his mouth; tasting the bacterially infested cheese, burrito, and other discarded items as he struggled to escape.

He closed his eyes and relived his first kiss with Henrietta Grutenschtein from Olympus City. Her lips were so soft, but the taste of her lipstick was horrendous. He remembered trying not to gag on the strawberry flavoring. He remembered being aroused, confused, excited, loved, and accepted all concomitantly. He remembered the Fourth of July show he attended with his parents. He could not get enough of the thunderous noise and powerful hues of the fiery scene. Seeing his parents actually holding hands, laughing, pointing, and talking to each other as if they were really in love. He remembered; he remembered it all so clearly, so vividly, almost unnaturally so. He did not want it to end. But his memories vanished as he heard it scuffling behind him in the blackness.

"Tonight," a male voice said. It was talking with the rest of them. It sounded like there were at least four of them: two girls, one boy, and he wasn't sure of the others. He knew his father was in there listening as well. Cameron tried to ignore them, but they followed him everywhere he went; talking constantly but too low to make out any of the words, with the exception of a short phrase here and there. He grabbed a pillow and stuffed it over his ears, but to no avail. They kept conversing; all of them talking at the same time, their voices amalgamating into a constant whirring that tingled like a buzzing in his ears that aggravated his soul. He grew angry and scared at the same time. He wasn't sure what to do. History had taught him that it was pointless to run. They always found him again—at church, school, with Sal, even in the shower. Always plotting, always secret, careful not to let too many of their words be heard.

"Yes, Cameron should," the female voice said.

What are they talking about? Cameron wondered, too scared to move his body. He was trying to pretend to be asleep, although he knew that wouldn't fool them.

However, when he did that, sometimes they'd leave him alone, and he didn't want to talk with any of them tonight. *This is my room. Why can't they just leave me to sleep in peace?* He heard a bump in the outer corridor.

"Who's there?" Cameron demanded as another bump came echoing through the silence of the night. The conversation from the unseen stopped abruptly as Cameron spoke, and all was still. The house cracked loudly, and Cameron listened as the old wood floor paneling bowed under the pressure of the human being who was now moving toward the bedroom door. Cameron lay paralyzed. He heard the door handle turning and listened to his heart pumping.

"Who's there?" he asked, his breathing violent and body sweaty. "Who is that?"

"Cameron?" Sal asked. "You still awake?"

"Yes," Cameron said, both irritated and relieved at the same time. "What're you doing here?"

"I'm sorry, baby. I didn't mean to frighten you. It's Tuesday night. You know tonight's when my shift ends early at the restaurant. I just wanted to sleep by you tonight, that's all. I didn't feel like being alone, you know? Now, move over. I'm tired. I'll see you in the morning."

"It's already Wednesday morning," Cameron said, eyeing the clock. "It's three thirty a.m."

"Whatever, baby," Sal said, slipping under the covers. Soon her breathing became relaxed and rhythmic. A light snore grew more pronounced across a twenty-minute span. Cameron could hear them start up after a while. Quietly at first, then louder after a while.

"It must be tonight," one of them said before dropping into a low and indecipherable speech pattern.

"You'll wake her," said another.

"Cameron," his father said to him more through an impression than in an audible tone. "Cameron, I know you can hear and understand me. Don't worry—no one else can. Only you can hear this. It is part of your special powers. Now blink twice if you understand me." Cameron took care to blink twice slowly but distinctly.

"Good. Now, I want to tell you something. I know what they're saying about you. I can hear every word they say, even though you can't. Did you know that? I can tell you what they're saying if you want. Would you like me to explain it to you? All you have to do is blink twice if you want me to explain what they're doing." Again, Cameron blinked twice.

"Okay, that's good enough for me. I'll tell you—I'll tell you what they're saying now. They're saying you can't do it. You can't get it done."

"Get what done?" Cameron asked through his mind.

"Your mission. The special mission asked of you to accomplish. You can't get it done, and that will make him very mad at you. That will make him hate you. Do you want that? Do you want God to *hate* you?"

"No! Of course not! I'd do anything to keep him from hating me!" Cameron screamed in his mind. "But I don't know what to do. I want to fulfill my mission, but I don't remember it. What was it?"

"You must correct the wrongs of the sexual demons

that lie everywhere. Like you did with me and your mom. You wished me away, and it happened. That was your fault. It is your fault that I'm dead. Now you must wish away others." Cameron's father put an image of John Joe into Cameron's mind.

"I hate him!" Cameron said, remembering the pictures he saw in the classroom. "I hate everything about him."

"Then you will wish him dead?" Cameron's father asked.

Cameron thought a moment before responding, "Does he have the ability to change?"

"Did I change, Cameron? You saw what I was like to your mother for how many years? You experienced me, watched me use her. Hitting her in the face. Hitting you in the face. Hearing things in the middle of the night. And did I change. Did I? No! Now, is that what you want for her?"

"Who?" Cameron asked. Cameron's father put a picture of Addy in his mind. Cameron's heart hardened. "No! I will not allow that to happen to her any longer. I will wish him dead now."

"Remember, you will be responsible for his death then. Are you ready for that? If not, your master will be disappointed in you, and you'll have to spend the rest of eternity in shame and in hell." Cameron listened to his father's words, then immediately wished John dead.

"Good boy, Cameron. You have done well today, but we are not through. You must also stop *her* from feeding into man's sexual desires."

"Who?" Cameron asked. Cameron's father put an image of Sal into his mind.

"No. She's done nothing wrong since I met her."

"She feeds into the addiction, Cameron. It's people like her who cause people like me to become what I did. Do you want that? If you do, you'll be allowing her to cause other little boys to watch their mommies being raped. Is that what you want?"

"No! Of course not, but that's why I took her off the streets! So she'd stop doing it. She'd stop engaging men that way. And she has stopped. She has an honest job now. And she treats me well."

"That's what she tells you," his father said.

"No! That's how it is. I will not wish her dead!"

"Fine. Then you'll not mind if I show you this. It's what she was doing tonight before she came over." Cameron's father put an explicit image in his mind.

"That can't be right."

"No, Cameron. It *is* true. She *is* a hooker. Once a hooker, always a hooker. You must wish her dead if you want to save her."

"How would that save her? If what you say to me is true, then she's already doomed to hell!"

"There are many levels of hell. True, she may not ever be able to go to heaven because of what she's already done. But if she continues to bring men down with her, she'll get worse and worse and be forced to agonize for more sins across the expanse of eternity. Is that what you want for her?"

"Of course not. I love her. I'd never do anything to harm her."

"But not doing anything to stop it *is* harming her. You're allowing her to sin. Would you allow her to run in front of a moving truck? No, of course not, so why are you allowing her to set herself up for even more eternal anguish? Is that what you want? You want her to suffer forever?"

"Of course not. No!"

"No?" his father asked.

"No!" Cameron said.

"Then you must wish her dead immediately."

Cameron began to silently cry as he lay listening to Sal's breathing and the conversation in the corner of the bedroom.

"Tonight," the female voice said. "He must do it tonight."

"Tonight!" the voices echoed. "He must kill her tonight!"

"Cameron, the time has come. You must wish her dead," his father insisted.

Cameron grabbed his temples and screamed internally into the night air. He turned and looked at his sleeping girlfriend and caressed her hair. She seemed to smile at him. "Out of love, Sal, I must wish you dead," he quietly sobbed into her left ear.

"Good," Cameron's father said above the tears of the sobbing youth. "You've done well tonight, but there's still more to do."

"What? I've already wished her dead. What else do you want me to do? Leave me alone. *Leave me alone!*"

"No, not until you save her and show me you love

me too. Cameron, you must act on your wishes. Now you must make them actualized. You may no longer use your power to just wish someone dead and it will happen. That only worked with me, but the rules are different now. Now *you* must be the one to cause life to end, so that life may go on and begin correctly for the many thousands of people these two would have corrupted either directly or indirectly. As a leader of a chosen people, you must do this to prove your faith, as all great spiritual leaders must do something equally difficult to prove their loyalty to God!"

Cameron felt a piercing pain in his forehead. He rubbed his scalp and squeezed his eyes as shut as he possibly could before opening his mind up to his father again.

"Then, Father, what must I do?"

CHAPTER FORTY-FIVE

John shuffled in his chair and pulled at the choking seat belt. Turning his head he gazed into the night sky and studied the blackness all around. *No cars anywhere tonight,* he thought, feeling nervous and uncomfortable. "This is like the creepiest road ever," he said to Merci and Addy, who were seated in the front of the car.

"It's nice," Merci said, then looking at Addy added, "just like you."

"Yeah, yeah. You're such a goof," she said, stealing a smile.

The trio rode along the old abandoned highway back toward town. John thought about the sermon they'd just heard. It was the last one they would have to attend for Doctor Haddelby's group project. Their report was to be given in ten days, and they hadn't met as an entire group even once to go over it. Actually, Cameron hadn't even attended the last two church services with them, which was annoying. On the other hand, John didn't mind Cameron's failure to appear given their recent history.

The little freak show had really crossed the line over the pictures incident, and it was all John could do to keep him from informing anyone about it. Of course, John figured he was so crazy no one would really believe him anyway. Cameron was probably one of the most disturbed people John had ever met, and he seemed to be getting worse. Not only was he odd, but over the last couple of weeks, his breath stank, his clothes stank, and his attitude stank. It just didn't seem like the lights were all on. He was always looking off into nothing, and if he did speak to you it was weird, and sometimes didn't even seem to make any sense. And when it did make sense, he'd just repeat himself. Then, still, he'd pull it together once in a while and knock your socks off by being normal.

John looked out the window and saw the ground become increasingly illuminated. *Wow, there's actually another car out here this time of night?* He looked up at Merci and Addy, who seemed lost in each other's presence. They appeared unable to notice anything else but themselves lately, and that was getting old to John. He looked back at the light, which was rapidly becoming more focused and bright. Suddenly the light broke to the left, and John watched as a fast-moving Geo Metro passed from behind their car and remerged in front of them, quickly disappearing into the darkened night. *That dude's got the right idea,* John groaned silently as he looked through Merci and Addy's fixed gazes to read the speedometer. *Fifty-seven miles per hour, gimme a break.*

"Hey, love birds, you wanna speed it up a little bit?" John said.

"Well, I don't know … are you ready for marriage, hon?" Merci said with a full corn-ball look into Addy's eyes, eliciting a charitable laugh from Addy.

Gag me, John thought. "You guys are killing me. And I don't want to be demanding or anything, but I once read somewhere that a good way to avoid death while traveling is for the driver to keep his eyes on the road."

John looked out the window again and saw the slivery moon cresting above the uneven mountain peaks, beckoning from the other side of the plains. The darkened mounds looked haunting yet commanding to John, and he wondered what it would be like to spend a summer amid their vistas, rivers, trees, and underbrush. *Maybe that's all I need; just a little time to get away by myself for a while.*

John didn't like the person he was becoming. Always so obsessed with sex and gratification—

and stalking women! What was that about? When and exactly how had he become so twisted? Or was it twisted? Maybe that's just how guys are. Look at Merci, for example; maybe he's not a stalker, but he'd sell his soul for access to Addy's body. Right? Wasn't that what it was really all about? What else is there in this life that's worth pursuing? God? Religion? Money? Fame? John had tried all of those things and found they only bring slow death to the soul.

They all show their ugly head, and it is *ugly*. It is cold. It is lifeless. It makes one feel helpless. And worst of all, it makes one feel lonely, disconnected from others. Such things are better left for someone else. But sex! That was a different story. Not because it takes care of problems, no! It has all of the problems of the former items. In fact, it probably creates more problems than any of the rest of them combined. But sex, because it is *so* much harder to satisfy. One can live with poverty. One can live with pain. One can live with destitution. But how can one live with the constant yearnings that come from a lack of sexual interaction? So if you don't want to kill yourself, you play the game to get access, like Merci does. If you don't have the body or skills to get access, then you do what John does, and that's how anyone would do it, if they were in his same spot.

John clicked off his seat belt and breathed in deeply for the first time on the trip since starting the ride home. Merci's station wagon twisted around a turn and started the long incline toward the summit of the mountain. John swiveled around and looked toward the valley behind him and saw the dimming lights of Garberville fading into the thick shadows.

"Hey, remind me, whose crazy idea was it to go all the way out to Garberville to do this church project tonight?" John asked as he twisted around again to look straight ahead.

"Cameron's," Merci said, grabbing Addy's hand.

"Ah, well then, makes sense," John said. He picked up his hands and imitated weighing scales. "Crazy wack job freak show of a nutcase: crazy idea. It's all coming together now."

"Ah, be nice to the little guy," Addy said. "I like him. It's not his fault he's strange. He's actually a pretty nice guy if you talk to him and get to know him."

"Nice, and *c-r-a-z-y*," John said. "Of course, you've never been good at seeing the wheat from the tares when it comes to guys."

"Let's see, wheat, tare," Addy said, pointing first to Merci and second to John. In response, John folded his lower lip in half and made a derisive gesture.

"Actually, what's crazy is that we listened to him. Remind me why we did that again?" John asked.

"To be nice. He came up with the idea all by himself, and I think we should reward him for that," Addy said.

"Okay—but crazy boy didn't even show up!"

"Well, but we tried. There's only so much you can do," Merci said.

The wagon forged ahead into the night toward the summit, finally reaching the top, and then started its descent down the long sloping two-lane road. All of the passengers in the car gazed across the breathtaking panorama of the city lights far below. No vehicle could be seen as far as the eye stretched. *It's so beautiful from up here,* John considered, remembering how much he loved to explore these kinds of scenes when he was a kid. He always felt on top of the world then, like he was untouchable; not even his father could abuse him when he was so high.

Despite the beauty, however, something strange and unsettling began to stir in John's mind, and he looked ahead of him again but saw nothing. "Does it just seem weird out here to me tonight?"

"What's that?" Merci asked, but without seeming to really care what it was John had said. John didn't respond and tried to shake the feeling that was growing in intensity. It began in his stomach and gave him shivers from the base of his back to the top of his neck. His heart started to race, increasing to the extent he could actually hear it pounding. It was an odd feeling. John rarely if ever got scared and didn't remember being this afraid since his father used to sneak into his room. Right now he was feeling terrified, but he had no reason to. In fact, it felt exactly like he used to before the molestation incidents would occur, as he heard his father climbing the stairs to his room. The signal of danger straight ahead.

"Seriously, guys, something's wrong. I don't feel right. There's something off…" he said. At the bottom of the mountainous slope a car's headlights appeared from around the bend.

"Are you serious?" Merci said with a glance over his shoulder as John repeated his worry.

"Stop saying that. You're startin' to creep me out," Addy said, the teasing drained from her tone.

John looked out the window uneasily. "I'm not trying to creep you out, just...something's wrong. I feel like maybe—," John felt too stupid to actually say he felt they should turn the car around, but that was the impression he kept feeling inside. Nervously he eyed the distant headlights of the mysterious car, and his stomach seemed to leap within.

"You feel like maybe what?" Addy asked.

John felt his eyes grow puffy and increasingly moist. His head throbbed, and he felt an inescapable sense of fear and panic. *What is wrong with me!* "Nothing. Forget it. Let's just hurry and get home as fast as we can."

Merci looked over his shoulder at his troubled friend. "You okay?"

John could hardly answer. The feeling of terror had grown too strong.

"I don't know, just...I'll be fine...just stop talking about it...forget...I said anything...just...hurry," John said as he gasped for breath. With embarrassment, he watched as Merci and Addy shared worried looks back and forth. Merci seemed to whisper to Addy a question.

As John turned to look out the window, his mildly hyperventilating mouth dropped, and his eyes grew wide as something human emerged from the forest trees but moved with inhuman speed toward the traveling wagon. With focused eyes and indescribable angst, John watched as the being seemed to call out John's name and signal for him to move the car in the opposite direction before fading into the open air.

"What was that?" John said, his eyes still wide and his voice shrill. Merci and Addy both jumped, and Merci swerved the car.

"What is wrong with you? You're freaking me out, man!" Merci yelled, steering the car back into the lane. "Seriously, what's going on with you? I've never seen you like this before."

John clutched at his chest and fought to slow his heart. "I ... don't know. Something ... something's not right! Something's wrong," he said, having great difficulty breathing. The impending effect of evil and fear was ubiquitous. The mysterious car below quickly traveled closer, sending shockwaves through John's body every time he looked upon it.

"Merci, do something! I think he's having a heart attack or something!" Addy said.

"He's probably just having a panic attack," Merci said. "That's exactly what I start lookin' like."

"That is no panic attack. There is something *seriously* wrong here. You have to help him! You need to do something!"

"Well, what? I don't know what to do! Do you have your cell phone? Maybe we can call 911?" Merci said. The approaching car's lights were nearer.

"I don't have one. John, do you?" Addy asked, turning around and grabbing his arm.

"No! And get in your seat belt!" John said.

"What?"

"Just do it!" John said as Addy sported a look of shock but slowly fell into her chair and clicked the belt around. John's mind was racing at lightning speed. He worried he was going to lose his capacity to remain conscious.

"Merci, I don't like this. This is really scaring me! Do something. Please!" Addy said.

"Like what? I'm drivin' as fast as I can, but we're on a mountain highway! It's not like I can go eighty!"

"I don't know, maybe we should stop the car, let him get some air or somethin'?"

"No, if it's in his head, he doesn't need air, but if it's really some kind of medical problem, then the best thing we can do is rush him to the hospital."

The lights of the oncoming car were now very close. John saw another humanlike figure on the side of the road running up to the wagon with one hand palm up and the other spinning in a circle and finally pointing behind them. Somehow, he thought he could hear him speaking to him, *Stop and turn around!*

"Did…you guys…see that?" John struggled to say in between breaths.

"See what?" Merci asked.

"That guy, in the robe on the side of the road. You had…to…see him. How could…you…miss him? He was…all…bright…like fire!" John said.

"Merci," Addy said, her voice a low whisper, tears running down her cheeks, "he's hallucinating! What're we going to do?" she raised her voice. "Hang on, John! Hang in there! Don't give up! Keep fightin' it! Hurry,

Merci!" The oncoming car's headlights disappeared behind a mountainous curve that temporarily took it out of the trio's visual plane.

"I don't know what to do!" Merci said. "Maybe we can see if whoever's in that car up ahead has a cell phone. If so, maybe we can get a helicopter up here or something."

"Okay, okay. Good idea! Why don't you stop 'em? Honk or somethin'!"

Stop them! Stop them! You mustn't meet up with the car! You mustn't meet up with the car! Said a voice deep within John's thoughts.

"No!" John forced out. "Turn the car around! I think we're in danger!" he shrieked into Merci and Addy's ears as he grabbed Merci's shoulder. Suddenly the light all around the car seemed to John to grow so bright as to catch the world in a fiery blaze. From every angle he could see in perfect portraiture each tree branch, rock, and mountainous detail as if a bolt of lightning had touched down on the other side of the passenger door. Descending from the heavens came a plummeting ball of fire that sparkled in an expanding ball of light that finally yielded a white-robed man standing resolutely in the middle of the road directly in front of the speeding station wagon.

"What is that?" Addy screamed as Merci hit the brakes and tried to swerve away from the being.

"Ah!" Merci shouted as he struggled to keep the car from jumping the road and off the cliff. The car fishtailed and then spun around several times before stopping perpendicular to the two-lane highway.

"Where did that guy run out from?" Merci yelled on the other side of a couple of quick breaths. Now unable to move with any voluntary control, John looked in terror out of his window and saw the once distant car fast approaching mere yards away.

Addy shrieked. "Does he see us?"

CHAPTER FORTY-SIX

"Cambo, slow down! You're going too fast!" Sal demanded as she tightened her seatbelt.

"No, don't slow down," Cameron's father yelled from the darkness of the night. "I've delivered them into your hands! I made this happen. This way, you kill them both. John is in that car, and he will die. Sal is in this car, and she will die, and your plan will be finished! You will be saved, and more importantly you will save countless others through their deaths! Speed up! They're just around the corner!" Time seemed to be going in slow motion. Cameron felt he could see every possible visual space. In his mind he could see the unsuspecting victims in their car, having no idea what was about to happen. Still, he couldn't shake the feeling that it was wrong.

"It's natural to feel it's wrong. God's work often goes against what we think is normal and right. Think of Moses, Jonah, Daniel. Think of Solomon! This is your quest! This is your challenge! Engage them and please your Maker! Please your Master, Cameron! Redeem yourself once and for all!"

As they rounded the mountainous curve, the wooded station wagon came into Cameron's sight, mysteriously sitting frozen, perpendicular in the road. Cameron grew wide-eyed at the sign. He hadn't known how it was going to happen, but he had exercised faith in the voices anyway, not knowing beforehand what he was going to do. He had come to the spot just like he was instructed, and now there they were. They really had been delivered to him. The Geo Metro sped toward the stalled vehicle. Cameron's hands began to sweat across the steering wheel, making it harder to grasp and steer.

"Cambo, watch out for that car!" Sal shrieked, flexing her legs into the floor and placing both hands on the dash of the small Geo.

"Do it!" his father said.

Cameron panicked as he realized he had only moments left to decide if he would carry out the mission.

"Don't, boy! Don't stop now!"

"Cambo, watch out!" Sal said. Cameron snapped his head toward Sal then back to look out the windshield. *There's still time!* he thought as he tried to turn the wheel in an attempt to swerve around the motionless vehicle, but his hands were frozen, unable to move at his command.

"Coward!" his father yelled as he held Cameron's hands and forced the Geo to stay on course for a collision with the stalled wagon.

"No!" Cameron said as he struggled to overpower his father's hands, but they were too strong. Cameron, disconnecting from himself, watched in horror at the faces screaming in terror as the Geo barreled into the side of the stalled wagon, sending the wood-paneled vehicle tearing across the road and through the safety fence, tumbling downward across the steep side of the mountain.

As he came back to consciousness, Cameron felt dazed and took some time to allow his vision to restore itself before remembering what had happened. His body ached, and he could feel himself bleeding in many places. His legs throbbed almost intolerably, and he struggled to get them out from under the steering wheel, which lay dangerously close to pinning him inside the car. Turning his head he saw Sal's bloodied cranium lying atop of the dashboard. Her hair was red streaked, and a pool of blood formed under her mouth.

"Sal," he tried to say, but his mouth hurt too much to speak. Suddenly the car made a popping noise and lurched backward.

"Cameron," he heard his father say quietly.

"Father," he answered back. "I'm scared!"

"Yes. Now, hurry. There's no time."

"No time for what?"

"You must get out. The car is going to fall."

Cameron surveyed the car's position and noted

that it was in fact leaning against the safety wall of the cliff itself.

"Get out, Son," his father said, grabbing Cameron's arms and pulling him out the driver's side door. Cameron groaned tremendously in reaction to the pain shooting throughout his body.

"Cameron, run! You must flee before they find you! They'll be coming soon for you, Son. Go!" his father commanded, forcing him down the switchback trail several feet from the crash site. "Hurry, here comes a car!" his father warned, showing Cameron headlights high above them at the top of the summit. "Hurry!"

He could hear his father yelling from farther and farther away as he took what seemed an eternity to descend the switchback trail, heading for the heavy underbrush at the bottom of the cliff. Suddenly, from high above him, he heard a thunderous noise. With pain, he turned and watched the Geo roll off the cliff and down the brushy slope to the valley plains below.

CHAPTER FORTY-SEVEN

John's mind awoke before his body. He lay in a foreign position and was unable to make sense of the numerous sensory signals being sent to his brain. He knew he was injured, but for the first several moments of his consciousness, he could not locate the specific discomfort he was feeling. It was as if he were feeling someone else's pain, far away, too removed to be overpowering but strong enough to dampen his own affective state.

Gradually his auditory world escalated from a low general hum to a grand cacophony of sounds; the creek mixing with an unidentified crackling, and the air howling through the treetops as it gushed from the mountainside. He moaned against the cold and pain as he struggled to open his eyes. With some effort he won the fight, and slowly he took in the scene of the crash. Some twenty feet away or so he identified Merci's old station wagon. It was lying on its top with one door flung open. *I must have been thrown out on the way down,* John reasoned as he tried to remember what happened. His thoughts were hazy at best, and he struggled to pick himself up. *Something's wrong with me,* he noted as his visual abilities faltered, momentarily fading and then coming on again. He examined the wagon to see what else he could recognize, but the darkness of the night was not friendly to perception.

John struggled with his bodily position and attempted to pick himself up. A large jolt of pain shot through his left arm as he tried to move, causing him to emit a loud yelp in protest of the pain. His head was throbbing, and his back significantly damaged. He wondered for a moment if he were paralyzed but reasoned he wouldn't feel anything if that were the case. With caution he picked up his upper body as much as he could and examined his position. He was lying approximately twenty feet from the wagon at the foot of a tree. Several branches lay around him. Under his head lay a door from the wagon, and to his dismay, he found that his left arm had been terribly cut and was lodged in between the door's window and a heavy tree branch, such that it was futile to attempt to move. His left leg was also trapped under a heavy branch, too heavy to simply kick off. If he could just position himself in a certain way underneath the branches, he was sure he could get it off him, but until he could free his arm, he was useless.

For several minutes he tried to wiggle his arm out of the window. Each attempt sent his body into near convulsions, so intense was the pain. Somehow he'd fallen into this position such that his left arm was not only trapped but was bending backward above his head, with the heavy log and metal frame using his elbow as a makeshift teeter-totter. He was afraid that if he struggled too much, he'd wind up causing permanent damage. He'd have to wait for someone to lift the branches off his legs first. Or maybe with careful contorting, he could pull his arm out the correct way so as to avoid breaking any bones, or at least any more bones than may already have been broken.

What happened? He began to itch terribly in his back, and in great agony he tried to reach the spot with his free hand, but it was useless. His mind flooded with thoughts of panic that he was trapped and unable to move, and he struggled against his racing heart and rapid breathing.

"Someone, help, please!" he attempted to say, but his voice was barely audible. Further, as he opened his mouth to speak, a warm liquid oozed onto his inner

palate, and he choked on the taste of his blood, trying to spit the substance outward. He realized that
there was a tremendous amount of blood across his
right eye as well, and his groin began to indicate it had
also suffered significant injury. Through stinging eyes
he once again tried to call for help, this time flaring
a painful piercing in his chest as he spoke. His cries
were answered by the constant movement of the creek
and nothing else.

John, get up, something seemed to say to him. It
was not a voice but almost a thought, and he didn't
know what to make of it.

Now I'm going crazy, he told himself as tears fell
across his cheeks.

*John, get up! Your friends are not dead, but they
need your help. Hurry!* the impression said again. John
became frightened and tried to look around to see if
someone was actually speaking with him.

"Who's there?" he demanded in a broken whisper,
but no answer came. "Who's talking to me?"

*John, get up! They're both going to die soon. You must
save them!* came the impression a third time. Suddenly
John's mind was opened to a panoramic scene of the
accident. He saw the Geo Metro smashing into their
wagon, and the wagon tumbling downward. He saw
himself being thrown out of the wooded vehicle as
it tumbled to the forest floor. He saw Merci trapped
inside the inverted wagon, with Addy lying halfway
out. Finally, he saw the Geo, some minutes later, tumbling downward and landing on the wagon.

See, you must hurry! Hurry! The small but powerful impression demanded.

This is crazy! John thought. *I must be hallucinating. I don't believe in God. I don't believe in telepathy. And I don't believe in ghosts. Besides, there's nothing I can do. I'm completely trapped, even if it were true. I need rescuing just as much as anyone,* he reasoned while trying once again to call for help.

This is your last chance to save them and yourself. Go rescue them now! Do whatever you must, but save them now! Came the feeling again.

No! There's nothing I can do. This is ridiculous! his mind screamed. His body however, could not be comforted. His heart rate was still skyrocketing, and he felt the blood around his face mingling with sweat. His whole body ached and yearned to move, but he could not dislodge himself from his trapped position. High above him he could see the crash site. The large mountainous wall was silhouetted against the starry skies and seemed so peaceful from his position far below. He noticed no other car teetering on the mountainside, and he reassured himself it was all in his head.

Still, he was uneasy about the experience and couldn't get it out of his mind. *How do I get myself out of this position?* he wondered, contemplating if there were any amazing gymnastics move he could commit to free either his leg or arm. *If I could only free my arm, then I know I could get that log off my leg. But how?* Grunting, he yanked his left arm as hard as he could to try and get it out from under the horrific position.

His elbow snapped against the branch and opened a fresh wound that poured blood onto the metal-wood mixture.

"Ah!" he growled, flexing his whole body awkwardly and streaming tears down his face. "I can't move it! There's nothing that can be done!" he said aloud, resting his aching body back on the ground and crying pathetically for what seemed like an eternity. Several clouds passed over his view, and he could see the heavenly lights peeking in and out of the misty vapors. *How did I ever get myself into this mess?* he wondered, cursing God in his mind. *I know you're not there, but if you were I wouldn't speak with you anyway. I hate you!* he screamed privately, thinking of his horrible life: the abuse, the destruction of his mother's emotional health, the loneliness, his sexual issues, and now this.

"Why would you do this to me?" he said, crying in large bursts of air and sobbing like a small child until being disturbed by an image on the hilltop. He turned his gaze toward the light and heard a crashing noise from high above. He could not believe his eyes: there was another vehicle jutting over the ledge. John could see the taillights; the car seemed to be stuck on something, but he could clearly see portions of it protruding the ledge of the drop-off from which he, Merci, and Addy had fallen.

Go now! The impression commanded, filling the depths of John's mind.

What do I do? What do I do? John thought, his mind racing desperately. All around the ground he searched with his free hand for something he could use as leverage to maybe give himself a little space in between the window and branch so that he might pull his arm through. In a panic he grabbed a large rock and tried hitting the door with his right arm, each hit sending a lightning bolt of pain through his body.

Suddenly his mind produced an image of breaking his arm in half then bending the arm back unnaturally so as to free himself. *I can't do that!* He looked up at the brooding car lights and back over at his arm. His grip tightened on the rock. With a grunt he brought the heavy rock down hard against his trapped arm, repeating the self-inflicted violence until he felt he would die from the pain. Dropping the rock he pathetically grabbed his left arm and bent it backward and away from the branch and up through the window. He sat up and cradled his arm and screamed helplessly to the unresponsive trees, feeling the pain was too intense to bear.

Hurry! The impression came again, somehow trumping the pain. John dropped his left arm, letting it fall awkwardly downward where it bled and drooped, broken. He grabbed the branch across his legs and scooted himself outward, finding success at freeing himself with just a few jerks. Tears still flowing, he attempted to stand on his feet but fell over with a rush of dizziness, landing on his broken arm. He screamed again into the frozen dark. *I can't do this! I can't do this! It hurts too much!*

Yes, you can! But you must hurry! the impression came again, more insistent. Somehow John rose to his feet and made his way toward the crash site. As he approached the wooded wagon, he saw Addy, her blouse ripped open exposing her bloodied chest, and her seemingly lifeless body halfway in and halfway out of the vehicle. For a brief moment, John felt a rush of intensity to look at her nakedness, but quickly he became disgusted with himself and, shrieking in rage at his thoughts, covered her chest up with her shirt before dropping to his rear behind her and grabbing her under the arms with his working arm. He scooted slowly and painfully away from the vehicle, and with terrific effort, rose to his feet, still holding the flopping body. He dragged her about a hundred feet away and hid her behind a large rock, stopping to pant for some time.

Get Merci, the impression demanded, and John immediately started toward his friend's position. After several steps, he discontinued his trek and gazed upward at the taillights above him. *Wait a minute. I'll have to crawl into the car to get him, and what if the car falls on me while I'm in there and we both die?* He looked back down at the broken vehicle. *Besides, maybe he's dead anyway, and I'm doing it all for nothing.* He closed his eyes and tried to think about what the right thing to do was. *But what if he's alive and I don't save him, and so he dies in the crash? How would I feel then?* he thought. *Course then I'd get Addy, especially after what I did here today.*

John closed his eyes and shook his head back and forth, hitting himself in the head with his functioning hand. *What is wrong with you?* he screamed silently while sprinting toward the wagon as fast as he could in his crippled way. Arriving at the wagon again, he half tripped and half flung himself onto the ground and crawled into the vehicle to grab Merci. Merci was wedged tightly into the seat. John threw his weight and effort into detaching the seat belt, which was taut against Merci's hanging body. Finding success, Merci fell with a large thump against the vehicle's ceiling, or what was left of it. With great pain and personal cost, John wrestled Merci out from around the seat belt harness and began to pull him through the open door.

From the heights above them, prickling fractures of ruptured air bellowed an ominous threat to the ears of the vulnerable and broken duo struggling to escape the demolished wagon, and John started to panic. With tremendous force he pulled at Merci's underarms and managed to get most of his upper body out of the car. John looked up at the suspended vehicle high above and couldn't tell if it had changed positions, but he also didn't want to wait to find out. He pulled the remainder of Merci's body out and somehow was able to get him atop of his shoulder, his arm around the back of his knees. John grew increasingly faint, and with wobbly legs he dashed away from the crash site toward the spot where he had laid Addy behind the large rock only moments prior. As he moved nearer the rock, he heard a tumbling chaos approaching with incomprehensible velocity from the towering highway ledge.

It's coming! John pushed his feet harder into the soil and felt the increase of wind pass his body as he moved Merci closer to the respite of the rock where

Addy's body lay without motion. With a cry and fading muscular control, John fell toward the approaching earth, landing with Merci behind Addy and the rock. As he felt the cold of the dirt on his stinging face, he heard the Geo slam into the wagon behind them, causing bright flames to illuminate the darkened sky, and popping John's eardrums under the terrific pressure. Several pieces of one or both of the automobiles flew across his fading visual plane and plummeted into the nearby trickling creek as John's eyes grew dark once again.

CHAPTER FORTY-EIGHT

Sal awoke to the terrible sound of the explosion and felt confused and disoriented. Her head hurt all over, and her neck was numb and tingly. *Where Am I?* she asked herself as she groped around the ground for answers. All she could feel were rocks and branches. It felt like she was on some sort of trail. *Where am I?* She looked up and could see the stars watching from their private distance. She turned her head and looked down the mountainside, staring in confusion at the large flames rising from ground. *What happened?* she puzzled until the madness of the experience came racing back.

Cameron! she shrieked in her mind as she remembered the crazed look in his eye and the fixed stare he had on the station wagon stalled in the middle of the road. *What did you do?* She shut her eyes briefly. *I need to help them!* she thought as she watched the flickering of the flames far down below. She attempted to raise herself up but was unable to move her body anywhere below the waist. *I can't move my legs.* She tried wiggling her toes and feet. *I can't move my feet!* She panicked, becoming terrified she might be paralyzed. Her head felt warm and sticky, her left eye was blurred from the caked blood that had hardened around her socket and streaked her forehead, nose, and mouth.

What am I going to do? She tried again to move her body upright. *Scream for help, Sal, scream for help!* She opened her mouth and emitted a loud shrill. She screamed as loud as she could for several minutes until she no longer was able to muster the breath. Defeated, she lay in silence for an eternity as the flames below raged and her breathing became deep and rhythmic once again. *Somebody help me,* she mentally pleaded, silently passing tears onto the ground below. She saw a car pass on the highway above, slow down, then race away. She wondered if she'd be able to last until the help arrived. She knew she'd lost a lot of blood. As time continued, Sal slipped in and out of consciousness, unsure if she were alive or dead, until she heard footsteps finally approaching her.

"Help! Help! Is there anyone out there?" The footsteps came closer. "I think I'm paralyzed. Please don't move me! I need help! Please, if anyone can hear me, please help!" she begged through her sobs.

"I'm here, please, whoever you are. Follow my

voice! I'm badly injured. Please, I need your help! *Please!*" Sally could almost here the footsteps on top of her. "Please, you're almost here. I'm over here. Please, can you hear me?"

"Stop yelling, I can hear you!" Cambo whispered intensely as he stood over her.

Sal's heart pounded out of control. She looked into Cambo's eyes and pleaded he not hurt her. "Please leave me alone, Cambo. You're not well. You're … not … " As she spoke she found her voice losing strength, her body disconnecting from her mind. Against the struggle to remain conscious, Cambo's face grew blurry and distant. She clutched her chest and tried kicking her feet, forgetting she was paralyzed. Her chest pain enveloped her body, and she saw images of her past begin to rush across her mind, scenes of a thousand memories somehow flashing as if for a final staging littering the fading flickers of her awareness. As Cambo's hands made their way to her body, she silently prayed in a way words would have only interfered, that a hero might save them all from their helpless conditions.

CHAPTER FORTY-NINE

Chief Murphy leaned his sweaty head against the chopper window, leaving a smudge against the tempered glass. *It's gonna be a long night,* he thought as he surveyed the dark ground below. Briefly he closed his eyes and listened to the boisterousness of the chopper blades as they sliced through the crisp air. *Thank heavens it's not snowing tonight,* he considered as he opened his eyes again and looked over at the helicopter pilot.

"How far out are we now?"

The pilot turned his face a bit toward the aging police chief and answered him without taking his eyes off the flight path. "Just a couple minutes out," he yelled. "Now, when we get there, there's no place close to land, so we're going to drop you right in through the tree line, okay? There's a slew of folks down there, and motorcycles can take you up or down the mountainside as you please."

Murphy nodded his head. "Sounds good," he confirmed as he sat back in his seat and adjusted the safety harness. The chief rather liked repelling, and it'd been a while since he'd performed the task, although he actually thought it might be easier to just land in one of the farm fields just outside the forest area and call a motorbike to take him in the mile or so. As they traveled farther away from the city and closer to the mountain range, the chopper dropped spontaneously about ten feet.

"Gonna be a little bumpy tonight, Chief," the pilot explained as the chopper fell downward again and slid violently to the right, concluding with a rough tremor that rattled the windows. "Don't worry, Chief, this is the fun part, and I've only had two beers tonight, well under the legal limit."

Chief Murphy looked over at the pilot with an unappreciative look as the pilot cackled. Pushing the main stick slightly forward and fidgeting with several gadgets, the pilot took the chopper down toward the tree line. As the helicopter descended, Murphy searched the grisly scene below. A modest fire flickered at the base of the mountain, with large clouds of smoke rising into the air. High above, a circus of emergency vehicles was hastily coordinating their rescue efforts and options.

The chief was anxious to know what happened. When he took off for his visit of the scene, preliminary information had merely indicated that a passing motorist had noticed skid marks on the road, some busted metal, and a gaping hole in the safety wall with flames down below. It seemed to the chief that the holidays always brought on accidents like this, and there was nothing worse in his mind than calling someone on Thanksgiving or Christmas and telling them their young daughter died on the way home from college; sorry, and better luck next time.

"Okay, this is it. Right down below and you should be in touch with the emergency response team who's working up the accident specs," the pilot said. "You're clear to go anytime."

"Who ruled this an accident?" the chief asked.

"Sorry, Murphy. I of course mean working up the incident specs," the pilot said.

Chief Murphy gave him a nod. "That's better. Hey, I want you to stick around and stay on com.

Shine your spotlight around the scene so we can make sure we're not missing anyone down there, all right?"

"Will do, Chief."

"Thanks," Murphy said, grabbing his rope and opening the chopper door. A surge of freezing air slapped him in the face. *Oh, that is just too cold,* he grimaced. Carefully he ducked his head and lowered himself onto the chopper's landing bar. Placing his right hand on the rope in front of him with his thumb on top and his left hand on the portion of his rope behind his back, he lowered himself back off the landing bar and let his body drop into the open air. The drop was easy and accomplished quickly, and upon reaching the ground, the chief whipped the rope a couple of times to signal to the pilot to retract the rope into the chopper. Duff approached the chief in haste.

"Murphy! Glad you could make it. How was the ride?" Duff asked, grabbing the chief's arm and walking him toward the crash center.

"Not as bumpy as my marriage. What do we got here?" Murphy asked, analyzing the scene on the ground and covering up his mouth to avoid the smoke. Duff handed him an air filter, which the chief positioned across his mouth.

"Well, I ain't gonna lie to you—it's ugly," Duff started.

"How ugly?"

"Not the worst we've worked together, but pretty bad."

"What happened?"

"Well, the inspection crew atop the mountain is

calling it an accident. Best they can tell from the pre-liminary analysis, car one comes barreling down the road from Garberville, loses control, sways out into the passing lane, freaks out, overcorrects, slams on the brakes. Next thing you know, car number one goes into a tailspin, winds up a broadside bulls eye for car number two, which smacks right into the stalled vehicle. Car number one slides across the road and pushes through the railing, rolling down to this posi-tion here," Duff pointed to the pile of cars.

"Now, here's where it just gets spooky. Somehow car number two winds up stopping in what must be neutral and backing into the safety railing, which seems to have buckled under the pressure, flies down the hillside, where it defies all statistical probability by landing smack dab on top of car number one. "

"Wait a minute. How do you know car number two rolled backward onto the railing? I mean, it lands right on the first car. To me it almost seems like it would have to be a suicidal idiot trying to dock his ship on the other car. I mean, what're the odds of it randomly falling on number one?"

"The odds, my guess, are at best a million to one, or maybe even just zero. But the inspection crew found a significant pile of taillight residue around the second safety rail break, and they really think that's what happened. 'Course, we all know they're wrong sometimes, but that's all I've got for you right now," Duff explained.

"What about survivors? Any found?"

Duff nodded his head. "Yeah, and this is where I'll

take 'It doesn't make any sense for a thousand, Alex.' We found a trio of survivors, all unconscious, and all of them badly bruised, some worse than others. Each one of them piled on top of one another about a hundred feet from the crash site."

The chief looked hesitantly at Duff for several long moments. "I don't know if I follow. This is all a little too—"

"Unbelievable?"

"Yes."

"Don't I know it. That's what I told you. Did you not get the whole *Jeopardy* thing, because that was meant to tell you it was weird, and even in a clever way too."

"Yeah, I got the *Jeopardy* thing, and it was a non-laugh by choice situation. In regards to the *police* business at hand, do you know if the three survivors were all from one car, or both, or what?"

"*Nada.* Fire crew lowered a hose from their highway position about ten minutes ago, but they're trying to be real cautious about using any water, so vehicle inspection has not been possible. I guess there was enough of a gas leak that they're afraid to spread anything flammable around. We'll just have to wait for the flames to die down. So far, other than catching portions of those trees over there, it's just been too cold for the fire to spread."

"Make of the vehicles?"

"*Nada* again. One on the bottom looks like it might be a wagon, and the top some compact cheap-o job. But I can't tell particulars until the heat goes down, allowing us to get in closer."

"What about the three folks behind the rock? They dead?"

"No, Chief," Duff said. "They're all alive with good vitals, believe it or not. And hey, Alzheimers, I already told you that they were *survivors,* which was meant to imply aliveness."

Ignoring the sarcasm the chief looked away from the site and up at the roadside high above, then back at the crash site again. "I don't believe it. In all my years I've never seen even one person live from a crash that steep. You gotta be kidding me."

"I wish I was," Duff said. The chief gave him a wondering look. "Okay, that's not exactly what I meant." Duff hastened to correct himself. "Let me try again. You said, 'You gotta be kidding me,' and what I meant to say was: nope, vitals are good. Guess someone was watching out for them. I don't want to fool you; they *are* beat up pretty bad. One has a busted-up arm, and all three have multiple lacerations to the head and body. They must've all gotten out before the bomb went off, though; not a one of them sports a burn mark."

"Amazing. Truly amazing," the chief said, looking back up at the mountain road again. "Honestly, how does someone live through that? It just doesn't even seem possible."

"I really don't know. But stranger things've happened," Duff said.

"Like what?" the chief asked. Duff responded with silence.

"What's the plan with the three survivors? How do we get them outta here?"

"They're being checked for spinal injuries as we speak. As soon as they're cleared, we're gonna have Clancy airlift 'em outta here."

The chief's face grew a look of confusion. "You say the safety railing broke in two places? Those things are supposed to be heavily fortified. What happened?"

Duff nodded his head. "Yeah. That whole section of highway's been on the repair list ever since that set of accidents the last couple of years. Counties all got in a fight over who's gonna pay for it, so they just keep patching it up instead of doing something permanent. Truth is that whole railing is barely hanging on. The dirt's pretty brittle underneath."

"Wonderful," Murphy said, shaking his head. "Okay, let me see the survivors."

"You got it," Duff said, leading the chief away from the crash site and toward the large rock fronting the survivors.

"Murphster. How's my man?" Spencer said as he spotted the chief.

"Good, Spence. Although we have to stop meetin' this way," the chief said, eyeing the survivors.

"Agreed."

"What's the work up?"

"Honestly, it's like nothin' this EMT has ever seen before. Vitals are good—heart, lungs, you name it. Epidermis is gouged and banged up here and there.

John Doe number one's the worst. Full fracture to his left elbow, which appears to have left it shattered. We got him stable and wrapped, however, and plenty of morphine for them all. The only thing we don't know is the potential neurological damage. But their luck is good tonight, so I'm pulling for 'em," Spencer said, looking up at the crash site far above. "'Course we have to get them down to General to really tell the extent of the damage. As always, I'm quite on edge about shock-induced convulsions and thermoregulation, particularly worried about internal bleeding. Jane Doe over there also appears to have lost a lot of blood, which has me concerned. Hospital's on alert, and we're just waiting for the okay to ship 'em out."

"Anything identifiable on 'em at all? Wallet, purse; anything like that?"

"Not yet, Chief. We'll float it to you or one of your officers the second we know anything on it."

"Okay, good work. Let me know the second anyone comes around. I'll be on com with the emergency channel. Have dispatch break into anything I'm doing if that happens, all right?"

"Aye, aye, Chief. Will do."

"All right, sounds good. Good work there, Spence," the chief said, turning back to Duff. "All right, here's what I want. Until we know what's going down, I want a full perimeter search of this mountainside. I want every bush, beer can, and urination spot examined twice before we wrap up shop, got it? Contact dispatch and have them send up whoever's on in the north region to assist."

"Why? What's the point of that? Emergency's got search and rescue out already. And we need the manpower back in the city. I mean, I'll do it, but what's your reasoning?"

The chief looked up at the crash site and once again pondered the unreality of anyone surviving the accident before answering, "Twenty-seven years is my reasoning. That's all. Every cop instinct I have is telling me that this is working out too perfect, and I don't like it. If there's a clue or something out of place here, I want to know. I can just feel it. There's more to this."

"Hey, you're the chief. I'm just going to do as I'm told," Duff said.

"Good. Hey, maybe you *will* be a good husband someday." The chief re-approached the lower crash scene. Searching the ground he noticed several sets of footprints and drag lines. *Hmmm, must be our hero's trail,* he thought, retracing some of the steps and noting the patches of blood here and there. After several moments he came upon a metal door, which he recognized easily as belonging to a wooded station wagon. He'd been in that car enough times as a young father to know it anywhere. Getting down on his hands and knees, he found a large rock covered in blood. *What the devil were you used for?* he wondered, taking a sample of the blood and tucking the vial away in his inner coat pocket. Shining his flashlight on the rock, he grew uneasy about the direction of the bloodlines, which suggested the rock may have been forced against a body in a repeated fashion. Quickly he took several pictures.

"Chief!" Smith's voice blasted on the radio channel. "Chief, come in!"

"Smith," the chief said, grabbing his radio. "What's up?"

"We found another body 'bout halfway up the mountain on the switchback trail. Black female, pretty well damaged. Lots of blood. Shirt torn off. Cuts all across her abdomen. Non-responsive. You wanna come take a look?"

"You betcha. What's your forty?"

"Take a look up the mountainside, and I'll keep flashing my flashlight till you get here. There should be a motorbike down there somewhere you can use to ascend the trail."

"Sounds good. Gimme a minute," the chief requested as he looked around for the motorbike. Finding one, he climbed on by swinging his cold leg over the seat, then grasping the handlebars with both hands. He fired it up, shifted into gear, and sped up the switchback trail toward the officer. When he was about twenty feet off, he cut the engine and laid the bike down so as not to disturb the victim.

"Charlie, what's the work up?" the chief asked as he approached.

"Hey, Chief. Not good for this one. Jane Doe is an African American female with multiple contusions and lacerations on both the face and body. She may have received severe injuries to both the frontal and left temporal lobes, as well as the hindbrain and spinal area. We need to get her an MRI STAT and rule out TBI with particular concern about CNS damage.

Vitals are poor. Heart is arrhythmic, pupils dilated, and she's nonresponsive essentially from the chest down. My guess is she's in shock and possibly paralyzed. I ordered a neck brace down from the roadside station above. I think she's the worst we got tonight."

"She was the driver of car number two," Murphy concluded.

"How do you figure?"

"Well, first, no one came to save her while the three down the hill seemed to band together. Second, it just makes sense. She didn't have time to brace for it, get her seatbelt on. She must've been thrown on the descent," Murphy said as a second motorist barreled down the switchback trail toward their locale.

"Chopper's on its way with a suspended bed transporter. Plan is to snap on the brace and take her straight to General. They're on standby with lots of blood right now."

"Sound's good," Murphy said as Charlie and his team carefully attached the newly arrived neck brace. Chief Murphy heard the chopper directly above and watched as the bed transporter came slowly down to their position.

"Okay, this is gonna be a little tricky. Let's do a log roll," Charlie instructed as every person available grabbed a portion of the victim and slowly turned her on her side, then onto the transporter bed. "Careful!" Charlie whispered as one of his team members fumbled a little in the loose debris. Once on, they strapped Velcro holders across the woman's face and body to keep her in place.

"All right, bring her up!" Charlie demanded as the group watched the body rise up into the arms of the assistant on the chopper, who directed the body into the inner containment area. In a flash, the helicopter banked left and around toward the downtown hospital.

CHAPTER FIFTY

About an hour after the sun had lazily drifted upward into the frosty air, Chief Murphy sipped on his coffee and surveyed the crash site. Something about this particular crash was troubling him, and he couldn't bring himself to go home. Trouble was he had no reason to believe that it was anything other than a crash. Forensics had already scanned the asphalt, and the general findings concluded a likely accident. In their best guess, the lead car got spooked by an animal or something then spun out and caused the second car to crash broadside into the lead car.

But Murphy didn't buy it. He had too much experience with hunches, instructive dreams, and unqualified feelings that wound up solving cases that he all too easily recognized the feelings he was having about this case. Regardless, he knew he couldn't tell anyone about it. No one would believe him. They never did. What was worse, he knew the guys would give him trouble for not buying it. In fact, he'd been ranting about his several conspiracy theories in the office of late, and he could tell a lot of them thought he was turning into a has-been detective, trying to live out his glory days.

Mmm, that feels good in this tired 'ole body, the chief thought as he shivered briefly while processing the warm substance trickling down his throat. With care he shifted the plastic cup from his right to his left hand and then brought his warm hand up to his face, planting it square over his nose. The sensation caused the tip of his nose to tingle, and he breathed in deep inside his small private space.

I wonder how my victims are doing, Murphy pondered as he dropped his hand and took another sip. His mind replayed the erratic scenes of the last several hours. A fire had broken out at the crash site, and it was all anyone could do to save the victims and get them all successfully airlifted without dying. Unfortunately, all of his men had to cease further inspection and throw their efforts in with the firemen who were busy chopping down trees and clearing a fireproof zone, a task made more difficult by the media and random spectators who demanded some of his staff to keep the investigation perimeter secure. Finally the fire was brought completely under control, and his men returned to the full-perimeter search, and now Murphy was ready to hear some results.

Another thirty minutes or so passed by when Jones came and awoke the chief in his slumped-over position under a pine tree.

"Chief, wake up," Jones said. The chief jerked

up, launching the remainder of his drink onto Jones's jacket. Jones jumped back and threw his arms out to the side for a moment then began to violently wipe off the liquid.

"*Aw!*" Jones griped as he did a half-jump, half-wiggle maneuver to try to force any loose drops onto the ground.

Chief Murphy laughed deeply and loudly, great big howls that seemed to roll out of his mouth like an opera singer descending in thirds from A to F major. "You *so* deserved that."

"Well, you deserve the personal insignia of my graduation ring on your fat forehead," Jones retorted, still wiping down the front of his coat.

"Yeah, yeah, what do you got for me?" Jones looked up for a moment with a blank look, as if not having any idea what the chief was talking about. Suddenly his eyes grew wide, and his face morphed from its angry and defiant expression to a look of excitement and disbelief.

"You're not gonna believe this, Chief. Fact is, I didn't believe it," Jones said.

"What, you idiot. Hurry up and tell me."

"The car specs came in. *Question one.* Was it a Geo like you suspected? *Answer:* yes. Year, make, and model? Couldn't be determined given the extensive damage and limited resources available as yet. However, several minutes ago, Officer Bryce recovered a license plate, which yours truly had central run through the computer, and guess what: nineteen ninety-five Geo Metro, beige, reported stolen approximately three months prior. Registered owner, one Mr. Cameron Bo. I believe you know this guy?"

"Yes, I do," the chief said. "And the plot thickens."

"Yes, it does," Jones said, smirking back at the aging chief. "We got him then. This is the guy you been looking to book, right? Let's go get him."

"No," the chief said, thinking silently for a moment. "No, not yet, that would be premature. There has to be more. First off, if he had anything to do with this, then he's not home. He's out here barfing up a lung or something, or dead." Murphy looked around the accident scene and the surrounding wooded area. "We should increase the scan. Have central send in more units, and search within a five-mile perimeter. I bet we find him in there. No way he's walking around fast after that fall," the chief reasoned, looking up the mountainside at the highway far above. "And close out the area now as an official crime scene."

"What if he wasn't in the crash? Maybe a hit for hire? You want me to send a couple of blues over to the house and pick him up there?"

"No, we don't got enough on him. We walk over there and take him in now, we might shake his confidence before we can book him on something legitimate. Make him split. So far, all we got is a crash scene and a suspect who, if he's not dead, will be able to effectively argue that his car was stolen." The chief's eyes grew wide as he remembered the woman recovered halfway up the switchback trail. "Hey, what's the ID on the victims? Any word yet?"

"I don't know, Chief. Everyone we had was working the fire. But I can find out."

"Yes. Do it," the chief affirmed. "When I met with Mr. Bo, he told me the car was stolen by a hooker. If memory serves I think he said her name was Sal or Sally or something. 'Course it might've just been a street name. Find out the woman's name who was recovered on the mountainside and cross-check it with my notes from the interview I had with Mr. Bo. And you let me know what you find immediately, got it?"

"Agreed. But this time I'm waking your tired butt up from a distance."

Laughing, the chief made his way over to the ground team as Jones sped off to his motorbike. "I'm packing it up, guys. Let me know if you get anything new, all right?"

"Will do, Chief," Smith replied. The chief crossed the roped area and settled himself on the motorbike he'd been using to get up and down the mountainside. For several minutes he rode up the steep slope, mostly on the trail, excepting where he felt he could cut a few corners here and there. The wind slapped against his face as his mind drifted to a warm scene of his hearth at home; blazing hot, with his boots off, and his blanket over him keeping him toasty warm. *Man, I'm getting old*, he thought as he crested the roadside ledge and motored onto the asphalt.

"I'm taking off!" he yelled to the high-ground team. One of them came running over with a large Ziploc bag.

"Chief!" the runner yelled. "Wait a sec!" The chief killed the engine and dismounted the bike.

"What do you got for me, Tessy?"

"We recovered one of the participant's wallets," Officer Tess explained. "Found it in the shrubs just off the mouth of the switchback trail. Belongs to an eighteen-year-old Caucasian male, one Cameron Bo. We just faxed the picture over to the hospital, and they responded back that it was a negative match; he's not any of the participants admitted this morning. Chief, I think he was the driver of vehicle two."

Murphy grabbed the bag from Tessy and looked directly into her eyes while patting her on the shoulder. "You know, I've a hunch you're correct."

CHAPTER FIFTY-ONE

Addy raised her hands to her head and scrunched her eyebrows. She groaned as she became aware of the widespread throbbing and aching in her body. Slowly she opened her eyes and waited for the images of life to come into focus. The end result was a depiction of a white room with several blinking gadgets and computer machines surrounding her bed, many of which could be heard emitting low-frequency sounds. On her arm was an IV with a heart monitor attached to her finger. Her right arm was in a cast, and her head felt bandaged.

I'm in a hospital, she thought. She rubbed her temples just under the bandage line for several moments and shut her eyes to try and de-escalate the disoriented feeling that overcame her. After some time, she re-opened her eyes and again started to process her surroundings. Memories of the accident came streaming into her mind, and she felt her body tensing up. *You made it, obviously. You're not dead. Calm down,* she told herself, feeling the muscles in her body relax slowly.

"Merci!" she suddenly said out loud. "Merci, where are you?" She pined out loud again, her eyes growing increasingly moist. *He's dead. He must be dead!* she languished, now in a full cry. "Merci!" she said one more time as a mass next to her bed began to rise.

"Addy?" Merci asked, his head appearing from underneath the blanket under which he'd been sleeping.

"Merci?" Addy said. Merci's face was heavily scarred, and he was wearing hospital attire.

"Addy! You're back!" he said, rushing to her side. "Thank God you're back. Thank God!" he said as they held each other as best they could, given Addy's medical equipment constraints.

"I love you!" Merci said with Addy repeating it. For several long moments they alternated from kissing and holding each other, their tears mixing on Addy's hospital pillow.

"Hey, welcome back," Doctor Carter saluted as he entered the door with a light knock. Addy looked over at the blond-haired man towering in the doorway.

"Hello ... " Addy said. The man strode over to the bed and put his hand on Addy's arm.

"I'm Doctor Carter. You don't know me, but we've been spending a lot of time together the past four days—although not as much as Mr. Bowku here. After he escaped his bed five times in one day, we decided to stop fighting him and let him sleep in here with you."

Merci caressed Addy's cheek and backed away a foot from the bed, still holding Addy's hand. "Let's let the doctor examine you," he said under his sniffles. Doctor Carter pulled out his stethoscope and placed it on several locations on Addy's body.

"That's it, breathe deep," Carter instructed. A sharp pain shot through Addy's left side.

"That hurts," she said.

"Where, right there?" Carter asked, lightly pushing on her left ribs.

"Uh huh," Addy answered, trying to breathe shallowly.

"Yes, well, you banged yourself up pretty bad there, and you even have a few hairline fractures on your ribs. You're going to need to take it easy for several weeks. Believe it or not, though, you and Merci both came out of this amazingly well. Your vitals are good. No serious breaks, with the exception of the right arm, which, as I'm sure you noticed, we already put in a cast. We found no evidence of serious internal bleeding, and your neuro signs have been good. Essentially, we've just been waiting for you to return to us so we can monitor you, give you some tests, check your memory, that kind of stuff. If every thing checks out, you should be outta here within the week. Okay? I know this is a lot to take in right now. But it is my experience patients like to hear this stuff right away. We'll talk more later, but the bottom line is, you're going to be fine, okay? So is your boyfriend. You'll both be out of here by early next week, okay?"

Addy closed her eyes and rubbed her head. "What about John?" she asked, opening her eyes and looking at the doctor. Doctor Carter raised his eyebrows and quickly dipped his head to the lower right and then back up again, before looking over at Merci with his mouth open. Merci moved in closer to Addy.

"They're not sure he's going to make it," Merci said quietly, squeezing her hands. "He's beat up pretty bad. I guess he's had a lot of internal damage."

Addy looked up at Merci and sobbed again. "We should've listened to him! It's our fault he's dead! He knew … he told us to turn back. He knew!"

Doctor Carter interrupted. "What did John know?"

Merci looked up at the doctor's bewildered face. "Nothing, Doctor. It's just, when we started home from the church sermon, John, well, he kind of freaked out and told us he had some bad feeling that we needed to turn back around. That's all. If we'd listened to him, I guess … "

"Oh. I see," the doctor said quietly. The three sat in silence for some time.

"I guess you think we're kind of nuts or something," Merci asked.

The doctor stood up.

"Not at all. Son, I've been a doctor for fifteen years in this hospital. If I had a dime for every time I heard something like that, well... let's just say I've heard it before. And I believe it. I've learned more about the limits of science as a doctor than I've learned about the power of science. Both of you are alive, and we're not giving up on John yet. I'd say that the only way to make sense of the fact that we're having this discussion after you fell off the Garberville Gap is that someone up there was taking care of you guys. Now I'll leave you two alone for just a minute while I grab a nurse, okay?" The doctor turned to exit the room. Merci looked down into Addy's eyes, and the two of them cried in tandem.

Addy wiped her face with her left hand. "We fell down the gap?" she asked. Merci nodded his head. Addy lay quietly for several moments. "That must be like a thousand feet. How does someone live through that?"

"I don't know," Merci said. "In fact, one of the nurses told me she remembered a couple dropping off about the same point last year, and when she arrived on the scene they were both dead. They never had a chance."

"So why did we live?" Addy asked. "What makes us special?" Merci shrugged his shoulders.

"I don't know. I guess I agree with the doctor. All I can think is there must be a God. There's just no other way of making sense of it. It must be God's handiwork."

"What, to save us and let other people die? That

doesn't make any sense." Merci shrugged his shoulders again.

"No, it doesn't, but it makes the most sense. There's just no other way to explain it. Everyone agrees we should be dead. There's just no other way!"

Addy sat quietly, thinking about what Merci had said. She looked back up at Merci's teary face and felt the urge to touch him. Slowly she wiped some of his tears away from his warm skin. "Well, I don't know what happened, but I'm very glad you're here," she said, holding his cheek in her hand.

He smiled and kissed her face. "Me too."

CHAPTER FIFTY-TWO

After several days Addy was up and moving around. She and Merci sat in John's room looking at Chief Murphy.

"Okay, so one more time. You're driving home, and John begins to suspect something's wrong. He tells you to turn around, but neither of you pay much attention to what he's saying. Why would he say that to you, do you think?"

"I don't know," Merci said. "We just figured he was having a panic attack or something. He was breathing all funny and ... "

"And ... what?" the chief said.

"I don't know, he just, he seemed to be awkward. That's all," Merci explained.

"So then what happened?" the chief said.

"Well, like we told you before, then he got kind of more freaked out, and we started panicking too," Addy said. "We thought maybe he was having a heart attack or something else at that point. We felt we didn't have much time to find help, and so we were gonna flag down the other vehicle and ask if they had a cell phone or something."

"Okay," Murphy said, nodding his head.

"Well, then, I don't know," Merci said. "There was like, this guy, or something standing in the middle of the road. I swerved to miss him, which I did. But then the car started fishtailing and spinning around, and next thing you know, we're stalled smack dab in the road looking at headlights."

"Both of you saw this guy?" the chief asked.

"Yes," Addy replied.

"What did the other car do when you stalled out in the middle of the road?" the chief asked.

"Well," Addy said, "I really don't remember much. I kind of remember it swerving, but it was too late."

"No, that's not what happened. I remember specifically. It swerved to the left to avoid us, then seemed to lose control itself, and the last thing I remember, the headlights were coming right at us," Merci said.

The three of them sat quietly for several minutes as Chief Murphy repeatedly flipped his notebook cover up and back down again. "Okay, thanks. That's all I got for you guys right now. Glad to see you're feeling better, Addy," he said, standing on his feet.

"Thank you," Addy said, holding Merci's hand in a vice grip. The chief made his way to the door.

"Oh, one more thing. Either of you remember anything at all in between the time you got hit and the time you woke up in the hospital?"

"No," Merci said.

"Nope. Sorry, Mr. Murphy," Addy replied.

"No, no, that's okay. I was just wondering. I'll catch you guys later. Bye now," the chief said, disappearing into the outer hall. Addy and Merci sat a good thirty minutes in silence, watching John's vitals on the various machines. His heart rate was stable at around eighty beats per minute. His periodic blood pressure was registering at about one twenty over eighty reliably. His breathing sounded symmetrical. Every once in a while his face would twitch, but Doctor Addison explained that was typical of coma patients and didn't necessarily indicate anything was improving. After some time Merci turned to Addy and placed his second hand over hers.

"There's something I've been meaning to tell you," he said, his voice solemn. "I probably should have already, but, I don't know, I guess you've seemed so frail these past couple days, and so reactive about John, that I was afraid of upsetting you even more."

"You're so worried about me all the time." Addy smiled, placing her hand on Merci's cheek. Merci grabbed her hand and brought it down onto his lap.

"It's about John," he said.

"What about John?"

"The police think that John is ... that he's the reason we're alive."

"What do you mean? I don't understand."

"I mean. Well ... that night, when the car crashed, they think John was thrown out. You and I were apparently trapped inside, unconscious. It seems that John somehow was able to drag us out to safety. He might've even broken his own arm to untangle himself and save us. He really risked his life for us."

Addy looked at Merci in disbelief. "How could anyone know this? John has been unconscious since he got to the hospital, right?"

Merci nodded his head. "Yeah, but the police did some tests, and they found his blood away from the crash site and on the rock they think he used to break his arm. The doctor also confirmed that his elbow was likely a self-inflicted wound, the way it was fractured," Merci said, grasping more tightly onto Addy's hand. "It appears he saved our lives."

The two of them sat quietly, staring at their friend, neither of them knowing what to say. Finally Addy released Merci's hand from hers and stood up, taking a step toward John's bed. Turning to face Merci, she asked him if he would leave her alone for a moment.

"Why? What're you going to do?"

"Nothing, just ... I just want to spend a minute alone and think, that's all. Okay?" she asked. Merci looked bewildered, but he shrugged his shoulders. He stood up and walked over to Addy, placing his arms around her.

"Whatever you need," he said, kissing her cheek and holding her in a tight hug for some time before stepping backward and disappearing out the door. Addy walked over to the door and closed it. She peeked out the window and watched as Merci departed down the hall toward the restroom. Turning, she walked across the room to John's bed. She pulled up a stool and sat next to him, looking down at his scuffed face. She reached out her hand and touched his. It felt warm. Placing her hands softly on his body, she lightly caressed the scars on his hand and arm, running her cuticles all the way up to his neck and face. Softly she glided her fingers through his hair and let giant tears fall upon his hospital gown.

"I'm sorry," she whispered into his ear. "I'm really sorry. We should've listened to you. But you saved us anyway. No one has ever done something like that for me before. Thank you. I'm sorry. Please don't die," she said as she leaned into his forehead and gave him a soft kiss.

CHAPTER FIFTY-THREE

Merci emerged from the restroom and walked toward the lounge. As he approached the small room, he overheard the voices of Chief Murphy and someone else conversing. Curious to hear what they had to say, he slowed his walk and stopped just shy of the door opening.

"Well, I don't know, Murph. I think we ought to question them. Maybe they know the suspect. Maybe they could give us something to go on."

"No," said the chief. "They're still recovering, and they don't need to hear about some fishing expedition we're calling a possible homicide. And yes, I said fishing expedition because that's all it is right now. It might actually turn out that the boy was telling the truth the whole time, and that the girl in room three ten really is the one responsible for the crash."

"But you don't believe that. You've been clamoring for the last three months that something fishy is going on with that Geo theft, and you don't expect me to believe that you really think that's bogus now. *I* don't think it's bogus now!" the first voice said.

"No," the chief said, "I *don't* expect that you'll think it's all bogus, but the fact is that it *isn't* substantiated, and until I know there's some real evidence behind it, I'm not willing to tell these poor kids they were part of a murder plot."

"Well, I'm sorry, Chief, but I just don't get you. I mean, how much more evidence do you need? We got evidence for premeditation because he reported the car stolen three plus months ago. Forensics ruled out three ten as the driver, given that her injuries matched a collision with the dashboard, not that of a person hitting a deployed airbag. Obviously someone else was driving the car, and as no one has seen the suspect go in or out of his home since the crash, in concert with the fact that his wallet was found at the site gives any jury in the world reason to convict. I say we put out the APB on him right now, debrief the surviving victims, and see if they know anything about him! Right now! I mean, what else do you need? A hammer to hit you right upside the head?"

"No, but I do need something you haven't got yet," the chief said.

"What's that?"

"A motive. You don't have a motive. And because you don't, all of your circumstantial evidence goes to crap because you can't convince anyone that he would've been motivated to do the crime. What do you have—a wallet and his car? Well, guess what, the suspect told me *personally* that a hooker took both his car and his wallet. A second report linked the car to a shooting involving a hooker and an unidentified youthful-looking male. So I, listening to you, take the case to court, and our DA stands up and tells the judge that we should have a trial because all of the circumstantial evidence points to our eighteen-year-old, youthful-looking suspect, who is missing his wallet and car, which were found on scene, and which indicate he should be convicted of murder. Which I think we would have to argue was premeditated because you can't sell the stolen car thing without selling premeditation.

"So, here I am telling this judge we have an eighteen-year-old kid who has the insight to report his car stolen, blame it on a hooker, pick up the *same* hooker months later, chase and follow a pack of young adults, wait for their car to stall and spin out, then run into them. Even if I could prove the circumstantial evidence was robust, then all the judge has to say to me is *why?* And I with my not-so-bright look on my face just gave the case away to the defending attorney, and the judge throws me and my crappy work out of his courtroom. So what do I need? I need a motive, Jonesy, that's what I need. I *do* think it was a homicide, somehow, but *why?* That's the part I can't figure out. So here's the plan: we don't talk to the victims about possible foul play yet, but as soon as we can figure out a possible reason *for* foul play, then we formally investigate it, okay? So you can talk to them, but *do not* indicate any names or any suspicions at this point, all right? I want this one clean."

Merci's mouth dropped and his eyes grew wide as he took some steps backward. He looked around the hall to see if anyone else was privy to the debate. *Homicide?* he thought, wondering what the chief was talking about. *I thought this was an accident!* His mind rapidly replayed the events of the night. *There is no way it could have been planned! Who would have known we were going to be spun out in the middle of the Garberville highway? Besides, it was nighttime. How would he be able to know it was our car instead of someone else's?* he wondered, unable to answer his own questions. He found a seat by the restrooms and thought over the conversation for some time. *Who would any of us know who would want to kill us anyway?*

For twenty minutes or more, he sat and pondered why something like this would happen on purpose, but he could not come up with any logical reason how someone could have set up the accident in such a way as it played out. Particularly he could not conceptualize a rational explanation for how any perpetrator could've gotten them to have stalled on the road.

Suddenly Merci remembered the man who had run out in front of them right before the crash. Parting his mouth he raised his eyelids and turned toward the lounge. Rising to his feet he darted across the lobby area and into the lounge, causing the chief to scoot his chair back and grasp his gun.

"Merci, you scared the living daylights out of me. What can we do for you, son?" the chief asked, dropping his hand off his weapon.

"I think I might know something about your suspect," Merci said, his mind on fire. The chief looked over at his partner and then back at Merci. "What're you talking about, son? What suspect?"

"The one you think might be responsible for the accident, or homicide, or whatever. Look, I'm sorry, but I overheard your conversation from the hall. I know you think this might have an element of foul play, and I think I might be able to help."

The chief scrunched his face and ran his hand through his coarse hair. He seemed to Merci to be very angry about being found out. "All right," he finally said, obviously unsure what else to say.

Merci took a few deep breaths to try to calm himself. "Well," he began as he looked up into Murphy's fixed stare, "I told you this before, but I didn't think of it then. To me, the hardest part to figure out would be the way someone would know that we were stalled. I mean, how do you plan someone going into a tailspin in the middle of the highway, if you plan on murdering them by automobile crash, right?"

"Okay, go on, son," the chief instructed.

"Then it hit me. Right before the crash, both Addy and I saw the same person dart in front of the car. It was literally seconds before the collision, which means the suspect must have planned it to happen that way. Whoever it was knew we'd have to swerve to miss him, and then we'd be unable to keep ourselves from the oncoming collision," Merci reasoned. "That's gotta be it."

The chief sat back in his chair and closed his eyes for several seconds. "You may be right, Merci, but if you are, the question still has to be asked why. *Why* would anyone have any reason to hurt someone in your car?"

Merci looked blankly at the police chief while thinking over the question. "Who's in room three ten?"

The chief looked back at Merci unflinchingly. "I'm not sure if it's such a good idea to tell you that, son?"

"Look, I'm not going to go blabbing it to anyone, okay? This thing, if it's an accident, I can live with it, you know? It happens. But if it was done on purpose, well, that's my girlfriend all beat up and my best friend lying comatose in the other room. All I want to do is bring justice to anyone who hurt them. I just want to help. That's all. I'll do whatever I can to help. Just like I did just now. Please, you can trust me. I would not do *anything* to jeopardize your investigation. Who's in three ten?"

The chief let out a bellow of air and brought his hands closer to his body while still letting them rest on the table. "You're taking this awfully well, you know. I'm not sure it's such a good idea to go down this road right now. We got plenty of time to talk."

Merci furrowed his brow and took in a deep breath. "Look, I haven't lived a sheltered life. None of us have. If we seem to be taking it well, we're not. To be honest, it's just another crapload of problems in a crappy life to begin with. Privately, we're all hurting. But we want to know what happened too. Like I said, that's my *girlfriend* in there. And the other guy is the one you think saved my life, and he might die because of that. Now I can and will break down about this later, but right now I have to believe time is essential, and we might be on to something. Please, I'm not going to do anything to three ten. I just want to be on the offensive. I won't even tell Addy about it. But I want to; no, I *need* to help. Please."

Murphy looked out the window of the small room before turning back to face Merci. "It's someone from the other vehicle. We think she may be linked to whatever's going on. Now, I'm trusting you, son, and don't mess with my trust. You are not to see this woman in any way unless assisted by myself or another officer at *our* request. You got it? I have guards at her door twenty-four-seven, and if any of them ever call me saying you're giving them guff, I won't be scared to push you about it, you get my drift?"

"Perfectly."

"Good."

"So, what's the deal with her? Is she knocked out too?"

"Well, honestly, she's not just out, but we're not sure if she's gonna make it. But if she does...well, maybe she can set the whole ordeal straight," Murphy said then added, "If you're religious, best thing you might be able to do to help is to pray for a miracle."

Merci considered the chief's comments and looked down at his scarred arms. "I'll try it, but I might be fresh out of favors with Him."

CHAPTER FIFTY-FOUR

Officer Lewis strode out from his position against the wall and surveyed the hallway and nearby lobby. All looked exactly the same as it did during the last fifteen-minute check, as well as the fifteen-minute check before that, and the fifteen-minute check before that. The nurses tending the station were busy answering calls. The patient on the bench was still sleeping with the blanket over his head. Doctors were still bustling up and down the hall periodically. Family members and other loved ones still congregated in the lobby waiting room to see their brother, son, sister, daughter, mother, or other family relation.

This is so ridiculous, he thought, moving back to

his position opposite Officer Smith. "All clear," he said as he backed into the wall and let his body slump against the drywall. *Murphy is way overdoing it on this one,* he thought as he looked over at Smith.

"Man, I could go for a cold drink right now, you know what I mean?" Lewis said, his eyes aglow.

"I'm not much of a drinker," Smith replied, his gaze alternating up and down the hall. Lewis sported an irritated look.

"Look, you don't have to be so Captain America, Frank. It's not like anyone's coming to get her. *She's in a coma,* remember? And we got a million people around. I think you can relax. If that lunatic does show his face around here, the only way to her is through us, and I guarantee you that ain't gonna happen. So why don't you loosen up a bit?"

Smith looked over at Lewis, then down the hall again. "Look, Lewis, I'm not trying to annoy you or anything. This is just how I am on the job. Serious threat or not. Guess it can be pretty annoying to others sometimes. But I can't turn it off, okay?"

"Well, hey, everyone has flaws. I'm just trying to have a conversation with you, that's all. This place blows. I've seen more action at a Greenpeace convention, you know?"

Smith emitted a brief laugh while checking the halls again. "So you think she's gonna make it?" Lewis shrugged his shoulders and pursed his lips momentarily, making a smacking sound as he began to reply.

"I don't know, to be honest. I overheard Doctor Sharon in there, and she didn't think it was looking too good."

"What did she say?"

"Just that she's been out for almost two weeks now, and that her chance of coming out of it slips a little every day she's non-reactive. Besides, even if she does come out of it, looks like she's pretty banged up. They say she's paralyzed."

"Well, guess she'll need a new career," Smith said.

"Yeah." Lewis said. "Of course that might not be a bad thing altogether."

"Yeah," Smith agreed. The two of them stood for a while, watching the bustling in the lobby. An elderly couple had walked in and was asked to be seated. The charge nurse was busily inscribing names on the master board. *I hate hospitals*, Lewis thought, closing his eyes and rubbing his temples.

Suddenly the doors burst open. A younger man with a pale white complexion and several scars across his face hovered menacingly at the threshold, each of his palms resting on a door.

"Where are they?" he yelled, looking over at the elderly couple in the waiting room. A hand flew over his shoulder and around his chest area. It belonged to a female hospital attendant.

"Hey, calm down!" the attendant said.

"Get offa me!" the man said, arching his back and elbowing the attendant in the face then turning and punching her in the stomach. The attendant grabbed her stomach and slouched to the ground, trying to catch her breath.

"Hey! Calm down, fella!" Officer Lewis ordered as he bolted toward the waiting room lobby.

"Outta my way, pig!" the man yelled as he leapt over the nurse's station desk and swung his arms wildly at the charge nurse, who went down easily and remained limp on the floor. A second, redheaded, petite nurse screamed and tried to escape, but the crazed man cut her off and tackled her against the hospital wall.

"Shut up!" he screamed in her ear, cupping a hand over her mouth and throwing her in front of him. "Shut up or I'll kill you. Don't test me, lady! I'll have no qualms killing you!"

Lewis slowed to a stop at the head of the nurse's station and lowered his hand to his gun. Quickly he unbuttoned his holster strap and carefully held his fingers on the gun handle while holding his other palm upward toward the attacker.

"You want me to do anything?" Smith yelled from down the hall. Without looking at him, Lewis signaled for him to stay put, while also motioning for the hospital security guards who had just shown up at the lobby entrance to stay on the other side of the double doors.

"That's right. You tell them all to stay away, or I'll kill her!" the man said, saliva dripping from his mouth onto the quivering nurse's hair.

"Now wait a minute. You're outnumbered, and you don't have a weapon. Why don't you just let the woman go, and we'll work this out together?" Lewis said.

"Shut up!" the crazed man thundered in return. "I don't need your stupid weapons. I've been given gifts from someone much, much more powerful than you, and I can do to you mortals as I please! If I wanted a mortal weapon to kill her with, I could use this!" he said, revealing the scissors he had in his left hand. Backing up against the nursing desk wall he opened the scissors and held the sharp side against the nurse's throat, careful to keep the nurse between himself and the officer.

Lewis put both of his hands in the air and took a couple of steps backward. "Hey, okay, we'll play by your rules. No reason to get hostile, and no reason to hurry. Everyone is listening to you now. Just tell us what you want," Lewis offered, noting that Smith had advanced down the hall, weapon drawn, to the corner of the wall just out of sight from the crazed man behind the nursing station desk.

"I want you to take me to them. That's what I want. No more games. I must end it now! You here me? Now!" he said as he brought the scissors closer against the exposed flesh of the nurse in front of him

"Look, friend. I have no reason not to trust you. I want to help you, and I have the power to do it; just lower the scissors a little, and we can talk. Okay? Can you do that?" Lewis asked, his voice calm and steady.

The man looked back at the officer and then nervously around at everyone else in the open area. "What are you all looking at? Stop looking at me!"

"Okay, okay, easy. They're looking away now, see? They're all going to turn around and face the other way."

"You too!" the man said.

"Oh, no. Not me. You and I talk. Everyone else looks away. That's the deal," Lewis said.

"I can make you look away. I can kill her too. I can kill you. I have special powers. I have a mission to accomplish, and you're getting in my way. Time is running out. I need to hurry. Faster! Stop talking to me and let me go, or I'll—"

Unexpectedly the nurse being held hostage grabbed the open scissor blade from her neck and forced them away, elbowing the assailant in the groin. Lewis immediately rushed forward, with Smith following toward her captor as the nurse dropped to her knees and screamed as she held up her bleeding hand, pouring red all over the tile floor.

"Stop right there! You're under arrest!" Lewis commanded to the assailant as he kicked the scissors out of his hand and fired a right hook at the hanging jaw of the captor. At the last possible moment, however, the assailant pivoted, causing Lewis to over-swing. Smith barreled into the man's chest and knocked him onto the ground. The man let out several shrill screams and violently swung his arms and legs into the open air at anything within contact.

"Ah!" Smith said as the man bit into his arm and wiggled loose. As he started to rise to his feet, however, the hospital security guards had made their way into the scene, and a massive dog pile of bodies clashed into one another in an attempt to stabilize the writhing man.

"We got him pinned!" one of the guards yelled as a doctor rushed in with a syringe, which he plunged into the man's body. For several long moments they held him as he still persisted in his violent wiggling, demanding to accomplish his mission, but soon the medicinal agent took effect and the moving declined. The man lay increasingly immobile and dissociated. Slowly the pile of bodies removed themselves one at a time, with Lewis clasping handcuffs on the man before rolling him over onto his back.

"Officer, I assure you this man doesn't need to be handcuffed. I gave him a very powerful sedative," the doctor said. Lewis gave the doctor a look as if to suggest he didn't care what the doctor thought. He depressed his shoulder radio button and called for dispatch to send in an officer to process the incident and take custody of the assailant.

"Officer, I'm not sure that's the right call. This man obviously belongs in the psych ward, not the prison. Release him to me, and we'll see to it he gets a thorough evaluation," the doctor said.

"When the officers get here, you can take it up with them and the psychiatric examiner," Lewis said. "Right now I got some accosted victims who might not want to see him simply be transferred to psych, okay?"

The doctor threw up his hands and then stepped away from the officers and began to examine the charge nurse, who was still unmoving on the floor.

"You okay, Smithy?" Lewis asked, taking a look at his bleeding arm.

"Yeah…" Smith said softly while cradling his arm. "That guy had one *monster* of a bite."

Lewis responded in-between heavy breaths. "Yeah. Too much excitement for me too. What was that all about, anyway?"

"I don't know. From the looks of 'em, though, I don't think he knows what that was all about either," Smith said.

Lewis's breathing was becoming more controlled again. "Yeah."

"What happened?" The charge nurse asked, finally conscious again. "Are we okay now?" she wondered aloud, seemingly dazed as the doctor put a hand on her forehead.

"Yes, ma'am. We got him. You okay?" Lewis asked, joining the doctor in helping her to her feet.

"Yes, I…I think so. I think I'm okay. But, what's that ringing?" she asked, bringing her hands to her ears as the doctor became distracted by the nurse with the hand wound from the scissors.

"I don't know, but he got you pretty good. Maybe you ought to take it easy," Lewis said.

"No! Be quiet a minute," she said, holding her finger to her lips. She stood listening for several seconds then turned her head to the emergency panel and noticed the blinking light on 310.

"Oh no!" the nurse shouted as she stood upright and pushed herself toward the room.

"What? What is it?" Lewis demanded, falling in step behind her.

"It's your patient. She's flat lined!" the nurse cried, whipping around the corner and down the hall.

"What? For how long?"

"I don't know. It must've happened during the scuffle. Quick, get the doctor!" she said as she clumsily made her way into Sal's room.

"Smith, get a doctor in here now!" Lewis ordered, racing into the room behind the nurse. To his horror he saw Sally Strathers on the floor, her IVs knocked over, and the bags of medicine punctured and leaking all around her. Her heart monitor was ringing as a constant horizontal line ran across the display. "What do you want me to do?" Lewis asked the nurse who was administering CPR.

"Clear the floor around her and start re-hanging those IVs!" the nurse ordered while counting from one to four, then breathing into Sal's mouth. Lewis desperately struggled to stand up the IV tree, but in his anxiety he knocked it over the opposite way and crashed the metal bars into the computer screen.

"Careful!" the nurse thundered in between her counting and breathing. Lewis finished clearing the broken containers and other obstacles as a team of doctors burst into the room. He stood back against the wall and watched helplessly as the medical staff worked Sally up. *C'mon, c'mon,* he thought, wondering what he would say to Chief Murphy.

"What do we got?" the attendee demanded.

"Thirty-something-year-old female in for TBI and multiple fractures secondary to vehicular accident. We just had a violent altercation in the waiting room where I was knocked unconscious. When I came to, I heard the distress signal and found her in this position flat lined," the charge nurse said.

"What're the readings just prior to the flat line?"

A female doctor pulled herself away from Sal's body and snatched the printout from the computer. As she pulled it up from the ground, however, the weight of the soggy lower half caused most of it to detach and fall to the floor. The doctor dropped to her knees and searched through the liquid-stained folded section until she found what she was looking for.

"Barbara, now!" the attendee snapped.

"Okay...looks like several large K complexes leading into a massive spike wave pattern just preceding the cardiac flat line. It appears she started seizing up, and must have fallen out of her bed dragging the IV down with her."

"How long?" the senior doctor asked.

"Duration of seizure looks about three minutes," she answered.

"Okay, guys, you heard her. There still might be time. Let's get her up," the attendee said.

"Doctor Cox, she's paralyzed," the charge nurse said.

"Doesn't matter. I have to stimulate her heart, and I can't do it in this pool of liquid. Now, on my count: one! Two! Three!" he said as the team hoisted her onto the hospital bed and then busily wiped down as much of the liquid as they could from both her and the bed while the charge nurse prepared the electrical paddles.

"Start her up," the lead doctor said, rubbing the paddles together and then applying them to Sal's chest and side. Sal's body jumped briefly before slumping back into a lifeless position. "Bump it up," the lead doctor commanded, applying the paddles again. Sal's heart rate remained unchanged.

"Why weren't the safety guards up on her bed?" the lead doctor asked.

The charge nurse remained in control of her reaction. "She is paralyzed, Doctor. We didn't think it was necessary."

"Again!" the doctor ordered, with similar results. "Well, what do you think now?" the doctor said. The nurse hung her head.

"Let's give her the max," the doctor ordered as he placed the paddles on her once again. Sal's body jerked violently, and then slumped back down onto the bed in a fixed position. Lewis and the team watched for several solemn minutes as the nurses and doctors kept pumping the heart. Finally the lead doctor called the time of death and the team slowly dissipated. As the charge nurse left to grab the custodial staff, Lewis looked up and saw Smith's horrified expression in the doorway.

CHAPTER FIFTY-FIVE

Cameron silently moved down the hall and tried to avoid eye contact with any of the hospital staff. He pulled his blanket over his head tightly and worked hard to not think about what his father had just made him do.

"You did the right thing," his father consoled him. "You did what you had to do. You had to save yourself to save others."

Another voice screamed at him, "Murderer! I saw you kill her, and I'm going to tell!"

Shut up! Cameron screamed inside his mind as he tried to scare the voices away.

"Murderer!" the voice screamed again, this time triggering a round of conversations that he could hear in stereo. Although he couldn't make out any of the words, he knew they were talking about him. He knew they were plotting how to frame him for the murder. He wouldn't let on that he was affected by any of it. He saw the nurse's station approaching, and he slowed his pace to virtually non-motion, so as to read the chart. The nurses were buzzing about the commotion that had occurred on the third floor.

"I told you the way would be shown to you if you were just patient," his father lectured. "You can trust in me, Son. You can always trust in me. You can't trust any of these people. Most of them aren't even real. Most of them are mannequins. Just spies that work for *them*. For the people who want to kill you and stop all of the good work we're going to do. Is that what you want? Of course not! That's why you did the right thing!"

"Murderer!" an amalgam of voices said. The smell in the hospital was overwhelming. Everywhere he went there were rotten eggs or overwhelming perfumes. He didn't know if he could take the smell anymore without throwing up.

"Murderer!" the voices screamed relentlessly. Someone touched him on his back, pushing him to go faster. As he approached the target room, he read the name on the chart and found what he was looking for:

Patient: Joe, John
Status: Critical
Room: 513

Cameron moved in a hastened step. "Murderer!" the voices cried at him again. He saw a picture of himself strangling John. He blinked and noticed that his heart was pounding profusely. *Why am I scared?* he thought as a bright light opened through the ceiling and shone upon him. His father descended out from it and hovered above his head. Instantly the image disappeared, and he saw himself strangling John again.

"I'm still here," his father said as Cameron entered John's room. "Do what you have to, Son! Don't let me down like you always did when I was alive. If you hadn't always let me down, I might not be dead. I might not've killed your mother that night. Don't disgrace me in my death as you did in my life!"

Maybe I'll pretend to be asleep again until the time is right, Cameron thought. He exited John's room and then walked by it several times. Stopping, he turned again and peeked around the corner. *No cops,* he thought, taking a step into the room.

"Murderer!"

Cameron stopped and covered his ears for a second, straining his face. "Shut up!" he whispered, unable to quiet the voices. He reentered the room and walked over to John's bed and looked at him sleeping.

"Do it now, Son!" his father pressured.

"Murderer!" the voices screamed. Cameron dry-heaved at the putrid smell of his mother's perfume mixing with the spoiled eggs.

"No, I'm not going to do it this time!" he said.

"Yes you are!" his father commanded. Cameron stood, unsure what to do. His mind told him to do it, but for some reason he couldn't seem to get his hands up. His whole body felt numb, emotionless. However, strangely, at the same time, he experienced what he considered must be the full range of emotions: fear, anger, lust, hatred, love, apathy, indifference. His head throbbed, and he clasped his hands around his temples and pushed as hard as he could into his head. *Stop it!* he screamed in his mind as he heard the cacophony of sounds mingling together with the smells, sights, emotions, and feelings to form a grand mosaic of aversive sensory experience.

Slowly he let his hands drop from his temples and fling off his face, suspended in the air over the comatose patient's exposed neck. Fighting himself, he felt his father's hands surround his own, forcing them into a cupping shape. Slowly his father forced Cameron's hands downward toward the victim's soft flesh. Feeling the warm skin under his cuticles and the fat rolls in between his fingers Cameron felt a rush of excitement and shame at the same time. His body was on fire, and his mind raced faster than he could keep up. It was almost like he was far distant from the scene, watching someone else perform the act but feeling all of the emotions to be felt himself.

Bearing down hard, he brought his face up against John's and began intensely closing off John's air passage, looking deeply into John's vacant face. Suddenly John's eyes opened, and a look of fear pierced through the air and into Cameron's center. Cameron felt John grab his hands as he released his grip around his neck and took a step backward, his heart racing so fast he thought it would soon explode. John raised his head a little with what appeared tremendous effort, his eyes still gazing upon the trembling Cameron. He opened his mouth and spoke in a low but sustained tone. "Leave me alone." After several seconds, John's head slumped back into unconsciousness on his pillow.

"Get out of here! Get out of here! Get out of here!" screamed the voices.

"They're coming to get you!" his father screamed to Cameron. Cameron grabbed his chest and gasped for air. His hands and arms uncoordinated, he pulled his blanket back over his head and, using all of his strength, raced outward toward the stairwell.

CHAPTER FIFTY-SIX

Doctor Haddelby knocked quietly on the open door to John's room, causing a tired Addy to turn her head in curiosity. Upon seeing the old man, her face lit up, and she flashed a warming smile. "Professor? What a surprise! Come in, come in."

The old man crept slowly forward, taking off his hat and holding it with both hands in front of his chest. "Ms. Siwel, I hope I'm not intruding. I phoned your home, and Mr. Bowku said I might find you here. I should've come earlier, but I didn't want to—"

Addy waved him off and made a spot for him on the couch opposite the chair on which she was sitting. "Nonsense. I'm very flattered you're here."

"How is Mr. Joe?" Haddelby asked. Addy looked over at her unconscious friend, glancing at his heart monitor and IV.

"I don't know. They're not sure if he's gonna make it," Addy said. The two sat in silence as thirty seconds faded away.

"How are you?" Haddelby asked.

Addy considered the question for some time. "Honestly?" she started, looking up at the old professor. "I don't know."

Haddelby cracked a subtle smile. "Would you believe me if I said I know the feeling?" Addy tilted her head and looked at the floor momentarily before returning her gaze to the aged professor's eye level.

"You mean, your wife?" Addy questioned to which Haddelby gave a singular nod.

"I have been meaning to apologize to you for that. Do you know that in forty-two years no one has ever actually approached me about why I was drinking at that bar? I guess when it happened people were too uncomfortable to ask, and then, over time, I just became another drunk passing a lonely night away."

"How can that be when you're so well known?"

"Oh, my darling, academic fame is not real fame. And that bar was far out of the city boundaries for a traveling professor. But enough about me. Really, I want to know, how are you?"

Addy shrugged her shoulders and fought the tears. "Like I said, I don't know how to answer that." Haddelby dropped his head and stared at the ground. With small effort, he made his way to the chair Addy had cleared for him and dropped his weight atop the cushioned seat.

"Addy, I'll be honest with you. I'm not going to have any great words of insight and wisdom here. But I can take a guess as to how you're feeling."

Addy felt a lump building in her throat. "How's that?"

"Well, just what any human being would feel. Confused, alone, misunderstood. Unable to block the images and thoughts from pouring in. Trying to keep the unwelcome experience from re-traumatizing you anew every day."

Addy struggled but lost the battle over an initial tear displacement. "Okay. You're pretty good at this."

"Do you mind if I ask what happened? I mean, I saw the news report, and the dean informed me you were involved. But I'm still not sure I understand. You fell off the Garberville Gap?"

Addy looked over at John's comatose face then back at the professor. "Honestly, I don't know exactly what happened. One minute we're just driving, and the next thing you know I'm waking up in the hospital. I mean, I don't even know if I can tell you what occurred in between. They keep making me talk about it, but would you know what I meant if I said the details seem to get more fuzzy the more I talk about it?"

"Yes, I think I would know exactly what you meant."

The two sat exchanging niceties back and forth for the better part of twenty minutes, Addy trying to fill in details and describe the difficult yet peculiar ease with which she and Merci had been recovering.

"Well, that's life for you," Haddelby advised, "just when you think you've got a handle on something. Just when you think you know how to react. *Boom!* Something grabs you, and you just don't know what to do with it. I wouldn't worry about the *right* way to react. You'll figure it out in time."

Addy nodded her head in agreement. "You know what bothers me the most? People keep treating me like I'm disabled or something now. Yet I don't feel disabled. In fact, I don't feel sad at all, just bitter. And I keep thinking to myself, be grateful for what you have. Be grateful for your life. But deep down inside all I can think is why did this happen to me? What did I do to deserve this?"

Haddelby leaned forward in his chair and put a hand on Addy's shoulder. "What did you do to deserve this? Nothing. You did nothing to deserve this. It was just random chance."

Addy looked at the floor to gather her thoughts

then leaned back, causing Haddelby's arm to disconnect from her shoulder. "You're the first person I've talked to who's said that."

"What, that it was random chance? Hmm, how very interesting. What has everybody else said?"

Addy shrugged her shoulders. "I don't know. It's different, but all the same as well. Everyone just keeps saying it was a miracle."

"A miracle?"

"Yeah."

Haddelby sported a strange look on his face. "Well, why would they say that? What's miraculous about being run into, falling a thousand feet or so, then waking up in the hospital all mangled? I don't think there is any miracle in that."

"Well, I guess they keep saying that we should've all died. Especially since it was so steep. I mean, what're the odds of that happening? And the way Merci and I recovered I'm told is extremely unusual—the way we're able to move around again and talk so quickly, coming out of comas and stuff functioning. I mean, how else do you explain all that? There's just no way."

Haddelby shifted in his chair. "Look, Addy, I don't want to corrupt your optimism, but the truth is that while I don't know what the odds are, you and Merci are living proof that there are odds. Science doesn't know everything yet, and probably never will. We are too barbaric to give ourselves the time to figure it all out. But every year somewhere in the world someone wakes up after being pronounced dead, or after thirty minutes without breathing, or someone falls off a cliff and lives. My lands, people have even been skydiving and their parachute fails to open, but still they live. Sure, they may break every bone in their body, but they still live, right? Miracles? Sure, I guess, if you want to call them that. But then what of the thousands and even millions of rapes and murders and acts of violence? If God supplies the miracles, then he must also supply the murderers. And why the murderers? Wouldn't it be easier to just take them all away? I mean, if there were no tragedies, there wouldn't need to be any miracles, right? So what's the point of a miracle? What is the function of tragedy? What do we learn from you being miraculously saved from certain death? That God has the power to save people after he savagely destroys them? That doesn't make any sense, now does it? So you or they may say miracle, but I say random chance. But I'm glad random chance was on your side, Addy."

Addy swallowed the lump in her throat and thought about what the old professor was saying. She had to admit it made some sense, but she didn't know. So much had happened; it would have to be a lot of random chance if it was probability and not God. Still, people win the lottery. Random chance happens. She looked over at John, wondering if he would wake up. She stroked his casted arm and thought of his efforts to save her and Merci. *Did you do all that for random chance?*

CHAPTER FIFTY-SEVEN

Chief Murphy looked blankly at the news report, vacantly gazing at the squawking news figure presenting the top stories in his polished suit and hairstyle.

"Police are still investigating the accident at the site of the Garberville Gap," the reporter began as a picture of the burning cars was replayed courtesy of a media helicopter covering the incident. "Police Chief Frank Murphy argued that while all signs point to an accident, they're still considering other possibilities. Murphy admitted to frustration with the case, as the chief suspect, Ms. Sally Strathers, passed away last week as the result of massive internal hemorrhaging. The police are continuing to request assistance in locating a person of interest they believe may have useful information. The unidentified male was seen seconds before the crash by two survivors of the incident, who indicated that the man had run out in front of their vehicle seconds before they collided with a Geo Metro, which had been reported stolen some three months prior."

Chief Murphy clicked off the set and sat for a while in the silence of his home. "Hemorrhaging!" he finally grumbled underneath his breath.

He didn't believe the hospital report at all regarding Sally Strathers's death. It seemed uncanny to him that the woman happened to die as the scuffle in the waiting room had occurred. It just seemed too interesting to him that the hospital didn't have any tape running at that time either. Smelled like a strategy for avoiding lawsuits to him. No matter, it wasn't like anything else was going his way anyhow. What did they have? Great circumstantial evidence that Cameron Bo was a killer. But why? The whole murder plan made no sense to Murphy, and if he couldn't even sell himself on a motive, he sure wasn't going to call the deputy attorney general and make a formal request. Still, there had to be something. He simply could not get this case out of his mind, no matter what he did. And the feelings were only getting more intense.

Reaching over to the nightstand, he grabbed the composite sketch from Merci's and Addy's descriptions. He noted the symmetrical features and towering presence of the image. *This doesn't look anything like Cameron Bo,* he thought, looking at the file photo of Bo. Still the only thing that made any sense was that Bo had run out in front of the speeding station wagon, hoping the vehicle would lose control and become a prime target. Or alternatively, that he'd hired someone else to do it while he was the driver. *What a stupid murder plan!* Murphy marveled within himself. *How can I go to the DAG with something this harebrained? It doesn't make any sense! After all, even if Cameron had hired someone to run out in front of the car to set up the Geo, who would be stupid enough to volunteer for that job? It was almost certain death! And even if someone would volunteer to do it, what idiot in the world would use a Geo Metro? The car's like tin foil!*

Murphy tossed the pictures on the table and leaned back in his recliner while watching the flames of the fire flickering in the hearth. *This whole case is ridiculous,* he thought as he let his upper eyelids meet their lower counterparts. In the other room, he could hear Lucy snoring softly. He thought of his son sleeping down the hall. *This is so stupid; I just need to give it up. That's what central wants anyway, and all the guys think I'm being superstitious. But still, what're the odds this stolen car gets in this accident with these people?*

The crackling fire and the stillness of the night air massaged the chief's senses as his bodily position became increasingly relaxed. His head fell forward onto his chest, and his right arm hung lifelessly off the armrest. He drifted into unconsciousness as he listened to his breath quietly entering and exiting his nasal cavity. From far away he could hear the crackling of the fire and screaming of voices. The image traveled closer and became frighteningly real. His whole visual plane was aglow with flickering fire strands and popping chemicals. He felt uneasy and sweaty and gasped for air amid the horrible scene. He called out for help, but he was only answered by more intense heat. Looking through the blaze, he saw the tops of pine trees swaying in the frozen wind. Snow fell from some of the majestic pines into the blaze where the chief was beginning to melt within the fervor.

With all of his physical faculties, he thrashed about in the fire, trying to climb out somehow, when suddenly his body took flight and he was lifted away from the scene out of a sunroof of a vehicle he had apparently been inside. Hovering over the crash site, he watched as the flames grew higher and more intense until finally the whole scene was as bright as the eye could imagine. Chief Murphy watched in horror as two others struggled in the blaze. *Save them!* Murphy pleaded, looking around for help. He tried moving from his position in the air, but that was useless. *Please, someone, save them from dying!* the chief asked again to the vacant sky. Down below he could see human feet and legs and hands boiling and burning to nothing, the sight's awfulness only superseded by the haunting and eerie moans coming from the immersed victims.

"Help me!" one of them called out toward the chief.

"I can't! I'm stuck here!" the chief answered pathetically, beginning to cry.

"Help me! Please!" the voice from the fiery scene demanded again.

"Someone help 'em. Call the fire department! Call the police!" Murphy begged to no one.

"You are the police. Help me. Find me! Save me!" a voice pleaded from the center of the roasting vehicle.

There's nothing I can do, the chief languished from his aerial position, his tears falling far below him to the ground.

"Yes there is. You can save me. You can save us both!" the voice said as the burning victims shot their boiling arms out into the night air and began to climb up a rope the chief was suddenly hanging from.

"Stop! Get away from me!" the chief ordered as he tried to climb higher on the rope. The burning victims were gaining on him fast. With ease the top victim reached the chief's position and grabbed his pant leg, the searing heat burning a hole through Murphy's leg.

"Save us!" the voice thundered as the victim climbed up the chief's legs, waist, stomach, and shoulders. "Save me!" the voice demanded again as it put its face up to the chief and looked him right in the eye. The chief screamed as he looked into the face of Cameron Bo. The face was bright and splintered, threatening to burst. Murphy let go of the rope and fell speedily downward into the open sunroof.

"Ah!" the chief said, jerking his body up on the recliner and looking into the hearth. Sweat fell heavily from his brow into his eyes, and his heart thumped wildly in his chest. Wrestling himself off his seat, he grabbed his jacket and cap and raced through the kitchen, looking for his car keys. Finding the keys, he slipped on his flip-flops and flung himself through the garage door and toward his car. Anxiously fumbling his keys, he turned the engine and forced the stick into reverse, stopping only long enough to shift before racing out into the nighttime landscape. Hardly a car was on the street, and Murphy's mind was racing faster than his cruiser.

"C'mon!" he yelled angrily at the off-ramp sign, which signaled his exit would be available in two miles. As the off ramp approached, Murphy cut a harsh right, leading the car down the worn side street and into the anterior of the police station. Blasting open his car door, Murphy bolted out of the car, across the entryway, and into the building toward his office, ignoring everyone looking his direction. He readied his keys for his office door and thrust them in as soon as his reach would allow him to contact the keyhole.

"C'mon!" he grumbled as the key refused to turn. He jiggled the knob several times, and the handle awkwardly turned a centimeter to the left, unlocking the door latch and allowing Murphy to burst into his office. Tossing his jacket off and slapping on the light, Murphy crazily searched through his working file folders and located a modest-sized manila folder entitled "Cameron Bo."

"C'mon! C'mon!" he repeated as he frantically thumbed through the loose papers and note pages. Finally he found the paper he was looking for and snatched it away from the main pack.

"Local vehicle plunged off the Garberville Road ... two individuals presumed dead ... coroner confirms ... bequeathed estate ... "

"No!" the chief uttered under his breath, going back and rereading the introductory paragraphs.

"Local vehicle plunged ... the victim's names were Dominique and Tasha Bo, time of death 10:37 p.m., November 21."

The chief reread the line again and fell into his chair. November 21.

He reread it over and over. Setting the paper down, he searched through the stack of papers for the date of last year's Thanksgiving. Finding the current year calendar, he checked the date of Cameron's parents' accident against the date of the current accident and found what he was looking for.

He's a ritualist, the chief thought. *How could I have missed that?* He looked at the two dates again. *He's a ritualist! A ritualist! That's my motive. There it is. Right there, in black and white! How could I have been so stupid as to not have checked this before? He has a bad Thanksgiving and spends the next year planning out the next Thanksgiving. His parents somehow the first year, then the hooker the next. He figures out I'll be on to him, so he sells me the line about his car and wallet being stolen, plants the wallet at the scene just to dare me to call him in, and blames the whole thing on the girl.* The chief rubbed his hands across his face and then picked up the paper and checked the dates again. *Pretty gutsy, indeed,* the chief thought, shaking his head. *Except for one thing: I never believed your story, pal.* The chief picked up the phone and called dispatch.

"Dispatch."

"Judy, Murphy here."

"Up pretty early this morning, Chief. What can I do for you?"

"Time to bring in Cameron Bo. Put an APB out for this kid. Follow the plan we worked out when this whole fiasco began, all right? Send in Clancy and Smith to check his house first, have Ann contact the media, and tell all patrols to begin active search as they cruise. I want this kid picked up five minutes ago. Got it?"

CHAPTER FIFTY-EIGHT

John opened his eyes and tried to fight the feeling to go back to sleep. His body moved in awkward, involuntary mannerisms.

"John? John?" he heard from a far away place. It was a female's voice followed by a male voice.

"I think he's waking up," he heard the male voice say. The voice sounded as if it were underwater.

"He's doing it!" he heard the female voice say.

All was blurry, though he could see contrasting blotches of dark against a white surrounding. The blotches appeared to be moving up and down slightly and shifting from side to side.

"John? Can you hear me?" the male voice said again, now a little clearer. John felt the voice was familiar, but he couldn't place it right away. His head felt nauseous, and his arms and legs threatened to break through whatever was under him.

"John, keep it up. Don't go away!" the female voice commanded. All went dark again.

Two hours later he felt his sentience reviving.

"John?" the female voice from before said.

"That's right, bud, keep it up!" said the male voice. John tried to turn his head and look toward the direction of the familiar voice, but instead his right hand jerked spasmodically. He recognized it now. It was Merci's voice.

"Merci," he tried to say, but his mouth was difficult to open, feeling as if it was actually impossible to open. As he tried to speak, he felt a cool pool of liquid run out of his mouth and down his cheek.

"He's speaking! Did you hear that, Doctor? How about that? That's pretty good, buddy! Take your time. We've got all day!" Merci said.

John lay motionless for ten minutes or more.

"That's right, John, take all the time you need. We're not going anywhere. If you can understand that, blink your eyes or raise a finger or something."

John blinked his eyes. In response, psychedelic patterns of whites, yellows, and blues danced across his visual plane.

"All right, two points. Good for you," a new voice said. "John, you don't know me, but I know you very well. I'm Doctor Carter. I've been taking care of you. Blink again if you understand that," John blinked again with great effort.

"Okay, let me tell you what has happened. You were in a car accident. Do you remember that? Blink if you do." John blinked again.

"You're doing a great job. Now, we're going to take this nice and slow. You had an accident, and it was pretty bad, and it left you pretty banged up. The good news is we got you into the hospital before anything seriously damaging happened, and we've been able to fix you up pretty good. Okay?" the doctor explained and waited for another blink. John struggled to say something again, but he couldn't get his mouth to move in accordance to his wishes. His leg kicked slightly.

"Look, are you having some problems getting your mouth to work?" the doctor asked. John blinked several times. "Okay, well that's normal. It's going to take a while for you to start having a return of voluntary control, so don't strain yourself. You've been in a coma for a while now, and some of your muscles have atrophied slightly. But your brain scans show no damage to the frontal cortex or temporal lobes, and your musculoskeletal structure by and large is quite responsive. Simply put, I'm confident we can get you back on your way again, okay? But we're going to have to take it slow. You're doing good right now. All your vitals are good. I just wanted to let you know so you can enjoy your friends, without worrying why you can't move well. You don't seem to be paralyzed or anything like that, so enjoy listening to your friends, and I am going to grab a nurse so we can start some tests on you, okay?"

John blinked.

"Good, give me five minutes. Addy and Merci have both been very excited to see you. They come every day and have taken turns working your body out along with the physical therapist. You'll be in good hands," the doctor said as he left the room.

John looked up at the two blobs who were looking increasingly like recognizable human beings. "Hi, John," Merci said, grabbing his hand and pulling a chair up to his face. "We've missed you, buddy. Welcome back."

"Welcome back," Addy said, grabbing John's other hand and placing her hand on his cheek. John looked into Addy's eyes as a drop of liquid escaped from his tear duct and ran down his face.

CHAPTER FIFTY-NINE

John finished off the applesauce and grape juice the nurse had wheeled in moments before. "Mr. Joe, you do seem to have a healthy appetite today," the nurse said as she strolled in through his open door.

"That's 'cause all you ever give me is the rehashed crap! I'm starvin' here!" John said, shoving the tray away from his body. "I told you, I don't need baby steps back to manly food. I want it now! How about one of those tasty Salisbury steaks the hospital is surely famous for?"

"No can do. Whether you're feeling good about it or not, Doctor Carter said no to solid foods right now. And you may have noticed that I'm a nurse, not a doctor. That means I do what he wants because then I won't get fired or sued for practicing medicine without a license."

"Well, all you evah gonna be is a nurse with that attitude," John said.

"Well, all you evah gonna be is dead with *that* attitude. Miracle recovery or not, I'll take your life in an instant if you give me lip."

"You sure you weren't supposed to be a shrink or something? You really have a way with people, you know?"

The nurse laughed. "I'll think about that. Hey, you need anything else, you just gimme a holler. Now try to rest up, okay?" the nurse instructed as she dropped her hand on John's shoulder momentarily before departing out of the open door. John reached back with his functional arm and adjusted the pillow behind him. With care he maneuvered the small pocket of cotton downward toward his middle back and then slowly tipped his body backward, careful not to rub the pillow with his back so as to misalign the position. *No!* He groaned within himself as he uncomfortably fell upon the pillow that was leaning awkwardly too far to the side.

"Can I help?" a woman's voice offered from the direction of the door. John looked up curiously, his bewildered face quickly breaking into a smile.

"Hey, you. Have a penchant for the physically handicapped or something? This makes three visits in three days," John joked to Addy, who made her way across the tiny room and pulled John's pillow to the center.

"That better?"

"Perfect," he said, letting an oversized breath out and relaxing into the pillow. He pulled his sheet up over his chest and turned his head toward his visitor. "So really, what brings you up here today?"

Addy pulled a chair up to John's side. "I don't know, just kept thinking you could probably use some company, that's all." Addy reached up and caught John's hand, carefully intertwining her fingers with his. John felt aroused and uncomfortable. He considered if he should address this finally.

"So what's with the hand thing? Finally come to your senses about that Merci guy?" John said, immediately embarrassed as the words departed his lips. Addy's face grew flush, and she quickly withdrew her hand and retreated it into her lap.

"You know, I'm sorry. I didn't even think about it. I guess I just got so used to doing that when you were in a coma that it's just automatic for me now. I'm sorry. Didn't mean to make you feel uncomfortable."

"Don't be," he said, maybe a little too quickly.

Addy smiled and looked down at her lap for a moment.

"John, I don't know how to say it, but I think you deserve to hear something. So I'm just going to say it, and if you ever try to talk to me about it again, I'll probably deny that we had this discussion, but I really don't think I can just not say this to you. So hear it is, okay?"

"Okay…"

"It's just—I know what you did for us. The police figured it out when you were sleeping, and besides, I read your statement to Chief Murphy after you woke up. You know, about saving m—," Addy lost her ability to speak momentarily as she choked on the emotions behind the words, "mine and Merci's lives. It was an incredibly brave thing that you did, and I don't think anyone has ever done anything that nice for me before."

Fighting tears, John awkwardly reached out to touch her face, and Addy responded by bringing her head onto his chest, which caused significant pain to John, but he didn't care. Addy let the tears flow wildly from her eyes, dampening John's gown.

"It's okay, it's okay. You weren't ever supposed to know about that. It's okay," he assured her as he ran his hand through her hair and fought a crying response more intensely. *Truth is, no one has ever done something like this for me before,* he thought as he looked at the sobbing woman distraught over the issue. He struggled to adjust himself and turn off the sexual impulses and feelings he was having. *Not now, John. Turn it off!* he ordered himself as he wiped a tear from his eye. After a long time, the two of them ceased crying and held each other silently.

"John," Addy finally said, "Can I ask you a question?"

"Sure," John said. Addy pulled herself off his chest and wiped her face down with her sleeve.

"Why did you do it? I mean, I know I've said some things, and … I mean, I know I haven't been that great to you. Why did you do it?"

John bristled at the direct confession. It made him sad. Moreover, he thought solemnly about the simple question and was unsure how to respond. "Well, actually, the truth is that I didn't really think about it. I don't know. The whole night is kind of a blur to be honest. I know that's not a great answer."

"Well, why were you freaking out? I mean, you really had me scared. I've *never* seen you anywhere near what you were like that night, right before the accident. I mean, I know it sounds stupid, but I thought you were dying or something. I didn't know what to do."

"I don't know. I wasn't dying, obviously, I just. I don't know. We were drivin' up the road, and all of a sudden I just got the most evil feeling, like something bad was coming our way, and I knew it. I just knew it! I actually didn't say anything for a long time because I knew it was so stupid. But I couldn't hide it. And besides, when I saw that creepy guy in the middle of the road, I knew something had to be wrong."

"Yeah, he was creepy," Addy said. "It's even creepier that the police think he was part of the plot to come after us. What do you think about that?"

"Honestly, I don't know. None of it makes sense to me."

"Me either. I mean, what kind of murder plot is that anyway? To just run in front of a car so they drive off the cliff?"

"Yeah, well, it's stupid, but it's smart too. Think about it. You run out in front of a car, chances are they're going to swerve, and when they do, they go off the cliff. There's virtually no way they're going to link it to you. Besides, on that curve, I bet nine out of ten cars jump the cliff before they can really put on the brakes. So in a way, it's like the perfect murder."

"Yeah," Addy said, dropping her head and looking silently at the ground. Outside the room a nurse called a doctor on the P.A. system. "Can I ask you another question?"

"Of course," John answered.

Addy looked deep into his eyes. John observed the redness in her eyes, and he felt pity for her. "Do you really believe what the police are saying about Cameron? I mean, do you really think he would try to kill us? What is that? What did we ever do to him? I just don't buy it."

John looked away from Addy and fixed his gaze on the ceiling tiles. "You know, honestly, if there is one thing I've learned in this world, it's that people do mean things to all people. The good and the bad are not safe, and sometimes there's just no rhyme or reason."

The clock ticked steadily as John and Addy passed contemplative minutes. The gory scene of the accident and his two friends trapped in the broken wagon replayed endlessly in John's mind. The oddness of the man in the road, and especially how he thought he saw a whole bunch of people or beings warning him to turn around, hurt his brain. Was he hallucinating or were they real? If he hallucinated the first couple, then why did Merci and Addy see the third? But even then, he thought it was an angel or something where Merci and Addy just saw a guy in front of the car. Nothing seemed to be right in John's mind about any of it.

"Addy," John said, his eyes closing and his feelings frail and vulnerable.

"Yes," Addy said.

"Would you hate me if I asked you to hold my hand again?"

Addy silently reached up and grabbed John's hand and pulled it to her mouth. With a kiss she dismissed it from her face and guided it back to his bedside, where she clutched onto it until John passed into slumber.

CHAPTER SIXTY

"All right everyone, take your places," Chief Murphy ordered as he entered the conference room. "Look, we don't have a lot of time, and I'm starting to get increasing heat about this case, so I want to solve it now. Got it? So first, some real quick introductions and setup. For those of you not familiar with me, I'm Chief Frank Murphy. To my right and going around we have Officer Jones, who is my eyes and ears. Anything you want to run by me you first run by him. Next over is our clerical person, Nancy Waters. Next to her are Detectives Randall, McLachlan, and Milton. Right there we have our IT guy, Phillip Sanders, and finally our psychological criminologist, Doctor Jacobs. Now, intros over, let's talk real quick about what we *do* have. Jones, give everyone a shakedown."

Jones opened his mouth, "All right, everyone, here's what you should already know: on the night of interest, an eighteen-year-old Caucasian male named Cameron Francis Bo is believed to have caused a serious vehicular accident resulting in one fatality and three critically injured victims. Here's what you may or may not know; on September eighth, Mr. Bo reported his nineteen ninety-five Geo Metro stolen. Several weeks later, on October first, a similar vehicle was reportedly involved in a random shooting in the red light district off the northeast quadrant of town. Chief Murphy visited Mr. Bo personally at his home on October twenty-first and interviewed Mr. Bo face-to-face, where he found him effusive, guarded, and 'generally odd.'"

"How did you find him odd?" Doctor Jacobs interrupted.

The chief looked over at the well-groomed doctor and studied his navy blue double-breasted suit and plain yellow tie. "He didn't make a lot of sense. He rambled a bit. Gave vague answers. Seemed a little paranoid to me."

Jacobs nodded and returned his look toward Officer Jones.

"Since the beginning of fall, Chief Murphy has received several anonymous calls from a male in distress that appears to be psychotic. These calls have become increasingly disturbing. We believe these calls are from Mr. Bo. The most disturbing of these calls was probably the last, which came in on November twenty-seventh, because on this call he no longer appeared committed to regulating his actions. I will now play you that message." Officer Jones picked up the remote control for the compact disc player and depressed the play button. A breathy recording of the phone call emerged. For the first ten seconds, only indecipherable utterances could be perceived. Finally a male voice whispered on the line.

"Don't save me now, Chief. It's beyond repair. Don't save me now," Jones clicked off the CD player as the caller hung up the line.

"Pardon me for interrupting again, but why do you put these calls to Bo?" Jacobs inquired.

"Well, all I can say is years of experience," the

chief said. "Obviously, the voice output was too soft to make a direct discriminative association, but it just makes sense."

"Why?" Jacobs pressed.

"Well, this just seems to be this guy's M.O."

"Why would this be his M.O.?" Jacobs asked.

"Because he's nuts. He's lost his mind. He's playing games with us."

"I don't buy it. The way you're putting it together, you're painting this guy as a schizophrenic, and by definition, schizophrenic disorders preclude insight," Jacobs said. The group looked blankly back at him. "In other words, if he really is schizophrenic, he usually wouldn't know that he's schizophrenic and especially would not ask for you to save him, or warn you that he's losing his mind."

"So what's your point?"

"My point is that if the guy really is schizophrenic, he is not sophisticated enough to have an M.O. If he is really premeditating, then he's faking being schizophrenic; that's what I'm trying to say," Jacobs said.

"Well, why would he try to fake being crazy?" Officer Jones challenged.

"Insanity plea," Detective McLachlan offered.

"Not likely. I mean, it is a valid hypothesis, but in reality very few people make the insanity defense. Anyone doing their homework, as it would seem this guy had if he were feigning crazy, would have to know that," Jacobs said.

"So why would he do it, then? Fake it, I mean," the chief asked.

"I don't know. I'm not saying he did. I'm simply saying that it would be unlikely that someone in an acute schizophrenic psychosis would one, recognize the state of hallucinatory and delusional behaviors and thought; two, communicate it in a meaningful way; and three, cover his tracks well enough so as to functionally premeditate and complete a sophisticated murder plot. Finally, even if I'm wrong, and he did do all of that sophisticated work under an extreme form of schizophrenia, how did this psychotic killer manage to survive the scene and flee without evidence?"

"Well, he didn't," Detective Randall said. "His wallet was found at the crime scene."

"True, but according to the previously noted visitation report by Chief Murphy, Mr. Bo quote 'insisted that he could not produce his driver's license because it had been stolen by his prostitute.' A prostitute that Mr. Bo claimed was named Sal, which coincidently was the name of the female you found on site, involving the Geo Metro that Mr. Bo reported she had stolen," Jacobs said.

"What are you, his defense lawyer?" McLachlan said.

"No, just a psychologist who doesn't believe it does the cause any good to surmise the tenets and facts of a case on weak theorizing. Now here's what I think. I think Mr. Bo *did* attempt to kill these people, but I do not think he's a serial killer or has an M.O. I think he's flying by the seat of his pants, and while I don't think he's schizophrenic, per se, I do think he is crazy—although not schizophrenic—and that is precisely why he is so elusive."

"I'm not following you," McLachlan said. "What're you saying in laymen's terms?"

"Look, my objection is that you're trying to paint this guy as the Hollywood schizophrenic. There are all kinds of psychotic disorders, and schizophrenia is just one of them. But to say someone is schizophrenic and has the insight to have an M.O. is preposterous. On the other hand, this guy is random in his actions and obviously disturbed, and that can be a form of psychotocism, just not schizophrenia in this case. So my first objection is that we need to be clear on our terms. Now my second beef is that if he is psychotic, then your setup is wrong and you have to throw out your thinking as normal. You just can't proceed with normal investigation techniques on someone who is a violent psychotic. You can't use criminal thinking to account for the actions of the insane. It ain't gonna work that way. That's what I'm trying to say. Some things in life are logically illogical."

"So you're saying there's no rhyme or reason to all Bo's doing?" Murphy said.

"No, I'm saying there's no *criminal* logic behind his actions. But I think there is plenty of psychotic rhyme and reason for what he's doing."

Murphy leaned back in his chair and threw his hands on top of his head. "I don't know if I accept your logic. Criminal is criminal. If he is crazy, then why is he breaking the law? There are plenty of ways to be crazy without framing a hooker for murder. I mean, are you trying to tell me he is innocent, that he has no idea what he is doing? That he's some victim of pretend thoughts and beliefs? That he's just not able to control any of his behaviors? I don't buy that. I don't care how nuts people get, no one has to murder."

"Well, of course not. But murder is only murder based on the way we think about the justification for murder. Murder is a made up construct of society. The actual behavior we call murder is simply ending a life, and that is something that happens all the time, for various justifications. Sixteen million soldiers in Hitler's Germany took the lives of millions of Jews, but they wouldn't call it murder because they thought it was justified by God. Millions of Native Americans were murdered and displaced by European-American settlers who felt it was justified. The point is criminal behavior is only criminal if the criminal knows it. If it is a game of cloak and dagger. If it is for the rush of breaking laws or effecting gain at the expense of your own accepted societal rules. And Cameron Bo doesn't seem to have anything to gain for what he is doing. In fact he was a good kid, wealthy, honor student, religious, extremely intelligent. This is not the profile of a sociopath. His life doesn't predict the kind of behaviors we think he is doing now. You are all simply approaching this the wrong way."

"Okay, suppose what you are saying is true. So what would we do different? What are you saying we are not doing, that if we did, our investigation would work? What is our action from this point out?" Murphy asked.

"Simple. Get in his head. Find out what makes him tick. Find out what he is running from, or running towards," Jacobs said. "In other words, accept that whatever Bo did, Bo had a logical reason in his own head for doing it, and that's what makes him very dangerous right now. If you do that, than maybe, just maybe you'll be lucky enough to find him before he finds some other helpless victim who has no idea who he or she is dealing with."

"But why would he be dangerous, if you're right? I mean, he already did whatever it was his crazy mind told him to. Sally Strathers is dead. He went after the college students. He did all the things under your theory his crazy mind should do. It should be over now," McLachlan said.

Doctor Jacobs leaned in close to the group and stabbed the table with his finger. "Oh, no. If my theory is true, then the fact that people didn't die that night means he will know that he didn't finish the job right. Essentially, if I'm right, he failed all over again, and this time I guarantee you there is no insight left. No conscience telling him he's crazy. In other words, he is now very, very dangerous because he is completely lost to his delusions and hallucinations. Whatever justification or buy-in to his craziness he had before, it is only likely to increase ten fold without therapy or medication. Right now, right at this very moment you should all be terrified about what this very dangerous man is capable of. If he could justify taking the lives of people he probably knew well and was probably friendly with, how much more should the rest of the world be worried, now that he is friendless and on his own, with only his private psychosis to rely on. I believe he tried to warn you of this himself," Jacobs said, leaning over and hitting the play button on the CD player.

"Don't save me now, Chief. It's beyond repair. Don't save me now."

CHAPTER SIXTY-ONE

Cameron lay shivering in between the large trash bins and watched the vagrants in the alley exchanging wine, humor, sexual favors, and aggression. It had been the same scene night after night, and he was learning more every second about who was good, bad, and unimportant.

"That one, right there," his father said. "That one is very bad. Yesterday he beat his child for drinking his last ounce of wine. No one should get away with that. You know that man is bad, don't you?"

Cameron agreed with his father telepathically, careful not to move his lips or his eyes for even a moment. That was important. He needed to remain unseen. Except for the involuntary shivers, he was completely invisible to everyone in the alley. At first, he'd thought it was impossible, but his father, as much as he hated to admit it, was correct. Somehow, the murder, and those several he had committed since, had given him more power. God had blessed him, probably because he was now more trustworthy. He had proven, night after night, that he could take the lives of the hopeless of the world of all ages and save them from themselves, or their horrible evils. He was brave enough to make decisions the rest of the weak world could not make. To assist God with the giving and taking of life. And because of this he could now be trusted with powers other persons couldn't, such as his invisibility cloak. Unfortunately, though, it only worked reliably on humans. The others could sometimes find him.

Stop it! he silently commanded his stomach as it growled into the frozen night air. Without moving his face or eyes, he checked his peripheral vision for any sign that the sound had given rise to suspicion he was being watched. No one bothered to look, however, causing Cameron to wonder if his sounds were also somehow muted from the rest of the world. No matter. He had a mission to perform, and when he got the sign from his father, he would know what to do, how to do it, and when. Until that time he'd have to simply wait.

Facets of his previous life would, at times, interrupt his focus on his mission. He remembered his warm bed, his relationship with Sal, and his love for his mother. Such thoughts could be of no use or goodness, however, and he simply needed to throw them out of his mind. He would never again have such a life, and he knew it. He was on God's errand now. And like the great prophets of the past—Paul, Peter, James, Moses—he must be tried.

He considered flying to another location. Several times when the workers of the restaurant had thrown away their trash he'd been worried about being detected, although his powers were too great for such mortals, and he knew it. He just needed to trust in himself, have some confidence, and all would be well. More scenes from his former life and of the accident in November flashed through his mind. He saw the image of Sal bloodied and bruised. He saw the picture they'd shown on the television screen in the restaurant with his face on it. He wondered if anyone would've recognized him had he not had on his invisibility cloak. Fortunately, he'd not been found. Certainly they would have punished him, as they do all prophets. They would have given him the chair, hung him, or lined him up in a firing squad. There is simply no way that anyone would understand the mission God had entrusted in him alone to execute.

A tear formed in his eye and made its way down his cold cheek. His thinking was flooded with memories of Sal. Her warm body, her soft face, her love of life and human interaction. His anger turned on these thoughts as he remembered her fornicating nature; her misery and trauma from her youth; her ignorance of right and wrong; and her tendency to perpetuate evil. From nowhere a demon told him she could have been saved, that she could have been remediated without death.

"Command that voice to be silent!" his father demanded. Cameron told his father through his mind that he did not have the power yet to silence demons.

He would simply have to allow them to speak with him, and he would prove that he was valiant enough to persevere even in the face of such treacherous rhetoric.

Far down the street a siren blared, and over the course of several minutes, the sound grew loud and nearer. As the fire truck passed, the flickering lights temporarily illuminated the alley, and Cameron could see that all had fallen asleep in his row. He would only need to wait several minutes to allow them to return to their slumber briefly interrupted by the fire truck, and then he could begin his scavenger hunt.

He didn't know how the others could survive. Being puny mortals they required sleep. All that Cameron required was a good source of fuel for his partially translated body. Sleep was no longer a requirement for him, although he sometimes elected to engage in sleep just because he enjoyed it.

After about ten minutes, he made his move. First, he'd test the waters and make sure no one was lying in wait for him. Having turned off the invisibility cloak, he slowly moved his eyes left to right. When no one moved, he opened and closed his mouth several times. Next, he let out a soft whisper. When no one responded, he then let out a loud whistle. Silence. It was time to move.

Carefully he stood up from his hiding place, positioning himself against the wall of the alley where possible. He was smart enough to only take about two steps every minute. He'd learned through sad experience several nights ago that the demons in the alley had sensors for anyone who took too many steps in too short of a time. Sliding his hands across the dirty brick exterior, he inched his way toward a man who'd passed out in the middle of a large pool of vomit. Carefully he opened the man's coat and found an empty bottle of whiskey inside. Reaching into the man's pockets, he pulled out a half-consumed granola bar the man had probably found in a trashcan. Cameron's stomach churned with disgust, and he thought of the many desirable vittles in his home cupboards and refrigerator.

"Forget about them," his father commanded. "They are part of another life now. And you should know better. You, like all of the great prophets, will be taken care of, but beggars can't be choosers, now can they? Unless they choose death."

Cameron's father put into his mind an image of Cameron being thrashed about by demons. He could hear himself screaming out in pain, his neck and body bleeding profusely from the attack. He then flashed to an image of himself burning in hell.

"Is that what you want?" his father asked. Cameron begged his father to keep him safe from such a fate. "Then eat the granola bar."

With that instruction so powerfully given, Cameron found it possible to ingest the bar, which reeked of halitosis and whiskey. He threw up a little in his mouth on the first bite but was able to keep it in long enough to swallow.

"You've done good, my boy," his father affirmed. Cameron moved on farther down the alley. He turned the corner and ventured down an adjunct alley toward another group of sleeping men. They were all huddled up with one another; their hands in their tattered parkas, trying to keep warm. Nestled in the middle of the several men was a large bag. Cameron knew that was where the demons liked to keep their power morsels. They would hide it there so no one else could see it.

With extreme care he leaned against the alley wall and stepped between their legs. Even though he knew it wouldn't help much, given his movements, he turned his invisibility cloak back on and spent several quiet minutes extending his arm out, grasping the bag, and slowly pulling it away from the group of men. Once he was a safe way down the alley, he ducked behind an unoccupied dumpster and rustled through the bag. In it he found a half-drunk soda bottle, a flask of wine, and several partially eaten sandwiches. He ate the sandwiches and drank the soda. He then stuffed the wine in his coat. Rummaging further through the bag, he found a few pairs of socks and a package of matches. He pocketed these items as well, moving one pair of socks over his cold hands.

Satisfied he'd found enough sustenance to last another day, he started the long walk back to his home.

Silently, and un-lauded by the world for his heroic deeds, he slipped back between the restaurant dumpsters and stared at the curious galactic symbol on the wall of the dumpster opposite where he lay. He found it appropriately distracting to follow the several circles endlessly looping around the centered dot, and he imagined the gratitude he would receive in the next life for the sacrifices he was making.

"You have done well," his father said as Cameron stared through unflinching eyes at the cold metal wall.

CHAPTER SIXTY-TWO

Through the large black speakers, an endless sea of yuletide melodies blared to the delight of all in the room. The fake Christmas tree with its blinking lights and decorative ornaments dazzled the visual senses of the three friends as they laughed, joked, and felt the presence of one another. Through all that happened, they had developed an understanding of one another—an identity. John had never felt an identity with anyone before, and he really liked it.

"I'm glad you guys came here tonight," John admitted, leaning back in his chair and observing the mess around the room. They'd spent the better half of the afternoon watching movies, opening cheap presents, playing cards, and eating pizza. The signs of habitation were everywhere.

"We're glad we came too," Merci affirmed, leaning forward to slap the side of John's legs a couple of times. The three friends sat in silence listening to Bing Crosby crooning a vintage version of "I'll Be Home for Christmas."

"I don't want Christmas to be over," Addy whined, snuggling her head deeper into Merci's chest as she half sat and half laid upon him.

"Me either," John agreed. Strangely he'd been enjoying himself this Christmas season, which was odd, since he didn't celebrate the day on the twenty-fifth of December as he should have. Christmas had been over for two weeks actually, but John, Addy, and Merci decided it might be therapeutic for them all to formally recognize the holiday together. And John was particularly touched when Addy had suggested they have their private get-together at John's place. As Bing Crosby held on to the final note in his master-piece, Addy sat up and wore a face of determination.

"All right, I don't want to ignore this anymore. Why have we never talked about it together?" she asked, stirring the lazily draped men from their relaxed positions.

"Talked about what?" John asked, looking over at Merci then back at Addy.

"Ah, come on. I don't want to play dumb anymore. We've never talked about it, and you know exactly what the 'it' is that I'm talkin' about. That night. That guy."

"Okay, someone's a little random tonight," Merci said.

"Yeah, well, I'm random every night, so what? I wanna know. Why don't we ever speak about it together? We haven't even talked about it once?"

John shifted in his recliner. Throwing his left hand up over his head, he unloaded a heavy breath and scrunched his face. Truth was he didn't know why he never brought up the issue to Merci or Addy. He guessed he felt a little stupid about it. It wasn't his most flattering moment when he began to have a heart attack and see things. Then when he had seen the sketch of the unidentified man composed from Merci and Addy's description of the guy they saw, he had a sobbing breakdown right in front of them. Since that time, none of them had spoken of the experience. It was as if they all knew it was out of bounds. Something accepted but not spoken; not to the police, not to the press, and definitely not to each other.

"What was it?" Addy asked. No one moved. "Seriously, what was it?"

"What do you mean 'what was it?'" Merci asked.

"Look, I don't want to pussyfoot around this anymore. What was that thing? Was it a man, or..." Addy said.

"I don't know," John said. The fire crackled. John let his gaze drift from the fire to the stockings lying randomly in front of the tree. Carefully he read the names and smiled big when he saw the stocking Addy had made for him. The log popped, and a spit of fire shot out from the hearth but was stopped by the metallic screen propped on top of the brickwork.

"Well, what exactly do you want to say about it?" Merci asked.

"I don't know—I don't have any plans. I just think, you know, that it's stupid we can't talk about it. I mean, the three of us survived some kind of attack I guess, and then recovered together, and have basically spent every moment together since, but we can't talk about the—"

"Attack?" Merci said. "I still don't know if I buy that. That whole theory just seems too farfetched to me."

"What's so farfetched about it? People attack each other somewhere in the world every day," Addy said.

"Sure, but by *car?* And by random ramming? How does that make any sense?" Merci asked.

"Well, Murphy thinks Cameron's crazy. So it doesn't have to make sense," John said.

"Fine," Merci continued, "the murder doesn't have to make sense, because he's crazy. But *the way he tried to murder* is what doesn't make any sense. I mean, how did he know it was us? What, was he following us? How did he just *happen* to ram into our car? There could've been any number of people on the road at that time."

"Well, but I told you I saw the Geo pass us when we started the incline to the Garberville Gap. He shot past us, and that's such a deserted road, he must've correctly figured it'd be us when he turned around and saw the headlights," John said. "Besides, it was his idea we go to Garberville in the first place. He obviously knew what he was doing."

"I don't know, I still have a hard time buying it. That's just too farfetched," said Merci. "Why not ram us from behind or something? That's what makes sense."

"Why must you have everything in the world make sense? There's a lot in the world that doesn't make sense," John said. "Why did the *Challenger* blow up the very first time a schoolteacher rode it? Why did the *Titanic* have to have just one extra hull breached than was permissible? Why did the radio operator have to fall asleep during the Pearl Harbor raid? Why did so many people just happen to not get on the airplanes when they had no good reason during the 9–11 attacks? Things happen. Why can't you just accept that it was a shoddy plan from a crazy person that happened to work out?"

"Because that's stupid. That's too much of a leap of faith. How did he know we'd be spun out? How did he *know* the car was ours? What? Did he, like, have the greatest calculator in the world, that could, like, pinpoint our exact location?"

"How did he know the car was ours? He passed us. He knew exactly where we were. Besides, who knows? He could've had a homing device. You can buy those practically at cost now on the Internet. I'm sure he had some way. Why does it matter?" John said.

"Fine. But even if it was a homing device, how in the world did he know we'd be spun out exactly as we were? How would he know *the precise* moment to come and ram us? And even then, why would he do that? He was likely to die! Wouldn't he try to kill us in a less dangerous way for himself?" Merci said.

"Well, like was said. He's crazy. He probably thought he wasn't going to die. It probably wasn't thought out well. And maybe..." Suddenly John found himself hesitating.

"Maybe what?" Merci asked.

"Maybe he never planned to hit us broadside," John said. The three sat quietly, contemplating the thought.

"You mean he planned to ram us head on? Why

would he do that?" Merci asked. "That just doesn't make any sense."

"Sure it does. That's what makes the most sense. I mean, think about it. Like you said, how did he know we were going to spin out? *We* didn't even know we were going to spin out until you swerved to miss the ... " John grew frustrated with himself as he found himself hesitating again.

"Well, but that's the point," said Merci. "That's why Murphy thinks he knew to hit us broadside. He ran out in front of us to make us swerve, then his girl-friend rammed us. That makes some sense."

"How does that make any sense?" Addy said. "How did he know we would swerve and stall for his girlfriend? A thousand different things could have happened. We could've just run off the road. We could have just swerved slightly and missed him. We could have run into the mountain wall. I think it makes no sense at all that way."

"Well, I think *none* of it makes sense. Like I said in the first place, maybe it was just a random accident. How else do you explain it? It just defies all of the laws of science!" Merci was fuming.

"And maybe that's the point," Addy said. Merci gave her a strange look. "I'm dead serious. Maybe that's the entire point. Like John was saying, this accident is too weird to be true. Maybe God wanted people to take notice. Maybe he has some sick and twisted plot to inflict upon us all, for his entertain-ment or something."

"Why does it have to be sick and twisted?" John asked.

Addy shrugged.

"I don't know," John argued, still trying to process Addy's interpretation. "I don't believe God chose Cameron to be crazy. I don't believe God forced Cameron to murder. I don't think God forces anyone to do anything like that. Maybe what happened just happened, and God tried to help in the least intrusive way possible."

"What are you even talking about?" Merci grumbled.

"I'm talking about God. Maybe he knew that we were all going to die. I mean, what're the chances of living through a head-on collision? The stats grow exponentially worse, right? Maybe that's why he sent … "

"Sent what?" Addy asked quietly.

"I don't know," John faltered. "Maybe that's why he sent someone to help us. To stop us. Like a messenger or something."

"A messenger? I don't know. That's just a little too *Star Trek* for me," Merci said.

"Well, what about this isn't *Star Trek*?" John said. The group fell into a temporary truce. The holiday hits kept playing. John sank back in his chair. "Well, *Star Trek* or not, I'll say what none of us want to. I think it was an angel. Think about it. It had to be. We're driving along, and I get this foreboding feeling. Then I see someone point us the opposite direction. I see someone who was obviously trying to get us to turn around. Then I see him again. And then the third time, all of us see him. Look, I'm the last one who would just go for a divine explanation, but it's hard to deny! I think God was trying to help us. I mean, we are all alive, right? Plus..." The three friends sat in silence while John gathered more courage. "Plus, there's more."

"What more? More you never told us?" Merci asked.

John nodded his head and fought the urge to cry.

"Well, what is it?" Addy asked.

"That night. That night when you were both, you know, in the car. I had a...like I saw stuff. Stuff that was going to happen in the future." Addy and Merci looked back at John, whose face was now flush, incredulously.

"What do you mean? Like you had visions?" Merci asked.

"Well, I don't honestly know what I would call it. But I saw stuff about the crash, before it happened, before the Geo fell from the cliff. I saw in the wagon, before I got to it. I saw you guys in the wagon."

"What about us?" Addy asked.

"About you dying," John said. Addy and Merci answered his statement with a profound silence.

"Look, I... it was like this. I woke up on the bottom of that mountainside in so much pain, I can't even describe it. But beyond the pain there was a consciousness. A knowing that I had to do something to help you two. I..." John was red faced. He let out a huge breath. "Man! I really feel like such an idiot saying all of this!" Addy reached over and grabbed John's hand while also holding Merci's.

"Look, I was sitting down there feeling sorry for myself. I thought I needed rescuing just as bad as anyone, so when the … *voices* … told me to go help you, I first thought I must be going crazy. I knew there wasn't a God. I knew he couldn't then be talking to me. I knew I was just in an accident and figured I must be crazy, that's all. But it didn't stop at voices. There were feelings too. It was like, like this piercing knowledge that if I didn't try to save you, you'd both be dead, and somehow I knew I needed to act, or, I don't know. Or there would be consequences for me. Like, spiritual consequences."

Addy squeezed John's hand harder. "So what did you do?"

"Nothing, I just sat there, yelling and screaming for help. But no one came. It was the loneliest feeling in the world. And just as I was going to defiantly give up on the feeling, that's when I saw—"

"Saw what?" Merci asked.

"Saw the vision. Of you both dying. I saw the car falling on top of you. Of you burning up in it. And of me being respons—," John was now in a full cry. He tried to wipe his tears off with his broken arm at first, seeming to forget it was in a cast. The velocity with which he brought the broken arm to his forehead called for a small injury to his cranium, which caused him even more pain and suffering. Addy let go of Merci's hand and fully embraced John, stroking his head and telling him it was okay. Merci leaned forward, obviously unsure of what role he could play in comforting his friend but ultimately only wearing a clear look of concern on his face.

Time trickled by slowly, then in volumes as the three friends sat silently, watching the fire die. After several hours Merci had fallen asleep, and John thought Addy might have as well, until she broached the silence with a whispered query.

"John, if it was an angel, why do you think *we* didn't see it the first time, or even the second time that you saw it?"

"I don't know," he said, matching her soft voice.

"Why didn't God just send the angel into the car to explain to us the danger or to tell us to turn around? I mean, if he really wanted to save us, why didn't he make it easier, like by telling us the day before, or even on the way up, not to go?"

John hadn't really thought of that before. He didn't have a good response.

"Why didn't God write a letter, or give us dreams, or tell us in person, or send a relative, stranger, or friend, or even a prophet to warn us? If he has the power to send an angel, why wouldn't he just snap his fingers and make the whole accident go away and force Cameron to have not done what he did? I mean, if he can send an angel, couldn't he just not allow the accident to happen? I mean, like you said, maybe he *was* saving us from a head-on collision, but is a broadside hit where we then fall off such a steep mountainside really any safer than head on? Why make it so weird if God is involved? I mean, I'm not saying it wasn't; maybe it was. I dunno. But if so, what's the point? What're we supposed to learn from that? What is so important about giving us puzzle pieces that we have to figure out on our own? I mean, that doesn't make any sense! I happily admit that I'm inept! I happily admit that I'm helpless! Is it some sick and twisted game he has to play for his own horrible sense of humor to fill his time?"

The bitter dialogue hung in the night air above the two late-night philosophers in a paralyzed space-time continuum, until John could see Addy's eyes closed and hear her emit a light snore. He stared at her face, her bosom, her stomach. He felt a strong urge to violate her and began to tremor. His entire soul became uncomfortably aroused, angered, provoked, belittled, passionate, self-deprecating, lust driven, and self-loathing all at the same time. He so badly wanted to touch her, overcome her. He at times didn't know if he could contain his physiological arousal, which was uncomfortably in full force. Time began to move away from him. Soon an hour, then two circled the clock, and he could not shut down either his desire for flesh or his sense of shame. He reached out and touched Addy's skin, and his body shivered with both disgust and delight; although mostly disgust.

I can't do this, he thought, briefly moving his hand up her body. He adjusted his seating on his chair and let out a big breath. Silently, he paused and listened for a minute as her breathing became more shallow and asymmetric, and contemplated what to do. *Oh, God, please help me to do the right thing, I feel so lost and confused,* he thought, now frozen in between violation and retreat. *How do I stop myself from this?* he wondered, saddened at his pathetic state. In his mind he looked over at the picture of Jesus he had just purchased and hung on his wall several days ago. *If you really exist, and really love me, and if you went through all of the trouble to save our lives, why wouldn't you take this sin away from me?*

CHAPTER SIXTY-THREE

Chief Murphy dreamed of terrible and frightening images. He saw figures burning in horrific displeasure. He saw children weeping and being brutally dismembered and disfigured. He saw mothers crying and begging for their lives. He saw fathers drunk and passed out and being choked in the midst of their vomit and incapacitation. He saw demons, evil, darkness, blood, fear, and terror. And he saw himself running in a vacuous space of never-ending substance. An enigmatic figure of authority without grounding; theorizing and speculating without product and case.

He also had another recurring dream, which troubled and bothered him but which he could not make sense of. In each dream, every night, and for several weeks, he would conclude these disturbing dreams with an evil and foreboding feeling something was genuine about them, and in each case, the dream had ended with the exact same sequence. Murphy would find himself seeing the horrible and disfigured images, followed by superimposed blackness that gave way to incomprehensible form. The form would then materialize into organized patterns that began larger than life and then moved away from his sight, turning into a holistic image of twisting curves and circular rings that ultimately ended in a planetary image where he could see not only the planet and planet's moons but also the ring path of the moons. As the first planet moved away, invariably a second appeared on its left, followed by a haunting image of a disheveled Cameron Bo nestled in between the two systems.

The chief awoke from his current dream drenched in sweat and breathing heavily. He looked at the clock and grew angry at himself for being unable to sleep. It was only 1:17 a.m., and Lucy was lost to her more peaceful images, dreams, and slumbering sounds. She'd become very accustomed to Murphy's late-night issues and seldom woke up these days to ask him what was the matter. She, like he, simply agreed it was a strange gift he'd received from God from his childhood. They didn't question it, and Murphy knew God was trying to communicate to him through this media once again, but how?

The infamous "how" question was the troubling part. What was it he was to know? He brought himself up from the bed and moved into the kitchen, pouring himself a bowl of cereal and digging into the first crunchy bite. *What is it?* he wondered. *What is it you want me to know?* he thought again as he thumbed through his notebook on the Bo case. It'd been over a month and a half, and still no sign of Bo. The force would not allow him any more manpower to observe Cameron's house, although they had searched every inch of it for a third time several days ago and found no trace he had returned. And they wouldn't find any evidence he'd returned. Cameron was lost. Lost to himself and lost to the city. There was no denying Doctor Jacob's theories on this case. He had read many of the transcripts himself and knew he was right. Cameron was psychotic, and floridly psychotic people are either under the watchful care of loved ones, inpatients in a psych ward, or they are homeless.

The city estimated that there were at least two thousand homeless persons living across the west side bridge alone, and there was simply no way they were going to peruse them all for Bo, although the chief had tried numerous times. He was beginning to give up hope of ever solving the case. But every time he got closer to that conclusion, he swore that God turned up the heat in his dreams, his obsessing, and his focus that Bo was out there, at large, and very dangerous.

At one point he thought he had seen him when investigating one of the rash of fire victims in the west side sector. State police had convinced Murphy they had a traveling arsonist who sometimes liked to kill for fun. Always vagrants, and always women and children. There had been about ten in the last three weeks found dead. The problem was that they couldn't tie the murders together into a comprehensible fashion because sometimes the bodies were bludgeoned, but other times it looked as if they had died from natural causes and were simply burned, maybe by a fearful husband or lover who couldn't stand to see his loved one violated as corpses in the perverse underground world of vagrant vices.

Still, Murphy was convinced that these killings had something to do with Bo himself. Even if Bo was not, and frankly Murphy didn't believe Bo was, the perpetrator, the images of the victims and Bo's image had blended in his dreams, and to Murphy this was a message of which to take note.

Murphy examined some of his past scribbling and tried to make sense of emerging patterns or themes. "December 30: burned children, three, young, one mother, whiskey flask. December 31: elderly woman found bludgeoned to death. January second: two burned children, older, two women dead in conjoint alley."

The dreams just didn't make sense to him, and especially the planetary issue didn't make sense. *Maybe it's a symbol of a fixed delusion of identity, Bo thinking he is from another planet?* Murphy rose from his chair and searched for his old book of astronomy. For about a half hour, he thumbed through the various pictures of galaxies and planets, trying to see if there were any that resembled the two he'd seen so many times of recent date, with Cameron's face in the middle.

Exasperated he slammed the book shut and headed out for his cruiser, careful to leave a note for Lucy explaining where he'd gone. In the garage he fired up the cruiser and waited as the door opener worked its magic. Once out, he depressed the remote button fastened to his sun visor and headed down the long path leading to the downtown area. He sang with Frank Sinatra, Doris Day, and Mel Torme. He complained during long commercials. He marveled at the beauty of the night air.

His mind wandered across his childhood, his parents, his college years, and his decades on the force. He thought of Lucy and how beautiful she was the day they were married. He considered the many times they had fought, the heartache they both felt when they were unable to have children, the pain and the tears of their life. He thought more on the beauty of their marriage, of the idea of marriage itself, and of life, and of all of the wonderful things it had to offer. The surprise they'd experienced when after years of infertility they had their singular miracle baby. And then there was the rest; the ugly, crass, and dreadful side of existence.

After some time he reached the west side district, and he carefully retrieved his gun from the glove compartment. He had been in trouble once before on the west side, years ago, when a gang approached his cruiser and demanded he get out of the vehicle. He had been trapped that day, unable to protect himself because he did not anticipate the speed of attack possible on a police car. He had a gun, in fact, guns, on him before he could react and had to give his position up. It was a mistake that nearly cost him his life, and it did cost him several weeks in the hospital.

With one hand on his pistol and the other on the wheel, Chief Murphy spent a couple of hours driving up and down the streets looking for anything that might give relief to his insomnia. But no relief came. No Bo came. No solace. He did see pain, misery, families, snow, and cold. He wondered how life could survive through all of this. How people get up and face another day, believe in a future, believe in a God, when all they know is squalor, vice, neglect, and pain.

Eventually Chief Murphy made his way out from the west side commerce district and engaged the freeway route back home. His mind again wandered through the past fifty years of memories, eliciting both smiles and tears from the seasoned officer. He thought on the purpose and meaning of life, on the philosophical issues raised in canonical Scriptures. He thought of the many people the world over without faith in these teachings and wondered about the purpose, nature, and destiny of God.

Eventually he reached his turnoff for home, but on a whim he continued to drive forward, reliving June memories in the middle of a cold winter. Re-experiencing the beauty of his first intimate experience with Lucy on their honeymoon, his first taste of ice cream in the fourth grade, his first promotion in the force, and his father's dying words on his fortieth birthday. The aging police chief wiped a tear from his eye and observed the solemnity of life, unsure of how to proceed from this point. He and Lucy were starting to have so many problems; he didn't know what to do about that. Crimes were getting so bad these days. People no longer believed in God or even in general morality. The rapes, kidnappings, murders, molestations, thefts, and fraud were so thick and pervasive, he didn't know if he could take another decade of it. He didn't know if he wanted to. Why was life so difficult at times? Where was the world headed? And what do we do with the Cameron Bos of the world? Is there such a thing as an insanity defense? Not in the law but in decency? Why would God, a perfect being, make something so imperfect as a Cameron Bo? Or divorce, death of a parent, disease, misery, sexual sin, pain, or suffering?

Once he reached the Garberville Gap, the tired police chief pulled his cruiser to the side of the road and let himself out by the railing, which still had not been repaired. He would need to make a note of it and harass the county to send a crew up here. This was a dangerous error on a dangerous stretch, which had more than its share of accidents over the past decades.

Murphy walked across the darkness to the spot where the railing stood before the accidents had occurred. He glanced into the hellish pit of blackness deep below and tried to imagine the thoughts, fears, and terror involved for Merci, John, Addy, and Sally that night. Although it wasn't very long ago, it seemed to have occurred in an ancient time, years before. He looked up at the city lights and mused upon the notion that each player, except Sally, was nestled in that busy metropolis, trying to move on with their lives. But each had to wrestle with the reality that the case was not solved. *And that,* the chief reasoned to himself, *is mostly your fault.*

Looking up at the stars briefly, the chief hung his

head, partly in reverence, and partly in shame. "Heavenly God, wherever you are, I could use some more help on this one. I'm trying my best, but I don't feel like I'm too good at this stuff anymore. I would sure appreciate a favor. Not for me. You been good to me in this life. But for the kids. Help them get some closure. Help them sleep better at night. And, I guess me too, if that's all right."

He looked up into the starry night. A shooting star crossed his gaze, then another. Chief Murphy's eyes fell with his mood into further quiet reflection as he listened to the nighttime rhythms all around him. The wind howling in the treetops, the distant motor vehicles moving along the sloping hillsides, and the feeling of darkness settling around him as he positioned himself atop his cruiser hood and stared into the blinking lights of the city far below. Somewhere, in all that blacktop and life, a killer was still to be found.

CHAPTER SIXTY-FOUR

Addy had never been more unsure of herself as she was when entering the confessional, but she had some big decisions to make, and she knew she needed advice before doing anything drastic. The priest, much to her surprise, did not open the confessional window right away, and the longer she sat alone in the room, the more stupid she felt. Just as she was about to leave, the window flew open, and she could see the silhouetted figure of an aged priest on the other side.

"I'm not Catholic," she blurted out, interrupting him in the middle of his introduction.

"I see," he said. "That is a problem that is easily remedied. But what can I do for you today, my dear?" he asked in a gentle and empathic voice.

"I don't know," she admitted. "I didn't know where else to go."

"Were your parents Catholic?"

"My parents didn't know me well, and vice versa. I wouldn't describe them as Christian in any way, or Catholic, or—I'm sorry, I didn't mean to offend you."

"You didn't, my dear. Catholics believe in Jesus, so I guess that makes us Christians, now doesn't it? Don't be bashful. What would you like to speak with me about tonight? Is there something troubling you in particular?"

"Yes," Addy said with an obvious anger. She wasn't sure why she was angry.

"Well, is it a sin you would like to confess to?"

"No, I just ... I have some questions."

"Well, this is not really the place for general doctrinal questions, but I'll be happy to give you a few minutes. Sound fair?"

Addy sat for a few moments, not sure how to respond. She was angry that the priest had dismissed her so readily without even hearing her out. *Weren't these guys trained to deal with people like me?* Her anger grew more steady and her breathing more pronounced.

"Uh oh, the old priest has upset the poor young

woman. I'll beg your pardon, dear. Sometimes I'm a little too by the book. Never mind time constraints. Why don't you tell me what's on your mind?"

"That's okay. I really don't want to have this discussion with someone who cares more about policy than people. Thank you for your time," she said, starting to rise.

"Coming to a confessional and unwilling to forgive another? That is an interesting paradox," the priest said.

Addy got the point and took it to heart. She sat back in her chair and started in on her questions. "Do you really believe in God?"

"Of course," the priest said.

"No I mean, *really*. Do you *really* believe there is some all-powerful being out there who knows everything and everyone? I mean, don't just give me a pat answer, I want to know. Do you honestly buy it all?"

"With every fiber of my being, my dear. It is more than just mere speculation; I am speaking of actual knowledge. There *is* a God, and you *will* meet him some day."

"How do you know that? I mean, honestly, how do you know, for real? And don't give me that old 'you can't see the air, but you know it's there cause you feel the wind' kind of thing. That's cute, but I'm talking about life-and-death issues here, and I want to cut the crap out and get down to the nitty-gritty. How do you *know* that God exists?"

"Because he does," the priest replied calmly and steadily. Addy sat dumbfounded at the sophomoric nature of his response. She wondered if he was taking her seriously. "I'm not trying to be trite with you, my dear. Why would you suppose I'd respond to you in such an opinion-driven and not proof-oriented manner?"

"I have no idea."

"Well, I'll tell you then. I did so because nothing I could say would be sufficient for you, would it? I could quote you Scripture, cite you anecdotal evidence, even explicate scientific theories that point to the evidence of God, and you would dismiss them all, wouldn't you? Sure you would. It's all been done before. Studies show that upon death, people consistently lose a fraction of weight. That can't be the soul leaving the body; it's just excrement or cessation of cellular movement. Studies indicate that numerous people, upon dying, report seeing tunnels of light. 'Well, that's just neural patterns slowly tapering off, causing a narrowing of the visual plane, which looks like tunnel vision. Numerous studies indicate the presence of auras through Kirlian photography. Oh, that's not a soul, that's simply microscopic matter dematerializing, and to think otherwise is archaic and voodoo."

The priest took a breath. "Now, you see what I mean? If you came here for me to prove the existence of God, you came to the wrong priest because I can never prove anything to you that you do not want to believe. Don't believe me? You check it out for yourself. Look at the interpretations of creationism and evolution, of spirituality and religion in the scientific community. You'll scarcely find a believing, renowned scientist who's not labeled a heretic, although they did exist at one time. Individuals like Einstein, who were beyond refute in their theorizing, including their theorizing of God. So that said, let me ask you a question. What is so important about whether or not there is a God that you came here to speak with me today, although you are not a member of this church?"

Addy considered the old priest's question for a moment before responding. "I want to know why God allows for pain and suffering?"

"Because that is very much part of life. You can't have pleasure without pain. Remember, God himself was not able to escape pain, neither emotional nor physical pain."

Addy shifted her weight and lifted herself off the chair slightly with her hands. "Well, I know someone who is going to make a decision soon that will impact his life in a tremendous manner."

"You are speaking of suicide, are you not?"

"Yes, sir."

"And this friend I assume is in no way you, such that you would especially deny it if I had a mental health worker speak with you?"

"Of course."

"Continue," the priest said with a deep breath.

"Well, this friend doesn't think he believes in God, but if he did, he wondered where he'd wind up after he killed himself."

"Well, that is not entirely easy to answer. If the friend believes or not it is immaterial. There is a God, and he will wind up being judged by God. Catholics believe the next life consists of a heaven, hell, and an in between state called purgatory. Where your friend winds up will depend very much on how suicide is defined—passive versus active suicide, his knowledge of religion and life in general, his clearness of thought going into suicide, irrevocable laws of heaven, and a myriad of other things. But, can I ask, why would your friend want to gamble with such a question if he does not know the outcome?"

"What do you mean?"

"Well, if your friend does not know about God, and is relatively young, say your age, and doesn't really have enough life experience to know any better, why would he gamble with committing what might be a huge sin? Perhaps a sin that God will interpret as being turned against, and one requiring eternal punishment?"

"You think God will throw someone in hell for suicide? That is the sickest thing I've ever heard."

"Now wait a minute. I didn't say that. I said God will require punishment. But that's not because he delights in punishing us, my dear. That's because he enforces what must be. And when we sin, we bring darkness and despair upon ourselves. And thus, we *give* ourselves punishment that *we* cannot take away."

Addy was sobbing at this point. She felt so helpless and confused. She didn't know what to do, and she didn't know what she was doing with this priest.

"There are a lot of people who can help … your friend. We have counselors, mental health professionals, people who really are quite good at answering some questions that maybe old priests have difficulty with."

"My friend wouldn't go to any of those people."

"Oh? Why not?"

"I don't know, but he won't. That's all. He doesn't trust them. They've hurt him before."

"Well, has this friend tried the Word of God before?"

"Many times."

Addy and the old man sat silently for some moments. "Mr. Priest, Father, or whatever—can I ask you just one more question? Then I promise I'll go."

"Of course. What is it, dear?"

"Let's say you're right and that God does exist. Let's say that there is a hell to come, and that suicide is not the way out. Let's say everything you say is true. That truth doesn't take away the fact that people in this life are raped, molested, murdered, abandoned, cheated on, homeless, crazy, and basically miserable no matter what they do. Why in the world would someone who supposedly loves us and calls us his children give anyone that kind of life?"

"You mean like why would God allow someone to beat, spit upon, try to destroy the reputation of, and crucify an innocent man, say someone like Jesus?" the old priest asked. Addy stared vacantly. The priest let out a bellow of air and leaned closer to the confessional window, placing his hand on the wiring. "My dear, that is a question as old as the church itself. And sad experience has taught me that anything I say, short of a five-hour lecture on technical doctrine, will not satisfy the individual in crisis. But I will say this. Look around you. Notice those who have accepted God. Look at those who interpret with an eye of faith. I'm not talking about people who believe there is a God, but rather those who actually believe God. Not those people who accept the idea of divinity while rejecting his atonement and his loving power to save.

"When you focus on true disciples, those who actually believe in his presence and his promises, you'll see this: mostly every person who sees the future with the eye of faith, that somehow there is a higher educable purpose in the plights of life; those who see trauma and cry and wrench and moan, but who underneath it all see the handprint of God and fight with all of their hearts, might, mind, and strength to replace bitterness with humility, meekness, and teachability; in short, those who believe God and believe they are in a plan of happiness that will lead them to a better place, those are the ones who land on their feet while all others tend to acquiesce into disconnection, bitterness, anger, and in some cases, apathy. Those latter are the ones most at risk for giving up, feeling hatred, unloved, unworthy, seeing no other way out."

Addy wept profoundly as the priest spoke. "But if loving and believing in God doesn't keep you from an eternity of sadness, anguish, and misery, what's the difference between heaven and hell? Belief and non-belief? The righteous and the wicked?"

"Oh, believe me, child. I have been a priest for a very long time and a human being even longer. Both personally and professionally, I can promise you there's a profound difference in the character and affect of those two groups. You may be right that there is not always a detectable difference in the trials of each group. But inside—in that place where no man has ever been able to take an adequate measurement, in that place where the sustenance and meaning of life is hidden—in that private chasm where the very soul of man defines his being, *that* is where the difference can be found between the heathen and the believer. And that difference carries them, both literally and figuratively, through all the trials they must endure, until one day there will be no hiding the difference of what each has become." The aged priest brought his wrinkled fist up as he briefly emitted a forceful cough.

"Now, you tell your friend he is welcome here any time. You tell your friend it is not worth it to die. And you tell your friend to hold on to faith. Even someone else's if he has nothing else at this time. It's not worth the gamble, the pain, and the tears. You tell your friend that he would not want to pass to the other side and find he was wrong in his calculated decision. There is more out there for him, and for us all, than that."

CHAPTER SIXTY-FIVE

"Well, let me put it this way, I don't know that I would go to a shrink if I had those kind of problems; no offense," Chief Murphy said.

"None taken, and likewise, I don't know that I would go to a cop if I were a victim of someone with those kinds of problems," Doctor Jacobs said.

"Touché."

Jacobs laughed. "Aw, don't worry, Chief. I'm just teasin'."

Murphy matched the laughter. "Well, I am sorry you don't get more than a free breakfast. You deserve more. The department is just very political, and I couldn't keep the investigation alive anymore. The case will still technically be open, but the reality is we're going to sit in the 'wait and see' mode for now. The higher ups just won't let me commit either the staff or the money to researching and investigating him anymore. But I wanted you to hear from me personally that you did a tremendous job here. And coming from me to a psychologist, that, I hope you realize, is really a mouthful."

"Well, I appreciate that. And truth is I think it *is* time to move on. We know about as much now about Cameron Bo as we're going to. Bottom line: he's crazy, doesn't know it anymore, and that makes him dangerous. But the good news is, and I'm convinced of this—although I know we might disagree here a little—I think your guy has a very good heart when he's stable. Everything he's accomplished in his public schooling career right up to the accident suggests that this was a good guy. Someone who really tried to make a difference in the world. I mean, the guy is feeding the homeless, visiting the sick and afflicted in rural areas, volunteering for mentoring programs, organizing human aid and relief clubs in high school. A real rare find, this kid."

"Murderer and psychotic."

"Well, yeah, he's a little that too. It's a real shame."

"He's more than a 'little' that. Just ask Sally Strathers."

"Yeah, you're right, but I still think it's a human tragedy."

Chief Murphy buried his head in his plate and smelled his bacon and egg meal. "Yeah, I guess. I got some other words for it."

Doctor Jacobs smiled. "Well, I guess I can see why you don't believe it. I probably wouldn't believe it either if I didn't work with this population and see the difference therapy and pharmaceuticals can bring to someone this psychotic. There really is no other word for it. It's a miracle."

The chief looked up from his bacon and eggs. "*Miracle*. That's an interesting word choice."

"Yes it is," Jacobs replied, taking a sip of his milk. "So, what does the big man around the police station do next?"

"Well, central's been caught up in the string of vagrant killings lately. They pretty much want me to spearhead that movement. They have a task force and all, and we're going to start conducting some systematic interviews, that kind of thing."

"Sounds interesting."

"Yeah, I think it will be. I'm always out to get a bad guy, homeless or no. Killers need to be found and stopped no matter where they reside, right?"

"Sure."

"Well, I'm sure we'll have room for a criminologist here and there. We might actually see each other again soon."

"I'd like that a lot," Jacobs replied, poking at his waffle.

"Say, before we go, I do have a question for you, if you don't mind."

"Shoot."

"Well, this is gonna sound funny after all the shots I took at your job."

"I wouldn't have it any other way with you, Chief. What's on your mind?"

"Well, don't laugh here, seriously. But what do you know about dream analysis?"

"Dream analysis? Not really my field. But I did have to study it extensively in grad school. What do you want to know?"

"I don't know. Anything to it, in your mind?"

"Not really. Freud thought it was important. He talked about things like manifest versus latent themes in dreams. He thought certain things meant aggression, others sex. Nothing ever really came of it. Hardcore scientist types have generally dismissed dreams as meaningful. Our best theories to date basically argue that dreams are random memories."

"Well, maybe dream analysis is not what I mean. What about dreams as predictors?"

"Oh, sort of prophetic dreams?"

The chief nodded his head.

"Oh, well that's a lot different, but the answer is

the same there as well. Science has never found evidence for 'em. You're on your own there."

"That's what I figured," Murphy grumbled as he leaned back in his chair. The doctor did the same.

"Well, Murphy, I guess this is it," Jacobs said, rising out of his chair. "'Till next time." Murphy stood and shook the doctor's hand.

"Yeah. 'Till next time. And hey, you were right, Doc. I don't care for the neighborhood that much, but I got to admit, the food here is great."

"Oh, tell the owner. He's a friend of mine. I've known him since college. Been coming here for over two decades now, back when it was The Dorm's Table. I always thought that was a stupid name. I told Tom that Atomic Café was a much better choice."

"I'd have to agree." The chief laughed. "See you later."

"Bye now."

Murphy watched the doctor as he walked across the café floor and disappeared out the doorway. Dropping his view back to his plate, he picked up his fork and played with his eggs some more, resisting the unofficial closure of the Cameron Bo case in his mind but knowing the department heads were right in moving along for now. There was just too much else going on in the world to ignore. Cameron Bo would have to wait his turn.

"Officer, can I get you anything else?" the waitress wondered as she began collecting the doctor's plate and drink.

"No, that'll be it," the chief said, giving the waitress enough cash to cover the meal and her tip.

"Thank you, sir, and have a good morning."

"Sure. You too."

Murphy leaned back in his chair and let his mind wander over the case and all that he'd done in the last several months to combat it. Here it was nearing the end of March, and they hadn't pulled up a significant lead in over a month. It was as if Cameron Bo had disappeared into thin air. There was no use trying to find him anymore. They would just have to wait for him to show up in trouble. That was the problem with big cities. They were the perfect place for crazy murderers to hide. Murphy thought that if the public knew how many murders went unsolved in big cities, they might move.

Murphy watched all of the people in the restaurant eating and talking or reading their papers. He'd never been to this side of town to have breakfast before. He didn't really like the west side. It was the kind of place cops didn't like to go because it just seemed like their cruiser couldn't sit anywhere for even two minutes without being vandalized. And of course the violence of the west side was something Murphy knew personally, and he didn't like the memory. But he'd be back here again. It was good food and at a good price too.

Grabbing his belongings, Chief Murphy stood up and made his slow exodus to the door. It felt strange; surreal even. In a way, he would sort of miss the case. It had haunted him for so many months now that he kind of saw it as much a part of his life as his recliner, his paper, his clothes. Reaching for the door, he thrust it open and started across the threshold.

"Officer!" the young waitress cried out. Murphy spun around slowly to see what she wanted.

"Looks like you left your planner," she said, holding up his black book and then setting it on the table before whirling around in the opposite direction and disappearing through the kitchen door.

"Thanks," he yelled after her, crossing the room again to his table. As he approached his scheduler, he extended his arm but tripped a little and knocked it to the ground, scattering several loose papers. With a groan he bent down, dropped to a knee and started chasing the papers back into their home. As he scooted the last page back into his small scheduler, he picked his head up and started the standing sequence but abruptly froze in place. Directly ahead of him something caught his eye, but he wasn't sure what. He was looking at a man speaking to his girlfriend or wife or someone. The man was facing off to his left, but framed on either side of his face was the Atomic Café's symbol, an atom. It took him a few moments, but then it came to him. He could feel it in his heart and mind. He recognized the symbols readily from the dreams. They weren't planets; they were atoms. This was the sign he was waiting for. Cameron Bo was here.

CHAPTER SIXTY-SIX

Chief Murphy stood up quickly, a little in shock. Regardless, he was still cognizant enough to place a hand on his gun. He spun around and examined every customer in detail. Bo was not in the main eatery. Slowly and consciously he made his way to the kitchen, first looking behind the counter.

"Can I help you with something else, Officer?" his waitress asked from across the room. He waved her off and put his fingers to his lips, to which she responded with an uncertain look. No one was behind the counter. Through the kitchen window he didn't see anyone but the cook. Pushing though the door, he noticed the kitchen gave way to a hall where the food storage area could be found.

"Officer, can I help you with something?" the cook asked as the dishwasher turned to look as well. Murphy also waved him off. Slowly he made his way down the hall and carefully opened the door to the storage area while unbuttoning his gun latch. No one was in there.

He stood straight and spun around, looking for anything else to examine. He made his way back to the front of the store and let himself out, ignoring the concerned staff and patrons of the restaurant. People bustled everywhere, but he did not see anyone that grabbed his attention. He stepped away from the café and read the sign, looking at the artwork. It was a large building, but only one story. No one would be living in any upstairs apartment. Still, Murphy knew the feeling he got when he saw the customer framed in the artwork on the wall. This was no accident. This was the message he had been prepared and waiting for. Cameron was near, and Murphy wasn't going anywhere until he found him.

The chief walked guardedly around the right of the building and checked the adjacent edifice. It was a Laundromat, and someone could be seen sitting quietly on the far side of the waiting area. With great care the aging police chief progressed toward the front glass door, eyeing the young man while grasping his weapon more tightly. Silently, yet firmly, he pushed the entry door open and glared at the young man facing the opposite direction. Oddly, no machines were engaged.

The man didn't move as the bell loosely tied around the door handle rang clumsily. Murphy partially pulled out his gun with his right hand and slightly raised his left hand, palm up, as he called out to the motionless person. "Listen, I'm a police officer. I need you to turn around nice and easy. No sudden movements. Do it now!"

The man didn't move.

"I said, this is a police officer. Turn around now and identify yourself," Murphy said. The man slowly turned his head and glared menacingly at Murphy.

"What do you want, pig?" the man said. Murphy's body relaxed, and he dropped his gun fully back into his holster.

"Nothin'. Forget about it, kid." Murphy sighed, his heart trying to slow down again. Looking first over his shoulder, Murphy made his way back out of the facility. On the side of the Laundromat was an alley, which the chief cautiously entered. This made sense to him. He figured the only way Bo could go on, as crazy as he must be right now, was to be homeless. Anywhere else he'd stick out too much. In the back streets, he was just another product of deinstitutionalization. Deliberately, Murphy made his way down the alley, carefully checking every vagrant for Bo's face. Recognition would be easy. He knew every inch of it. He had studied the police photos so well he could probably recognize Bo better than his own reflection. Bo was not to be found in the first alley, however. Murphy made a left turn at the alley intersection and started across the backside of the Atomic Café. The alley was plastered with graffiti and trash. Murphy carefully reached down and lifted the blanket off the face of a snoring vagrant. It was not Bo. A mother huddled with her children behind a dumpster off to the right.

"Please, Officer, don't take my babies away from me! Please! Please!" she said. Without taking his eyes off the path in front of him he waved her off and proceeded forward. The next intersection of alleys was trouble. There was a large group of vagrants off to the right, but several large dumpsters off to the left, against the alley wall. Murphy thought for a moment, considering if he should remain alone, or whether he risked being mocked by calling in backup for his hunch. Playing the safe card, he called central and ordered Officer Jones specifically to be dispatched to the area.

"Okay, Chief. Officer Jones is en route, ETA fifteen minutes, hold your position."

"Thanks, LuAnn," Murphy said back into his communication piece. Something about the dumpsters on the left had his attention, and he inched forward to see what it was. He approached the dumpsters circularly, coming around the front of them in an arch-like fashion. Into his sight came a man—or woman; Murphy couldn't tell because its upper half was under a blanket—presumably asleep in a seated position between the dumpsters.

On each side of the vagrant, the dumpsters sported the Atomic Café symbol, whose sight caused Murphy's nervous system to light on fire. His hand tight again around his gun handle, the chief inched toward the citizen and commanded him or her to wake up and take off the blanket. When nothing happened, he repeated his request, but a response was again not found. Taking his gun out of its holster and aiming it toward the vagrant, he approached and grabbed the blanket with his left hand while holding the gun in his right hand.

"Now, I'm gonna remove this blanket real slow. No surprises or sudden movements. I just need to identify you."

With great caution the officer removed the blanket, slowly revealing a dirty young indigent with stains and scars across his hands and blood messed in his matted hair. The man was looking down at the ground. His hands were twitching, and he seemed to be humming something.

"Stand up and identify yourself."

The man did not move.

"Stand up and identify yourself, now!"

Again, the man sat motionless.

"Cameron, stand up now!" the chief said, both hands on the pistol that was dead center at the vagrant's head. But the man did not move. He just sat there, humming to himself, staring blankly at the ground. The angle was such that Murphy could not get a fix on his face. But the rest of him did look like Cameron's profile. The vagrants down across the other side of the alley had fled elsewhere when they heard the officer yelling. Only Murphy and the indigent now shared each other's company, sandwiched between commerce and trash receptacles.

"Sir, I'm going to ask you only one last time, and then I'm going to cuff you, and take you to the precinct. Identify yourself, *now!*"

The man sat rigidly, undaunted by the officer's commands. Murphy moved in easily but slowly. With the gun still pointed at the man, he dropped one hand to his cuffs, and unloosed them from his belt.

"I'm sorry, sir, but I am going to have to take you downtown now for refusing to comply with an officer." As Murphy began to quote his Miranda rights, he moved in close enough to touch the young man. His hands trembling a little, he reached out and cuffed the vagrant's right hand.

Suddenly the man pulled Murphy off balance, the

chief's body clumsily rushing forward and colliding with the young man, who growled and shrieked something indecipherable. Murphy lost his breath as the man beat him again and again in the head and stomach, knocking his gun loose and bringing him down coldly upon the concrete and dumpster walls. The pain in Murphy's head was ringing as he looked up and saw the unmistakable face of Cameron Bo. Cameron reached into the sky and brought his elbow down on the crown of the chief's head and then kicked the aging officer in the center of his abdomen, causing the chief's world to fade.

CHAPTER SIXTY-SEVEN

When his consciousness came back, Chief of Police Frank Murphy opened his eyes and forced himself to stand, found his gun, and spit some blood onto the floor. He took a few steps forward but then vomited his egg breakfast onto the dirty concrete. Catching his breath and wiping the blood off his face, a groaning Murphy started down the alley after Bo, toward the alley intersection, drawing near to the wall as he approached the corner. From his spot he could tell that Bo could not have easily gone off to the left or straight, and the traffic was much too busy to have easily crossed the street. Gun in hand, Murphy peeked around the right corner wall and then slipped into the alleyway.

The mother with her small children was gone, although the sleeping vagrant still lay on the floor. Murphy's head was throbbing, and his vision was not well. Bo had injured him, and he knew he was no longer at peak performance. Had Bo taken his gun, he didn't know what he would do. But his gun gave him confidence and the upper hand to proceed. Quickly this time, instead of cautiously, Murphy ripped the blanket off the now protesting vagrant, ruling out Cameron as being underneath. Murphy looked, gun first, into the dumpsters, one by one, but he did not find Bo inside. As he approached the corner of the Laundromat alley, he looked down the opposite way and also did not find his man. That again left the alley to the right, and Murphy braced himself for another possible altercation. Peeking around the corner first, Murphy then committed his body, gun pointing forward, into the narrow lane. But the alley was empty; Cameron was nowhere to be found.

Where could he have gone? Chief Murphy wondered against bleeding wounds and aching muscles. Quickly he spun around and considered his options. After a brief delay, he spotted something odd at the end of the alley opposite his. There lay a pile of glass he didn't remember seeing before. Murphy ran toward the glass and saw that it was underneath the fire escape where a broken window hung several feet above it. Looking behind him, Murphy reasoned that the only way to reach the window was to access the fire escape ladder, and the only way to access the ladder would be to strategically maneuver his body against the nearby dumpster and brick wall, which did have several holes possibly big enough to place a foot into.

Holstering his gun, Murphy grabbed a hold of the brick ridge and carefully set his foot into the first hole. With a jump and a little luck, he was able to reach a second grasping, and finally a third, just enough to reach the lower rung of the ladder. As he grabbed the ladder, a mixture of his velocity and gravity brought the metal bars down upon him and the top ridge of the dumpster, upon which they both fell, pressing against his bruised ribs and meaty abdomen. With a painful protest, but still holding onto the bars, he fixed himself into a standing position and hoisted himself up the topside of the ladder rungs and ultimately onto the fire escape landing.

As he approached the window, he reached for his gun. He paused, however, as an overwhelming feeling came upon him, somehow telling him to throw the gun down to the ground. Interpreting the impulse as a product of his aching body and fading brain power, he pulled the gun out and aimed it forward while taking a step. Again the impulse came to toss the gun down below. He resisted again, however, knowing such a maneuver could get him suspended from the force, as well as to make it possible for another to access his firearm, if not cause it to discharge when contacting the floor from such a high elevation.

He took another step forward to the window. Now the impression was screaming to him to throw over his pistol, to the point that his physical faculties were nearly overwhelmed. *Now!* A voice in his head shrieked as he impulsively tossed the firearm over the railing and down to the alley below. As he let go of the gun, he felt Cameron's feet hit the back of his head. The chief flung helplessly forward into the rusting railing, which knocked the wind out of him.

"I'll kill him! I'll kill him for you, Father! He's the work of the devil! He's the minion of Satan, and I'll kill him now in the name of the heavens!" Cameron said as he thrust knuckles into the shoulders and back of the police chief over and again. Wailing out in agony, Chief Murphy tried to pin Bo's hand against his body as Bo clawed after the vacant holster where Murphy's firearm was not.

"Get offa me!" Murphy groaned, but to no avail. The young man attacked viciously and rabidly, tearing at the police chief's clothes and striking him now primarily with elbows and head butts on the back of the chief's head.

"Where's your gun?" Cameron screamed in the chief's face as he brought his hands around the old man's neck and started to lessen the distance between his palms. Murphy grabbed Cameron's arms and dug his thumbnails into the underside of Cameron's wrists, causing Cameron to howl in pain. As the two struggled, the dangling handcuff knocked Chief Murphy in the chest.

Stop fighting the choking and grab the cuff! the impression came again as a vision of the guard rail was put into Murphy's mind. Murphy struggled for another few seconds against Cameron's grip, afraid to let go as he felt himself growing weaker.

Grab the cuff! the impression came again. With a wave of fear, Murphy let go of Cameron's hands; his neck making a croaking noise as Cameron's full strength was upon it. As his eyes began to protrude their sockets, Murphy grabbed the dangling cuff with both hands, and arching his back to knock Bo off balance, he thrust his weight toward the rail, which he could not see. The cuff missed, and he tried a second, third, and fourth time, all the while with Bo fighting against him.

Finally, with a desperate prayer for help, Chief Murphy closed his eyes and gave every ounce of strength he had left into his thrust, his hands finding the railing. Bo looked up as the cuff latched around the metal, and he released his grip on Murphy, snatching the keys out of the chief's pockets and searching for a way to unlock himself. Murphy choked out several deep breaths before he could finally get on his feet; Cameron completely distracted in his pursuit to find the right key.

Still panting, Murphy reached inside himself, and with all the energy he could muster, he threw his bleeding fist into the back of Cameron's head, knocking his body forcefully against the rail, which then bounced backwards and fell motionless to the floor. Retrieving his keys from the unconscious vagrant, he sat down against the railing and tried to catch his breath. *Jones will be here soon,* he told himself. *Hurry up, Jonesy.*

CHAPTER SIXTY-EIGHT

Addy sat avoiding the eyes of the many on-lookers seated in front of her.

"Honey, you okay?" Merci asked, his voice soft and low. She turned her head and found her boyfriend's eyes and melted in his protection and compassion. Discreetly, she smiled at him. Her body shook in a warming manner as he grabbed her hand, leaving her to muse on why such a simple act could actually make her feel better about the speech she knew she must soon give, even though she didn't know what in the world she was going to say. Doctor Haddelby had asked her, John, and Merci to come as guest speakers to his class and share their feelings about religion in the context of the past November accident—or murder. She still had a hard time calling it that. She referred to it as an incident in conversation, but underneath she knew it was more than that, and that bothered her.

John and Merci had flatly refused to comply with Doctor Haddelby's wishes, and they even seemed offended by the invitation. Addy, however, felt she needed to use the opportunity to make a clean break. She looked over at her lover and best friend solemnly, picturing him lonely and destitute. She considered that she might even use this speech to explain to him her final emotional standing in this world. A last performance before death. One last event before journeying to the land of emptiness and forgotten memories, including the painful memories no one wished to remember anyway. Memories of failure, abuse, rape, heartache, and now murder. She squeezed Merci's hand tighter while fighting the urge to cry. *And memories of hurting a loved one, keeping him back from true happiness. Keeping him against his better judgment from a life of true mercy.*

Addy looked away from her loved one and into the spacious crowd. She recognized everyone in the stands. There was the jock, the nerd, the blonde, the rocker. She saw the preachers, the teachers, the bullies, and the creeps. She laughed at the mods, smirked at the GQs, and stared blankly at herself—the invisible ones looking down at the floor while wondering if there is even a point in being here today.

There were so many invisible ones—would they all come to the same conclusion she had about life? Not likely. They'd be smarter than she'd been. They'd all be able to carry on. The world needed them. Like oxygen, they might not be noticed, but they were essential to survival. They filled jobs, had children. They loved and lost and loved some more. They provided the world with the next generation of thrills, jocks, geeks, mods, preachers, and nobodies.

Wiping a second tear, Addy told herself she had to regain control. She had to keep focused. For only ten minutes she had to matter to the world. She didn't fully understand why. In fact, she knew that she wouldn't be of any use to the audience members. Who was *she* to talk to them about religion? Or rather the grand delusion of religion? She had come to realize herself that it was all a hoax. Well, at least she'd come to realize that it was either a hoax, or something she didn't want to be part of. She didn't want anything to do with a deity who would let her suffer, bleed, wallow in pain, and waste away in dumpiness and heartache. She didn't want to have feelings to feel. She wished to be inanimate. She wished to be alone, so she might never know the bitterness of departure, of connection gone bad, of happiness gone lonely and miserable and depressed. In short, she did not want to be human but dead. And soon, she would be, and there was only one more miserable thing to say about it. Now was the time she had to speak.

She looked up at Doctor Haddelby; watched how he masterfully controlled the crowd. She grew angry at him for a moment, picturing his pathetic figure at countless bars, drinking the hypocrisy of his poisoned life. He was, in her mind, as corrupt and murky as the philosophy he preached. Although she had to admit, each time she felt this way about either of them, she felt a ping in her soul, a terrible feeling that perhaps she was wrong about it all. This feeling angered her, made her more than angry, livid. She wanted to simply forget it all—throw it all into the wind. Ignore the pain and anger and depart this life numb and emotionless.

But she couldn't bring herself to do it. She didn't know why, but deep down, underneath all the bitterness, pain, anger, and tears, her heart held a secret from her mind. She did believe it. She believed there was a God. She believed there was a point to life. She believed there was a hope for Doctor Haddelby and his dismembered wife. She believed there was a larger plan, something she could not comprehend, even though she was a part of that plan. She believed it all. And because she believed it all, secretly, in her sub-conscious, she was bitter.

Doctor Haddelby's loud voice jerked her out from her ponderings with his rambling laughter. "Well, enough of the jocularity. Now, I want you all to give me your attention. No doubt you all know we have a special guest today. And no doubt she is in no need of social introductions. Nonetheless, I would like to introduce you to her.

"Addy Siwel is a living testament to the goodness of life. I use the word *testament* in the archaic sense. Not simply a cluster of factual sentiments, Addy's life is a covenant-based interaction. Her life is laden with philosophy, caretaking, and love. All who know her know her to be a humble seeker of truth without regard to the place or time that truth is found. I am going to embarrass her a bit by admitting to you that she has a shy nature and disposition; however, I am confident you will not let that impede your ability to hear whatever message she has prepared for you today. Addy, can you come up here please?"

Addy released her grip of Merci and slowly rose from her chair. As she rose the audience burst into a round of applause, and every eye was upon her. The applause shocked her, causing her to jump slightly and survey the audience. One by one the audience rose to their feet. *What are they doing?* Addy thought, com-pletely bewildered.

"That's right," Haddelby said. "Come here, Addy." Addy turned toward the old man again and took several steps toward him. He was smiling at her, and he thrust his arm around her and shook her shoulder rapidly up and down. Leaning over he whispered into her ear.

"I've told them a lot about you. They're all interested in your story. You are among friends here."

Addy withdrew into herself and felt very nervous. She was starting to regret her commitment to speak to these people. The unanticipated attention was making the whole experience much worse. She definitely had not sought attention, nor asked Haddelby to pressure the audience to like her and stand up for her. She felt completely stupid and horribly embarrassed. As such, she tried to wriggle out of Haddelby's grip and shrink to the door, but Haddelby sensed her escape plan and drew her in even tighter.

"Now, I am going to surprise everyone here and shut up. But first, let me say something about this young woman, something I did not tell you on Wednesday at our last class meeting. In all of my years teaching, I have never had a student who has touched me so much as this one before you. I am here to tell you that if ever a religious person existed on the earth, with a heart meek enough and charitable enough to see the face of deity, that person would be Addy Siwel. Now, Addy has agreed to come today and share her thoughts on her religious project, something she was never able to do prior to this, due to the well-known crash that occurred some half-year ago. You should all be so fortunate as to avoid this kind of life-altering incident. Nothing affects the religious mind quite like a fatal or near-fatal occurrence. Nothing affects the religious mind like a murder. Nothing … well, Addy, I am going to sit down and let you explain it to them."

Haddelby stepped aside and handed Addy the microphone he'd been speaking in. She grabbed the warm metal staff of the amplification device and stared into the dark, foamy receiver. As she looked up from the microphone and became aware of the awkward quiet that had fallen over the crowd, she looked at the blank faces and searched her mind for something to say, but nothing came.

The pain in her stomach grew increasingly intense as the silence escalated into deafening levels. Some of the students, not knowing what else to do, stared at the ground, while others seemed to glance back and forth between Addy and Haddelby, as if pleading with him to step up and end the awkward silence. Haddelby, however, was cool and collected. He seemed as calm and tranquil as a baby in his mother's arms, looking at Addy but seeing something beyond, something in the distance far away. Suddenly, from the middle of the class, someone raised his hand. Unsure what else to do, Addy pointed to him and asked him what he wanted.

"Well," he said, "I'll just be real frank. Doctor Haddelby has told us all semester that the most important thing we can do is determine if there is a higher purpose to life than simply existence. If you would be willing, I would like to know what you've decided. Is there a God?"

Addy stared at the young man. She didn't know

how to respond to him. Truth was she had never answered the question for real, although, again, deep down, she had a hard time denying the truth that she thought to be real. Frankly, that there was a God, and he had abandoned her. Addy sucked all the air she could fit in her lungs before answering.

"Well, that's a good question. Is there a God? I don't know. I suppose it depends on what your definition of God is. I do believe there's a God. I guess. That's the truth. No matter how hard I want to believe otherwise, the conclusion is always the same: I don't believe it. I don't believe that we are evolved from monkeys. I don't believe we are the crowning products of a random evolutionary scheme, because I think the whole idea of evolution is hopelessly flawed. Not as a useful theory, but flawed as an overall theory. Flawed as a theory for the creation of life in and of itself.

"The problem, though, is that so is religion flawed. Religion is seriously flawed and doesn't seem to be helping us anymore. Look at the world. Turn on the news. What do you hear? There are constant struggles in the Middle East. Our cities are full of mischief, hatred, and violence. Teen pregnancy is ridiculous while drugs and violence are everywhere. The major world religions have had scandal after scandal, and the political leaders of the day seem to give counsel to the churches, not the other way around."

Addy looked up at the audience with a quivering gait while also gaining in boldness. "I'll tell you what I've concluded in my life, even though I admit I don't know why any of you would care to know. But here it is. I believe that God—that God is dead. God is dead to me, to you, to all of us. How else do you explain it? In this world full of hate and murder, rape, hunger, racism, and loneliness, there is simply no way that God could possibly be monitoring us! How could a perfect God create such imperfection? We must be castaways, projects for some misunderstood plan. How else do you explain life? How else do you explain the pains of death? You can't! And to try would be delusional. A delusion of grand proportions. This is my conclusion, and my response to your question. It is, simply, that life is pain."

Addy finished her answer and noticed that she was sobbing. The sensation was surreal, foreign, and unnoticed. She had no idea when she began to cry. The entire scene felt awkward, uncomfortable. She simply didn't know what to make of the words originating from her mouth. She didn't know why Doctor Haddelby had called her, why he had built her up to his students. Was it because she looked like his past wife, or did he have some other motive? Most of all she didn't know exactly what to do in this moment where she had just given such an awful and blasphemous yet honest monologue to the shocked and uncomfortable students.

What do I do? she asked herself while examining the empty eyes and mouths and heads and bodies all staring at her. Suddenly, rising with defiant posture, she noticed Merci, standing perfectly erect, his face fixed and determined, walking in an undeviating path toward her. Addy turned and looked desperately at her companion. She gazed into his eyes and tried to communicate something to him, although she didn't know what.

"Addy, I love you. But everything you just said I disagree with," he said gently, turning to the audience and raising his voice as if to address congress. "In fact, not only do I disagree, I passionately refute everything you just said. And I couldn't sit and watch these people see you this way and think you were some hapless person stumbling through the awful throes of life.

"The last thing I would profess to be is some expert on religion, in any sense. I'm just a guy. Not even a good guy. In fact, I was too spineless to agree to come here today and address you like Addy did. I simply showed up to support Addy because I was too afraid to tell you *my* real feelings. *My* real fears, and shames, and questions about life. But I'm addressing you all now, and I refuse to endorse what Addy had to say about this life.

"Sure, life does suck, sometimes. Even a lot of the times. But does that mean there isn't a God? Does that mean we're human waste? A throwaway project not worth divine attention? That God abandoned us? I just can't believe that. Life can be and is a beautiful place! Life is a place where we *feel*. Where we love, lose, win, and reflect on happy times during sad times. Does that mean there is no God? That we must be destined to live out our lives in misery, only to vanish into nothingness? No! I don't accept that!

"Why can't we accept that sometimes there is no happiness, while sometimes there is only happiness?

And that's okay. Why do we think of God as a being who spends one minute to the next just smiling in his or her eternally blissful state? That isn't authentic. That isn't logical. I believe in a God who is like us! A God who gets up every day, if he or she has to get up, and decides once again to engage in his or her godly duties. I believe in a God who loves, and shares, and does everything he or she can for us. But maybe we've always tended to oversell his powers in a weird way. Maybe we have tried to sell a God who never is sad, who never cries, who never wonders if it's all worth it.

"And I say, why? Why would we do that? Doesn't it make more sense that God would be just like us, only perfected? I mean, think about it. Why would God create us and give us misery if that were an unnecessary thing to feel? Why would he subject us to emotions that were unimportant and unnecessary? I don't believe he would! Why can't it all be part of the package? Why can't God be a being who's learned to see the good and the bad together, inseparably a part of the emotions and commonalities that intertwines us all? That gives us experience? That makes us whole?

"Again, I do not claim to be some kind of religion expert, but isn't that the whole point of Adam and Eve? Wasn't the whole point that they choose for us a mechanism for happiness and pain? That before the fall they were unable to experience pleasure because they didn't know sadness? That before they could know the value of bread, they would have to sweat for it?"

"But why sweat for it?" Doctor Haddelby said, causing Merci to turn with the class and sport a bewildered look. "Why sweat for bread when you're God? If I have a power tool, why would I let my son labor unceasingly with a manual saw? If I have air-conditioning, why would I force my family to live in the heat? If I have access to the cure for cancer, why would I let my spouse die a discomfiting death? Why would I do that?

"You say life is beautiful. Sounds like a pathetic statement from an insignificant mongrel who has never experienced the world. Now, don't get me wrong. I don't actually think you a mongrel, but I do think you insignificant, as do I think myself insignificant." Haddelby turned to the class as a whole. "In this class I've always tried to instill in you a sense of the importance of critical thinking. Not the scientific method, which for all of its hoopla is just another limited methodology too often used for shameful exploitation of the human condition. But rather I've tried to instill in you the ability to consider and analyze data free of your own biased assumptions. An ability to look directly into the spoon of horrific reality and open your mouth to swallow it whole." The old professor turned back to Merci. "And now look at you. You spew your emotion-filled dogma in my presence as reckless as Peter, Paul, Siddhartha, Muhammad, and other delusional thinkers of history past.

"Let me ask you. You in the audience, undoubtedly, shocked to hear my atheistic interpretations. You should feel lucky. It is the first time I have admitted this to a class." He looked back at Addy. "Although some of you have heard it more privately. But here it is. I disagree with you, Mr. Bowku! Your premises are as shallow and lacking in substance as is your narrative this evening. No amount of pontificating redeems your arguments from the blatant and salient miseries of life.

"The truth is God does not exist. And, yes, I agree with Ms. Siwel that to think otherwise is delusional. A grand delusion of epic proportions! And I'll prove it. In fact, simply think about it. How many of you, if told there was an unseen force out there that no one had ever seen but was responsible for life itself, would actually believe it? I mean, think about that for a minute! You're told by someone that an indescribable object is actually responsible for generating and perpetuating life, and you're actually going to believe it? No! Of course not! Why do we allow such juvenility when it comes to the meaning of life? Why do we allow such idiocy when it comes to our 'eternal' natures? There is no life after death! There is no life prior to life! There is no ultimate home! *That* is why none of you have seen God, or angels, or deceased ones! *That* is why none of you have knowledge about the past or future beyond this world! And *that* is why none of you may have hope about the human condition! In then end, then, all there is, is sadness and despair, and mortality, and murder, and..." the old man took off his glasses and rubbed his watery eyes, "and deceased loved ones."

The statement floated out of Haddelby's mouth like the dying groans of the severely beaten, and hung over the class as an uninterruptible sadness.

"The problem is that religion is elusive and untrue. And it always will be. And it will always be utilitarian. Used for what men desire. It is the ultimate rationalization, the ultimate con. It is the ultimate evil, as ironic as that statement may be. That, Mr. Bowku, is what Ms. Siwel is trying to say. And that is what you do not get because it is too real and honest for you. It ruins your hope that all of your pain, your misery, and your sadness have reasons, when in the end, they do not. They're just another part of an illogical and unrelenting world of misery, sadness, and despair."

The time on the clock signaled that class had officially ended, but no one dared leave the room. The three debaters held their ground—each teary, each solemn, each unsure of how to proceed. The class sat nervously, anticipating what would happen next. Finally, Merci took a step toward the doctor and compassionately grabbed him by the arm.

CHAPTER SIXTY-NINE

"Dr. Haddelby, I'm sorry your wife died, but I don't buy it," Merci said while looking directly into the old professor's weepy eyes. "That is just not true! Religion is not a delusion! It's not a dream! I believe in God! And I believe in life. Yeah, life is hard! Yeah, life is pain! And yeah, sometimes life is even miserable! I can admit that. But there's more to life than all that pain. You know it, and I know it. Why don't we kill ourselves right now if all you say is true? And I answer, because we want to hold on to life. There is something about it that keeps us from letting go. Something about it that is beautiful and refined and pure. Life *is* good. And good *is* God. Life is a playground of happiness, not a cemetery for joy.

"You say religion's a delusion. A grand delusion of epic proportions. I'm sorry, but I disagree. Religion is not the delusion, but non-belief is the delusion! The grand delusion is in the thinking of those who would ignore the evidences of God that are everywhere. Think about it! In every culture across the world, there's a belief in God. Every culture from the beginning of time! Religious symbols like the Star of David have been discovered in archeological digs the world over in every human time period. There really was a Jesus Christ who walked the earth and performed miracles, and a Muhammad, and a Buddha, and there really are billions who follow and worship their teachings. Is this all untrue? Is this really coincidence? Is this really delusional?

"The atheist points to pain and misery to defy god. True, I don't have answers for why these are around, other than that which I've already said. But what of love? Why evolve love? Ever think of that? Sure, some have. They say love is some kind of survival of the fittest type of thing. Or some kind of protective emotion that isn't real. But that falls short every time I look into the eyes of the one I care about, feel her breath, or marvel that she would want to spend her time with me. Think of pride, of familial ties, of desires for world peace, of human interaction, of patriotism, mercy, and *altruism*. How do you evolve that? How do you evolve altruism? How do you explain the ultimate sacrifice of altruism with evolution? Or without the idea of God?

"You in the audience. Your teacher asked you to consider the ridiculousness of believing in a God whom none of you can see or hear or touch. But I ask you: if you do not, why? We learned in this class from this professor that more than 90 percent of the world population believes in God. If you don't, why did you lose your faith? Because of despair? Is that now the test of truth? If it doesn't feel good or if it doesn't solve human suffering it cannot be true? What else do we hold to that standard? That's ridiculous." Merci turned back to Addy.

"I can't tell you how I know that I love you. But I know I do. And no scientist can prove it. It's the stuff of unseen knowledge, but it's as real as anything ever handled or documented." He turned back to the class again. "Why is it so easy for us to accept unseen feelings as love, but we cannot trust the feelings of knowing, of faith, that tells us there is a God? Why must I be considered delusional if something more powerful than any textbook I've ever read testifies to me with every red blood cell in my body that there exists a living, breathing God somewhere out there? Why is the heart less important than the mind? Why is faith in the unseen truths of the world less valued than the scientific teachings of human beings, beings who have a knack for getting it wrong as much as getting it right in the world of science?

"I guess what I am saying is I just don't buy it. I don't buy any of it. The grand delusion is not faith, but the lack of it. That is delusional. The thought that mankind—people who can't even save themselves from aging and cancer or even figure out how to make contact with the next planet over—is not in need of religion to explain the endless worlds and magnificence of the universe is delusional to me, and I refuse to be part of that thinking."

Merci took a step back and looked into the crowd once again and then turned and looked at Addy. Deliberately he strode over to her spot and grabbed her by the hands. With care he descended to one knee and fished a small velvet container out of his pocket. Opening it, he revealed a modest one-quarter-karat diamond firmly placed on a golden band.

"Addy," Merci said. He had her full attention. Addy's heart raced, her body caught on fire, and her head transferred from tense to constricted, the pressure threatening to overtake her consciousness. "I was going to have this talk with you privately, later tonight, after dinner. But after hearing that speech, I…I want to show you that this world can be a place of joy, as you've already shown me every day for the last many months. If you can believe…if…if you can see a place in your heart where maybe the world can have meaning, and where two people can be connected through time and space and human existence both here and beyond. If you can see that, and I pray you can, then please, please fulfill my every aspect of being and grant me the honor of being forever associated with your name. Addy, please choose *life,* and me in that life. I don't want to spend another day without you. Please, marry me."

Addy's face grew contorted, and she burst into droves of tears. Her body shook, and her entire being flared with passion, excitement, movement, and love. Smiling underneath the watery mess of her face, she first nodded her head, then whispered acceptance into Merci's ears.

"Thank you! Thank you for this! Thank you!" Merci said as the two embraced and hugged to the thunderous clapping of the students, who after a time began filing out of the room, after thanking and congratulating the two lovers who were oblivious to the crowds, preferring to kiss and hug privately in the center of pandemonium.

When the class, the debate, and the tears faded, the two young lovers finally broke their trance, and Addy looked over Merci's right shoulder, fixating on the singular student who remained in his chair. Deeply seated, far away in the back row, John rose to his feet, his face red and flush with tears and emotion. Slowly, he made his way up to the couple and shook their hands while offering them his warmest congratulations.

CHAPTER SEVENTY

John grimaced through his tears as he made his way to his apartment door. With ferocity he ripped his house keys out of his pocket and threw them at the door, which he kicked mightily upon reaching. Leaning his head against the door, he squeezed his brow tightly as he cried silently against the miseries of the world. Bending down, he grabbed his key chain, and with both hands he pulled the house key against the metal ring as hard as he could, ultimately causing his palm to slip and tear across the ridges of the underside of the key.

Finally thrusting the now slightly bloody house key into the doorknob, he kicked open the wood and threw his wallet at the living room wall. With tremendous force he yanked the house key outward and again threw his keys, this time into the kitchen, where they collided with a pot that sprayed in every direction. Turning around, he slammed the front door intensely. The door hit the frame so forcefully that it popped back open again, and a surprised John caught it on the rebound. Turning his affect back from shock to hatred, he bent down a little and rammed the door into the frame, leaning his whole body against it long after he heard the click signaling it had latched successfully. He slumped down the door's side onto the entryway linoleum and sobbed for thirty minutes like a rejected child, asking God why he was alive through all of the emotion, hatred, anger, tears, and snot.

When God did not answer, he felt his blood boil, and he got up on his hands and knees and looked directly at the couch. Driven by disgust and adrenaline, he launched into the couch, burying his right foot into the couch cushion, which flew up and ricocheted off the living room wall. Catching the cushion in mid-air, he pulled it apart as hard as he could until he ripped the fabric and stuffing flew out across his head.

Spitting out all of the stuffing, he tossed the fabric and then ripped the next cushion, his muscles starting to ache. With a clenched fist, he rammed his hand into his right temple, then again and again. When he could take no more pain to his head, he turned his anger toward the wall and shoved his fist through the soft exterior and into the inner crossbeam. He yelled out in further pain and momentarily nursed his hand until the bitterness transformed his empathy from sadness to numbness. As the numbness enveloped, he spent several minutes tossing things about the kitchen and bathroom, after which he found himself sobbing on his bedroom floor and self-loathing in pity.

As he laid moaning and wailing, his eyes came upon the religious emblems he had recently turned to for guidance and help. He felt something from deep within stirring, and hatred growing wildly. Rising up to his desk, he grabbed his Bible and impulsively ripped up his Scriptures, throwing the rent halves at his religious pictures on the wall, screaming that he hated God and life and everything he had been through. When all was said and done, he lay bleeding on the floor in front of his computer, alternating between moaning, crying, and thinking thoughts of death.

"Why would you do this to me? Why? Why? I thought you were supposed to love me. Why would you rape me? Why would you leave me alone in this world, fat, ugly, rejected, unloved?"

His tears turned convulsive, and he wept bitterly for another hour until he fell asleep. Waking again several hours later, he felt himself aching and bruised. His arm needed bandaging and was full of blood-caked wounds. He sobbed again and wondered what to do.

Rolling his head his eyes came upon a picture of Jesus that he'd thrown to the ground, causing the glass to shatter. The picture, while now embedded in broken glass, revealed an intriguing angle of the Messiah's face, which exhibited the quality of being both accepting and rejecting of the onlooker. John struggled to his knees and groped his way across the floor to the painting. Once he finally reached the depiction, he carefully brushed off the glass and removed the painting from its frame.

"Why would you do this to me?" he asked the painting, the tears strolling down again, but this time not in bitterness, but defeat. Darkness filled the house, and the only illumination came from the open bathroom nightlight in the hallway. John passed the night looking at the picture and thinking. He thought about the argument in Haddelby's class. He pondered over Addy and Merci and his parents and the murder attempt and all else in his life that seemed to go wrong.

Somewhere in the early morning he stopped crying, and in the dim light, he caught sight of the photo album he'd collected of Addy from his late-night outings, which seemed so long ago. Clicking on the lamp, he walked over to the album and thumbed through the pictures one by one. With each view he grew increasingly disgusted and self-loathing. With each page he saw less and less hope for his life or future. As he closed the book, he sat back and picked up the picture of Jesus once again.

"What am I supposed to do with my life?" he asked, trying to decide which look Jesus was giving him.

CHAPTER SEVENTY-ONE

Cameron Bo looked across the table and stared at the empty chair opposite him. His mind was flooded with the horrible images of the past year, and he wiped tears away from his warm face. *I am a most despicable human being,* he thought, seeing the faces of terror in his mind as he imagined his victims burning to death or screaming down the hill or suffocating. *How could I be human?* Cameron's attention was quickly shifted away from his thoughts as he heard the door lock click briefly, followed by a low-decibel buzzing sound. Through the small rectangular window, he observed the graying, middle-aged man staring back at him. *I wonder what he's thinking right now,* Cameron pondered as Chief Murphy slid across the threshold of the door and approached with his hand outwardly extended.

"Mr. Bo," the chief of police said, grasping Cameron's hand with a tight professional grip. "You mind if I sit?" he asked as he hovered in a half sitting, half standing position with his eyes raised toward Cameron.

"By all means, Mr. Chief. It's your jail anyway, right?"

"Well, not exactly. Now, what can I do for you?" the chief inquired. Cameron shifted uncomfortably in his chair.

"Well, I'll get straight to the point. First, I owe you quite the apology for what I did to you, and I am sorry for that. You deserve more than words, but I don't know what else to give at this point."

"Your full confession might be a worthy token."

Cameron looked down at the table then up at Murphy again. "Well, that's the second point. I've decided to cooperate with your investigation."

Chief Murphy stared blankly at Cameron as if trying to process his comments. "Say again?"

"I've decided to cooperate with your investigation. I'm happy to answer any questions you'd like to ask."

"I thought you were convinced that we made the whole thing up to frame you, entrap you in some plot?" Murphy said.

"I did. A long time ago. Months ago, in fact, before I was stabilized on my meds. Now, with all the therapy, well, I can see the level of ridiculousness in such statements. I would like to cooperate now."

"Look, I'll tell you what—we should really have an attorney present. Why don't we go grab one right now, the jail has someone who can assist you, and I'll get a tape recorder, and then we can do this properly?"

"No. No lawyers. I don't like lawyers. They just tell you what to do, and they don't believe anything you say anyway."

Murphy dropped his head and let out a sigh. With a backward scoot he gathered space to stand.

"Well, Mr. Bo, thank you for your time. If you have no other requests, I'm going to have you returned to D block now," the chief said as he stood up and pushed his seat back in. Cameron sat looking at the fleeing man, confused.

"Wait!" Cameron said as Murphy put his hand on the door. The chief stood rigidly for several seconds, finally turning his body with blatant impatience.

"What, Mr. Bo?" Murphy responded.

"It's just that … I thought, I mean, I guess I figured you would be happy."

Chief Murphy tilted his head and took a step to the table. "You thought I would be happy?"

Cameron nodded his head.

"Happy?" Murphy repeated, this time low and flat. "Now you tell me why I should be happy?"

"Because, I thought you'd be happy I decided to do the right thing. I want to help."

"The right thing, huh? Yeah, I'm sure. That's what

you want, to do the right thing. How stupid do you think I am?"

"I don't think you're stupid."

"Right. So this is the part where I say nice try, and you say 'so long,'" Murphy said, turning toward the door again.

"Nice try? Nice try to do what? I'm serious about tryin' to do the right thing. What kind of police chief are you? I'm sure when the papers get a hold of your refusal to work with me, you'll regret treating me this way. I am a human being, you know. Even if you don't like crazy people, that doesn't give you license to violate my rights. *I* am not an idiot," Cameron said, his face flush and his heart racing.

"An idiot?" Murphy screamed, matching the young man's irritated tone. "Oh no, I *definitely* don't think *you* are an idiot. In fact I know you aren't an idiot. One sixty-two IQ score on the best adult IQ test on the market. Outstanding verbal and motor skills. Top of your high school class. Considered a child prodigy by your father, who was also considered gifted by most of his instructors both at the public and private school level. You won fifteen awards from Young Scientists, including seven back-to-back awards in the academic decathlon. You had offers at Yale, Harvard, Minnesota, UCLA, Oxford, and Berkeley, which you turned down because you decided to go on a killing spree causing indescribable suffering to who knows how many people. Further, the warden here is 'very impressed' with your impeccable behavior record, and the therapists all indicate that your medical management has improved your psychiatric condition. So much so that you have your wits about you to the degree that you are able to check out and read sophisticated professional articles from the prison library.

"For example, I met with the librarian's office shortly before meeting with you, and guess what they told me? You've had your nose in case law and the state's legal code every chance you could for the past three months. I perused the rolls and found that indeed you had been actively reading the law, and I was interested to find that you even checked out a certain volume with a certain case, where a sophisticated criminal suckered an unwitting police officer to record his testimony that he was guilty to seven counts of murder, only on the stand, the defendant swore he was coerced by force into testifying without a lawyer present, and the entire case was thrown out. Whitney versus Vermont, nineteen seventy-eight. So, no, I don't think you're an idiot. In fact, just the opposite; I think you've used your intelligence successfully to dupe people into thinking you're crazy, victimized, and sorry. Only after nearly three decades of putting up with thugs like you, I don't care. You're going to fry just like that little homeless boy did. Yeah, bet you didn't think I knew about that one. And who knows how many others. That's right, evidence or not, we both know what I'm talking about. And you're going to answer to God in the next life, someone you won't be able to fool!"

The chief was leaning over the table on his clenched fists, his red face sweating and snarling at Cameron, as if daring him to respond. Cameron burst into tears, leaned forward, and looked into the chief's eyes and opened his mouth, speaking slowly and evenly.

"Trying to defend oneself does not make one sadistic. And you don't need to stand there and lecture me about morality. I guarantee no one in this world is more familiar with the consequences and pain involved in the taking of another's life than I am. I'm telling you I am here to work with you because what I did was reprehensible, and all I want to do is to relieve anyone of any further unnecessary suffering if still possible. It is the least I can do. It is something I'm obligated to do under God!"

The two sat staring across the table, daring the other to break the gaze and play the next poker chip. Finally the chief retracted his head position and stood erectly in front of the young prisoner.

"You disgust me," he said coldly and low. "People like you are the worst kind of scum on the planet."

Cameron watched as the police chief made his way back toward the room's door. *Stop him!* he told himself, wondering what he could still say to convince him of his sincerity. In desperation, he looked above him and said a quick prayer. Suddenly he looked toward the exiting officer. "Chief, wait! I want to know if you believe in God!" The officer paused momentarily before shooting an angry glance over his shoulder.

"Usually, until I meet people like you. Then I start wondering quite a bit about the idea of a meaningful life."

"Let me ask you one question, and then I won't try to stop you from leaving," Cameron said. The officer didn't move. "Why do you think I reported the car stolen?"

Chief Murphy stared blankly at Cameron without flinching, seeming to be intrigued by the question.

"Why? Why would I report the car stolen? Have you figured that one out yet?"

"I have a guess," Chief Murphy said.

"What? What is it?"

"'Cause you get off on the danger of being caught."

"Well, I can assure you that was not it. I can promise you that the *last* thing I wanted to do was to be caught. Why do you think I never went back to my house, if I was looking to flirt with being caught? I was frightened to death to live like a vagrant on the city streets in the dead of winter. Sense of adventure? No, that was certainly not it!"

The chief didn't move.

"Why do you think I stole the car, and why would I call you asking for help?"

"But never revealing your identity," the chief said.

Cameron looked down at the table sadly. "No, I didn't, and I wish I had, then I might have avoided—"

"The brutal murder of who knows how many victims?"

Cameron looked up at the officer's stone face. "Yes."

"Well then, why? You tell me, Mr. Conscience. Why did you report the car stolen? Insurance claims, thought it would help your case? You want to help me and come clean with everything, here's your test. You be dead honest with me as to why you reported that car stolen. Why you looked me straight in the eye and told me that some hooker who you later killed was the car thief? Huh? 'Cause you know, I would think your suggestion that you were looking for help falls to the wayside when you frame another person for murder, don't you?"

Cameron pictured Sal and fought desperately the tears forming, trying to burst to the surface. "Yes," he said. "I suppose it would."

"Good answer," Chief Murphy said, taking a step back into the room and resting his hat on the table while he sat down. "You just earned yourself another fifteen seconds, so don't blow it with your next response. I do want to know. Why? I don't know. Guess I've just spent too much of my life on this stupid case, and I'd like an answer or two. So here's the deal: you tell me straight, and I'll hang out with you some more. So think carefully before you speak. When you're ready, you tell me. You tell me why you reported that car stolen."

Cameron leaned away from the table and struggled to keep his voice even. He thought of that night so long ago. He thought of the voices and the hallucinations and the awful feeling of loneliness and terror. He thought of Sal, of Merci, of John, of Addy, of the little children he murdered in the alley. He thought of his sweet mother and his horrible father. He thought of all of the yelling and screaming and forcing. He remembered the night he found out they had died, how devastated he was. How frustrated he was with himself. He relived all of the pain and confusion and frustration of having lost his mind.

"I don't know," he said through his multiple tears. "I don't know why this would happen! Why would I do all of this? Please don't leave; I don't want to live with these secrets anymore. I can't—I need to get them out of this," he said, hitting his head. "I am telling the truth when I say it. You want to know why I did all of these things? I don't know, okay! I don't know! I can't even describe to you how my mind was working one year ago. Truth is I don't even remember it that well. I don't! All I can remember is pain and suffering, and dying faces, and flames and terror and loneliness. Okay? I can't give you motive. I can't!"

Chief Murphy looked at the young man for a long time without speaking, listening to his cries. Finally, after several minutes, Cameron looked up again into the officer's cold eyes.

"What I can tell you is this. The key to it all, for me, is in the car. The car, for me, makes sense of the whole situation."

"How do you figure?"

"Well, what led you to me? I mean, seriously, what gave it away to you that I was your man? Why were you so interested in interviewing me that day so long ago? I remember that. For some reason I remember every detail. I can see you there, on my front steps. Taking it all in. I can hear you breathing, see you looking right through me, hinting that you knew more than I'd let on, letting me know you were watching me. I remember everything about that day, right up to the way your hair was combed, and let me tell you, that is saying something for me. It's as if you knew what I were about to do, even though I didn't know it yet. That was before I'd done anything or knew I would do anything. So here's my question to you: why were you so interested in that car theft report?"

Murphy shrugged his shoulders. "I'm a police officer. I'm interested in all crimes under my responsibility. And I personally write down every stolen car just so I can remember it better, that's all. It's just what I do."

"Malarkey!" Cameron said. "I did look this up. There are over two thousand car thefts a year in this city."

"Yes, but that's not all in my vicinity—"

"Fine, but the truth is that something about you couldn't put it to rest. I know, I've read the interviews in *The Sun*. I've heard the officers talking in the halls. Everyone knows you're a cop who acts on instinct. Why? Why did you pursue the car so much? *Why?*"

Chief Murphy sat back and eyeballed the prisoner. Cameron sat frozen, returning his gaze. "Why?" Cameron asked again, more broken and meek this time.

"You want to know why?"

"Very much so."

"Well, fine, I'll tell you why. It's no secret. I felt a prompting, that's why."

"A divine prompting?" Cameron asked.

Murphy shrugged.

"Do you know why?"

"No. That's just how it works with me. I get

promptings. Now, any other questions for me, Mr. Bo?" The chief grabbed his hat.

"Just a comment. Just—I thought you were going to say that. I thought you were going to sit there and tell me that you got a prompting, you know why?"

"Why?"

"Because promptings happen. You know, Chief? I used to be a missionary, did you know that? I went on a lot of minimissions for my church, and there is one thing I learned that people hate to argue against, and that is promptings. You can get all of the scientists, all of the atheists, all of the people in the world who pooh-pooh religion, and the one thing they can never explain is promptings. Feelings. Gut instincts that turn out to be so true it's eerie. I used to say to the unbelievers, you can trash the idea of God all you want, but then *you* are the one stuck with explaining how divine feelings occur."

"So what's your point?"

"My point is I knew you were gonna say that promptings led you to the car. Why? Because I get promptings too! I get promptings for me to act in ways I don't understand, and then I follow them. And I got a prompting several months before it all went down, even before I had completely lost my mind. And you know what that prompting was? That prompting was to report my car stolen! Which I did! And I didn't know why!"

"To frame a hooker, that's why," the chief said.

"No it's not! I had no idea how that was all going to turn out. I don't deny that I wound up using it to my advantage, but I didn't know at the time why I was reporting my car stolen! I was driving around in that 'stolen' car all the time for heaven's sake! If I'm some mastermind, why would I do that?" he looked up at the chief's confused face. "Why would I do that?"

"I don't know," the chief said. "Because you're a freak?"

Cameron ignored the dig and stood up and wiped a tear from his eye. Nervously he raised a hand to his chin and turned about, pacing toward the corner of the room.

"Chief," he said, looking at the corner of the wall. "I think I might know why I did that." Cameron turned to face the chief and leaned against the wall.

"I think I reported the car stolen because I believe that there is a God who loves me just as much as he loves you. And I think that he knew I was going to commit murders and could not be stopped, so he *prompted* me to report that car stolen."

The chief let out a big sigh and grabbed his hat once more. "Wow! I've got to tell you that I thought I'd heard it all, but this ... you really are a piece of work! You know that?" the chief stood up, shaking his head. "I just don't get you people," he said. "Why? Why would you think something like this? I mean, tell me, really, just out of pure curiosity. I gotta know. Why do you honestly think God would *help* you murder his own children? Do you *not* think that sounds a little weird? I mean, c'mon! How could you think that? You killed at least two people, who knows how many more, and you have the gall to blaspheme the name of deity to my face by telling me, while medicated, that you still had a divine errand to perform? You sicken me."

The chief's tired old jaw line was now quivering, his forehead bulging a colossal vein that threatened to break through the skin at any moment. Cameron looked back into the old police officer's eyes, unflinching.

"No, Chief, not for me. That's not what the prompting was for. Not to help me murder; you got it all wrong. For you."

"What are you talkin' about?"

"I'm talkin' about this. I think I was prompted to report it for you. You were the right cop at the right time. You were religious. Everyone that knows you knows that. You listened, you paid attention to the whispering of God's voice, and you followed those promptings right to me. That is how it worked. If you didn't have the car, you couldn't have tracked me. You wouldn't have known how to make heads or tails of it all. I could have blamed the prostitute, said she stole the car that night, and no one would have been the wiser. That car was what brought this case to a close.

"Don't you see? Everything about this case smacks of religion. Don't you see that? Everything about this case is bizarre and sensational! How does evolution explain that? How does science explain that? How does police work as usual explain that? Think of it, Chief. This story is way too harebrained for logic, and science, and sense! And yet it is played out all across the world, every day, in one form or another. I mean, maybe not always in murder and psychoticism, but in the sheer unbelieveability of it all! Random stories of heroism, of children lifting objects that outweigh them, of people feeling prompted to take alternate routes home only to hear of fatal accidents they would have surely been victim too had they gone their typical way. Of two-year-olds dialing 911 when no one ever told them how! I think that is the point, that God does have his hand in the world."

Chief Murphy took a step away and shook his head back and forth with great anger. "*You* mean to stand here and lecture *me* on God!" Murphy said. "How dare you! I have never heard anything more blasphemous in my life than the profanities you're breathing right now! My God isn't an accomplice to murder! In any form! My God doesn't have to make his point by hurting others!"

"Then why did the Son of God have to die with great pain?" Cameron said. "Hurting, pain, murder, rape, molestation, and embezzlement happen every day, Chief, and your God allows that. But *allows* is the key! You're missing the point if you think I'm saying that God forces or causes murder. No! But it does happen. I don't think God forced me to be crazy, but crazy happened. And I think God loves me, as he does you, as he does someone with Alzheimer's, as he does someone with mental retardation, as he does anyone in over their head in this cold world. And this cold world is a world of secularism, of intellectualism, of 'we got it all figured out so we don't need God.' But then once in a while something too random, too bizarre, too enigmatic, too inexplicable; something out of this world happens, and we're at a loss for how to explain it. But it doesn't make it any less real. I did go crazy. I did report the car stolen. I did ram those college students. You did get promptings, and you did find me. You're getting caught up in the wrong details, Chief. The real story is in the hidden details. It's in the promptings to the Chief Murphys, and it's in the bizarre reporting of the car being stolen. In the end, *that* is what brought this case to a close. *That* is what ended the crime spree. *That* is what ended the suffering of everyone involved."

Cameron looked at the ground as his voice grew shaky. "*That* is what I pray will ultimately end my personal suffering. So, no, I don't think that God was trying to help me murder. No. Never. No, I think just the opposite. I think God was trying to save me, and you, and all of us. Cliché or not, God *does* work in mysterious ways. And for this, I wish to work with you. For this I am ready to admit to anything I've done wrong. Now the question is, what are you going to do? And before you answer, maybe you should look beyond all that hate, beyond all that suspicion, beyond all that 'mental health is crap' attitude, and beyond all that you see when you look at me, and instead listen to that small voice that got us here in the first place."

Cameron looked up at Murphy as his voice grew more gentle and slow. "So, Chief, what say you? Huh? Hate or faith? Blindness or see? This is not going to end here, you know. There will be a trial, and there will be testimony. I'm not pleading guilty because I believe I *was* crazy, and I wanted you to know that. But I am offering you my services. I will help you track the callous murders of that paranoid freak I used to be. So now it's simply a matter of how you would like to proceed, and I'm curious what you'll choose. Do you believe God works not just in you, but He could also whisper promptings to the deliriously insane? What are you going to choose? In the end, what will *you* see? In the end, where lies your belief?"

CHAPTER SEVENTY-TWO

Addy leaned over and picked up the new book. "Look, Merci. I guess he was really serious." Holding the book up to her face she quickly read the title, *Burying God.* Merci turned around and peaked over Addy's shoulders to spy the object of her focus.

"That our Doctor Haddelby's book?"

"Yep," Addy confirmed, opening up the book and reading the dedication page. "To all my students over the years whom I've blinded with my ignorance. I now tell the truth, and ironically, it was once said that truth can make us free." Addy snapped the book shut and placed it back on the sales display.

"Wow," Merci said. "I guess he isn't keeping his secret anymore. I wonder if it bugs him that you and I wound up becoming so religious."

Addy looked up at Merci and smiled. She'd learned by now not to argue with him about God. Ever since the engagement, he was full of faith and hope for their lives. She didn't want to ruin it all with her pessimism. But she did not believe in God. How could she, given what'd happened to her? Not only in the last year, but all of her life long. The abuse, the solitude, the anger, the bitterness, the depression, the teasing, the sexual and emotional dysfunction, and now the traumatic accident. She just didn't buy that it could all be real.

"Hon, what're you thinking about?" Merci asked. "I'm guessing how much you loved our honeymoon in Vegas?"

Addy laughed and threw her arms around him, squeezing him tightly. She thought about the Vegas trip, about how nice Merci had been. She thought about it the entire way home from the store, how much she'll miss being together, and how much she enjoyed being a new, young married couple, so full of love and hopes and dreams. It was fun to pretend. But Addy knew the reality, and she knew that Merci didn't. It was all about to change. Forever. For the better. Merci opened Addy's door and picked her up clean away from the car.

"What're you doing?" Addy asked as she let her arms drape around his neck.

"Well, you didn't think I was going to let you cross the threshold of our first apartment together, in our new life, without me carrying you, now did you?"

"Well, it might've crossed my mind," Addy joked as she let her head rest on Merci's chest and kissed his neck. "I love you," she whispered, beginning to tear up.

"I love you too," Merci said. As they crossed the door entrance and living room, Merci sped down the hall and up the stairs toward the bedroom.

"How about we settle into our apartment right now?" he asked, leaning in to kiss her again. Addy opened her mouth and caressed his calloused lips with her soft mouth. The two exchanged passionate gestures while locked in each other's gaze when Addy pulled her head away from Merci and looked deep into his eyes.

"Can I ask you something?" she wondered aloud, her voice shaking.

"Honey, we're married. You can ask me anything you want to. Anything at all."

Addy raised her hand to his head and held it there. "Is there anything I could do to make you not love me anymore?"

The two stared at each other for a long second before Merci spoke. "Other than castrate me?"

"I'm serious. I want to know the truth. Especially if the answer is yes. I mean, that would be hard to hear. But I really need to know. And I need you to promise me. Do you promise to say the truth?"

"Yes. Yes, of course. Hey, what's this about?"

"Nothing, I just need to know. Right now. Tell me. Is there *anything* I could do to you to make you stop loving me? Search deep. Anything at all?" Addy pleaded, her eyes frantically searching his. Merci grabbed her head with both his hands and slowly kissed her mouth.

"No. Nothing. Even if you beat me, cheated on

me, killed me, threw me away. I wouldn't like any of that, but I could never not love you. As long as I exist, you will always be the center of my world," he said, unflinching as he spoke with a simple yet piercing response. Addy began to cry fervently and pulled him into her arms tightly.

"Thank you," she whispered into his ears. "Thank you for marrying me. I love you. I want you to know that no matter whatever happens to me or you, I will always love you. It's all I can give you. I have nothing else but my love, but it's yours to keep forever. I love you! I love you! I love you!"

They sat holding each other, kissing on and off for hours, until Addy finally fell asleep. When she woke up several hours later, she found the other side of the bed empty, a note on the pillow.

> "Dear Wife, it's your husband, Merci (I know, I know. It's redundant, but I don't think I'm ever going to be sick of calling you my wife or saying I'm your husband). Anyway, I had to go in and check things out at work. After that, I'm going to run a few errands. I have a surprise for you when I get home. Be a few hours, but be ready to get dressed up when I get home. Love, Merci, your husband (there it is again! Aagh!)

Addy smiled and cried at the same time when reading the note, and she brought it to her face and kissed it with her mouth. She knew this was her moment. After going to the bathroom she took a shower, the whole time asking herself if she were doing the right thing. She was. At least, that's how she felt about it.

Slipping out of the shower, she put on her jeans and a T-shirt, then sat on her bed and looked around. She noted the date on the calendar, her mind retreating back a year ago. How different life was then! She tried to think of Merci in a year from now, or two, or three, with his new wife and children. Addy sobbed as she thought of him raising children. She knew he was going to be such a good father, and all she had ever wanted to be was a mother. It was the one thing she thought she was good at, the one thing people told her she had a talent for. But it didn't matter now. All was different. All was hopeless. All was lost. Just a few minutes and it would be done.

She leaned over and pulled the box of pills out of her suitcase and read the label. She thought it funny she was using the warnings as an indication of which pills would be the best to take. She selected one, then two different types, just in case. Popping open the lid, she took the remainder of the first bottle, which probably had about twenty pills in it. The second only had thirteen. She gagged as she put the second batch into her mouth, and already her throat felt tingly. Tears flowed consistently and intensely down her face as she found a pen and paper to write Merci a final parting note.

> "Dear beloved Merci, I know this will be a shock to you. But what I do today I do for love. I do for you, my love. You said you would never hate me; you said it moments ago, before I passed to sleep. Now that I pass to sleep again, I hope you will still keep your promise. I only want the best things in life for you. I only want to make you happy. I realized

some time ago that this dream could not happen with me around. I am such a drag, such a barnacle, such a pull on your ship. You can sail so far … I am sorry to have brought you pain and suffering. I am sorry to have brought you into this. Go on with your dream of God and hope and family, and be happy in that dream forever."

Addy's body was starting to feel very strange; her head exploded with pain and euphoria at the same time. She felt herself beginning to feel faint. *Finish the letter, Addy. You owe him at least that.*

"I'm not sure I'm going to be able to finish this in time. I'm starting to fade. I'll be brief. You are so full of love and hope, and I'm so full of misery and shame. I decided a long time ago, at church. You were there, taking it in, while I was getting increasingly bitter. I never believed. That is the truth, and the truth is the accident only brought that out of me, at a time I needed it to. Truth is, I believe we only get one shot at this life, and so why should you waste it on me? Do what you want with your life, and don't regret me. I love you. Find better than me because that's what you deserve. Love, your (brief) but eternally grateful wife, Addy."

Addy was dry heaving. Her stomach rumbled fiercely, and her esophagus was on fire. She sat on the floor and studied the way her mind was beginning to fade. She had no concept of time anymore. She had no concept of much anymore. Suddenly there was a noise downstairs.

"Honey, I'm home!" she heard Merci say from the

bottom of the stairs. She looked at the open door and panicked. She could not let him see her this way. She tried standing up, but her legs faltered.

"Honey? Where are you? You still in bed?" Merci called from the kitchen. Addy's heart was on fire. *I must ... close ... the door!* she ordered herself, commanding her legs to carry her. Unsteadily, yet swiftly, she lurched from object to object, losing balance with each lunge.

"That's it. I'm coming up to get you! You know you can't keep a newlywed male away from his wife for too long!" Merci hollered up the stairs. Addy reached the wall next to the door as she heard him start up the foot of the steps. *Do it now!* she commanded herself as she thrust her hand out for the doorknob. For a flicker of time she saw his bright face, eager and excited to see his bride. She smiled to see his face one more time before she slammed the door shut and locked him out.

"Addy!" she heard him scream from the other side of the door pane. "Addy, what's wrong? Addy! Why is your nose bleeding? Is someone in there? You'd better not hurt her or so help me, I'll kill you. I'll kill you!" he screamed as he thumped into the door.

All was starting to fade from before her eyes. The light grew softer, the sound more distant, the colors more vague. In the obfuscated scene she could see the door fling open, Merci breaking the latch. She could hear him screaming out in horror as he picked her up off the ground and listened to her heart. By the time he called 911 she could barely detect sound; all was quiet. All was without noise of any kind. Like a silent movie, full of busy pictures but no lines. Finally she could see her husband's face. He was crying and seemed to be blaring at her to hold on. A tear fell from his face to hers; a last connection. She read his lips telling her that the ambulance was on its way. Faintly, she thought she might even be hearing the siren as all grew dark and cold.

CHAPTER SEVENTY-THREE

John parked his car and looked across the beautiful vista. From the mountainous scene, he could see the large, white clouds spilling across the frozen sky. The city far below was bursting with activity, with everyone getting ready to see old friends, relatives, and neighbors. John imagined them visiting for summer vacations, lighting off fireworks on the fourth of July, eating Thanksgiving dinner, opening Christmas presents.

Leaning into the door and pulling the latch, John made his way out of his car and onto the street. The wind howled, and John felt a chill run through his body. Shaking off the cold, he retreated to the back of the car and opened the trunk with his key. Once open, he rifled through his belongings and grabbed the large backpack from the midst of his spare tire, water bottles, and various objects that had found their way into the miniature dumping ground he called his trunk.

John slammed the trunk shut and listened to the wind moving solitarily across the road. He looked at his watch and the position of the sun and decided he'd better get started down. Strolling across the street, John was vigilant to every sound, sight, noise, smell, and movement. He seemed to be processing everything with superhuman capability. A bird cawed from far away, eliciting an attentive glance from the sober-minded backpacker. John listened as the sound stretched across the atmosphere, meeting its demise with the oncoming gust, sounding like nature screaming through the pines for someone to help.

As he reached the upper crash site, he stooped down and felt the asphalt, carefully rubbing his fingers across the bruised highway. A few feet away, he found a small piece of Merci's wood-paneled wagon still lying on the shoulder. John sat on the ground and held the broken part in his hand, wondering what portion of the car it belonged to. The sun disappeared behind a large cloud, and John zipped his jacket up all the way to his chin. He looked up into the blue sky and marveled at the unceasing space, his mind full of serious philosophical thoughts.

Turning his attention toward the entrance to the switchback trail, he rose to his feet and became directional. He was not in a rush but also was ready to go. He had waited for this moment long enough. He had waited all of his life for this moment. John reached into his pocket and retrieved the small black handgun that had been sitting on his home mantle for the last three years and examined it. He pulled the clip out and peered at the full load, smiling as he thrust it back into the chamber and reset the gun into his pocket. Sticking his thumbs under his chest straps, he crossed the railing and began his descent toward the site that had changed his life one year ago.

A strange sense came over John as he became increasingly closer to the lower crash site. His mind flooded with the painful images of the crash and the many long nights and conversations between he, Merci, and Addy, trying to make sense of it all. A tear fell down his face as he recalled the bruising rock, the vacant looks on his friends' faces as he pulled them away from the grisly scene, and the look of sadness on Cameron's face in the photographs of his being arrested. He actually felt sorry for the little guy. It wasn't really his fault he was crazy. At least that was the way John felt about it. *No matter now,* John thought, slipping his hand into his pocket and feeling the metal of the gun. *Nothing like that will ever get to me again.*

After a long passing, John reached the base of the mountainside and smiled as he viewed the area where the wagon had landed. In his mind he imagined the voices of the past rushing around to help put out the fires and save him and his friends. John smiled as he considered the frantic firefighters and police officers who had worked so hard to revive them all. He continued smirking as he thought of the nurses and doctors and countless friends, relatives, neighborhood visitors, and even the community vigil that was held outside his apartment complex when the community had found out about his "heroism" in saving his friends. *People are always so superficial,* John thought. *They run around blindly, thinking they're engaged in some great cause, and it's all in vain. They're wasting their lives, just as I've spent so much time searching for meaning in my life and never finding it. Always focusing on the wrong thing. 'Till now.*

John paused and stood motionless as he reached the fragmented door where he had lain 365 days before. He examined the small space and imagined his pathetic condition as trapped inside of the door. Running his hand over the scar on his elbow, it was more than he could endure. Large drops of water fell from his eyes, and he cried loudly and intensely for the better part of ten minutes, kneeling on top of the door.

Finally, he slipped off his backpack and laid himself down in the doorframe, in the position he imagined he must have been in that night. His memory was still a little foggy on the exact details, but his arm fit easily into the open window slot.

"Ouch!" he said as he contracted his arm and saw the blood running out from his open wrist. *Guess that's what I get,* he reasoned as he carefully pulled his arm out of the window, successfully avoiding contact with any other shards of glass. Sitting at the site he closed his eyes and breathed in deeply, savoring the wintry pine smell. He then opened his eyes and looked far into the heavens.

"I won't waste the life you gave me anymore," he

said reverently as he stared into the vastness of the atmosphere, far above the pine tops. John retrieved his gun and unzipped his backpack. Carefully, he opened the clip and one by one threw the shells as far as he could into the forest shrubbery. Next he stood up and threw the clip. With care he detached the note taped to the trigger and unfolded the small paper. *Are you sure there is no other way?* he read. John tore the paper in half and tossed the gun as far into the wooded foliage as his muscles would allow.

Turning toward the backpack, he retrieved the lighter fluid, box of matches, and then finally his stack of magazines and private pictures. Setting the fluid and matches aside, he thumbed briefly through the stack of magazines and observed the scantily clad women and explicit images on their covers. *How could I have ever gotten to this point?* he wondered, the tears flowing again.

"I will never waste my life again," he repeated, looking first at the magazine covers and then up at the sky.

"I will never waste my life again!" he shouted, fist raised, saturated with a mixture of respect, humility, elation, and sorrow. His voice rose above the tree line and seemed somehow to echo in the distance. He thought of the scriptural passage from the Bible, "Go thy way and sin no more; thy faith hath made thee whole." John's entire body shivered and contorted not from the cold, but from the deep and personal emotions he was feeling. Never had he felt so positive and alive. Never had he felt so clean and pure.

Grabbing the lighter fluid, he threw the magazines one by one into the open door frame where his arm had been bruised, and he set out to finally heal himself from that painful day. With fervor he squirted nearly the entire small bottle of lighter fluid onto the pornographic magazines and pictures while images of his father crept into his mind.

"I will never waste my life again!" he yelled even louder and with more conviction to the images and through gritted teeth. Panting, he grabbed out of his backpack the binder he had put together of Addy. One by one he ripped the pictures and images out and threw them into the now fervent blaze. As he threw the last magazine and picture into the flames, he stood back and felt the warmth of the fire and watched as the yellow flames zigzagged high into the air, as if within the flickers John could see his old life dying and his new life beginning.

As the fire erased and purged the sins of his past, John followed the smoke trail as it ascended into the heavens. Without averting his gaze, he retrieved his small notepad and a pen. Dropping his eyes from the heavens, he read the words he had inscribed early that morning.

"This year you gave me my life anew; now, I give it back to you." His eyes full of tears, he forced his pen directly atop the space of the paper where he had printed his name, and with deliberateness he sealed the contract with his signature.

"Thank you for second chances," he said to his Maker high above. "Or even thirds or fourths."

He stared back at the fire and his signed contract

and enjoyed the wind, the climate, the beauty of the scene, and the brilliance of life itself, in a way he never thought imaginable for someone as pathetic as he had been.

As the fire died down, absent fanfare or press, he laid the notebook on the ground next to the smoldering ashes and looked up at his vehicle far above. Without letting his head drop from the end of the path before him, he cautiously but resolutely took his first step up the long, steep mountain trail.

listen|imagine|view|experience

AUDIO BOOK DOWNLOAD INCLUDED WITH THIS BOOK!

In your hands you hold a complete digital entertainment package. In addition to the paper version, you receive a free download of the audio version of this book. Simply use the code listed below when visiting our website. Once downloaded to your computer, you can listen to the book through your computer's speakers, burn it to an audio CD or save the file to your portable music device (such as Apple's popular iPod) and listen on the go!

How to get your free audio book digital download:

1. Visit www.tatepublishing.com and click on the e|LIVE logo on the home page.
2. Enter the following coupon code: 32fb-38ce-148c-0d15-761a-c76c-335e-ed2e
3. Download the audio book from your e|LIVE digital locker and begin enjoying your new digital entertainment package today!